SCYTHE & SPARROW

THE RUINOUS LOVE TRILOGY

SCYTHE & SPARROW

BRYNNE WEAVER

SLOWBURN
A zando IMPRINT

NEW YORK

zaNdo

Copyright © 2025 by Brynne Weaver

Zando supports the right to free expression and the value of copyright.
The purpose of copyright is to encourage writers and artists to produce
the creative works that enrich our culture. Thank you for buying an
authorized edition of this book and for complying with copyright laws
by not reproducing, scanning, uploading, or distributing this book or
any part of it without permission. If you would like permission to use
material from the book (other than for brief quotations embodied in
reviews), please contact connect@zandoprojects.com.

Slowburn is an imprint of Zando.
zandoprojects.com

First Edition: February 2025

Cover design by Quamber Designs
Text design by Pauline Neuwirth, Neuwirth & Associates, Inc.

The publisher does not have control over and is not responsible for
author or other third-party websites (or their content).

Library of Congress Control Number: 2024949155

978-1-63893-181-2 (Trade paperback)
978-1-63893-265-9 (B&N Exclusive Edition)
978-1-63893-286-4 (Walmart Edition)
978-1-63893-182-9 (ebook)

10 9 8 7 6 5 4 3 2 1
Manufactured in the United States of America

CONTENT & TRIGGER WARNINGS

As much as *Scythe & Sparrow* is a dark romantic comedy and will hopefully make you laugh through the madness, it's still dark! Please read responsibly. If you have any questions about this list, please don't hesitate to contact me at brynneweaverbooks.com or on one of my social media platforms (I'm most active on Instagram and TikTok).

- Eyeballs . . . again. If it's any consolation, I don't know why I keep writing them into books because eyeball shit freaks me the fuck out
- Also eyelids. Yep. We're there now
- I'm not sure as I really *ruin* cotton candy as much as maybe just defile it
- Possibly sausages and/or hot dogs
- Ill-advised use of staple guns
- Are drug-addicted raccoons a trigger? Debate!
- Clowns
- Sexy clowns
- Medical trauma including serious injury, ambulances, open fractures, puncture wounds, blood loss, hospitals, surgical recovery
- Impaling (not the sexy kind, but okay . . . that too)

- References to domestic physical abuse (not depicted), psychological/emotional abuse, sexual harassment, threats and intimidation, misogyny
- Injured dog—but if you've read *Leather & Lark*, you already know Bentley will be fine! He's too grumpy and badass to die
- Parental neglect, child physical abuse (not depicted)
- Numerous weapons and sharp objects, including knives, guns, baseball bats, metal hooks, an edge beveler—you should be used to these by now
- Detailed sex scenes, which include (but are not limited to): adult toys, primal kink, cum kink, anal, rough sex, sexual acts in public
- Explicit and colorful language, including a lot of "blasphemy." Don't say I didn't warn you!
- There is a lot of injury and death . . . it's a book about a doctor and a serial killer falling in love, so I feel like that's probably a given

Please note, if you're the kind of reader who likes to skip epilogues, I humbly request that you make an exception! There are no babies or pregnancies, but there might be another surprise or two that you won't want to miss. Just trust me! (*"But the ice cream!"* you say. *"The pizza! The beer and smoothies and fancy calcium!"* I know, I know—but just trust me *this time*. Haha!)

For those of you who read *B&B* and *L&L* and said,
"Hell, I've already endured the ice cream and pizza,
I might as well keep going" . . . you truly are my people.
This one's for you!

PLAYLIST

Scan a QR code to listen:

APPLE MUSIC

SPOTIFY

CHAPTER ONE: Ace of Cups
"Handmade Heaven," MARINA
"The Inversion," Joywave

CHAPTER TWO: Oath
"Mess Is Mine," Vance Joy
"Fight to Feel Alive," Erin McCarley

CHAPTER THREE: Stranded
"Lost & Far from Home," Katie Costello
"My Heart," The Perishers

CHAPTER FOUR: Prairie Princess
"The Daylight," Andrew Belle
"Next Time," Greg Laswell
"Silenced By the Night," Keane

CHAPTER FIVE: Left Unsaid
"Traveling at the Speed of Light," Joywave
"Never Be Alone," The Last Royals
"In a Week," (feat. Karen Cowley), Hozier

CHAPTER SIX: Shadows
"Orca," Wintersleep
"Look After You," Aron Wright
"Darker Side," RHODES

CHAPTER SEVEN: Ta-Da
"Man's World," MARINA
"Fun Never Ends," Barns Courtney

CHAPTER EIGHT: Push to Shove
"Roses R Red," CRAY
"Shutdown," Joywave
"Minuet for a Cheap Piano," A Winged Victory for the Sullen

CHAPTER NINE: Sutures
"You Haunt Me," Sir Sly
"Evelyn," Gregory Alan Isakov
"Reflections," TWO LANES

CHAPTER TEN: Renegade
"Every Window Is A Mirror," Joywave
"Is It Any Wonder?," Keane
"San Francisco," Gregory Alan Isakov

CHAPTER ELEVEN: Beast Mode
"Too Young To Die," Barns Courtney
"Take It on Faith," Matt Mays

CHAPTER TWELVE: Reduction
"Strangers," Wave & Rome
"Sister," Andrew Belle

CHAPTER THIRTEEN: Scratch

"Helium," Glass Animals

"THE GREATEST," Billie Eilish

"Fear and Loathing," MARINA

CHAPTER FOURTEEN: Reckless

"The Few Things" (with Charlotte Lawrence), JP Saxe

"Pieces," Andrew Belle

CHAPTER FIFTEEN: Descent

"Twist," Dizzy

"First," Cold War Kids

"Cold Night," Begonia

CHAPTER SIXTEEN: Surfacing

"Horizon," Andrew Belle

"All Comes Crashing," Metric

"Realization," TWO LANES

CHAPTER SEVENTEEN: Stroke of Luck

"I Know What You're Thinking And It's Awful," The Dears

"Shrike," Hozier

"Butterflies" (feat. AURORA), Tom Odell

CHAPTER EIGHTEEN: Hurdles

"Fun," Sir Sly

"Nuclear War," Sara Jackson-Holman

"watch what i do," CRAY

CHAPTER NINETEEN: Confection

"About Love," MARINA

"We're All Gonna Die," CRAY

CHAPTER TWENTY: Claws

"Coming Apart," Joywave

"The Aviator," Stars of Track and Field

"Wandering Wolf," Wave & Rome

CHAPTER TWENTY-ONE: Haunted
"I Love You But I Love Me More," MARINA
"Mayday!!! Fiesta Fever" (feat. Alex Ebert), AWOLNATION
"Content," Joywave

CHAPTER TWENTY-TWO: Dark Corners
"Come Back For Me," Jaymes Young
"Monsoon," Sara Jackson-Holman
"Au Revoir," OneRepublic

CHAPTER TWENTY-THREE: Untethered
"Arches," Agnes Obel
"Master & A Hound," Gregory Alan Isakov
"Sweet Apocalypse," Lambert

CHAPTER TWENTY-FOUR: Battlegrounds
"Into the Fire," Erin McCarley
"Particles," Ólafur Arnalds & Nanna
"Hold On," Chord Overstreet

CHAPTER TWENTY-FIVE: Out of Time
"Stranger," Katie Costello
"Viva La Vida," Sofia Karlberg

CHAPTER TWENTY-SIX: Script
"Can I Exist," MISSIO
"Cardiology," Sara Jackson-Holman
"For You," Greg Laswell

CHAPTER TWENTY-SEVEN: Three of Swords
"Fall For Me," Sleep Token
"Quietly Yours," Birdy
"The Shade," Metric

EPILOGUE ONE: Maps

"Close To You," Gracie Abrams

"Maps," Yeah Yeah Yeahs

"Re-Arrange Again," Erin McCarley

EPILOGUE TWO: Blade of Rage

"Serial Killer," Slayyyter

BONUS CHAPTER: Suspend

"Official," Charli XCX

"Kiss Me," (feat. Rina Sawayama), Empress Of

SCYTHE &
SPARROW

ACE OF CUPS

Rose

If you hit someone in the back of the head hard enough, you can pop their eyeballs right out of their face.

Or at least, that's what I read somewhere. And that's what I'm thinking as I shuffle my tarot deck, glaring at the sketchy-looking asshole thirty feet away as he pours alcohol from a flask into his soda and takes a long gulp. He wipes away the excess from his chin with the sleeve of his plaid shirt. A burp quickly follows, and then he shoves half his hot dog into his fuck-ugly gob before he takes another swig.

I could whack that big ol' egghead so hard his marbles spring right out of their sockets.

And the woman sitting across from me? I bet she wouldn't mind one bit.

I tamp down a dark grin and hope to fuck she hasn't noticed the devious glint in my expression. But even despite the murdery vibes I'm probably giving off, and the distractions of Silveria

Circus beyond the open door of my tarot tent, her attention seems stuck on the cards, all her concentration glued to them as I shuffle. There's no light at all in her eyes, one of them rimmed with a fading black bruise.

Blood surges in my veins as I force my gaze not to creep back to the man. *Her* man.

When her attention finally lifts from the repetitive motion of my hands, and she starts twisting in her seat to catch sight of him, I abruptly stop shuffling to slap the deck down on the table. She startles more than seems normal, just like I thought she would. Just like I hoped she wouldn't.

"Sorry," I say, and I mean it. She looks at me with fear in her eyes. *Real* fear. But she gives me a weak smile. "What's your name?"

"Lucy," she says.

"All right, Lucy. So I won't ask you what your question is. But I want you to keep it in mind."

Lucy nods. I turn over the first card. I already know what it will be. Its edges are worn with use and the image has faded with time.

"Ace of Cups," I say as I lay the card on the table and push it closer to her. She looks from the image to me, a question in her crinkled brow. "It represents following your inner voice. What does it tell you? What do you want?"

There's only one thing I hope she'll say: *to take flight.*

But she doesn't say it.

"I don't know," she says, her voice barely more than a whisper. Disappointment lodges itself like a thorn beneath my skin as she twists her fingers on the table, her simple gold wedding band scratched and dull. "Matt wants to buy another plot of land to farm next year, but I want to put some money away for the kids. Maybe it'd be nice to get out of Nebraska for a week, take the kids to see my mom and not be fretting about the price of gas. Is that the kind of thing you mean . . . ?"

"Maybe." I shrug and pick up the deck, giving it another shuffle. This time, I won't guide the Ace of Cups to the top of the pile. I'll let it tell her whatever she needs to hear. "What's important is what it means to *you*. Let's restart, and you keep that in mind."

I do Lucy's reading. Seven of Cups. Page of Cups. Two of Wands. Signals of change, that choices for her future are there, if she's ready to have faith and embrace them. I'm not even sure if she's open to receiving a message from my cards. I've barely finished the reading when her three kids pile into the tent, two girls and a boy, their faces sticky and stained with candy. They talk over one another, each wanting to be the first to tell her about the rides or the games or the upcoming performances. *They have clowns, Mama. Mama, did you see the fire-breather? I saw a game where you can win a stuffy, Mama, come see. Mama, Mama, Mama—*

"Kids," a gruff voice interrupts at the entrance of my tarot tent. Their thin bodies go still and rigid at his sharp tone. Lucy's eyes widen across from me. She doesn't let her gaze linger, but I still see it. The dull smear of chronic terror in her eyes. The way it deadens her expression before she turns away. I look up to the man in my doorway, his spiked soda gripped in one hand, a fistful of ride tickets in the other. "Go on, take 'em. Meet your ma at the big top in an hour for the show."

The oldest child, the boy, reaches for the tickets and grasps them to his chest as though they could be torn from him just as easily as they were given. "Thank you, Papa."

The kids edge past their father, where he stands unmoving in the entrance of the tent. He watches them disappear into the crowd before turning his attention our way. Bloodshot eyes fixed to his wife, he drains his plastic cup and drops it on the ground. "Let's go."

Lucy nods once and stands. She places a twenty-dollar bill on the table with a brittle smile and a whisper of thanks. I'd like to give her the reading for free, but I know men like hers. They're volatile. Willing to jump down a woman's throat for the smallest perceived slight, like pity or charity. I learned a long time ago to stick to the exchange of value, even if he might yell at her later for spending money on something as frivolous as a message from the universe.

Lucy leaves the tent. Her husband watches her go.

And then he turns to me.

"You shouldn't go fillin' her head with crazy fuckin' ideas," he says through a sneer. "She's already got enough of those."

I pick up my tarot cards and shuffle them. My heart scrapes my bones with every furious beat, but I keep my movement fluid, my outward appearance calm. "I take it you don't want a reading."

"What did you tell her?"

The man takes a step into my tent to loom over my table with a menacing glare. I lean back in my chair. My shuffling slows to a halt. We pin our gazes to each other. "Same shit I tell everyone who comes in here," I lie. "Follow your dreams. Trust your heart. Good things lie in your future."

"You're right about that." A dark smile tugs at the corners of the man's lips as he whips the twenty-dollar bill off the table and makes a point of folding it in front of me. "Good things do lie in my future."

With a tip of his head, he slides the bill into his pocket and walks away, heading for the nearest refreshments stand, where one of his equally shady friends is standing. I glare after him until finally I close my eyes, trying to clear him from my thoughts, refocusing my energy as I resume shuffling my cards. I reach for my selenite crystal to cleanse the deck and sever the connection between us, but my thoughts keep wandering to Lucy. The image of the purple halo around her eye returns, no matter how hard I try to push it away. The deadened look in her eyes haunts me. I've seen that look so many times before. In the women who have come to draw the Ace of Cups. In my mother. In the mirror.

I take a deep breath. I draw my first card with a question in my mind.

Lucy didn't ask for help. But she needs it. What should I do?

I turn over the first card and open my eyes.

The Tower. Upheaval. Sudden change.

I tilt my head and draw another.

Two of Wands. There are opportunities if you're willing to venture beyond your castle walls. The land beyond might be rocky, but it's vibrant. Take a risk. Try something new. A meaningful life is built from choices.

"Hmm. I think I see where this is going, and that wasn't what I was asking."

Knight of Cups. The arrival of romantic love.

"*Stop it.* My question was about smashing that dickhead's skull in. Not falling in love or some bullshit. Tell me about my actual question."

I shuffle the cards again. I keep my question in mind and draw the first card.

The Tower.

"Fucksakes, Gransie. Give it a rest." A deep breath floods my lungs as I fidget with the edge of the card and look out at the fairgrounds beyond the door of my tent. I should really be getting out of here. Leave this exchange behind. Get myself changed and ready for my upcoming performance in the big top. Zooming through the Globe of Death on a motorcycle with two other performers doesn't leave any room for error, and I need to be focused. But Lucy's husband is still in my line of sight. And then Bazyli walks by. I'll take that as the sign I was looking for.

"*Baz*," I bark out, stopping the teenager in his tracks. His gangly limbs are tanned and marred with grease. "Come here."

Sparks virtually shoot from his eyes. His lips stretch around a gap-toothed smile. "Gonna cost ya."

"I haven't even told you what I want yet."

"Still gonna cost ya."

I roll my eyes and Baz grins as he saunters into my tent with all the cockiness of a typical fifteen-year-old. I nod toward the fairgrounds. He follows my gaze. "The guy out there with the plaid shirt next to the grease joint."

"The guy with the head that looks like an egg?"

"Yeah. I need his details. Just the driver's license. And twenty bucks if he's got cash in his wallet."

Baz's attention latches to my hands as I shuffle the Tower card back into my deck. "I'm not a thief. I'm a *magician*," he says, and with a flutter of his hands, a flower appears on his palm. "The only thing I steal is hearts."

I roll my eyes and Baz grins as he gives me the flower. "I know you're not a thief. But Egghead over there is. He just stole twenty bucks from me and I want you to give it back to his wife over there. The one with the blond hair and blue top." I nod toward Lucy in the distance as she makes her way alone toward a concession stand. "She'll have three kids with her in the tent during the show. I want you to get the money back to her and the license to me."

Baz faces me, his eyes narrowing. "Whatever you're up to, I could help, you know."

"You are helping. By getting me that license."

"I'll do it for free if you let me help."

"No dice, kiddo. Your mom will string me up by the throat from the trapeze. Just get me that license. I'll buy you a Venom comic."

Baz shrugs. He twists the toe of his shoe into the trampled grass, trying to keep his attention away from me. "I have most of them."

"Not from the Dark Origins series." Baz's eyes snap to mine. I try to repress a smile at the longing he can't hide. "I know you're missing the last two. I'll get them for you."

"Okay . . . but I also get to borrow your inflatable pool."

I scrunch my nose and tilt my head. "Sure . . . I guess . . ."

"And I need bananas."

"All right—"

"And a pineapple. Some of those little cocktail stick things too."

"What the hell?" It's not unusual for the other circus performers and crew to send me out for random items or treats from the towns we stop in. I'm one of the few who has a second vehicle to escape the grounds with. I don't have to uproot my whole home just to go to the store. But that means I've had requests for an assortment of shit. Condoms, frequently. Pregnancy tests too. Vegetables in season. Fresh croissants from a local baker. Books. Whiskey. But . . . "A pineapple?"

"Mom said she'd get me a PlayStation when she finally gets a vacation. Since there's a fat chance of that, I thought I'd bring the vacation to her." Baz crosses his arms and squares up his stance as though he's about to go into battle. "Take it or leave it, Rose."

I thrust my hand in his direction, my heart a little warmer than it was before. "Deal. Just be careful, yeah? Egghead is trouble."

Baz nods and pumps my hand once and then he's gone, darting off to fulfill his mission. I watch as he weaves his way through children with their popcorn and cotton candy and stuffed animals, and teenagers chattering about the best rides, and the couples who come from the haunted house, laughing with embarrassment about how much our actors scared them in dark corners. These are the moments I usually love about my home with Silveria Circus. Moments of magic, as small as they might be.

But today, the only magic I'm after is the dark and dangerous kind.

I watch as Baz maneuvers close to the two men. My heart rolls against my ribs as he comes up behind Lucy's husband and pulls his wallet from his back pocket when the man is occupied with a laugh. When Baz has it in his hand, he pivots a turn, just long enough to open the wallet and pull the license from its slot. The money is next, and he slips it into his jeans before he finishes his spin. Within a handful of heartbeats, the wallet is back in the man's pocket.

Grabbing my tarot deck and selenite, I leave the tent, turning the OPEN sign at the entrance to CLOSED as I go, even though I'm about to miss another reading or two as another woman closes in on the tent with a twenty-dollar bill clutched between her fingers. I catch the brief flash of disappointment on her face, but Baz never leaves my field of vision. And I don't leave his. We pass each other as I head in the direction of my RV. I barely feel it, only noticing because I know to expect it. A slight brush of a touch at my hip.

When I enter my motor home, I pull the license from my pocket. *Matthew Cranwell.* I open my phone and check his address on the map of Nebraska. Twenty miles away, close to Elmsdale, the next town over. One with a bigger grocery store than Hartford. Maybe more hope of finding a good quality pineapple. I run my thumb over the photo of Matt's weathered face. With a faint grin etched across my lips, I change into my leather pants and tank top, slipping his driver's license into the interior pocket of my motorcycle jacket.

It's the first evening of performances here in Hartford, and the big top is packed with locals who have come from the surrounding network of towns to see the show. And Silveria Circus prides itself on a great show. I watch from behind the curtain as José Silveria introduces each performer. The clowns, with their miniature cars and their juggling act and their slapstick comedy routine. Santiago the Surreal, a magician who wows the audience with a series of tricks that he keeps as a closely guarded secret. Baz helps with the routine, always an eager apprentice, the only person Santiago trusts with his secrets. There are trapeze artists and aerial silk acrobats, Baz's mother, Zofia, the lead performer of their group. The only animals we have are Cheryl's troop of trained poodles, and they always delight the kids, especially when she calls for volunteers from the audience. And last up, the final act, is always me and the twins, Adrian and Alin. The Globe of Death. The scent of the metal mesh and exhaust fumes, the flood of adrenaline. The roar of our bikes as we speed through the cage that seems too small to fit all three of us. The rush of the cheering crowd. I love the speed and the risk. Maybe I love it a little bit too much. Because, sometimes, it feels like not enough.

I roll out of the cage after our set is done, stopping between Adrian and Alin as we wave to the audience. Matt Cranwell's license burns in my pocket as though it's branding my flesh.

The moment I can slip away, I do.

I exchange my dirt bike for my Triumph, my performance helmet for my custom painted ICON, pocket my mini tool set, and then head to Elmsdale, the lowering sun chasing me through the straight, flat roads. I'm a whirlwind through the grocery store, grabbing bananas and a sad-looking pineapple and anything else that looks remotely tropical, along with a flimsy tube of cocktail sticks. When I've paid, I stuff them in my fraying backpack, resolving to find a better one at a future stop.

On my way out of the shop I bring up my phone and double-check Matt Cranwell's address, entering it into the map. The route is straightforward on the grid network of small-town streets. He can't be any more than ten minutes out of town. The weather is perfect, the sun still high enough that if I do a little drive-by to scope it out, I'll still be back at the fairgrounds before dark.

The memory of the Tower card lies over my vision of the map like an opaque film. My nose scrunches. I stop next to my bike and slide my phone into the mobile holder mounted to my handlebars.

Maybe this is a bit insane. It's not my usual gig. But I've really wanted to change things up lately. I know I need to. I've known it for a while. If I'm going to keep helping women like Lucy to *take flight*, it's not enough to just give them the means to do it anymore. If I'm going to go for it, I should really *go for it*, you know? Rev it up. Full throttle. Motorcycle references aside, it's not right to be on the sidelines of the action anymore. I might be supplying the means to right a few wrongs, but I've always been a step removed from the actual *doing*.

I glance down at the tiny carnation tattooed on my wrist. My fingers trace the initials next to it. *V.R.* I can't let what happened last year happen again. Not *ever*.

Not only is it wrong to pass off the responsibility of ending a life to someone who might be ill-prepared to do it, it's a bit boring too. I want to take someone like Matt Cranwell down with my own two hands.

At least, I think I do.

No. I *for sure* do. It's right . . . *ish* . . . and I definitely have the urge, and maybe that will scratch the itch deep inside my brain that craves *more*.

Besides, there's nothing saying I need to do it right this second. I just have to swing by and scope the place out. And then I've got a few days to make my move and we'll be on to the next town. The next show. Always a next woman who lives in fear. Who asks for my help in coded messages and worried glances. A next man to take down.

I swing a leg over my bike and start the engine and then pull away from the parking lot and onto the country roads.

It doesn't take long before I'm rolling to a stop just before an expanse of cornfields and a gravel driveway that leads to a small farmhouse and outbuildings. I park in a dip in the road where my

11

bike will be obscured by cornstalks. My heart jumps up my throat as I pull off my helmet and just listen.

There's nothing.

I'm not sure what I expected. Maybe an obvious sign. But nothing seems to come. I just stand at the end of that driveway and stare at the small but well-kept house that could be anyone's. Swing set in the yard. Bicycles discarded on the lawn. A catcher's mitt and a baseball bat next to raised beds of a vegetable garden. Flowers in hanging pots, a flag flapping in the breeze. An all-American country home.

For a moment, I wonder if I have the wrong house. Or maybe I imagined everything I thought I saw back in the tarot tent.

And then I hear yelling.

A screen door slams. The kids leave the house and head for their bikes, picking them up to peddle away from the chaos with their bare feet. They disappear around the back of the property. The yelling continues inside as though they never left. I can't make out the words. But the rage in his voice is clear. Louder and louder until it feels like the windows will crack. The house is alive with it. And then a crash, something thrown inside. And a scream.

I'm halfway up the driveway before I realize what I'm doing. But it's too late to stop now. I pull my helmet back on and the mirrored visor down. I pass the raised vegetable beds and scoop up the aluminum baseball bat just as the screen door slams and Matt comes stalking onto the porch. I freeze but he doesn't even notice me, his attention locked on the phone in his hands. He trudges down the steps, a scowl imprinted in his weathered features, and starts walking toward the truck parked next to the house.

My grip tightens around the bat.

I could stop. Duck into the cornstalks and hide. He'll turn around at any moment and see me. It will be unavoidable as soon as he gets into the vehicle. Unless I hide *now*.

But there's one thing that keeps playing on repeat in my thoughts. *The show can't start until you jump.*

So I take my chance.

I stay on the grass as I rush toward him. Footsteps light. Tiptoes. Bat ready. He's nearing the front of the truck. His eyes are still on the screen. I'm closing in and he still doesn't know it.

My heart rams my bones. My breaths are quick with terror and exhilaration. My visor fogs at the edges.

I take my first step on the gravel and Matt's head whips around. A second step and he drops his phone. I raise the bat. On the third step I bring it down on his head.

But Matt is already moving.

I hit him but the blow doesn't strike hard enough. He ducks and drops, and the contact only angers him. It's not enough to bring him down. So I swing again. This time he catches the bat.

"What the fuck," he snarls. He rips the weapon from my hand and wraps his palms around the grip. "Fucking bitch."

A moment of unsteadiness on my feet is all he needs. He swings the bat as hard as he can. It hits my lower leg with the force of a lightning strike.

I fall to the ground. Flat on my back. Gasping for air. For a brief, glorious moment, I feel no pain.

And then it consumes me like an electric shock.

Shattering agony climbs from my lower leg and up my thigh and through my body until it erupts in a choked sob. I gulp a breath of air. Not enough comes in through my helmet. What

13

does carry through it is the scent of piña colada, the smashed fruit that's tumbled from my torn backpack, the seams split with the force of my fall. It's cruel. Sickening sweetness and blinding pain.

The bat comes down a second time and hits my thigh. But I barely feel it. The pain in my lower leg is so overwhelming that a third hit feels like a dull thud.

I see Matt Cranwell's eyes through my visor. Just a heartbeat. Long enough to see determination. Malice. Even the cold thrill of a kill. The whole universe slows to a crawl as he raises the bat above his head. He's positioned over my injured leg. If he hits my lower leg again, I know I'll pass out. And then he'll kill me.

My hand scrapes across the gravel. Nails dig into the dirt. I gather a fistful of sand and stone, and just as he's about to take his swing, I toss it in Matt Cranwell's face.

He pitches over at the waist with a frustrated cry, lowering the bat to work the gravel from his eyes. I tear the weapon from his grip, but he's quick enough to grab it back, even with his eyes watering, leaking dusty tears down his face. I kick his hand with my good foot and the bat flies into the cornfield. Before he can regain his composure, I kick his leg at the knee, and he tumbles down to my level.

I claw my way backward. My left hand slides through the slime of a mashed banana. Matt Cranwell crawls after me, half-blind with dust and rage. He reaches forward and I scramble around me for something to grab on to. A weapon. A shred of hope. Anything.

I sweep my hand though the gravel and a sharp point digs into my palm. I glance over just long enough to spot the cocktail sticks strewn next to my fingers. A bunch of them rest in the shattered plastic tube.

I grab them just as Cranwell wraps his hand around the ankle of my busted leg and tugs.

The scream I let loose is agony and feral rage and desperation. I pitch forward, the spikes clutched in my fist. And I drive their pointed ends right into Matt Cranwell's eye.

He cries out. Releases my ankle. Squirms in the dust, a shaking hand hovering over his face. He turns in my direction as he thrashes from the pain he can't escape. Blood tumbles over his lashes and down his cheek in a viscous crimson rivulet. Three cocktail sticks jut from his eye like a macabre kindergarten craft. Their little flags quiver with his shock. His lid tries to blink, a reflex he can't stop. Every motion of his eyelid hits the highest wooden skewer and he jolts with a fresh hit of pain. He's screaming. Screaming a sound I've never heard before.

My stomach churns and I retch in my helmet. I manage to swallow the vomit down, but just barely.

I have to get the fuck out of here.

I turn myself over and push up onto my good foot, the other dragging behind me as I limp to the bottom of the driveway. Matt is still yelling behind me, curses and pleas that tumble after me down the gravel track.

Tears stream down my face. My molars clamp tight, ready to crack. Every hop I take forces my broken leg to take the pressure of the step. Agony. It's fucking *agony*. A spike of pain that drives from my heel to my thigh. That threatens to bring me down.

"Keep fucking going," I whisper as I flip my visor open. My first breath of fresh air is the only thing that keeps me upright.

I don't know what happens when you get poked in the eye with a fistful of cocktail sticks. His other eye might be squeezed shut.

15

Or maybe he'll be able to fight through the pain and run after me. But I can't think about that shit now. I just have to get to my bike. Hold on to the hope that I can get away.

When I get to the bottom of the driveway, I glance toward the farm. Matt Cranwell is on his hands and knees, still yelling and cursing, spitting venom and dripping blood onto the gravel. And then I look toward the house. Lucy is there, standing behind the screen door. A silhouette. I can't see her face, but I can feel her eyes on me. She can't see me clearly from this distance, not with the helmet obscuring most of my face. She doesn't know me well enough to recognize me from my clothes or my mannerisms. She knows something life-altering has happened, that something is very wrong with this moment, her husband screaming in distress on the driveway. But it's not him she's watching. It's me.

She closes the door and disappears inside the house.

I leave Matt where he belongs, rolling in the dirt. I hobble to my motorcycle. When I swing my leg over the seat, something catches against the inside of my leather pants. Pain ripples up my leg. But I keep going. I start the engine. Close my hand around the clutch. Change gears and pull back the throttle and get the fuck away from this farm.

I don't know where to go.

I just follow my instinct and ride.

OATH

Fionn

I'm rounding the corner for home, walking briskly after my evening run. It'll be the perfect night to sit on the porch with the glass of Weller bourbon I've definitely earned, not just from this run but from the unholy combination of Fran Richard's ingrown toenail and Harold McEnroe's massive boil that I had to deal with at the clinic today. My little house is within sight when an alert comes through on my watch.

Motion detected at front door.

"Fucking Barbara," I hiss as I pivot on my heel and retrace my path into town. I pull up my phone to open the video doorbell app. "I know it's you, you fucking crazy—"

I stop dead in my tracks. It's . . . it's definitely not Barbara at the office.

There's a woman I don't recognize on the camera. Dark hair. Leather jacket. I can't make out distinct features of her face before she looks away down the street. But she's unsteady on her feet. Probably drunk. Maybe someone who's come into town for the circus and had too much fun at the beer garden down the road from the fairgrounds. I consider pressing the button to speak to her, and though my thumb hovers over the circle, I don't touch it. Maybe I should set the alarm I hardly ever use now, thanks to Barbara triggering it one too many times in the middle of the night. *I should call the police*, I think as I start walking, staring at my screen. But I don't do that either.

Not even when she somehow manages to open the locked door.

"*Shit.*"

I pocket my phone and run.

I do the math in my head as I sprint in the direction of the clinic. I've just finished a long run and can't push much faster than a 5:30-minutes-per-mile pace, so I'll be there in seven minutes and nine seconds. I'm sure I'll make it to the office in less time than that if I push as hard as I can.

But it feels like an hour. My lungs burn. My heart riots. I slow to a walk as I round the last corner and a wave of nausea rolls in my stomach.

There are no lights on in the clinic. Nothing to indicate anyone is inside except the faint smear of a bloody handprint on the door handle. A motorcycle with a dented fuel tank lies on its side in the grass. The key is still in the ignition, the polished chrome engine ticking as it cools. A black helmet painted with orange and yellow hibiscus flowers sits discarded on the walkway to the door.

I clasp a hand to the back of my neck, my skin slick with sweat. I look down one end of the road. Then the other. Then back again. There's no one else on the street. I take my phone from my pocket and grip it tightly.

"Fuck it."

I turn on my phone's flashlight and stalk toward the door. It's unlocked. I pan the light across the floor where it reflects on a bloody boot print. A streak of crimson paints the tiles in a long track that snakes though the waiting room. It passes the reception desk. Curves down the hallway like a horror script. *This way to your violent death.*

And like any idiot in any horror film ever made, I follow it, stopping at the mouth of the corridor that leads to the exam rooms.

There's no sound. No smell aside from the astringent burn of antiseptic that clings to the back of my throat. No light except for the red emergency exit sign at the end of the hall.

I guide my flashlight to follow the blood on the floor. It leads beneath the closed door of Exam Room 3.

With a single deep breath, I follow. I hold that breath as I press my ear to the door. Nothing comes from the other side, not even when I push it open and it meets resistance. A boot. A limp leg. A woman who doesn't stir.

My thoughts snap like a glow stick. From darkness to light. I hit the switch for the overhead fluorescents. Urgency and training propel me into the room, and I drop to my knees beside the woman lying on my exam room floor.

A makeshift tourniquet made from her shirt is tied around her right thigh. A fresh one from the cabinet is loosely knotted just beneath it, as though she couldn't tighten it with her waning strength. Medical supplies are scattered across the floor. Gauze bandages. Sterile cloth. A pair of scissors. Blood trickles down her calf and pools on the floor. The scent of pineapple and banana is a sweet contradiction to the broken bone that pokes through the torn flesh of her lower leg. Her leather pants are cut all the way up to the wound, as though she got as far as exposing the fracture and couldn't bear it anymore.

"Miss. *Miss*," I say. She's turned away from me, her dark hair strewn across her face. I press my palm to her cool cheek and turn her head in my direction. Rapid, shallow breaths spill past her parted lips. I rest two fingers against her pulse as I tap her cheek with the other hand. "Come on, miss. Wake up."

Her brow crinkles. Thick, dark lashes flutter. She groans. Her eyes open, inky pools of pain and suffering. I need her conscious, but I hate the agony I see painted in her features. Regret twists like a hot pin lodged deep in a cavern of my heart, a feeling I learned to shut away a long time ago so I can do my job. But somehow, when her eyes fuse to mine, that long-forgotten piece of me comes alive in the dark. And then she grabs my hand where it rests on her throat. She squeezes. Locks me into a moment that feels eternal. "Help," she whispers, and then her hand slips from mine.

I stare at her for just a moment. A heartbeat. A blink.

And then I get to work.

I pull a wallet from her jacket and dial 911 as I stride from the room to grab ice packs from the freezer. I relay the details of the woman's license and condition to the dispatcher. *Twenty-six-year-old female, unconscious, possible motorcycle accident.* When I return to the exam room, she's still unconscious, and I place the ice packs and my phone on the counter so I can hook her up to the blood pressure monitor. *Lower leg open fracture. Blood loss. Hypotensive blood pressure. Her pulse is climbing.*

I've gotten a line in for an IV and tied a proper tourniquet around her leg by the time the ambulance arrives. But she still doesn't wake up. Not when the paramedics fit a brace around her leg. Not when we lift her onto the gurney. Not even when we load her into the back of the ambulance and the motion jostles her. I take her hand and tell myself it's so I'll know if she wakes up. And eventually, she does. Her eyes flutter open and latch onto mine, and regret pierces me again. The paramedic across from me fits the oxygen mask to her face, and the plastic fogs with her increasingly rapid breaths as the pain settles into her consciousness.

"I'm Dr. Kane," I say as I squeeze her hand, her palm cool and clammy. "You're on the way to the hospital. Is your name Rose?"

She nods in the emergency neck brace.

"Try to remain still. Do you remember what happened?"

She presses her eyes shut, but not fast enough to veil the flash of panic in her eyes. "Yes," she says, though I can barely hear her over the wail of the sirens.

"Was it a motorcycle accident?"

Rose's eyes snap open. The crease between her brows deepens. There's a brief pause before she says, "Yes. I . . . I hit a slippery patch and crashed."

"Do you have any pain in your back or neck? Anything else aside from your leg?"

"No."

The paramedic cuts away Rose's makeshift tourniquet and a fresh waft of piña colada floods my nostrils. I lower my voice and lean a little close when I ask, "Have you been drinking?"

"*Fuck* no," she says. Her nose scrunches beneath the mask, and she reaches up to lower it despite my protest. "Are you, like, a *real* doctor?"

I blink at her. "Yes . . . ?"

"You don't sound sure."

"I'm pretty sure. Put your mask back on—"

"You look like a TV doctor. Dr. McSpicy or something. What are your credentials?"

I look over at the paramedic who tries to chew her grin into submission. "You only gave her morphine, right?"

"Why are you in activewear?" Rose barrels on.

The paramedic snorts.

"Are you one of those CrossFit guys? You look like a CrossFit guy."

I try to say no as the paramedic says, "Doc is *definitely* one of those CrossFit guys. My husband calls him Dr. Beast Mode."

Rose's cackle becomes a wince as the paramedic repositions fresh ice packs around the wound. Her grip tightens on my hand. "Who are you?" I ask the paramedic across Rose's body. "Have we met?"

She smirks as she checks the infusion pump. "I'm Alice. I live around the corner from you on Elwood Street. My husband, Danny, is a personal trainer at the gym . . . ?"

"Right, of course. *Danny*," I reply convincingly.

Rose grins, her dark eyes pinned to Alice. "He has no fucking idea who you mean."

"I know."

"How long have you lived in Hartford?" My glare shifts from the paramedic down to Rose and softens—but only into wariness. Her blood pressure has improved a little with the fluids. But pain still carves its marks across her features, creasing little lines into the sides of her nose and between her brows. I try to pull my hand from hers so I can get a better look at her leg, but she doesn't let go. "How long, Doc?"

I shake my head just a little to clear it, as though I might free myself from the way she looks at me. "Until we get to the hospital . . . ?"

"No. *How long have you lived in Hartford?* Or maybe we should go back to the credentials question. I don't want you amputating the wrong leg. Do you have short-term memory loss?"

Her faint smile is full of pity and mischief. But her dark eyes betray her. They're searching. Filled with distress. Filled with fear.

"No one's amputating your leg," I reply, gently squeezing her hand.

Ross swallows. She tries to keep her face set in a neutral mask, but the heart rate monitor betrays her. "But the bone is *sticking out.* What if—"

"I promise you, Rose. No one is amputating your leg." Rose's liquid eyes stay fused to mine, dark pools of molten chocolate. I slip her mask back up over her nose and mouth. Even though she says nothing in reply, I realize her words have been repeating in my mind since the moment she passed out in my exam room. *Help. Help. Help.* "I'll assist with the surgery," I say. "I'll be right there with you."

Rose tries to nod again, and I place my free palm on her forehead, where her bangs cling to her skin. I tell myself I'm just doing it to keep her still. But something aches beneath my bones when she closes her eyes and a tear rolls down her temple. When I pull my palm away, I let my fingertips graze the streak it leaves behind.

What the fuck, Kane. Get your shit together.

I refocus on her vitals. Try to concentrate only on the blood pressure monitor and the steady beat of her quickened pulse. I can't count the number of procedures I've done or medications I've administered or patients I've treated in my short career so far. But there's only been one whose hand I've held in an ambulance. Only one whom I've brought through the emergency bay, one for whom I've sat in the blue vinyl chairs outside the imaging ward to wait for her X-rays, my knee bouncing with impatience. Only one for whom I've asked to scrub in at the surgical suite so I could assist the orthopedic surgeon with the hours-long internal fixation procedure. So I could be there to reassure her that I would keep my promise as she fell unconscious on the surgical table.

Only one whose whispered plea for help still keeps me here at the hospital, hovering near her bed in the recovery room, her chart clasped in my hands even though I've read it enough times that I could recite it from memory.

Rose Evans.

I'm absently staring at her sleeping form, her leg splinted and suspended. I wonder if she's comfortable. If she's warm enough. If she'll have a nightmare about the accident. Maybe I should get the nurses to check on her again. Make sure her other minor injuries have been properly addressed.

I'm so engrossed in my thoughts that I don't notice Dr. Chopra until she's standing right next to me.

"Know her?" she asks. She pulls her reading glasses down from where they're nestled in her silver hair so she can skim the details of Rose's chart. I shake my head. She presses her lips into a line, the fine wrinkles around them deepening. "Thought you might, given the request to scrub in."

"She showed up at my office in Hartford. I felt . . ." I trail off. I'm not sure what I felt. Something unfamiliar and urgent. Unexpected. "I felt compelled to stay."

Dr. Chopra nods in my periphery. "Some patients are like that. Reminding us why we chose our path. Maybe you might want to scrub in more often? We could always use the help."

A smile teases the corners of my lips. "I thought you'd given up asking."

"It only took me four years to wear you down. Now that I know it can be done, don't think I'm going to stop."

"I'm afraid I'll have to disappoint you," I say as I cross my arms and straighten my spine.

"Shame. I know it's not as exciting as Mass General must have been, but we do still get some interesting surgical cases in the boonies. I had one tonight shortly before you came in. A patient of yours according to his records, actually. Belligerent prick, if you ask me. Cranmore? Cranburn?"

"*Cranwell?* You had Matt Cranwell in here?" I ask, and Dr. Chopra nods. "Yeah, I don't think you're far off with the belligerent prick assessment. What was he in for?"

"He had a handful of cocktail sticks in his eye."

"He . . . *what?*" Dr. Chopra lifts a shoulder. My brow furrows as I turn to face her. "He wasn't transported out to a level-one trauma center?"

"No. There was no salvaging the eye. Dr. Mitchell performed the surgery. Must have been an interesting story, but the delightful Mr. Cranwell wasn't willing to share." Dr. Chopra passes Rose's chart back to me with a faint, weary smile. "You should go home and get some rest. When are you in next?"

"Thursday night," I say absentmindedly as I stare down at Rose's name on the chart.

"See you then," Dr. Chopra replies, and then she disappears, leaving me on my own with my sleeping patient.

The one who smelled like piña colada. The one who didn't call an ambulance despite her injury, choosing to break into my clinic instead. Who seemed surprised when I asked her if it was a motorcycle accident.

I head to where Rose's clothes are folded on the vinyl chair next to her bed. Only her boots and her black leather jacket are left. Everything else was cut from her body. There's a small black pouch in one pocket. Inside it are metal tools, some of them streaked with dried blood. Realizing they must be the tools she used to break into my clinic, I put them back. Her wallet is still in the inside jacket pocket, and I take it out next. I pull out her license, the one I skimmed for vital details when I was on the phone with the emergency dispatcher. The card is registered in the state of Texas, an address in Odessa. I look through the rest of her wallet but there's not much to find, just a debit and credit card and twenty dollars in cash. Nothing that confirms or denies the twinge of intuition that creeps through my guts.

At least, not until I replace her wallet inside her jacket and my fingers graze another card, one that's loose in the interior pocket.

Another driver's license. One belonging to a man.

Matthew Cranwell.

STRANDED

Rose

Day three of being stuck in this bed.

Zofia brought Baz with her yesterday and tried her best to cheer me up by saying my stay in this hospital is like a less-fun version of a holiday, minus the beach. Or the sand. Or the hot guys. So that was a fail. Baz just rolled his eyes and laid his first three Venom Dark Origins comics and my tarot deck next to the medication button that rests untouched beside my hand. Then he asked the question that's been haunting me worse than the smell of the hot dog stand in a mid-August heat wave: *When are you getting out of here?*

Not soon enough.

And now, as José Silveria stands near the foot of my bed, his hat clutched between his weathered hands, I'm faced with the hard reality of exactly what *not soon enough* really means.

"What about the bottle stand? Or the balloon-and-dart? I can totally handle one of the games, I swear," I say, trying not to sound desperate. Judging by the way José sighs and fidgets with the brim of his hat, I'm failing.

"Rose, you can barely stand up. How long does it take you to get from here to the bathroom?" I frown. Ten minutes doesn't sound like a great answer, so I say nothing at all. "We can't stay in Hartford any longer or we'll be late for our dates in Grand Island. I can't take you with us, Rose. You need to stay and recover."

"But—"

"I know you. You won't look after yourself and you can't say no to anyone when they ask for help. Jim'll be lugging equipment or stacking boxes, and you'll be out there on one leg, trying to do it for him."

"That's not true."

"What about the time you busted your fingers in that crash two years ago?"

I cringe and tighten my left hand into a fist to hide how permanently crooked my pinkie is. "What about it?"

"Did you or did you not offer to help fix the curtain and end up stapling it to your hand?"

"Unrelated. One was an accident. The other was . . . also an accident."

José sighs and offers me a smile lit with the warmth that's earned him his much-deserved reputation as the loveable ringmaster of Silveria Circus. "We will always welcome you back. *When you're healed.* But right now, you need a chance to recover." José rests one hand on my good ankle. His eyes are always so kind with their crinkled edges and warm mahogany hues. Even when he's breaking my heart. "You'll come back as soon as you're given the all clear. This isn't forever. It's just for right now."

I nod.

His words echo in my mind as though my subconscious is desperate to cling to them and make them real. But even thinking about how long *just for right now* could be has my chest tightening and my eyes stinging. I've been with Silveria for so long, I can almost convince myself that I've forgotten the other life I left behind. I was just a kid, only fifteen when I joined the tour. Silveria has been my home. My family. And though I know he's right, and I don't want to make this harder on José than I'm sure it is, I can't help but feel discarded.

I shrug and give José a smile, but when I sniffle, his expression draws tight with regret. "Yeah, it's cool. I get it," I say as I clear my throat and push myself up a little higher, trying not to wince when my leg jostles in the foam block that keeps it suspended off the mattress. "I'll be fine. I'll catch up when I can."

José gives me a smile, one that doesn't quite reach his eyes. They might even be a little glassy, and that splits the cracks in my heart even wider. "Jim set your RV up at the Prairie Princess Campground just outside of town."

"Sounds like a classy joint," I deadpan.

"There's a hookup there but we filled the generator with gas, just in case."

I nod, unwilling to trust my voice to make words.

José takes a breath, probably preparing to launch into the thousand reasons why this unexpected time off is a "good thing," and how maybe I'm overdue for some time off, but he's cut off when Dr. Kane strides into the room.

And *oh holy fuck*, but he's ten times hotter than I remember from the first time we met. He's so pretty that it almost shocks me out of the burning ache in my chest at the circus leaving me behind. At least until I realize I probably look about as appealing as a bag of dicks. I think it actually makes my leg hurt less just to look at him with all his doctory seriousness and his stethoscope and his ridiculous good looks. His rich brown hair is swept into place. His sapphire eyes catch the afternoon sun that filters through the blinds. No activewear today, but I can still make out the athletic build beneath his white coat and pressed blue shirt and camel-colored pants. He glances from the tablet he clutches to me, then to José, then to José's hand where it rests on my ankle.

His eyes narrow for just a heartbeat before his expression smooths. "I'm sorry to interrupt. I'm Dr. Kane," he says as he extends a hand to José.

"José Silveria. Thank you for taking such good care of my Rose." Dr. Kane's expression is unreadable as he gives José a single nod. But José? I already know what he's about to say. The delight is written all over his face. "Rose is my *pequeño gorrión*. My little sparrow. One of my best performers."

"At the circus," I say flatly. "I work at the circus."

"Oh. That's—"

"Tell me, are you married, Dr. Kane?"

I suppress a groan. Dr. Kane clears his throat, clearly thrown off, though I find it hard to believe he hasn't heard overbearing questions like this before. "To my work," he answers.

José chuckles and shakes his head. "I know how that goes. I used to be the same."

"You're still the same," I say. "Speaking of which, don't you have somewhere to be? You should be getting out of here or you'll be setting up in the dark tonight."

Part of me doesn't want him to go. I wish more than anything that he'd pull up a seat and tell me stories of his younger years growing up in the circus, how he inherited a dying show and made it into a spectacle. I wish he'd tell me a lullaby of memories. That I'd wake up in my own bed, and that the last few days were nothing more than a dream that will be forgotten. But I also want to rip the Band-Aid from the wound. The longer José stays, the more likely I am to feel it, that hole in my chest that I don't think will ever truly be filled, no matter how much I try to shore up its crumbling edges.

There's not much I can get past José. He pushes between Dr. Kane and the bed to come to my side and press a kiss to my cheek. When he straightens, his eyes soften, the wrinkles that fan from their corners deepening with his smile. My nose stings, but I force the rising tears into submission. "Take care of yourself, *pequeño gorrión*. Give yourself some time. As much as you need." I give him a jerk of a nod, and then José turns, extending a hand to Dr. Kane. "Thank you for your help, Dr. Kane."

The doctor accepts the offered handshake, though he seems unsure, like he's caught on José's words. Before I can decode his expression, José draws him into a back-clapping hug. He whispers something to Dr. Kane, and the doctor's eyes land on me, a blue that cuts through my layers to land somewhere deep and dark, where that hole seems to crumble a little more along its edges. Dr. Kane gives a slight nod in reply, then José gives him a final clap and lets him go. He turns at the threshold and gives me a wink. And then that's it. José is gone, the wound left behind a little too fresh to cover beneath an apathetic mask.

Dr. Kane watches the door for a long moment, the tablet still clutched in his hands, his analytical stare locked on the space José

31

just occupied. Then he turns to me, and the ache of abandonment I feel must linger in my face, because he immediately flashes me a smile that's supposed to be reassuring but comes off as anything but.

"Is my leg going to fall off, Doc?"

A crease appears between his brows. "What? No."

"You look like you're going to tell me it's rotting and about to fall off."

"It's going to be fine," he says, nodding to my leg where it's splinted and suspended on a foam block. "We put pearls in it."

"Pearls?" I snort a laugh. "You're into pearling? No offense, but you don't strike me as the type, Doc."

Dr. Kane blinks at me as though he's trying to decipher a foreign language. His expression suddenly clears, and he muffles a startled cough into his fist. "Um, antibiotic pearls. In your leg."

"That's a relief. We're seriously going to have to revisit your credentials otherwise. Probably with a lawyer."

The hot doctor's cheeks blush in the most adorable shade of crimson. He runs a hand through his perfect hair and though it mostly falls right back into place, I feel an unexpected sense of satisfaction at seeing a few wayward strands that refuse to comply.

"How's the pain?"

"Fine," I lie.

"Have you been taking pain medication?"

"Not really. I'm okay."

"Have you been sleeping?"

"Sure."

"Eating?"

I follow the doctor's gaze to where it's stuck on the half-eaten turkey sandwich that sits on the nightstand next to my bed.

"Um . . ." My stomach audibly growls, filling the silence between us. "I'm not sure that really classifies as food."

Dr. Kane frowns at me. "You need to keep up your strength. Proper nutrition will help your body repair itself and fight off infection."

"Well," I say as I push myself up higher on my bed, "you can let me out of here and I promise the first thing I'll do is seek out real food."

His frown deepens and he sets the tablet down on a side table. "How about we see how things are healing," he says, and grabs a pair of latex gloves before approaching the side of the bed. He tells me everything he's going to do before he does it. *I'm going to take the splint off. I'm going to remove the dressing and have a look at the incision.* His words are clinical and unfussy, but his hands are warm and gentle on my swollen leg. There's a kindness in his touch that runs deeper than this professional persona. But he seems different from the man whose hand I held in the ambulance. Like that version is the real one, trapped beneath this polished veneer.

"I'm sorry about your clinic," I say quietly as I think back on that moment we met. "I wanted to make it to the hospital."

"Why didn't you call an ambulance?" he asks, not taking his eyes from the wound he inspects.

"I thought it would be faster if I took myself."

"You could have called from the clinic. Or found someone to help you along the way." Dr. Kane turns his sharp gaze to me, scouring my face with analytical intensity. "There was no one around when you had your accident?"

I shake my head.

33

"Where did you crash?"

Panic twists through my veins, a burst of adrenaline that has nowhere to go. I swallow it down and try to stay still. "A side road. Not sure which one. I'm not really familiar with the area."

"Did anyone see your crash?" he asks, glancing at me as he prods around the incision. He probably thinks he's being stoic and unreadable, but I don't miss the way his eyes narrow a fraction.

"Nope, don't think so."

"What about—"

"Dr. Kane," a second doctor says, cutting short his next words as she enters the room, a nurse drifting in her wake with a cart of supplies. "I thought you weren't due in until Thursday. This is a nice surprise."

"Dr. Chopra," he says with a deferential nod. I swear I catch a fleeting blush on his cheekbones when he turns to face her. A spark seems to catch in her eye, a little light behind her glasses. I guess I'm not the only one who noticed the hint of color in his face. "I thought I'd pick up an extra shift."

"How's our patient?"

"Getting there," he says. He gestures to my leg as Dr. Chopra joins him to look down at my incision. Everything is still swollen, not that I want to look too closely. They chatter about blood values and medications as Dr. Chopra picks up the tablet and reviews my file. Dr. Kane presses a final time around the incision before he seems to almost reluctantly admit to Dr. Chopra that "everything seems stable."

"Excellent," she says, reading through the notes before she passes the tablet back to him. "In that case, I think we can probably discharge you tomorrow afternoon, Rose. Nurse Naomi here can help you with a bath now and put a fresh dressing on that incision."

With a brief smile, she departs, and Dr. Kane shifts on his feet as though he's a metal fleck unable to resist her magnetic pull as she strides toward the door. His gaze bounces between me and the nurse, and then finally settles on me. "I'm not in tomorrow," he says, and I don't know how to respond, the silence lingering a little longer than it should. "I hope you feel better soon."

"Thank you. For everything. Truly."

With a curt nod in reply and a final beat of delay, he turns and strides away. Naomi and I watch the door, and I half expect him to come back in and say whatever seemed to be weighing on his mind those final moments before he left. But he doesn't reappear.

Naomi turns my way with a brittle smile, shifting a lock of dark curly hair behind her ear. "Let's get you up," she says, and raises the head of my mattress. There's a stretched silence as she helps me to sit up, a tense pause as though she's not ready to help me down from the bed.

"Everything okay?" I ask. Her hand is trembling around mine.

"Yes."

"Are you sure . . . ?"

Her attention darts toward the door and back to me. Her eyes are so dark they're nearly black, but in them I can see every shade of fear and pain I've come to know in women who ask for my help. I know what she's about to say when she leans closer and whispers, "I saw you at the circus. You're the tarot reader, aren't you?"

I nod.

"The Sparrow." It's a reverential prayer. The sound of hope that I've come to know. A secret kinship, bonded by suffering that transcends blood.

I remember her face now, the woman who was approaching my tent with a rolled twenty-dollar bill in her hand. A spike of chemical impulse hits my veins. Everything sharpens: the details of the room. The sounds of staff who pass in the corridor. The smell of antiseptic and industrial cleaner. The spark in Naomi's eyes when I reach for the deck on my side table.

I shuffle my cards.

"If we've got a minute, maybe I can give you a quick reading before the bath." I know the card I'm looking for by feel, by the fray at the edges, by the crease at one corner. I flip it over. "Ace of Cups," I say. "It represents following your inner voice. What does it tell you? What do you want?"

The hope brightens in Naomi's eyes, and my heart responds with a quickened beat.

"To take flight," she says.

I smile. And though Naomi's spirit might be bruised, it's not broken. I can see it in the way she smiles back.

I draw the next card. Maybe it's not what you'd expect. It's not Death. It's not the Knight of Swords. Not harbingers of chaos. I draw the Star. Hope on the horizon. Because in killing, there can be living. There can be rebirth.

Naomi shares her secrets in whispered notes. Stories of a man. One who demeans her. Belittles her. One who threatens her and harms her and controls her. One she can't break away from, not on her own. She asks me for help. And my heart swells until it aches.

Because I know this is something I can give, even if it takes a little time.

My thumb caresses the tattoo at my wrist.

I might have been abandoned here, left in a cage. Maybe my wings have been clipped. But I can still fly.

PRAIRIE PRINCESS

ROSE

There aren't many people around the Prairie Princess Campground when the taxi drops me off on the gravel driveway, the driver waiting patiently as I wrangle my aluminum crutches out the car door and shimmy my way free of the vehicle. There's only a smattering of motor homes. I guess it's not super popular to camp in a flat grass field outside Hartford, population 3,501. The taxi drives away and leaves me to the sound of children in the playground, all three of them pinning me with unnerving stares, the metronomic squeak of the ancient swings a sad melody within the downtrodden campground. I pause long enough to give them a half-hearted wave. All three stop swinging in a synchronized, sudden halt of motion. They don't wave back.

"That's . . . yikes," I whisper. "That's just fucking weird."

One of them tilts her head as though listening, even though there's no fucking way she heard me at this distance, and then all three resume their swinging at the exact same moment.

"I guess at least I know how I'll die." I swallow the sudden tightness choking up my throat and start to hobble my way across the unkempt gravel, my leg throbbing. My RV stands out among the others strewn across the clearing. Big ol' Dorothy might be closing in on thirty years old, but she's pretty as hell, with polished chrome bumpers and a custom paint job of a flock of sparrows over a sunset of pink and yellow and orange. I've put every spare penny into Dorothy's needs. She's my year-round home. But this is the first time I've ever walked up to my RV and wished I had something more permanent. Maybe the kind of place where it's not so easy for the rest of your home to just go and leave you behind.

"You're just being sore. You'll be back on the tour in no time," I whisper above the clink and rattle of my crutches. "You'll be fine on your own. You're not afraid of the murder children. Because you're a fierce, independent woman."

And I believe that too. At least, I do until I stop at the door of my motor home.

"Fuck."

It's hot as Satan's ball sack out here beneath the unobstructed prairie sun, and all I want to do is get inside so I can lie down and, let's be real, probably ugly-cry myself to sleep. Problem is, I don't know how to do that with crutches and a brace through a narrow door that's two feet off the ground and a set of narrow steps on the inside. I've never thought about buying folding or temporary stairs to get in. It wasn't something I ever needed.

My shoulders sag as I press my weight into the padding of the crutches, my body already protesting this foreign way of moving.

I'm blinking away exhausted tears when I hear a vehicle slowly roll to a stop behind me. I sweep a quick pass of my thumb beneath my lashes and then grip onto the handle of my crutches with renewed determination. I don't need people staring. I hobble closer and slide the key into the lock and turn it. And then a large hand reaches above me and pulls the door open.

I startle, losing my balance as I turn, the sun blinding as I look toward the man standing behind me. He grasps my arm to keep me from falling. "I'm so sorry," he says, his voice instantly familiar. He drops his hold on me just as quickly as it was given and moves back a step. "I didn't mean to startle you."

"McSpicy . . . ?" I squint at him, my gaze darting toward the classic Ford F-250 parked nearby, my motorcycle strapped upright in the bed. "What are you doing here?"

"Scaring the shit out of you, by the looks of things. I'm sorry about that." He glances toward the open door and the narrow stairs that lead into my home and frowns. When he turns his attention back to me, the intensity of his narrowed eyes burrows beneath my skin to heat it. "I heard you were released this morning instead of the afternoon, so I thought I'd bring your bike back and check on you. How are you doing?"

I could lie, if I just had a bit more in me to do it. But something about this man makes me want to tell him more than I should. Maybe it's the way he watches me, his eyes fixed to mine, the door held open for me, his other hand lifted just a little as though he's ready to catch me if I stumble.

"It's been a shitty few days," I say, my voice thinner than I hoped it would be.

Dr. Kane's expression softens. His hold on the door relaxes a little and it creaks on its hinges. "Yeah. I can imagine."

"I'll manage."

"I have no doubt."

"Really? Because you sound like you have *many* doubts."

He looks toward the motor home and shrugs. "I have doubts about the stairs." When his attention returns to me, a smile tugs at one corner of his lips, his eyes a lighter shade of blue in the bright sun. "I don't have any about you. I mean—your ability to look after yourself, of course."

I bite down on a weary grin, though he doesn't see it, not with the way his eyes dart to the shadowed interior of my motor home, then the gravel beneath us, then back to his vehicle as though he can't wait to get into it and drive away.

"You should probably have some doubts about me, Doc," I say, catching his gaze when it flicks back to me. "But I'll still manage. Thanks for bringing my bike back. I'm afraid I can't help you unload it, though."

"I can do that," he says, and I nod my thanks, gripping onto my crutch handles as I refocus on the entrance of my motor home. It's going to be even hotter in there than it is out here. Dorothy's been baking in the sun, but I'm desperate to peel off my leather jacket and strip down to my underwear and sleep until tomorrow. When I get to the step, I set my crutches against the side of the vehicle and grip the interior handle of the stairs. With the doc holding the door open, I hoist myself inside but hiss a curse when I bump my splint against the ledge on my way up.

"I'm good," I grit out. Dr. Kane scrutinizes me as I pivot on my

41

good foot to face him, his forehead crinkling at my forced smile. I reach back out the door for my crutches, but instead of grabbing them, I knock them over like dominoes.

"Well," I say as we both stare down at them where they mock me from the ground, both mostly hidden beneath the motor home. "That . . . wasn't great."

"Not a strong start, no."

"I'll manage."

"I can tell."

"You're not really helping."

My deadpan joke seems to slap Dr. Kane out of his own thoughts and into action. "I'm sorry," he says, his voice barely more than a whisper. He lets the door close gently, resting it against my elbow before he bends to collect my crutches. His faded gray T-shirt pulls tight across his back as he leans forward to pull them from beneath the motor home. Hard planes of muscle bracket his spine, his shoulders broad and defined beneath the thin cotton.

I swallow when he straightens to his full height and stands before me. I'm a hint taller than him where I stand on my little landing inside the motor home, but he still seems to take up all the space in my field of vision.

"Thank you," I say, a little breathless. I wrap a hand around one of the crutches and try to pull it toward me, but he doesn't relinquish it. "I'll manage."

"Yeah, I heard that. But you'd manage better at my house," he blurts out. His eyes widen as though the words have escaped his control.

"Um . . . what . . . ?"

"I mean . . . you should come to my house. This setup," he says, waving his free hand toward my home, "it's not ideal. You can barely get into it."

"I just need some practice."

"You don't have air-conditioning."

"I do . . ." Sort of. When Dorothy is moving and the windows are open. Also, when she feels like it. Which is basically never.

The doc gives me a suspicious frown. For a moment, I'm not sure if I said my thoughts out loud. "What about a shower?"

"I'm sure they filled my water tank before they left," I say, scanning the grounds beyond his shoulder. "And when it runs out, there's a communal shower over there."

Dr. Kane turns to follow my gaze to a small wooden cottage with a SHOWER sign painted on the side, the building's green paint as faded as the unmowed prairie grass surrounding it.

"Looks totally safe."

"They only murder people in there on the weekends."

Dr. Kane faces me once more, his expression both wary and clinical. "You need to look after that incision and come back in a week to get the stitches out and the cast put on," he says. "You can manage that?"

I swallow down the assurances that would only be half-truths at best. With every moment that passes, I'm increasingly nervous about being the star in what is clearly a horror movie entitled *Prairie Princess Campground: The Grisly Murder of Rose Evans*, but I don't really want some guy I barely know to realize that. As much as McSpicy is hot as fuck and seems genuinely sweet, I'm used to looking after myself. And it's tough enough to face the fact that I can't get around the way I'm used to without a constant reminder that I need help.

"Rose . . ." A darkness settles into the hollows beneath Dr. Kane's eyes. He searches my face, hunting for something, like he's weighing options and pathways set before him. The longer the silence stretches on, the more I long to fill it. When I shift to rest my swollen foot on the step behind me, he takes a sharp breath. "Matthew Cranwell."

I try to keep my expression neutral. But we both know he caught me off guard. "Who?" I say a beat later than I should have.

"Matt Cranwell," he repeats. "Do you know him?"

I swallow. Shake my head.

A shadow falls across his features, even in the bright light. Dr. Kane never averts his gaze, even when I try to break the connection and look away. He's still right there, taking up the space in my door, sucking up all the energy that seems to crackle between us in the hot summer air.

The suspended moment seems to stretch long enough that I can imagine every thought and accusation that's probably swirling in his head. He leans closer, his voice a lethal whisper when he says, "Did he do this to you?"

I want to back away. But I don't move. I want to shake my head, but I can't seem to make myself do that either. I'm like a fawn, unable to run when danger discovers it hidden in the grass.

"I suspect you're not the only person he's hurt," Dr. Kane says. His shirt stretches over his biceps, the muscles more tense than they need to be for the simple action of running his hand through his hair. Strands fall across his brow, his forehead creased in a frown. "Do you want to tell me what really happened that night?"

Each breath I take is so shallow, it might not even exist. My heart riots in my chest. I still can't shake my head, even though it could be the difference between me and the back of a police car. *Be tough. Be tough be tough be tough. You drive a fucking motorcycle in a metal cage in front of an audience of two hundred people in a goddamn circus. The fucking Globe of Death, for fucksakes. Don't cry, Rose Evans. Don't you fucking cry.*

I totally fucking cry.

A single tear slips past my lashes, sliding down my burning cheek. The crease softens between his brows as the doctor watches me sweep it away with a frustrated flick of my fingers. "I'd better go. Thank you, Doc," I say, trying to pull the door closed behind me. But he doesn't let it go.

"Rose, he's not the kind of person you want to fuck with." His expression darkens, and it feels as though there's no escaping his warning. "He was a Lincoln County deputy before he got himself suspended a few years back, something about an arrest that got out of hand. From what I heard, it was the last straw in a string of bad behavior on the job. Now he spends most of his time between two places. His farm outside Elmsdale, and the Fergusons' grain mill. Which is literally *next door*," he says, gesturing toward the back of my motor home. I look in the direction he's pointing, but I see . . . nothing. Nothing but wheat fields beyond the fence that encompasses the campground, with no structures and no landmarks visible. When I turn back to the doc with a question in my crinkled nose and furrowed brow, he rolls his eyes. "Okay, *fine*. Next door is a few miles that way, but it's still next door. Technically."

I can't say I love the idea of Matt being in my neighborhood, even if that neighborhood is a bunch of plants and a view for miles, an unobstructed perspective that makes it hard for him to sneak up on me. But I'm guessing he's a crafty motherfucker, even if he is down an eye.

My stomach flips uncomfortably. I stare blankly at the horizon, my mind trapped on the memory as I replay the image of driving the cocktail sticks into his face.

"I can help you."

The softness in Dr. Kane's voice pulls me away from the imagery, a soothing caress, so unlike the violence of that night. When I turn to him, something about the curves and angles of his face seems pleading. "It's safer in Hartford. I hardly ever see him there, only at the clinic once or twice a year. Elmsdale is closer for him." The doctor's eyes don't leave mine as he pulls something from his pocket and holds it between us. Matt's license. "Come and stay with me. I have a guest room. A hot shower. Functional air-conditioning. Edible food. I even know a thing or two about looking after injuries."

I blink at him, processing his words as he patiently waits for me to catch up. "I'm out of work," I finally say, dropping my gaze to the splint that encases my leg. "I can't pay you."

"I'm not asking you to."

Dr. Kane passes me the license. With a tentative hand, I grasp the edge, but I don't pull it away.

"You're not going to serial kill me in my sleep, are you?" I ask, narrowing my eyes. I've only asked him that to make him laugh. For any other man I barely know, it would be a legitimate question. But there's something about Dr. Kane that puts me at ease. Maybe it's the way he held my hand in the ambulance. May it's the way he holds this damning piece of evidence between us, one that could so easily be used to put me in jail. But I think it's just an essence, like a vibration in the air, something I can't touch or taste. Something I just know. I'm safe with him.

A grin slowly ignites in his full lips. "You're not going to serial kill *me* in my sleep, are you?"

I shake my head.

"Good. Then why don't you pack up some of your essentials and we get the fuck out of here. This place gives me *Children of the Corn* vibes," he says as he looks toward the seemingly feral group of kids on the swings.

"Same, honestly. Except that's wheat, not corn."

"It's still crops. And creepy kids. That's enough for me."

With an unsure smile, I pull the license free of his hand and slide it into the interior pocket of my jacket. He unloads my motorcycle as I water my plants and throw a few changes of clothes into a backpack. When I get back to the door, he takes the bag from me and slings it over a shoulder. Before I can struggle my way down from the ledge, Dr. Kane slides a strong arm around my waist and lifts me out of the RV, igniting an electric charge that skitters through my chest and dances along my ribs. I feel as though I'm floating in the bracket of his muscular grasp, like it takes no effort on his part to take my weight. When he sets me down, it's done carefully, slowly. He offers me his arm for balance and waits until I'm steady on my foot before he passes me my crutches. And even when we leave, he walks with me, matching my slow pace when he could easily stride ahead.

I don't remember the last time a man walked me to the passenger side of a vehicle. Or opened the door for me. Or got my belongings situated before carefully helping me inside. I don't remember anyone buckling me in. Not ever. But he does all those things, chatting the whole time, telling me about the truck and his house and the town. He flashes me a fleeting smile before he closes the door, and I can't recall ever feeling the way I feel now about such a simple gesture.

Dr. Kane slips into the driver's seat and keys the engine. He shifts it into gear, but keeps his foot on the brake as he turns to look at me. "Anything I should know before we do this?"

That electric charge I just felt? It seems to burn in my guts. I shake my head again.

"Okay. Good," he says, and then we roll away from my motor home and the Prairie Princess Campground.

I should stop him. Place my hand on the sun-kissed, corded muscle of his forearm as he reaches forward to turn up the volume on the radio. Tell him what really happened with Matt. I should shatter this moment. I should do it now, before it shatters me.

The truth rises to the surface. But it doesn't quite break through.

LEFT UNSAID

Fionn

What the fuck am I doing?

I've asked myself that at least thirty times on the drive home from the campground. I've tried not to let it show that this thought is consuming me. I've kept up conversation, trying to distract myself from this mantra that repeats itself on a loop beneath my inner monologue. But now that I've lifted Rose out of the passenger seat and set her down on the walkway to my home, it blares through my mind like an air-raid siren.

What the fuck am I doing?

Helping. That's what I'm doing. She asked for help, and something about her desperate request has embedded into me, a thorn that's lodged deep in my mind. The strange thing is, I can't remember any patient having asked me before, not like that. Symptoms. Histories. Medications. I've heard family ancestries, passed down in the building blocks that make each one of us unique. I've heard fear and gratitude. But I've never heard that simple plea for help. Not until Rose.

And she needs it.

Rose struggles up the steep stairs to my door on her crutches, the locomotion still unfamiliar to her. She hisses a string of curses. I want to simply pick her up and deposit her on the landing, but I hover behind her instead, waiting for her to work out the best way to maneuver on her own. When she gets to the narrow porch, she turns toward me and offers a weary but triumphant smile. I try not to be spellbound by it, but I think I fail.

"Well," she says, snagging my attention away from her full lips and back to her eyes where it belongs. "That kind of sucked. Hope I don't have to get anywhere quickly."

"You did well."

"Would have been easier if you just picked me up."

"Umm." I grip a hand over the back of my neck, trying to recall if I actually said my thoughts out loud. "Probably . . . ?"

"Maybe you should make me an adult-sized BabyBjörn and just carry me around strapped to your chest," she barrels on, a teasing glimmer bright in her mahogany eyes. "Can you imagine? Trips to the grocery store would be fucking hilarious. If you have a sewing machine, I can totally make that happen."

What the fuck am I doing? I think again, but this time the question has taken on a whole new meaning.

Rose is standing on my porch grinning at me like a little demon. Sure, she asked me for help, but I don't really know this woman. What if she's a complete weirdo? Or worse, *dangerous?* Unhinged? I know so many dangerous, unhinged people that maybe my barometer for that shit is broken. She certainly didn't seem like it the first few times we met, with those big brown eyes rimmed with thick dark lashes and her angelic face framed with chocolate fringe, the waves untamable as they cascaded over her shoulders. But there's a mischievous streak in her that I think is maybe just a little fissure that leads to an endless well of chaos.

Her expression softens, and I wonder for the second time if I've spilled my thoughts into the world. I swear she's climbed into my head when she says, "Don't look so mortified, Doc. I just get extra weird when I'm nervous and you're standing there being all doctory and shit. I'm only joking."

"I knew that—"

"Probably having second thoughts about letting me in your house now though, right?"

Maybe. "No."

"That was totally a maybe. It's cool, I'll be one hundred percent fine with the corn children, trust me," she says, flashing me a smile as she firms her grip on the crutches and swings closer to the stairs.

"Hold up." My palm is wrapped around her wrist before I can even string together the arguments about whether or not I should touch her so casually. Rose's eyes linger on the point of contact. I should let go, especially with the way she stares down at my hand as though we're soldered together and she can't work out how or when it happened. "I'm not having second thoughts. Just . . . please. Come in."

Though I uncurl my fingers from her wrist, the loss of that touch resonates in my skin.

I open the door. And for a moment, she hesitates. Then, with a faint smile that evaporates in a halo of nerves, she turns and passes over the threshold.

"It's a nice house," Rose says as she swings her way into my living room, the click of the crutches filling the space with a metallic melody. She casts me a brief smile over her shoulder. As though drawn by a magnetic force, she maneuvers closer to the coffee table until she bends to pick up the crocheted coaster resting on the surface. It was the very first thing I ever crocheted. The pattern is imperfect. Some holes are larger than others.

I'm not sure what she must be thinking as she inspects the cream-colored yarn. She holds on to it as she pans her gaze across the overstuffed couches and chairs, then toward the simple kitchen that still clings to a 1950s vibe despite the new paint and counter-tops, and then the dining table where only one place mat rests on the surface.

Jesus fucking Christ.

Seeing my home through someone else's eyes is humbling. Literally one place mat. And a single crocheted coaster. What the fuck must she be thinking?

Probably the same thing my dickhead older brothers think about my life here in Hartford, Nebraska. And it's the first time I really acknowledge that they might be on to something. Lachlan was right. I'm knee-deep in my peak "Hallmark Sad Man Cinderwhatever" era.

"It's really nice," Rose says again as she sets the coaster down.

"You think so?"

"Yeah." When she turns to face me, her smile seems genuine. Maybe a little melancholy. She puts on a brighter smile when she says, "I really do. Feels like a proper grown-up home. Something befitting of Dr. McSpicy Kane."

I snort a laugh and set her bag down next to the couch as I head past her to the kitchen. "Just call me Fionn."

Rose replicates the pronunciation. When I look over, she's watching me, her dark eyes fixed to mine as though searching for something. "I'm sorry if I'm upending your life. Cramping your style or whatnot."

"You're not." Part of me wants to admit to what she must already be thinking—that despite her polite words, there's nothing much to upend. Now that she's suddenly appeared, I realize how minimal my life has become. How monochrome. It's just work. Gym. More gym and more work. A monthly appearance tending to the wounded fighters at the Blood Brothers barn. My only real socialization has been with Sandra and her club of crocheters every week, and that only started for me a few months ago. I guess that's what I wanted when I moved here. Maybe not the crocheting, but the solitude. And yet, this is the first time I've wondered if I don't want the result I've successfully achieved.

I clear my throat as though it will rid me of these questions I don't feel ready to explore. "Want something to eat?"

Rose's stomach responds before she has a chance to, releasing an audible growl. "That would be great, thank you."

I bring out my blender from the cupboard and set it on the counter, then rummage in the freezer for frozen greens. Rose taps her way to the table, setting the crutches against its edge. I look up when she drags a chair back and lets herself down with a heavy sigh. She lifts her injured leg onto the chair next to her and closes her eyes, tilting her head back to rub her neck, the shimmering sliver of flesh on her chest exposed by the low V-neck T-shirt she's wearing. I've definitely been avoiding even the remote potential for romantic encounters way too long if that tiny slice of flesh threatens to upend all my attention. I look away, though it's harder to do than it should be. I start cutting oranges just to keep my focus where it belongs.

"How long have you lived here?" she asks, and there's a shuffling sound that draws my gaze back to her. She has a deck of cards in her hands, their edges bent and softened with use.

"Just over four years now." I watch as she nods and sets the deck on the table. "I was in Boston before that."

"Is that the accent I hear?"

"No. I was born in Ireland."

She nods again and flips a card over, leaning closer to examine its details. "You left when you were young. Thirteen, right?"

My hand stops midway to delivering oranges to the blender. My head tilts. "How'd you know that?"

Rose looks at me and grins, her eyes devious and sparkling. "Magic." I'm just about to pepper her with questions when she shrugs and drops her gaze to the card. "Or maybe it was just a lucky guess. Figured you were old enough to keep the accent, young enough for it to soften. Thirteen seemed about right." She flips a second card and hums a low note.

"Tarot?" I ask, and she nods without looking up. "Is this what you do at the circus?"

"Yeah, in part. But mostly I'm the Sparrow in the Cage," she says theatrically, framing her last words with jazz hands. She glances up just long enough to catch my confusion. "I ride a motorcycle in the Globe of Death." I open my mouth to ask her a thousand questions, but she turns the conversation back on me before I have the chance. "So, you ended up in Nebraska in an attempt to avoid romantic relationships?"

I snort a laugh, picking up a carrot to start peeling it. "Let me guess. You came up with that one due to the bachelor vibes of the house. Was it the doily that gave me away?"

"No, but I do have questions about that."

"I'm getting the impression you have *many* questions." I plop the carrot into the blender and watch as Rose examines a third card and shakes her head. "How did you know about that?"

Rose pins me with a stare that slides right into me. One that burrows in. Drills beneath layers that suddenly seem too thin to hide behind. I don't just feel looked at or assessed. I feel *seen*. And after a moment that seems like it's pulled too tight by an invisible hand, her expression smooths, as though she's found what she's looking for. "Magic," she says, and with a wisp of a sad smile, she takes the cards and shuffles them back into the deck. "How's that working out for you? Being here, I mean. Getting away from Boston."

"I don't know." I slowly start to peel another carrot. I can feel her eyes, the weight of her watchful gaze. She says nothing, just waits to see which way I'll take her question. And part of me wants to elaborate on the honest answer I just gave her. But I don't. "What about you, how's the circus working out for you?"

Rose breathes a laugh, but I can sense the disappointment in it. "Not so well now, I guess. They all left." When I look up, she does a little shimmy on her chair, wiggling her fingers before she pulls what seems to be a white crystal charm in the shape of a bird from her jacket pocket. She makes a slicing motion through the air in front of her and then places the object on her deck. Though I want to ask her about it, I don't, already feeling thrown off course by her presence without broaching the realm of crystals and divination.

I clear my throat, trying to regain my sense of balance when I ask, "How old were you when you joined Silveria?"

Rose's smile fades, turning brittle at the edges. "Fifteen."

"Pretty young," I say, and she nods once. "Why?"

"Had nowhere else to go." Rose shrugs as she pockets the crystal and shuffles her cards. "When Silveria Circus came to town, I took half the money I'd saved and spent all day there. Next day, I took the other half. Third and final day, I went straight to José and begged him for a job. He didn't say yes, but he didn't say no. When they pulled up stakes to leave, I hitched a lift with one of the crew." Her expression is brighter when she looks up at me, blowing a strand of hair from her eyes. "I worked and he fed me. I proved I was tough, and he paid me."

"So, what, you just . . . left home?"

"No," she says. "I just left."

I want to ask her what she means, but the light seems momentarily lost from her eyes. I watch as she flips over a card and hums a thoughtful note. "Do you enjoy it?" I finally ask, unsure if I should be scraping away at her past when the present is already enough of a mess to dissect.

"Normally it's great. I get to travel. I love the troupe. I'm always seeing new places. Meeting new people. But I guess it's not so great when something like *this* happens," she says as she gestures to her leg.

"Does stuff like that happen often?"

"No. Not to me."

"What about stuff like Matt Cranwell?"

Everything in the room goes still.

I feel like I'd be able to sense our heartbeats in the air if I reached out with my palm. Rose says nothing. Doesn't even blink. I can't read much from her expression, but part of me already wants to rewind time and reel those words back into my mouth. I don't know this woman. Whatever happened is none of my business, whether she's staying here or not. Prying into her life is unfair. I've offered my home, without anything in return. Not even secrets.

I'm about to apologize when Rose says, "Not exactly. No."

My gaze lingers on her for a long moment and then I give her a nod before I focus my attention back to the blender and the smoothie. When it's ready, I grab two glasses from the cupboard and fill them with the thick liquid, taking them to the table with a pair of metal straws. I pull the chair back from the end with the single place mat, Rose's eyes on me through every motion.

"I'm sorry. It's none of my business," I say as I pass her the smoothie, though she doesn't move or even break her gaze from mine.

"I'm staying in your house. You have a right to know the kind of person under your roof."

"Listen," I say, curling my hand around my glass to stop myself from touching her, the sudden impulse taking me by surprise. "I've had some suspicions about Cranwell. I don't see him often but when I do, there's something about him. An instinct I have about the kind of man he is, you know? I realize that's not a very scientific thing for a doctor to say. I shouldn't be telling you any of this, really." I shake my head and lean back, studying Rose's face. Those dark eyes. Those full lips that press tight as though fighting to hold on to whatever thoughts and worries are curling through her mind. "I just . . . *know* it. He's a dangerous person. And if he did this to you—"

"You were right. When you asked at my RV. I'm the one who stabbed him in the eyeball," Rose blurts out. Her eyes are enormous. So big I almost laugh. I don't think I've ever met anyone who could express so much with just her eyes. And now, the rich shades of chocolate seem liquid with fear.

"I kind of thought so," I reply, and impossibly, her eyes get even bigger as pink infuses her cheeks. "The essence of piña colada was a bit of a clue. But the license really sealed the deal."

Rose swallows. Nods. But she doesn't crack a smile despite the joke and the grin that still lingers on my lips. "I should go. I don't want to bring trouble to your doorstep or make you uncomfortable in your own home." When Rose clamors to lift her braced leg from the chair next to her, I grab her wrist.

"Stay. Please."

Even her wrist is tense beneath my grip. I can feel the strain of her tendons, the hammer of her pulse against my fingertips. Every cell in Rose is ready to run, or more accurately hobble her way out of my house. And I should be letting her. If I were a better man, I would be driving her to the police station. Or at the very least, back to the creepy campground. But I have absolutely no desire to do either of those things.

Though still eyeing me with wariness, Rose settles at least a little in her chair.

I don't let go of her when I say, "Did Matt Cranwell injure you, Rose?"

She doesn't say the words. Only nods. Barely a perceptible admission. And that faint, simple movement is enough to set my

58

blood aflame. The only thing anchoring me to this room and keeping me from fulfilling a sudden dark urge to strip the skin from his face is *her*. Her warm skin beneath my palm. Her scent lingering in the air, a faint note of cinnamon sugar and chocolate and a hint of spice.

"He didn't see my face. I was wearing a full-face motorcycle helmet and the visor was down," she whispers. She looks at her leg for a long moment before she returns her attention to me. "It was a baseball bat. Not a motorcycle accident."

"He *hit you*? With a fucking baseball bat?" Rose nods. "Why didn't you call the police?"

"I didn't want to make things even harder for his wife, Lucy," she says with a shrug as she looks down, as though she can't bear to maintain the thread of contact between us. "If she hasn't called the police already, there's a reason. Maybe she's not ready. Or she's afraid of the consequences." Rose meets my eyes once more, and this time they're fierce, lit with dark determination. "He's hitting his wife, Doc. And I don't regret what I did. If I could do it again, I'd make sure he never made it to the hospital in the first place."

She says it with such absolute certainty that I don't doubt every word is true.

My blood turns viscous, lava in my veins.

I've seen Lucy Cranwell only once at my clinic, when she brought one of their kids in for a chest infection six months ago. She was quiet. Shy. Polite. It wouldn't have been a memorable encounter aside from a single comment she made as she pulled out her phone to send a text. It stuck in my brain like a barb, but at the time I didn't know why, so I only turned it over long enough in my thoughts to dismiss it.

"I just have to text Matthew," she'd said, darting an apologetic glance to me. "He always likes to know where I am."

I let go of Rose's wrist to drag my hand down my face.

My focus slides to the door of my house and sticks there. It's begging me to walk through it. To get in my truck and drive. To not stop until I'm at Cranwell's house. And after that . . . ?

I shut off those thoughts before I can fall into madness. They're vines that will twist and turn and trap me in a dangerous life I can't escape. I've seen it happen. It's in my brothers, Lachlan and Rowan. I've felt those same urges constrict around me. But I've learned to put those desires into a box where they will wither, forgotten. Starved of light.

"He might not have seen me," Rose says, pulling me back to the present, "but how many women show up randomly in a small town with a busted-up leg? It won't take him long to find me, if he wants to. I really do appreciate your offer to bring me here, but I probably shouldn't have accepted. I really don't want you to be in harm's way. You've done so much for me already. We haven't even talked about the break-in or the mess I made at your clinic."

Rose's expression is sheepish but there's something mischievous about it too, as though she might enjoy leaving a little chaos in her wake.

"To be honest, I was relieved it wasn't the raccoon again. Do you know how hard it is to get a codeine-addicted raccoon out of a ventilation system? Fucking hard."

Rose's expression brightens. "I kind of wouldn't mind watching Dr. McSpicy rolling up his sleeves and getting into fisticuffs with a crazed trash panda."

"*Fisticuffs.*" I snort. "Well, chances are you will. It happens more often than it should." The light that seems to linger in Rose's eyes starts to dim. When she glances toward the door, I lay my hand on hers despite the voice in my head that tells me not to. "Listen. Cranwell lives outside the next town over." *So what? It's fifteen minutes away. And you've already told her this.* "He hardly comes here." *It's not like you keep tabs on him, dumbass.* "Doesn't have many friends." *No fucking idea how many friends he has. Could be friends with the whole fucking county for all I know.* I take a deep breath that fills every crevice in my lungs. "Please just stay. I promise I'll bring you to the clinic so you can watch me get my ass handed to me the next time the trash panda infiltrates the fortress. I'll be worried about you with the corn children if you go back."

Rose says nothing, just keeps her eyes locked on mine as she leans forward and wraps her lips around the straw. For a brief moment, fantasies about those plush lips flash through my mind, but they're cut short when she takes her first sip of the smoothie, and her expression transforms to one of thinly veiled disgust.

"And I'll maybe stay away from the green smoothies," I say with a grin as she slides the glass in my direction. I could tease her for the abashed look she gives me, but instead I take the glass to the kitchen and return to offer her my hand. "Come on, I'll show you your room."

She looks at my palm as though trying to work out a mystery, and it takes her a long moment to slide her hand onto mine, watching it as she does, as though this small action is a revelation. When she stands, I help take her weight until she's balanced and ready for her crutches, and then she follows me down the hallway.

"I figured this one would be better," I say as we stop outside the second of two guest rooms and I push the door open. "The other one has an en suite but it's narrow. This way, you can have the main bathroom to yourself and this tub is a little lower so will be easier for you to manage. I'll be right across the hall if you need anything. Is that okay?"

Rose swings her way into the bedroom. Her gaze pans across the details, everything bland and in monochrome. Everything except the new floral bedspread in shades of coral pink and cornflower blue, two deep yellow pillows leaning against the wrought-iron headboard. Her gaze lingers on the bed. Maybe she sees the fold lines still pressed into the fabric from when I bought it just this morning. Maybe she realizes I bought it just for her, in the hopes she might agree to stay.

Rose turns her smile toward me. The warmth of it hits me like a dart to the chest.

"Yeah," she finally says. "I think that's okay."

SHADOWS

Fionn

"What are you doing with this information, Dr. Kane?"

I rest an elbow on my desk at the clinic and rub my forehead. Lachlan is not a man to be fucked with. Especially not when you're his youngest brother. "It's not that big of a deal. Cranwell is a piece of shit and he's been up to no good. I want to know how big of a piece of shit he really is."

"Christ Jesus," he groans on the other end of the line. "This isn't about a woman, is it?"

"No."

"Why not?"

I sigh.

"Maybe it should be," he continues, his voice gruff yet teasing. "Get you out of your Hallmark Sad Man Cinderwhatever era."

"Whether it has anything to do with a woman or not, you wouldn't be happy either way, you broody asshat. Why bother meddling in the first place?" A dark smile of triumph tugs at my lips when Lachlan grunts on the other end of the line. "How's *your* love life going, since you're so invested in mine? Still fucking your way through Boston with abandon, or have you finally run out of women who will put up with your ornery attitude?"

"Shut up, ya feckin' gobshite," he hisses. "I have not been 'fucking my way through Boston,' I'll have you know. Ever since that Halloween party where you spent the night drinking away your feckin' sorrows only to throw them up again in my feckin' sink the next morning, I've decided to remove myself from the dating scene in the hopes I don't wind up as much of a dumbass as you." He *tsks*, though I can tell he's enjoying every minute of forcing me to relive my fall from grace that weekend. "Couldn't even make it the extra two feet to hurl in the toilet like a normal adult man. You had to clog my feckin' *sink*."

He loves reminding me of that night, I think in the hopes that I'll become so annoyed by his teasing that I'll move back home just to prove to him I can take it in person. But when the city is home to your almost-fiancée and the shattered remains of the life you thought you wanted, one-upping your overbearing brother simply to stop him from taking the piss out of you just isn't sufficient motivation.

"You know, Lachlan, every time you tell me that story, you remind me why I think Nebraska might be growing on me." Lachlan grumbles something in Irish and I grin, a smile that fades as my focus returns to the true purpose of my call. "Now that you've gotten that out of your system, I need to know about Matthew Cranwell."

Lachlan sighs, and I hear typing in the background. My brother might claim to hate his side gig as a contract killer, but he'd still be the first to admit that his access to information and resources does come in handy from time to time. "Fine. I had Conor pull some information together like you asked. There wasn't much, so don't get too excited, yeah?"

I nod, though he can't see me, and grab my pen and paper. Lachlan rattles off Cranwell's birthdate and location, his social security number, the date of his marriage to Lucy, and the names of his three kids. There are bank details, debts. His suspension from the Lincoln County Sheriff's Office for his role in an aggravated assault six years ago, a bar fight that got out of hand. Since then, he's had a surprisingly minimal police record for someone as unpleasant as he seems to be, just a drunk-and-disorderly citation from last year. I've already gone through his medical history, but Lachlan mentions the high points anyway, including the eye surgery. There's nothing that unearths the true depths of Matthew Cranwell's darkness. No grand reveal. No damning mark.

But my instinct tells me the darkness is much deeper than what we can see.

"That's all I've got," Lachlan says, and I imagine him tapping his silver rings along the edge of the desk in the Leviathan office, a place he's told me about but never shown me, always wanting to keep me and Rowan at arm's length from his batshit crazy boss, Leander. "Anything else you want to know?"

Temptation bubbles to the surface. *I could ask about Rose.*

I know so little about her. How does one become a motorcycle circus performer, anyway? What series of choices would lead her there? Where has she been? What has she seen and done?

Her name is right there on my tongue. But I don't say it. Not only because I want to unravel her mysteries for myself, but because I can't bear the thought of putting her at risk. My brother would never knowingly hurt her—he might be an assassin, but at least he has a conscience. But Leander Mayes? Not so much. He would fuck anyone up if it provided him enough gain to justify the effort, whether it's power, or connections, or money. I can't stomach the thought of Rose being anywhere on Leviathan's radar.

"No. Thank you. This has been helpful," I finally say.

"Not *too* helpful, I hope."

"Just helpful enough."

Lachlan hums a thoughtful note into the phone, and then we say our goodbyes. I stare down at my notes for a long while, reading and rereading the information until I'm confident I've memorized it before I take it to the shredder and destroy it.

And then I grab my jacket and leave.

It takes just over fifteen minutes to get to Elmsdale. A few more to get to his farm. I drive past it, just a hint slower than the speed limit, and park by the poplar trees that border the northwest corner of the field that stretches from the front of his house where my truck will be hidden by the dense foliage.

I open my door and take a deep breath of the impending storm.

The first drops of rain pelt my jacket as I walk the shoulder of the deserted highway toward Matt Cranwell's driveway, my eyes never leaving the house. There's no light on inside the home to fight the encroaching darkness of the massive thunderstorm that rolls toward us. At first, it seems deserted. And then I hear the whine of a grinder coming from the barn.

I stop and just stand there, watching the place. It looks like any other farm. A simple house. Toys in the yard. Outbuildings and equipment. I'm not sure what I'm even doing here, staring at someone's house as the sporadic drops of rain gradually become a downpour. Someone could see me, even with the storm covering the land with an early film of darkness. *What the fuck am I doing?*

There's a flash of lightning, illuminating something lying at the edge of the driveway. It's peeking from between the first stalks of corn at the edge of the field.

An aluminum baseball bat.

In another flash of light, I imagine every moment of Rose's injury. The way Matt Cranwell must have struck her. The force of his blow. The rage and malice painted across his face. Her agonized scream. I hear and see it all. I *feel* it. Just like I'm standing right there, watching it unfold.

Help.

Before I truly realize what I'm doing, I'm halfway up the drive and there's no turning back. My gaze slices to that bat, the dented metal beaded with rain. My hands curl into fists. It takes every last thread of my restraint not to pick it up as I pass.

When I'm a few feet from the barn, the grinder stops, leaving only the quiet crackle of an old radio behind. I halt, but the thought of backtracking down the driveway doesn't cross my mind. I just wait in the rain, listening as something heavy collides with metal. A handful of words passes through the narrow wedge of the open door, the tone gritty, the sentence disjointed. Cranwell is talking to himself, but beyond the occasional swear, I can't make out much of what he's saying. A moment later, a ratchet ticks as it tightens a bolt, and I take the opportunity to move closer to the light and peer inside.

Cranwell faces away from me. I haven't met him many times, but I remember enough to recognize him, particularly with the strap of an eye patch biting into shining flesh at the back of his head. There's a buzz of an incoming call on the phone lying on the metal frame next to him. I watch as he wipes a hand on his overalls and answers on speaker.

"What do you want," he bites out, not a question but a demand.

"I need to run to the pharmacy before it closes. Macie's cough—"

"I thought I told you to make dinner."

There's a pause. I hear a child cough in the background of silence. I'd be willing to bet my medical license that she has bronchitis. "Yes, I'm sorry."

"Then go make it." Matt presses the screen to end the call and refocuses on the engine. "You will be, you dumb bitch."

My blood surges, a wildfire in my veins. Heartbeats roar in my ears. I close my eyes, lost in a moment of memory. An image of a man much like Cranwell. Filled with hate and loathing. My father.

His face is so clear in my memory despite the years that have passed. There was rage in it the night he attacked us for the last time. I can vividly recall the split flesh of Rowan's lip and Lachlan's scream, the tip of his finger missing, a pulsing spurt of crimson blood left in its place. I can picture every detail of my father's back as he turned it on me, ready to deliver another blow to whichever one of my brothers was willing to face him next. And I still remember the weight of the knife I had hidden in my hand . . .

"*Sonofabitch*," Matt hisses. I dart back into the shadows. But it's the banged-up utility terrain vehicle that he's talking to. It isn't me. He bends over the engine and cranks the ratchet. "Dumb ol' piece of shit."

That's right. You are *a dumb ol' piece of shit.*

I slide back into the light and watch as Cranwell reaches deeper into the network of metal, his arm buried to the shoulder. I pull the sleeve of my jacket over my hand and push the door open to step inside the barn.

There's a table to my left where the grinder sits discarded on a stainless steel worktop, the surface dull with scratches and spatters of grease. Tools are strewn next to it. A rusty hammer. A set of screwdrivers. A roll of steel wire and a hacksaw.

My fingers wrap around the matte blue handle of a wrench and I lift it from the table.

Lightning flashes beyond the windows, the glass caked with a film of dust. Thunder rattles the walls a heartbeat later, so loud it feels like the world is breaking apart. Cranwell's back is still to me, his hand buried in the belly of the engine. Thunder and rain. The radio drones a soothing melody. We're blanketed in sound. Our own cocoon.

One hit is all it would take. No one would hear him scream.

My hand tightens around the wrench as I take a step closer.

I see Rose's face. Her fear. He did this to her. Just like he hurts his wife. Maybe his kids too. And he'll keep doing it, just like my own father did. It never gets better. It just gets worse. The only thing that stopped my father was death. The same will be true of Matt Cranwell.

I could do it. I could deliver the blow that ends his miserable life.

Something creaks in the shadows on the other side of the room, and I stop, frozen in time.

"Papa. I fed the chickens."

I duck behind the end of the table, pressing my body against the wall, the wrench still gripped in my hand. There's a grunt from

Cranwell, a clank of tools. "Good," he grunts. "Get out of the rain. You can help me with this piece of shit."

There are some shuffled footsteps, the sound of a raincoat being discarded somewhere. I peer around the corner of my hiding place and watch as Cranwell hands his son a flashlight and tells him to climb up on the frame to hold the light above the engine. The boy does as he's told, and the two of them peer down into the heart of the vehicle, only a few words passing between them as Cranwell twists the ratchet in the engine.

What the fuck am I doing?

Hands shaking, I turn back into the shadows and press my eyes closed. This question seems inescapable. More multifaceted than I ever realized it could be. I'm a *doctor*, for fucksakes. I chose my profession specifically so that I could right the wrong I can never take back. I am a *good* man. Not a dangerous one. So what the fuck am I doing even thinking about killing a man I barely know? What the hell is wrong with me?

With one last glance around the corner, I carefully set the wrench down on the worktop and slink back to the open door. I leave the barn. Jog down the driveway. I don't glance at the bat as I go and keep my eyes instead on the road ahead.

When I walk through the door of my house a short while later, I shed my damp jacket and soaked boots before heading to the kitchen. My fingers still tremble as I drop an ice cube into a glass and fill it halfway with bourbon. I knock back the amber liquid. The burn slides down my throat. It does nothing to destroy the image of Matt Cranwell in the barn, his back hunched as he worked on the engine, the wrench beckoning me with urges I once thought I'd overcome. My hand still feels empty without it, the rage in my flesh not cooled by the chilled glass in my palm.

I pour myself another and take the bottle with me as I head toward my room.

"You motherfucking baby. Get your shit together," Rose's voice says as I pass the bathroom. My steps falter and I pause outside the door. "Not so fucking tough after all, are you? Well, you'd better suck it up if you wanna be a—"

"Rose?" I knock on the door, and the volley of vitriol stops immediately. "Are you all right in there?"

There's a long pause. "Yeah . . . ?"

"You sure?"

"No . . . ?"

"Can I come in?"

Another pause. I hear water lapping at the edges of the tub and then the rustling of fabric. "Okay . . ."

When I open the door, Rose is sitting on the edge of the tub in a robe, her crutches discarded on the floor, her brace resting on the counter next to the sink. Water glistens on her chest and her good leg, but her injured one is dry except for the edges of the wound dressing where its pulled back at one corner.

"What's going on?" I ask as I set my glass and the bottle down next to her brace. Rose's cheeks flush with a crimson glow and she looks toward the floor. My heart cracks a little when she meets my gaze but only briefly, like she can't bear to hold it.

"You told me to take the bandage off today," she says, her voice softer than I've ever heard it. Even when she's exhausted, her words normally have a sharp edge or a teasing warmth. "It's harder than I thought it would be."

"That's okay. I can help. That's why you're here. Remember?" She gives me an encouraging smile, and for a moment, I forget what I nearly did tonight. I crouch in front of her, patting my knee for her to rest her ankle on. She does, gingerly, and I rub my hands together to warm them, an action that causes a flicker of a crease between her brows as she watches. "Does it hurt?"

Rose shrugs and looks away, a hard swallow shifting in the column of her throat. "A bit."

"It's okay if this stuff bothers you."

"It doesn't," she says firmly, though it's not entirely convincing and she knows it. With a resigned sigh, she says, "The bone sticking out was just a bit . . . much. It's hard to forget."

"That's understandable." I tug a little at the edge of the adhesive tape and she hisses as it pulls the hairs that have grown beneath it.

"The fur is really adding to the experience for me."

I snort. "What?"

"Look." She plunks her other foot on my knee to compare the difference between her freshly shaven skin still glowing from the hot water and the leg she hasn't touched, the fine dark hairs glinting in the dim light. She points to her swollen leg, the marks of the brace still imprinted on her flesh. "Fur."

I nearly say something stupid, like *I like carpet*, or *Fur is hot*, or probably fifty other dumbass options that suddenly cancel out anything professional or, God forbid, clever. I clear my throat and try to focus on the bandage, lifting one edge enough to check that the stitches haven't stuck to the surface of the gauze.

"Fur is human."

"Fur hurts like a bitch when it gets stuck in tape."

"Just wait until you get the cast."

"It'll hurt?"

"No. But once we take it off, you might be able to braid it."

"Doc," she says through a giggle as she prods me with her toes. "You're supposed to be helping."

"I *am* helping. I'm distracting you so I can do *this*," I declare as I tear off the bandage.

"*Motherfucker!*" she shrieks. She grips my wrist and laughs, her eyes wide. I know I'm grinning at her like a fucking fool, but I can't seem to make myself stop. "I'm ninety-nine percent sure you have no credentials at all, and you won your stethoscope at the Duck Pond game."

Rose lets go of my wrist only to whack me on the arm and then lean back, her smile slowly fading. It takes me a moment to realize mine has evaporated too. The ease of her touch makes it hard to hold on to words I shouldn't say. It's a struggle to quell the sudden urge to tell her how beautifully her skin glows in this light, or how funny and unique she is, or how grateful I am for the warmth of her touch, her presence. Just like I try not to think about how she's naked under this plush robe. The hand she rests on her lap is the only thing keeping it from falling completely open.

"Maybe you've got a little vicious streak hidden away in you, Dr. Kane," Rose says, and my thoughts of her body give way to images of Matthew Cranwell's barn. I can still feel the weight of the wrench in my hand, the burn of rage in my veins. I don't know if it's something about my expression that changes, or if she just senses the shift in the air, but Rose grabs my hand. She opens my palm and lays a damp sponge there. "But you've got a kind streak too. And I like them both. Equally."

Rose's smile is soft, her eyes warm. I try my best to smile back. To focus on the simple actions of care and healing. I clean her wound with a gentle hand, each press of the sponge against the incision a ritual. I seek comfort in giving it. The man I chose to be when I entered medical school? That's still the man I am.

But she's right. Maybe I do have a vicious streak. And I need to remember that. Because it doesn't seem so disconnected from the rest of me anymore.

TA-DA

Rose

"How does it feel?" Fionn asks as I swing next to him through the sliding hospital doors, my brand-new fiberglass cast wrapped with black tape. It encases my entire lower leg, all the way from my knee to the ball of my foot, replacing the temporary brace now that my stitches are out.

"It's okay. A little weird, but I'll get used to it." Fionn smiles and I try to do the same in reply, but I'm still feeling a little too queasy to put in much effort. I made the mistake of watching as he clipped and tugged the first two sutures free of my flesh. I had to look away as he took the rest of them out.

But I shouldn't be too hard on myself. The stitches probably just brought back the memory of all that pain and adrenaline. Fuck, that was gross. I remember sitting on the floor of his clinic, cutting the bottom of my pant leg so I could get a better look at the injury. The last thing I recall before waking up in the ambulance is the splintered bone that jutted from the split skin. And that's it aside from a hazy moment of seeing his face haloed by a bright light, an image that might be nothing more than a dream.

"You sure you'll be okay for a couple of hours while I finish up here?"

"Yeah," I reply, squinting down the road in the direction of downtown Weyburn. "I feel like I've hobbled around most of Hartford now. It would be good to explore someplace new."

Fionn watches me, a crease notched between his brows as his eyes scour my face. Sometimes, I feel like there's a heat in his gaze that lingers in my skin. And then with a blink, it always disappears, as though he's shuttered it away, keeping that little flame hidden in the dark. "Be careful?" he says, as though it's a question he's not sure he should ask. Though he tries to keep his tone clinical and detached, I still sense a thread of worry woven in the notes.

"Definitely. It might do me some good to move around," I reply.

"Any trouble whatsoever, call me."

"Yeah, of course. I'll be fine."

With a flash of a smile that seems to do little to reassure him, I swing my way across the parking lot of MacLean Memorial Hospital toward the empty sidewalk that will lead me to the shops. I glance back toward the entrance before turning the corner. I don't expect Fionn to be standing there, his arms crossed over his white coat. But he is. And I don't expect my heart to turn over when he raises a hand to wave at me. But it does.

I give him a nod, and then I keep going.

By the fifth block, I start to regret my life choices.

I've gotten pretty good at maneuvering around with my crutches. The whole *tick-swing-step* rhythm is almost musical. But there's only so much crutch-music a girl wants to make before it becomes crutch-torture. My armpits are starting to chafe. The bistro a few blocks in the distance might as well be miles away. I need to rest for a minute, preferably somewhere with air-conditioning and maybe an iced latte.

I squint at the sandwich board of a store on the next block. SHIRETON HUNTING AND FISHING SUPPLY.

That'll do.

I hobble my way to the small brick building, the first in the businesses that stretch along both sides of the tree-lined Main Street. When I pull the door open, the scent of leather and rubber and synthetic pine greets me. There are high-visibility orange vests. There's camo print in every format of green and beige blobs. Fishing rods. Hooks and bait and fake fish and plastic worms. And knives. Short. Long. Serrated. Smooth. Matte, powder-coated in black. Shining silver, polished to a mirror finish.

The shop owner is a grizzled-looking old man with buzzed white hair and trenches of wrinkles that cut patterns through his skin. He looks up from his fishing magazine and gives me a nod as he flicks a glance down to my cast. I've become used to the repetitive questions and I have a practiced response ready to slide off my tongue. But he doesn't ask. He just gives me a curt but not unkind "Good morning," dips his fingers into a tin of snuff, and slides a pinch of the mahogany tobacco between his lip and lower teeth before he returns to his magazine.

I hobble down one of the long aisles and lose myself in the cool air and the rows of glass cases, taking my time to appreciate the finer details of every blade.

". . . didn't I tell you that? I thought I fucking told you that," a man snarls at the end of one of the aisles, his body hidden by a rack of waders and waterproof jackets. "You are so fucking stupid."

I glance toward the front desk, but I don't think the shop owner heard, or if he did, he doesn't let on. The man on the phone snaps out a few more disparaging comments as I creep down the aisle next to his. When he temporarily halts his tirade, I hear a woman's muffled voice on the other end of the line, though I can't make out what she says. Only the tone. Placating. Pinched with fear.

"I don't fucking care, Naomi."

My spine goes rigid. I'm standing in front of a stack of waders hanging from an aisle rack, but I'm not really looking at them. Instead, I'm picturing the nurse, Naomi, and the way her smile never reached her eyes when I pulled her cards at the hospital. I'm seeing the dullness of the light in them, like they were too haunted to shine. I'm hearing her voice, the thinnest thread of hope in her words when I asked what the Ace of Cups meant to her. *To take flight.* I know exactly who this man is. What he's done. And where he needs to go.

A burst of wicked glee explodes through my cells. I glance down at my cast. Maybe my bad luck wasn't so bad after all.

"It's your problem," the man continues, snapping me back into the moment. "And if you're not careful, I can make it even *more* of your problem. Unless you suddenly don't care if those photos of you make their way around town . . . ?" There's a quiet plea from the other end of the line. "I told you already that I'm going out tonight, and I swear to fucking God, if you aren't there when I get back, I'm going to—"

I part the waders with sudden force, the hangers grating against the metal rod. A man my age startles, the phone held a few inches from his face as he looks at me with wide, steel-blue eyes. "I'll call you back," he says.

And then a slow grin spreads across his lips.

Just to look at him, he's handsome enough, in an unfussy kind of way. Tousled dark hair. Stubble on an angular jaw. Those silvery eyes that light up when he smiles. I'm sure he's gotten away with all kinds of trouble with that smile. And he knows it.

"Hi," he says, his voice rich and smooth. I give him a faint nod.

He waggles his phone and gives me a sheepish tilt of his head. "Sorry about that. Work thing. You know, people not doing their jobs and stuff. Trust me, they deserved it."

"Yeah," I deadpan, though he doesn't seem to notice my sarcastic tone. "I'm sure they did. Bet they won't fuck up again."

His expression lightens and he takes a deep breath. "I hope you're right." He jerks his head down to my leg. "What'd you do?"

I lean forward through the waders and cup my hand over my mouth. His eyes glimmer with anticipation of a secret shared. "I broke it trying to kill a guy."

I wink and he laughs, delight filling the aisle. "Now that's a story I'd like to hear more about sometime. Name's Eric." He pauses, as though I'm going to give him my name in return. When I don't, it brightens the gleam in his eyes. "You like fishing?"

"Something like that," I reply, and his lips curl.

I shrug and start hobbling my way back over to the knives. Eric follows, watching from the other side of the glass case as I turn my attention to the weapons just out of reach.

"Do you have a secret fishing hole? I could use some tips if so. Haven't caught anything all week. Maybe you could show me sometime."

I look up at him, tilting my head. A slow, predatory grin creeps across my lips. "I think Naomi would mind. Don't you?"

Eric's smile finally cracks, though doesn't disappear completely. He scoffs, pausing as though giving me one last chance to come to my senses. Then he rolls his eyes. "Dumb bitch," he mutters, loud enough for only me to hear.

I stay where I am, my hands curled into tight fists, my nails etching crescents into the padding of my crutches as I watch him stride toward the counter. The shop owner sets his magazine down, his expression unreadable as his eyes flick to mine. "Afternoon. What can I get for you?"

"I'll take a box of Winchester 350 Legends," Eric says.

The old man lets out a grunt, his eyes narrowing. "It ain't hunting season. Shouldn't you be getting fishing gear?"

"I am. Gonna shoot the fish right out of the river. Just don't go tellin' the sheriff. Not my fault if a deer gets in the way of my shot."

With another grunt, the shop owner unlocks a display behind him to take a black box from the shelf, the ammunition inside shifting in a deadly whisper. I linger at the glass case even though the urge to jump on Eric's back and strangle him with my bare hands breaks over me in waves. Why does a man like that get whatever he wants? Get away with whatever he wants? Hurt anyone and anything he wants? I stare down at the knives and they seem to whisper in their cases, reflecting their possibilities back at me.

It doesn't have to be that way.

I'm still staring down into the acid-etched patterns on the steel of a hunting blade when I hear the door open and close as Eric leaves. Shuffling footsteps follow and come to a stop at my side.

"Stay away from that guy. He's a piece of shit," the old man says as he unlocks the glass case and passes me the exact knife I'm looking at in the row of blades, as though it's whispered to him as much as it has to me.

"Kinda got that impression." I take the knife he offers by the handle and turn it over to examine the swirling patterns of the Damascus steel blade. As the shop owner takes out the sheath and runs me through some of the specs, I glance through the front window. Eric is across the street, waving to a group of people our age. He opens the rear door of a black truck and tosses the box of ammunition on the back seat before he walks toward the liquor store. "It's perfect," I say, interrupting the old man. "I'll take it."

The shop owner rings up my order, and I slap down enough cash to cover the total. I don't wait for the couple of dollars of change. With my new sheathed blade gripped between my teeth, I hobble my way toward the door at speed. The old man behind the counter must see a lot of oddities in his shop, because he merely grunts a goodbye as I limp into the merciless summer sun.

I scan the street. There's no one around other than the group Eric just parted with, and they're already a block away, their backs to me. No one even looks my way as I cross the road and throw open the unlocked rear driver's side door of Eric's Dodge Ram 1500 truck. It's a bit of a mess, thank fuck, with a box of tools and some empty soda cans and a grease-stained set of overalls strewn across the seat. It might be a bit gross, but it makes it even less likely that he'll notice me. I shove my crutches in across the footwells, and then I heave myself inside and cover myself with a blanket that smells faintly of mildew and diesel. I clutch my new blade to my chest, and then I wait.

It's only a few moments before I hear the tailgate drop and a couple of cases of beer slide onto the bed beneath the tonneau cover. There's some rummaging, and a moment later, the tailgate slams shut. My heart crashes against my bones as heavy boots smack the asphalt. With a grunt, Eric gets into the truck, clicks his seat belt into place, and a moment later we're gliding away from the curb to the sound of country music and Eric's off-key whistle. I hear the hiss of a can opening as he cracks a beer, as though that's perfectly normal. Where are we headed? I have no fucking idea. But I'm sure it will be an adventure.

That's how I have to think of it. *An adventure.*

Last time I tried to kill a man, it didn't go well because I wasn't prepared. Not that I'm really prepared now, but at least I have more of the element of surprise. And a better weapon too. Does the thought of those cocktail sticks quivering in Matt Cranwell's eyeball still make me nauseated? Sure, a little, though right now it could also be Eric's driving and this mildewy smell from the blanket. But the only way I'm going to get good at this is to practice on a deserving candidate. And it seems like everyone around here knows that Eric fits the bill.

Okay, the shop guy is just one person, but he's old and grumpy as fuck, and if he doesn't like Eric, that should count for the opinion of most of the town. So practice on Eric, I shall.

I just have to psych myself up.

And that's what I do as we head through the town. I imagine how this time it's going to go smoothly. He'll park. I'll spring up. I'll slice his jugular. End scene. Maybe one or two doubts start to creep in, like how I'm going to dispose of the body, for one. I figure most problems can be solved with fire. Getting back to town might be another issue, especially now as we pick up speed and the town roads turn to country highways. But then Eric opens his third beer of the journey and places a call to Naomi to spend the next ten minutes berating her, and I can hear the broken notes of hopelessness and exhaustion heavy in her voice. I realize the issue of how to get home is a problem I can solve when I'm done, even if it takes all day to hobble my way back into town.

Gravel crunches beneath the tires as we take a right turn onto a side road. Then another turn onto an uneven surface, as though the road is rarely used and difficult to traverse. Eric hums along to a song on the radio, seemingly unbothered by the terrain, or his shitty-as-fuck attitude, or anything at all, really. At least, until a phone rings.

My phone.

Van Halen. "Somebody Get Me a Doctor." I know Fionn's name and face will be lighting up the screen. I scramble to silence the phone, but it slips from my pocket and drops between the rungs of my crutches, hitting the footwell with a damning thump.

"What the *fuck*," Eric screeches as the vehicle swerves on the uneven road.

It's now or never.

I toss the blanket aside as I burst from my hiding place, my shining new blade clutched tight in my fist.

"*Ta-da*, motherfucker."

PUSH TO SHOVE

Rose

Eric screeches an octave higher than I thought possible, his eyes wide as they connect with mine in the rearview mirror. The truck careens off the road and into a field, and before he can figure out what to tackle first, I take my chance. I punch the point of my blade into the side of his neck and *push*. The sharpened steel slides into his flesh to the sound of his startled, liquid cry, and then I whip it back out in a rush of blood.

A garbled, choking cough fills the truck as blood sprays from the wound in pulsing bursts, coating *everything*. The windows. The seats. The hand he holds to the gaping wound. *Me.*

My stomach heaves and I puke on the smelly old blanket.

"Holy shit, that is so fucking gross," I hiss as I shove the blanket aside. Eric is squirming in his seat but growing weaker with every moment that passes, his gurgling breaths shallow and labored. The truck rolls on through the field but it's slowing down, bumping along through the prairie grass at a pace that's not much faster than a walk. Eric is still gulping for air as I look through the blood-spattered windshield to get my bearings.

In the distance, there are more fields of long grasses, their tips bleached by the summer sun. Just beyond the front bumper is a shallow, washed-out thread of dry sand that must form a little creek in heavy rains. And in between?

A steep drop into a river.

Fuck.

"Gotta run," I say as I sheathe my blade and open the rear driver's side door, tossing one of my crutches into the grass. Eric gurgles and I struggle to swallow another wave of nausea when our eyes meet in the rearview. His face is smeared with blood, his skin pale. His half-lidded eyes are pleading. "Don't look at me like that," I snarl. "You know you're a piece of shit."

Eric slumps forward against the steering wheel and the truck keeps bumbling along. I toss my knife and my other crutch out the door, pocket my now silent phone, and jump out, landing in the grass with an aching thud. I roll over to watch as the truck nears the drop-off, veering into the sandy trail of the dried creek bed.

The vehicle slows. And it slows some more. *No no no, get in the river.* But the front wheels slide to the side, mere feet from the drop-off. The truck sinks into the sand. And then stops moving forward altogether.

The engine still runs and country music drones from the open door, the man in the driver's seat motionless.

"*Fuck.*"

I grab my knife first, because one can never be too careful, of course, and more important, I just paid a shit ton of money for this thing and it's already proved itself worth every penny. It takes a minute to figure out the position of the straps, but I manage to harness it against my back. Then I gather my crutches and hobble to the truck to figure out what to do.

When I open the door, the scent of hot blood and piss and shit smack me in the face. I undo Eric's seat belt and shove him toward the center console until his bloodied torso and floppy arms drop toward the passenger seat.

"I'm not sure I'm cut out for this," I admit as I haul myself onto the rail and use my crutch to press down on the accelerator. The wheels spin and drop deeper into the sand. I try shifting the truck into reverse, but that doesn't get me anywhere either. My phone rings on my seventh attempt to free the vehicle, when the realization has crept in that I am well and truly *fucked*. I cut the engine and brace myself in the hope that my gut feeling is right about the good doctor being not-so-good, even though I have nothing to go on lately that my instincts are in any way reliable. "Hi, Dr. Kane."

A warm chuckle flows through the line. "You've been living at my house for a week. Fionn is fine."

"Right. Fionn . . ."

"What's the matter? Is something wrong?"

I squint out across the ravine that's just a few short feet away, yet feels unreachable. "I'm in a bit of a quandary. I got the jump on a fleabag townie and it kind of . . . backfired."

There's a pause. "You . . . what . . . ?"

"Got the jump. On a townie. He was a fleabag."

"What do you mean by 'got the jump' on him?"

I cast a frown at the cooling body. *Well, here goes.* "Maybe you should just come and take a look. I could use a hand. Or two. I'll drop you a pin. It's probably best to keep it to yourself."

Fionn takes a sharp breath to ask a question, but I hang up with a cringe and quickly drop him a pin before I pocket my phone.

"Well," I say as I pat Eric's lifeless arm. "This whole experience could have gone better, probably. But I didn't pass out, so I'll take that as a win. And you brought celebratory beer."

Before the nausea creeps in once more, I gather my crutches and slam the doors shut before I limp my way to the back of the truck. I pop the tailgate down and grab a can of Coors Light from the cooler. Fionn blows up my phone with calls I don't answer and texts I mostly ignore. There's only one response I can give to his barrage of questions: *You'll see what I mean when you get here.*

Thirty minutes later, I spot his truck barreling down the deserted road, a cloud of dust billowing in his wake. He slows when he nears the location of the dropped pin, but it takes him a moment to spot me waving from the bed of the truck, the vehicle clearly not where anyone would expect it to be. Fionn stops and cuts the engine, then marches in my direction, steps that slow and nearly halt as he takes in the state of my clothes. And then he's running straight for me.

"Jesus, Rose," he says, his Irish accent breaking free as panic etches lines in his face. "What happened? Are you hurt?"

"I'm fine." Though I give him a reassuring smile, it does nothing to untangle the knot of anxiety that twists my guts. Fionn's eyes travel over every inch of me, searching for injuries that he won't find. "I had a slight incident."

"Slight incident," he echoes, though it seems to take a second for the words to click together in his thoughts, his focus still consumed by hunting for the source of the blood. "What do you mean, 'slight incident'?"

"There was this guy—" is all I manage to get out before Fionn's gripped my shoulders, his eyes molten as they pierce right into me.

"Some guy did this to you?"

"No. Not exactly." I look away to the tinted rear windows of the truck, but when I turn back, Fionn's still watching me with an intensity that scorches the chambers of my heart. "This guy was really a piece of shit. I was in a shop and he was threatening a woman over the phone, and then he tried to come on to me with some lame-ass line about a fishing hole or some shit, I dunno, I don't know shit about fish—"

"The point, Rose."

"The point is, I . . ." I look to the grass. The sky. The ravine. The truck, though it seems to mock me. I shrug, trying to shrink from the weight of Fionn's gaze that still burns a hole into my face. When I finally meet his eyes once more, I cringe. "I started it."

"*You* started it . . ."

"Yeah."

"Aren't you supposed to say *he* started it?"

"Probably. Maybe he *did* start it with the whole dickhead-phone-call-fish-loser thing. So, more accurately, I guess I finished it . . . ?"

Fionn lets go of my arms. He takes a step back and runs a hand through his hair, his expression slack as though the blossoming epiphany has wiped it clean of emotion. He walks to the front of the vehicle and opens the driver's side door, and I hear the sharp intake of breath, the curses on the next exhale. The truck jostles as he steps up on the driver's side and checks for signs of life. I already know there's nothing to find.

There's a long, terrifying, heavy silence. A redtail hawk cries in the sky above, the only sound on the windswept plains.

I try to look as nonthreatening as possible as Fionn slowly returns to the tailgate. I hold out a sweaty can of beer as an offering. "Would you like one?" Fionn stares at the dried blood streaked across my skin, though the condensation has rehydrated some of it. The aluminum is smeared with crimson streaks. He watches as I hastily wipe the can and my palm on my jean shorts and offer it to him again. "He won't miss it," I suggest. "Might as well."

"What . . . the fuck . . . is happening?" he asks. I want to remind him that he's a smart guy, he can probably figure it out. But I chew my lip and just wait for him to voice a few conclusions. "Did you . . . kill him?"

"Umm, *yes*. But he's not a good guy."

"And you called me to help you to what . . . get rid of him?"

I shrug. "I got a little stuck. And you specifically said, 'Any trouble whatsoever, call me.' This is 'trouble whatsoever.'"

"I didn't mean *killing* someone and disposing of their body."

"I did the killing part. I just need a little help with the disposal."

Fionn lets out an exasperated sigh. "'Body disposal' was not on my list of trouble."

"You should have clarified that from the beginning." I push the beer in his direction. Fionn drags his hands down his face and looks toward the sky as though angels might swoop down and save him. But the more I watch him and try to decode the series of cogs and wheels that must be turning in the confines of his skull, the more I realize a critical detail. "You're not freaking out."

Fionn turns his gaze to me, his eyes narrowing. "I am on the inside."

"Not that much. And you said '*killing*,' not 'murdering.'"

"Same thing."

"Not really."

He folds his arms across his chest and squares off in front of me. "Explain."

"Killing is like, 'Someone is dead because of me, but maybe it's an *oops*—'"

Fionn snorts. "I highly doubt this is an 'oops.'"

"—But murder is like, 'I totally meant to do that.'"

"Did you mean to do it?"

"That's not the point."

"It's not?" he asks. I lift a shoulder, and Fionn's head tilts. "Then what could possibly be the point if it's not you *fucking killed* someone?"

"You said 'killed,' and 'killed' is nicer." I slosh the beer side to side in a last-chance gesture, but when he doesn't take it, I stuff it in the front pocket of my plaid shirt. "Your loss. Follow me, Doc," I say, positioning my crutches so I can safely hop down from the tailgate. Fionn moves closer as though he can't stop the urge to offer his help, but he does stop himself, in the end. He halts just shy of taking my arm and then stands back to watch as I swing my way to the driver's door. When I pull it open, he's still standing where I left him. "I'm not going to hurt you. I just wanna show you something."

Fionn looks toward his vehicle parked on the dirt road. I'm sure the pull is strong to get away from here, to go back to life the way it was before I appeared like some kind of fever dream. Part of him probably wants to crawl back into the shadows and imagine this is all just a strange nightmare that might cling to his consciousness for a few days before it fades from memory. I know what it's like to hide, and I know what it's like to be found. It can be exhilarating to be seen. And it can be terrifying to be exposed.

"I guarantee I don't enjoy this as much as you'd think," I say, pulling the beer from my pocket and cracking it open. I take a long swig in an effort to swallow the churning unease that creeps up my throat. With a deep sigh, Fionn turns toward me and stops at my side.

"That's reassuring."

I give him a tentative smile that isn't returned, and then take a deep breath and hold it, setting my beer down on the dash. I turn toward Eric's body to start patting him down for his phone. When I tug his torso into place to sit upright on the driver's seat, I find it in his front pocket. As with pretty much everything in the truck, it's covered with blood, so I wipe it off on my shorts.

"That's good. Make sure you get the evidence really embedded in the fibers," Fionn says.

"In for a penny, in for a pound." I turn back to the corpse and hover the screen in front of his face but it doesn't unlock. When I use the edge of his shirt to wipe the blood from his skin, that doesn't work either.

"His eyes need to be open for the face ID to work," Fionn says flatly.

"How about now?" I pull his eyelids open and try again, but still nothing. "Bear with me a minute, Doc." Leaving my crutches to rest against the open door, I hop off the rail and over to the rear of the cab, climbing onto the back seat to rummage through the box of tools. With a squeak of triumph, I find the perfect tool to help.

"Sweet Jesus. *Rose—*"

"Call it circus ingenuity," I say as I hop back to the front of the vehicle with my prize in my hand. I climb onto the rail and hold open one of Eric's eyelids with one hand, lining up the staple gun with his lash line. "Last time I used one of these, I stapled a curtain to my hand, so let's hope for the best."

Fionn's whispered curses fall into the backdrop as I press the handle down, pop a staple into his eyelid to attach it to the flesh below his brow, and then turn to retch. "You might want to find another hobby," he offers.

I cough. Retch again. Take a few deep breaths and a swig of the beer sitting on the dash. "I'm good."

"Have you had this reaction to blood and gore before?"

"Not really . . . though maybe now that you mention it, I did pass out during the curtain incident. Woke up to Jim flapping my arm around like a wing."

"What about when I found you passed out on the floor in my exam room?"

"Well, I thought that one didn't count, all things considered."

"I think it still counts."

With a fleeting smile and shrug, I turn back to my task and repeat the process with Eric's other eyelid. Pop. Staple. Retch. Blood seeps over the surface of his eyes, so when I've managed to subdue the urge to vomit, I take my can of beer from the dash and pour a line of liquid across his brow to wash it away.

"Dear God," Fionn says, and it comes out more like a resigned groan than any true shock. "This is a fucking travesty."

"I know, right? What a waste of good beer on this asshole."

"That's not exactly what I meant."

Though I toss him a grin as I dab Eric's eyeballs and face dry, Fionn only frowns, a deep sigh lifting his chest and his muscled shoulders. "Okay," I say, then prod one side of Eric's lips to make a lopsided smile that falls as soon as I let go. I hold the device up to his face and this time, it finally unlocks the home screen. "*Success.*"

I slide off the rail and open his text messages. Half the snippets displayed only confirm what I already know, that he was cheating on Naomi with multiple women. *Hey baby! What are you doing tonight? Want to come over? I miss you . . .*

And then I open his text exchange with Naomi.

The rage I feel as I skim the conversation has me wishing I could do it all over again. Make him suffer. Bleed longer. Staple his eyes open and let him fall over that cliff while he was still alive, so he could feel concentrated fear, distilled to its purest form. Naomi must have lived in fear every day. Fear of being with him. Of being without him. Fear of leaving only to face his retribution. Any doubts I might have had about what I've done are erased when I read his threats and insults, his backhanded, controlling compliments and his unhinged, narcissistic outbursts.

My nose stings when I think of the suffering Naomi must have endured every day when she woke to this reality, her chest tightening as consciousness took hold, her stomach hollow. I remember that feeling. How worry and hopelessness can carve out your center, leaving you scraped clean. How every waking moment becomes corrupted by the kind of dread that pulses just beneath your skin, a second heartbeat humming in the dark.

I clear my throat, but it does nothing to dislodge the knot that pulls tighter around my every breath. "He's been abusing Naomi Whittaker, the nurse at the hospital," I whisper, offering the phone to Fionn. "Threats. Intimidation. He struck her recently. She told me while I was there."

The shock in Fionn's face is replaced with the slow dawn of epiphany. "You mean, just like Matthew Cranwell has been abusing Lucy," he says, and it's not a question but a carefully delivered statement of fact.

"Something like that."

"Did you start that fight too?"

I shrug. "I guess it depends on how you look at it, Doc."

He watches me for a moment, a crease between his brows. With a tentative hand, he takes the mobile, but he seems reluctant to remove his gaze from mine. Maybe it's the glassy sheen he sees in my eyes. The way tears gather on my lash line. I nod to the phone and force a smile. "Go ahead, before it locks and I have to rinse his eyeballs with beer again."

Fionn's brows pull tighter. And then he looks down at the phone.

I see every minute change. The flush of crimson that dusts his cheeks. The way his pulse quickens on the side of his neck. The parting of his lips, the subtle shake of his head. He scrolls through the messages, once. Twice. Three times, and he's probably read more now than I have. He sees something that makes his fingers tense around the phone before he locks it and slides it into his pocket as though he can't stand to look at it another moment longer.

He unbuttons the cuff of one of his sleeves, rolling the pressed gray fabric up his forearm, his muscles tense. "Keep watch on the road," he says as he repeats the motion with his other sleeve, his voice gruff, his eyes never straying from mine. "If you see a cloud of dust in either direction, tell me."

I nod once and he takes a step closer, our connection unbroken as he reaches for the half-full can of beer to take a long sip. And then he turns and stalks away. He pulls a small knife from his pocket, unfolding it as he bends to unscrew the cap on the tire valve. He presses the tip of the blade to the core and air hisses from the tire. When Fionn has finished airing down each one, he returns to my side, repocketing the blade. "Start it up, wheels to the left, put it in four-wheel drive. When I tell you, give it just a little gas."

"Okay."

He heads to the back of the truck and prepares to push as I press the brake with my crutch. I start the engine, shifting it into drive. When he's ready, he gives me the signal, and with the slow, steady crawl of the deflated tires and his rhythmic pushing, the truck finally glides free of the sand. I stay on the rail until we near the edge, and then I take my crutch off the accelerator and let it crawl forward.

"Eyes on the prize, dickhead," I say, and with a final salute to Eric's dead body, I hop down from the vehicle, taking Fionn's waiting hand as he slams the door shut with the other. The truck rolls to the cliff edge and we follow to watch it tumble down the steep embankment, gathering momentum. It hits a boulder and flips, then cartwheels end over end until it smacks the surface of the slow gray current to sink into the silty gloom.

"Investigators are really going to have questions if the body turns up with his eyes stapled open," Fionn says as the last tire disappears from view. Bubbles pop in the swirling eddies and we watch in silence until the last one dies, and the water resumes its slow procession. He turns to face me then, and I'm not sure how to read the mask that watches me back. There are hardly any clues to what he must be thinking, just a feathering of the muscle along his jaw. A haunted spark in his eyes, like a candle nearly burned to the end of its wick, fighting to hold off the dark. He must realize I'm trying to read him because he breaks our connection and bends to retrieve the crutch I dropped when I took his offered hand. "Let's hope he never turns up," he finally says.

We don't talk. Not as he helps me into his car, even though he doesn't need to. Not when he turns the truck around to head back to the main road. Neither one of us remarks on the thunderstorm that looms in the distance, or how its black heart bursts with bright streaks of light in the palest shade of pink. It's beautiful, and I want to say it out loud. But I don't.

It isn't until we're on the other side of Weyburn and well past the town limits that Fionn pulls Eric's phone from his pocket. He wipes it clean. And then he veers to the center of the empty highway and tosses it out the window into the ditch on the opposite side of the road.

And he doesn't look back.

SUTURES

Fionn

I never thought I'd find crocheting meditative and soothing. But here we are.

I'm sure my brothers would have a field day if they knew that I was holed up in my room like a hermit, spending my Saturday night crocheting a fucking blanket. But I guess they equally take the piss out of me for my "gym obsession," or as Lachlan likes to call it, my "Dr. Bellend gym-bro phase." And Rowan would be chiming in with some unhelpful suggestions, or even worse, he'd take up crocheting just long enough to make me a mankini for my birthday. While Lachlan is a broody asshat, Rowan is fucking nuts, and will go to literally any lengths to make a point or get what he wants, no matter how reckless or ridiculous or absurd. The two of them together are the worst, and the torment would be never-ending if they found out all the details of my life at present.

Especially seeing as how the most beautiful but admittedly also terrifying woman I've ever met is sleeping in the room across from mine, and I've done nothing but try to force myself to avoid her as much as possible.

I haven't been doing a great job of it either.

Even when I'm at work or running through town or at the gym, Rose will suddenly appear in my thoughts. I'll hear her voice, that desperate, whispered *help* still a barb in my mind. Or I'll see her face, like her startled expression when I pulled the door of her motor home open for her, the way her eyes glimmered in the summer sun when she realized it was me. I came here to Hartford in the hope that I would isolate myself from the things that made me weak, that made me want to poke and prod the hidden dark corners of my mind. But from the moment Rose showed up, she's invaded my thoughts as though she's stripping my immunity, cell by cell.

But it's not me I'm worried about.

It's *her.*

I lower the blanket I'm working on and pan my gaze across the room. Simple furniture. Nondescript paintings. Impersonal details on display, all of it dull and unoriginal. Nothing that would provoke any emotion or raise any concern. Nothing you'd look at and think, *This belongs to a man who covered up a murder yesterday.* Or, *This belongs to a man who nearly bludgeoned a farmer to death with a wrench.* And certainly not, *This belongs to a man who killed his own father, and nobody knows it was him.*

I set the blanket aside and brace my elbows on my knees, pressing my palms to my eyes as though it will push those thoughts back where they belong.

But they never truly fade away.

I still see my father in his drunken and drug-induced rage, still remember with vivid clarity the disappointment I felt when he returned after a week of being missing, those glorious few days when I'd started to believe he'd finally been killed as the ultimate consequence of his shitty life choices. After all, I was the one who discovered who he owed, who he stole from. It was me who thought if I let the Mayes family know that he'd taken money from them, they would get rid of my father for good. With every day that had passed that week, I realized I didn't feel the way any decent person would for selling out their own father. Me? I felt relief. Even *pride.* I felt fucking invincible.

But I was just a kid.

I underestimated my father's ability to get himself out of trouble. All that growing hope and serenity I felt was suddenly washed away when he reappeared on Saturday afternoon, slurring and cursing as he shoved my brother Rowan into the kitchen of our childhood home in Sligo, demanding a meal. He smacked Rowan across the face when my brother protested. When I tried to intervene, he shoved me against the counter and knocked my head against the cupboard hard enough that I saw stars. But through the flashing light, I still caught the way my brother's eyes turned black with rage. How he looked to Lachlan where he stood in the living room, his fists curled at his sides. It was as though there was a secret switch that had been flipped between them with that fleeting look. When the last conflict with my father erupted, I slipped a knife into my hand when no one was looking. And I remember how a single word stood out like a beacon as my brothers kicked off the brawl that would end Callum Kane's miserable life.

Finally, I thought.

Finally.

Even now, I still feel the rush of adrenaline. Hoping that it would be the end. *Knowing* it, as though it were part of my blood and bone, my DNA.

I've spent every day since trying to prove those instincts wrong. I've tried to be worthy of my brothers' devotion, to be worthy of their sacrifices. I've wanted to make up for my role in his death that day, one my brothers didn't even realize I played. And yesterday, it was like I simply . . . *succumbed.*

With a deep sigh, I check my watch. Eleven thirty. Eric Donovan has been dead for over twenty-four hours. If he hasn't been reported missing already, it's not going to take much longer. The tracks of our vehicles would have been washed away by last night's downpour, if anyone even bothers to look on that deserted patch of land. His vehicle is submerged beneath murky gray water. Maybe, if we're lucky, he'll never be found. Wouldn't a normal person feel remorse?

I don't.

That's the real reason I'm avoiding the woman across the hall. Because despite what she's done, I'm not afraid *of* her. I'm afraid *for* her.

And I think about that as I set my crochet project in my bag and slide into bed, chasing sleep. I don't feel remorse. My last conscious thoughts are questions that have no answers. What if I've spent all these years trying to cultivate something within me that just doesn't exist? What if I'm just as much of a monster as the man who made me?

When I wake the next morning after a night of restless dreams, Rose is either asleep or out. Both of these options are strange. She's usually up by six, always before me unless I've taken on an early shift at the hospital. I've gotten used to the smell of waffles and maple syrup and bacon in the morning, and though she makes enough for both of us every time, I always opt for a probiotic shake. But the scent has become welcoming. It feels like home. And Rose seems to enjoy spending the mornings in, making conversation that I try to keep to a minimum, or laying out the cards of her tarot deck to stare down at them with a crease between her brows. She plays with her wavy fringe when she has trouble interpreting their meaning. Sometimes she whispers "ta-da" and twinkles her fingers when she figures it out. Or she hums off-key. Or talks to the deck. Or catches my eye and grins at me as though she knew all along that I was watching like the fucking blue-balled hermit I am. I try to stay professional. Detached. But I feel like I'm caught in her orbit, sucked in by her gravitational pull.

And now I'm trying to sense that gravitational pull from outside her door, like some kind of fucking weirdo stalker.

I hear . . . nothing.

I rap the door with my knuckles, softly at first. When no sound comes from the other side, I knock again, a little louder this time. "Rose . . . ?"

Against my better judgment, I open her door. And it's like I've stepped into a room that belongs to someone else's house.

The bedspread I bought for her is perfectly smoothed across the mattress. The yellow pillows are propped against the headboard. But there are extra pillows too, not just a few but maybe half a dozen of them, in floral patterns and stripes and polka dots that are all mismatched yet somehow work together perfectly. There are framed photos and knickknacks on the nightstand. There's a painting I don't recognize that's propped up on the dresser. And plants. Plants *everywhere*. A monstera near the bed. Ivy on the shelf. Orchids on the windowsill. Three spider plants hang suspended from the curtain rod. In a matter of a few days, and entirely without my realizing it, Rose has transformed a once bland and lifeless room into something that feels like a home.

It leaves me with many, *many* questions. Such as, *Where the fuck did she get all these plants? And when? How? She couldn't have done it by herself. So who helped her?*

And where the fuck is she? And why does it worry me so goddamn much that she's not here?

I stop in front of one of the plants lined up on the dresser next to a mortar and pestle, the inner surface of the bowl stained with purple streaks. The first plant I don't recognize. It has small indigo flowers and glossy dark berries. Beside it, there's a small shrub with blossoms that look like pale pink stars. The third plant in the row has hood-shaped purple flowers clustered around a vertical stem. This one I know. It's monkshood, also known as wolfsbane. A highly poisonous plant.

I take a few more steps into the room and lean in to look at the photos on the nightstand. Teenage Rose in her motorcycle gear, flanked by twin boys. Rose a few years older, her arm around a woman in an elaborate costume. One of José Silveria, standing proud beneath a curved sign of lights. *Silveria Circus*, it says. His voice surfaces from a few weeks ago, when he wrapped me in an unexpected embrace in Rose's hospital room. *Take good care of our Rose*, he'd said. *She needs this. She just doesn't know it yet.*

I don't know if anyone needs a broken leg or a hospital stay or to be left behind in an unfamiliar town. But I nodded anyway.

I'm about to leave when I notice a postcard from Colorado Springs leaning against one of the frames. I turn it over.

Dear Sparrow,

I wanted to thank you. I was afraid. But I was more afraid of what would happen if I never took flight. Thank you for giving me my wings back.

Sincerely,
M

I can't know for sure what the note means. But I think after the last few days, and given the row of plants on her dresser, I might have a clue.

I take one last look around the hidden garden of my guest room and leave, stalking out of the house with my bag of yarn and my half-finished blanket and my crochet hooks slung over my shoulder.

When I make it to Sandra's house four blocks away, I don't know if I'd rather turn around and go home to stew in my morose confusion or immerse myself in the Suture Sisters gossip in the fragile hope of taking my mind off Rose.

And that hope is immediately shattered when I enter Sandra's home.

"Hey, Doc. How's it hangin'?"

I come to a dead stop in Sandra's foyer, my jaw slack, my expression dumbfounded. Rose is surrounded by the Suture Sisters crochet group, her leg propped up on an ottoman and a backpack resting next to her on the floor. A sly grin spreads across Rose's face as she watches me standing motionless like a malfunctioning robot, my brain seemingly detached from my body.

"Dr. Kane," Sandra says, and I finally break my gaze away from Rose when the host of our club swans into view. Her petite hand wraps around my wrist and she tows me into the living room. "Your friend Rose has come to join us today. Turns out, she's an avid crocheter, did you know that?"

"No," I reply as she leads me to the chair across from Rose and passes me a glass of lemonade. "I did not know that."

"I wouldn't say 'avid,' necessarily." Rose's eyes don't leave mine as she leans forward to grab her bag from the floor and opens it, withdrawing a ball of black yarn and a set of crochet hooks. "My gran taught me growing up, and I like to dabble from time to time. But I might be a little out of practice. I'm probably not as good as Doc."

The other Suture Sisters eat that shit up. Maude and Tina let out synchronized *aww*s from where they sit on a velvet love seat as Liza, the group's most voracious gossip, snorts a laugh, reaching over to pat Rose's arm with her liver-spotted hand. "You're far too kind, Rosie dear."

Rose doesn't correct her on the mispronunciation of her name. Quite the opposite, in fact. With the way she beams a devious little smirk at me, I'm pretty sure she's already earned "Rosie" as a nickname, despite the fact she's been here all of two seconds and doesn't know these women. How the fuck did she get here and *why the hell is this simultaneously grinding my gears and adorable and hot as fuck?* It's like she's set off a bomb in my thoughts, and now they're scattered everywhere, a mess I can't hope to make sense of.

And she's loving every second of it.

"I've seen your doilies," Rose whispers, her eyes still latched to mine, innocent and wide, though the gleam in them is pure mischief. "I thought the one in the living room was really good."

"Bless your heart," Sandra says as she tops up Rose's lemonade. Then she sits down next to Maude, who's the quietest of the bunch, her focus captured by the work of her hands. "Dr. Kane—"

"Fionn, please."

"*Fionn.* You didn't tell us you had such a delightful young lady staying at your home."

Maude and Tina share a weighted glance. Liza grins down into her yarn.

"Yes . . . well . . ." I clear my throat, trying to avoid the burn of Rose's gaze on my face. I pull my yarn and hooks from my bag, laying them out on my lap before I start my first stitch. "Rose had an accident and needed a place to recover. So, here we are."

"She told us. A motorcycle accident. Such a shame, but you can stay as long as you like—"

"I'll have to get back to the circus as soon as I'm healed," Rose interjects, as though she's saving me from an explanation I'm ill-prepared to give. To be honest, I've felt ill-prepared for all the moments that have passed since I walked through Sandra's door this morning, but I feel even more blindsided by the wave of disappointment at the prospect of her departure. "I'm sure Fionn will grow tired of my antics soon enough anyway."

I snort.

"Nonsense, dear. I'm pretty sure our good doctor has had more excitement in the last few days than he has in the last few years. Isn't that right, dear?" Sandra says, her gray eyebrows hiked halfway up her forehead as she pins her gaze on me.

Before I can answer, Liza leans forward in her chair, her eyes darting from one person to the next. "Speaking of excitement, have you heard about that Donovan boy?"

My heart stops beating and drops through my guts. When I look at Rose, the color has drained from her face, but she does an admirable job of staying composed as the Suture Sisters speak over one another with questions that Liza can't keep up with to answer. *Christina Donovan's boy? The one in Weyburn? I thought she had two boys, which one is it? Did someone finally throw them in jail?*

"Eric. The younger one. He's missing," Liza finally gets out, and the other women gasp and *tsk*. "Last anyone saw him, he was buying some beer. Told some friends he was going fishing but didn't say where. He never showed up for work and he's not answering his phone. Just . . . disappeared."

Panic still crawls through my veins, but at least my heart restarts when it settles in that he hasn't been found. I make some agreeable noises when they say how sad it is for Christina or that he probably just went on a bender and will turn up in a day or two, but I don't miss Maude's muttered words beneath the fray: "Let's hope he doesn't come back." I'm so focused on catching every shred of the rapid-fire chatter that it takes me a moment to feel the weight of Rose's attention on my face. When I meet her gaze, I see worry in her eyes, and then determination. And frankly, it's the latter that truly scares me.

The conversation is still churning when Rose taps Sandra on the arm and pushes her crochet work toward her for inspection. "Do you think this yarn will be strong enough?"

I take a sip of my lemonade, trying to swallow the dread that's crept up my throat as Sandra scrutinizes Rose's pattern with a furrowed brow. "That depends," she says. "What are you making, dear?"

"A sex swing."

Lemonade shoots up my nose and burns. I cough and sputter my way through what would otherwise be a moment of suspended silence. But that only lasts for a blessed few seconds before I'm surrounded by a flurry of voices that tosses me into an alternate reality.

"You'll need a softer heft for that. Maybe try the MillaMia merino."

"You might want to consider a tighter crochet stitch."

"Is it for you?" Maude asks without looking up. "Or does it need to take the weight of an adult man? Like, say"—her eyes flick to me—"maybe the doctor's size?"

I drag a hand down my face as though it will scrape away my blush. "Jesus, Maude—"

"I don't know," Rose says as she looks toward the ceiling, tapping her lip with the end of her crochet hook. "Maybe . . . ? I'm not sure."

"What about Tencel bamboo yarn? Soft *and* strong."

"Did you find a pattern?"

Rose shrugs. I die a little. "I was just going to wing it."

"I have a pattern for a pot hanger," Liza chimes in, pulling her bag onto her lap so she can rummage through the contents. She finds a magazine and flips it open, pointing to a photo of a crocheted hanging planter. "You could use this, maybe make leg holes *right here*. Ooh, and what about an extra pair of hanging handles and ankle braces?"

Sandra leans over to scrutinize the pattern, adjusting her reading glasses. "My Bernard could make you a wooden frame. It'll have to be good and strong, don't want something like that collapsing when you're taking it for a ride, you know?"

"Yeah," Rose says, taking the magazine from Liza, her smile barely subdued, her eyes glinting with amusement as they flow over the page in her hands. In a sudden flurry of motion, she tosses it in my direction and it smacks me in the face, falling open on my lap. "What do you think, Doc?"

I should probably give her a sharp glance, a cutting look. Say something about how I'm technically still her doctor, or at least offer a bland and noncommittal response. But as I look down at the photo of the crocheted hanger, I can actually picture it. Picture *her*. Her tongue leaving a trail of moisture across her lower lip. Her legs spread wide, her pussy glistening with arousal in the dim light of my room. Those dark eyes of hers, full of desire, feral with need for my—

"So? Think it'll work?"

When I look up, it's the first time I see a glimmer of apprehension flash across Rose's face. I clear my throat, the trace of a burn still lingering from the lemonade. "I think . . ." I trail off, drawing out her doubt before I finally give her the barest hint of a conspiratorial smile. "I think you should use a thermal stitch for the base. It's sturdy. Could support the weight of a six-foot-four adult male. Theoretically."

Rose's eyes dance in the morning light that streams through the blinds. "Even all Beast Mode muscly?"

I swallow a laugh as I set the magazine aside and resume my stitches. Though I try not to blush, I'm probably failing, judging by the heat coursing beneath my skin. "I mean, *theoretically*."

There's a single beat of silence, and then the women around me *cackle*. Though it takes a minute for my smile to really break free, it still does when I spot Maude dabbing at tears with the tissue she always keeps folded beneath her bra strap, or when Tina wheezes "sex swing" and laughs so hard she has to shuffle to the bathroom.

"Well, *thank God*," Liza says as she pulls a flask from her bag and dumps a generous splash of vodka into her lemonade, stirring the mixture with the end of her crochet hook. "We were starting to wonder if you were going to run off back to Ireland and join the priesthood."

I roll my eyes. "I'm not joining the priesthood."

"Valid concern." Liza shrugs and downs a third of her glass. "We'd be heartbroken to lose you. Especially when you've finally come out of your shell a little bit these last two weeks."

I try to think back on last week's meeting and what I said or did that was any different than the times I've been here before. I know I didn't explicitly say anything about how Rose broke into my clinic, or how I rode with her in the ambulance to the hospital. But maybe I did open up a little more than usual when I told them about scrubbing in for a surgery. Maybe I did say something about a patient I was worried about. A case that was weighing on my mind.

Liza smiles as though she can see where my thoughts have gone, and the conversation eventually veers to other topics, other gossip. We spend a couple hours there, and I finish the blanket I intend to donate to the hospital and then start a new one, soliciting guidance from the group for the difficult jasmine stitch. When noon rolls around, everyone packs up, and I help Rose to her feet before I take her bag alongside my own and we leave to a chorus of final advice about the sex swing.

At first, we walk in silence. It's hard to know how to start. What to say. I know I'm good at diagnosing illnesses and treating injuries and the precision and science of medicine. But with Rose, I feel out of my depth. Do I start with the Suture Sisters? Or the whole sex swing fiasco? Or do I go head-on with tackling the subject of Eric Donovan?

But while I'm overthinking my options in silence, Rose just dives right in. "Hey," she says.

A brief smile passes my lips. Maybe it doesn't have to be so complicated. "Hey."

"I like the Suture Sisters."

"Yeah. They're . . . entertaining. Not what I expected when I went to my first meeting. I thought I'd be stitching up wounds for a women's fight club or roller derby, not . . . just . . . *stitching*." I glance down my shoulder at her and Rose is grinning, clearly pleased with herself. "How'd you find out about that?"

"I saw a flyer on the bulletin board outside Wesley Pharmacy the other day. Thought I might check it out. Imagine my surprise when I called and Sandra mentioned your name."

"You were not surprised at all, were you?"

"The doily kind of gave you away."

"Much less lethally cool than the piña colada scent giving away an eyeball-stabbing incident."

Rose shrugs around her crutch pads. "I dunno. Those crochet hooks could do some damage."

"And while we're on the topic of crochet, a sex swing? Seriously?"

"I figured it would be a good distraction. It worked."

"You're nuts."

"I've been living with you for a week, and I killed a guy *yesterday* and you're just figuring that out now? I still think we need to revisit the conversation about your credentials, Dr. Kane." Though I try to give her a chastising look, it doesn't really stick, not when I see so much worry and unease hidden beneath her teasing smile. "Can I ask you a question?"

"Always," I say.

It takes her a long moment of watching me before she says, "You could have turned me in. Or called the cops. You could have driven me straight to the station."

I shrug when she says nothing further. "I could have, sure."

"So why didn't you? Why did you help me?"

"Because you asked me to," I say, and her whispered plea in my clinic resurrects itself from where it lies just beneath the surface of my thoughts. I'm sure she has no idea how much it has stuck with me. How sometimes I still hear it in my dreams.

Rose watches me, doubt written into the crease that appears between her brows. "Most people would have said no."

"I might look like most people. But I'm not."

"Trust me," she says with an eye roll, "you *do not* look like most people." A dusting of blush rises in her cheek, and she turns away. Even though I know I shouldn't let it, my heart still flips over in my chest with this quiet admission that she might look at me and like what she sees. Rose waits until her blush is gone before she faces me once more. "This whole thing with Eric . . . the river . . . What if this all goes tits up?"

What if it does?

I've asked myself that many times over the past two days. Tried to imagine what life would be like if anyone discovered my role in Eric Donovan's demise. But the thing that surprises me the most is how much I think about the opposite question. "What if it doesn't?"

"But you could get in so much shit."

"You could get in even more shit."

"Yeah," Rose says, drawing the word out. "That's definitely the truth."

"This thing with guys like Eric . . . have you been at it for a while?" I ask, thinking of the plants and the postcard with the cryptic note on her dresser.

"Kind of." Her head swivels, and she squints into the distance, her gaze landing across the street on a couple plucking weeds from a flower bed near their driveway. "Maybe not the time and place to get into details, but I used to just supply the means, if you know what I'm talking about. But now I'm trying to take on a more . . . active . . . role. Didn't work out once."

"You mean Matt?"

Rose shakes her head and looks away, but not before I catch a glimpse of a glassy sheen in her eyes. My hand tightens around the straps of our bags to keep myself from reaching for her. Before I can say anything reassuring, she takes a deep and cleansing breath, then manufactures a brittle smile. "Anyway," she says, clearing her throat, "I don't want to make you uncomfortable in your own home. Would you like me to go?"

"Stop asking me that. Please. I'm not uncomfortable with you there." I leave out the part about how strange it was to wake up to her absence today. Or how much I like what she's done to the guest room. "I'm not used to it. But I don't dislike it."

"Round of applause for Dr. McSpicy Beast Mode on his exemplary performance of a compliment," Rose booms in a theatrical ringmaster tone, pausing long enough to let go of a crutch and sweep her hand toward an imaginary audience. "And now for our next magic trick, witness Rose Evans's disappearing self-esteem."

Though I snort a laugh at the *oohs* and *aahs* she mimics from her circus spectators, my stomach still drops with the weight of her words. "I like *you*—"

"I can sure tell—"

"It just . . . takes some getting used to, having someone else in my home. Not because of the . . . thing . . . that happened. I mean, just generally. I've become accustomed to being alone, I guess." I shrug and I can feel her watching, the way she hunts through my expression like she can burrow right into my mind. And sometimes, I think she does. She gets inside and pulls every loose thread, unraveling sutures through old wounds, opening them up to look inside. It's as though she's tearing my thoughts apart, stitch by stitch, until I don't recognize the pattern of who I'm supposed to be.

"What was she like?" Rose asks softly. My steps slow and she matches my pace. When I look down at her with a question tugging at my brows, she gives me a sad smile. "The woman who broke your heart. What was she like?"

My step falters on a crack in the pavement. How does she figure me out like this? I don't have anything of Claire in my home, I left it all behind when I fled Boston. There's nothing she could have found, no one here who even knows the story. But she seems so sure, and something about that confidence in her deductions makes me want to tell her the truth. On paper, Rose is dangerous.

A murderer. And I'm an accessory to her crime. But she doesn't *feel* like someone to fear. She feels like someone to trust. And that scares me.

I let out a long breath, a thin stream of air between pursed lips. "She was . . ."

The opposite of you.

I shake my head. Try again. "She was someone I'd known for a long time. We met in college. She was the work hard, play hard type. She always wanted her life to look perfect. But she craved a bit of chaos underneath."

"Can't say I blame her there," Rose says as she swings along on her crutches beside me. "I mean, I live in a literal circus for fucksakes. Not sure what's more chaotic than traveling across the country and riding around in the Globe of Death for a living."

"At least that's chaos with a purpose. I think Claire's chaos was purely to fuck shit up and watch everyone else scramble in the aftermath. At the time, I thought she was exciting. She had this pristine life with an unpredictable twist. I thought she was what I wanted." I look across the street where kids are playing in a sprinkler on a lawn, their bikes discarded on the sidewalk. Farther down, neighbors chat across a hedge, sharing a midmorning beer. I know there is an underbelly of darkness in small towns just like in big cities. But something about Hartford feels comforting, even if it might be an illusion. "Looking back, I'm not sure I knew what I wanted at all. So I came here to clear my head. Guess I'm still figuring it all out."

"And how's that going for you?"

I laugh, hiking the straps of our bags up higher on my shoulder. "Up until a couple of weeks ago, it seemed to be going fine. And then the circus came to town, and nothing's been the same since."

Rose's eyes dance, the color warming to a dark amber hue in the summer sun. "I'm sorry about that."

"I'm not," I reply. I catch the flicker of surprise across her face before she grins. "I mean, it was kind of boring until you came around. Although you could make it slightly less boring, and I'd be okay with that."

"But you have a drug-addicted raccoon that haunts your office. How boring could it possibly be?"

"You'd be surprised." We fall into a moment of silence, and though Rose usually fills those quiet chasms, this time she doesn't. It's as though she knows there's more I want to say, but she doesn't want to push me into it. "I proposed to her," I finally admit, something I don't usually share with anyone. "She said no."

"The raccoon?" I guffaw a laugh and Rose's eyes sparkle with delight. "Such a shame. I would have loved to come to the wedding."

"You could have been the officiant."

"Even better."

"The only caveat is that it would have been circus themed, so you'd have needed a clown costume."

"Sign me the fuck up."

Our smiles slowly fade. Memories take hold in the silence. Pain dulls with time, but can still linger, waiting to be polished so it can shine once more. "I'm sorry that someone broke your heart," Rose says, and her voice is so soft and melancholy that I look over at her.

"Thank you." I don't tell her I'm not sorry. That I spent a long time in mourning, not for losing Claire, but for how my whole reality seemed to shatter the moment I got down on one knee and she said no. I thought I loved her, and maybe I did love the *idea* of her. But more than that, I wanted the life I had envisioned for us. A safe and secure and straightforward marriage. A surgical career in one of the best hospitals in the country. What my brothers had fought so hard and so long for me to have. A perfect life. Atonement for the sin I had committed, a final twist of the key to lock my secret away. Proof that I am a good man, deserving of a good life. That moment I got down on one knee and Claire Peller said no, that she wanted a future with someone more exciting, darker, someone more . . . real . . . it tore me apart. Just not in the way everyone believes.

Maybe I was never deserving of all the things I thought I wanted. And that key? It just never turned.

And I'm starting to wonder what would happen if I just opened the door.

RENEGADE

Rose

Fionn's sitting in the armchair, a bag of disgusting-looking de-hydrated vegetable chips in his lap, his crochet project tucked at his side, his legs crossed at the ankles on the ottoman as a new reality-dating show plays on his TV. His shorts come just above the knee but they've ridden higher with the way he's sitting. Since when have I been attracted to a guy's legs? Since now, I guess. His are all tanned and muscly with just the right amount of hair that's bleached from all his time running in the sun. I want to touch them. But of course, I don't. I also want to tell him that it's so fucking sexy that he's sitting here with his yarn not even hiding the fact that he's as into *Surviving Love* as I am. Why is that sexy? I have no fucking idea. But here we are.

"Val and Mitchell better win this thing, or I'm going to be pissed," he says as his favorite couple appears on the screen.

I tamp down a grin, pretending to focus on my own crochet project, which I guess will be a sex swing after all because why not? Sandra called the other day to let me know that her husband was making me a frame, even though it's probably not going to see much use since I'm on the driest dry spell ever. "I think Dani and Renegade are going to win."

Fionn snorts. "*Renegade.* What kind of a fucking douchebag name is that?"

"A made-up one."

"My point exactly. He deserves to lose for the name alone."

"Hate it all you want, Doc. He's still going to win."

Fionn gives me a piercing glare and I grin. God, I love that expression on him, when his eyes go lethal, their blue darkening to a deeper hue. There's a hunter in there somewhere. I just know it. I can imagine him letting that beast out to play. Chasing me. Catching me. Holding me down and tearing my clothes and—

A notification comes through on Fionn's phone, a sound I don't recognize. He whips it from the side table and frowns at the screen. A look of shock passes over his face and he darts to his feet, scattering his dried veggies across the floor.

"Fucking *Barbara*," he hisses.

I grab a crutch and hop up onto my good foot. "Yeah, *fucking Barbara*. Let's fuck her up," I say, whipping my knife from the sheath at my back. "Who's Barbara?"

"The raccoon."

I blink at him as Fionn pockets his phone and strides to the table to grab his truck keys. "Aww, I don't want to fuck her up. She sounds cute."

"Trust me, she's not so cute when she's gotten into the medication cabinet. Or the break room. Or basically anywhere." Fionn marches to the door and throws it open, then turns to give me a questioning look over his shoulder. "Well? Are you coming or what?"

He smiles, and it's so bright, so beautiful, maybe even just a little bit unhinged, that I feel like I'm lit from the inside. I sheathe my knife and grab my other crutch and hobble toward him. His grin grows even more magnetic, a feat that doesn't seem possible. I pass him to step onto the landing, and before I can attempt the stairs, he sweeps me up with a strong arm across my waist and doesn't set me down until we're next to the truck.

"She might look cute," he says as he helps me up into the vehicle, "but don't let her deceive you. She'll tear your face off to get what she wants."

I force a mischievous grin as he settles my injured leg into the footwell, trying not to think about what it might be like for him to toss me around when he lifts me so effortlessly, or what his hands might feel like gripped so tightly to my hips that he leaves fingerprints on my skin. "Are you talking about me, or the raccoon?"

Fionn huffs. "Both, probably. So I guess you'll be evenly matched."

He tosses my crutches onto the back seat and jogs around to the driver's side, throwing the truck into reverse the moment it's started so he can peel out of the driveway with a squeal of tires.

"So, how did you come to name a raccoon Barbara, anyway?" I ask as we turn onto Main Street.

"Kind of randomly, to be honest. It just seemed to suit her."

"Any idea how the hell she's getting into the clinic?"

"Witchcraft is my guess," Fionn says as we watch a pair of state troopers drive in the opposite direction. We turn off Main Street and onto Stanley Drive, the side street where the clinic is located. I twist in my seat and watch as the troopers continue on their path. "They must be opening the search for Eric at Humboldt Lake. From what I heard, that's his favorite fishing spot."

I swallow. "Where'd you hear that, exactly?"

"One of the search volunteers. He came to my clinic yesterday." Though I'm not looking at him, I can feel Fionn's eyes bore into the side of my face. "Why? What's wrong?"

"The shopkeeper at Shireton. He saw me and Eric talking when Eric bought bullets and I bought my knife. He knew Eric wasn't about to go fishing."

"Gerald. Yeah, I know him." Fionn's hand is a sudden warmth over mine, and I search his face when he breaks his gaze from the road to glance at me. "If Gerald was going to say something, he would have done it by now. Of anyone who could have drawn a connection between you and Eric, he's probably the least likely to bring that to the cops. He plays by the rules, but it doesn't mean he has any fondness at all for law enforcement. It'll be okay."

I sit back in my seat. I know enough about the area now to know that Humboldt Lake is about twenty miles out of Hartford, in the opposite direction of Weyburn. That puts it at least a good forty or fifty miles from Eric's watery tomb at the bottom of the Platte River.

By the time we park at Fionn's clinic, the burst of adrenaline from seeing the police vehicles has subsided. Maybe it's a false sense of security, but knowing the authorities are focusing their attention so far off course, I feel a measure of relief. I can't say Fionn feels the same. Not with the way his brows knit together, or the momentary pause he takes when he exits the vehicle to look back toward Main Street as though the cruisers might appear. When he comes to my side to help me down, the smile he gives me is a faint echo of the one from his doorstep only a few minutes ago.

"Don't worry," he says. "As long as no one else realizes he was intending to hunt and not fish, he's going to be hard to find. And even if they do, who knows where he might have gone."

"I'm not worried." I probably should be. I'm sure that's what Fionn is thinking too. But something about it feels *right*, no matter what happens next or what consequences I might have to face. Sometimes, I think *right* might not be *good*. And *wrong* might not be *bad*. Even before I joined Silveria Circus, I'd started to question what kind of people drew those lines around our lives, and whose benefit those boundaries are really for. Because the more women I meet like me, the more I believe the rules were never made with us in mind.

With a single, decisive nod, Fionn passes me my crutches before grabbing a backpack from the rear seat. When we get to the entrance of the clinic, he brings up the app on his phone, disarming the security system before he checks each of the internal cameras. "I don't see her," he says as he pulls the keys from his pocket and unlocks the door.

"Is there a back entrance?" I ask, and he nods. "I'll take the keys and go in that way. We can corner her. Or, if we're lucky, she's already gone."

Fionn levels me with a flat look as he drops the keys onto my waiting palm and then slides the backpack from his shoulder to rummage through its interior. He passes me a pair of gardening gloves. "Trust me. She's not gone. She's lying in wait to ambush us."

"Okay," I say as I shift my shoulders back. "Where's the comms device?"

Fionn's eyes narrow as he hands me a beach towel.

"Walkie-talkie? Riot gear? Lasers? Surely you brought lasers, right? You're not expecting we can take down an assassin raccoon with nothing more than a towel, are you?"

Fionn pulls on his own gloves and sighs. "Just . . . be careful."

"Copy that."

I grin at Fionn's exaggerated eye roll and pocket the keys before I pull the gloves on. With the towel tossed over my shoulder, I make my way to the back of the clinic, making note of any potential entry points where Barbara might be gaining access into the building. A vent near the peak of the roof catches my eye, and though the grill looks like it's in place, I'd be willing to bet money that she's figured out a way to get past it.

"You might be tricky," I say to myself as I unlock the door, "but you're not circus-level tricky, Barbara."

I step inside the air-conditioned building, shutting the door behind me with a quiet *snick*. The storage room I've entered is silent and dark. To my right, there are shelves with boxes of office supplies and latex gloves, masks and paper towels. To my left is an unlit hallway that must lead toward the exam rooms.

"Marco," I call out as I flip on the storage room light. I lean my crutches against a wall and shift some boxes on a shelf, half expecting the raccoon to jump on my face. "*Marco.*" My phone buzzes in my pocket, and I pull off a glove and check the device.

| Polo.

Shhh. She'll hear you.

Loosen up, McSpicy. You're
worse than a bongo board in a
blowdown.

. . . . .

I have no idea what that means.

You know, the tent master? In a
circus? During a storm that blows
all the tents down?

. . . I'm still lost, but we'll come back
to that later. DON'T LET BARBARA
SENSE YOUR FEAR. It makes her more
aggressive.

I grin at the screen and pocket the device before taking up my
crutches and starting toward the corridor.

And then I hear it. A rustling in the distance.

I dart as fast as I can to the mouth of the darkened corridor and
lock eyes with the raccoon.

Barbara stands upright on her hind legs. Neither of us moves.
She looks at me as though weighing her odds for coming out of a
fight on top. And then, with her beady black eyes pinned to mine
and her front paws folded against her chest, she walks on her back
legs into the room at the end of the hall.

"Oh my God. That's both creepy and adorable. *Barbara, get back here.*" I chase after the sound of her chattering call, losing my momentum when the towel slips from my shoulder and tangles around my crutches. There's a momentary clattering of tiny nails on stainless steel, but all has gone eerily quiet by the time I regain my balance and make it to the darkened threshold. When I hit the light switch and look around the staff break room, Barbara is nowhere to be seen. "What the hell . . . ? Doc . . . Doc . . ."

Fionn's rushing footfalls draw to a halt just behind me. "*No, Rose,*" he says, his voice desperate. "She's drawn to sound."

I pivot to face him and roll my eyes. "Doc, you make her sound like a fucking velociraptor—"

"*Duck!*"

I turn just in time to see an angry ball of fur launching toward me from a shelf just above eye level. My crutches fall. My hands fly to my head. I dodge and spin on my good foot to watch as Barbara connects with Fionn's face.

I toss the towel over them both.

"*Why?*" the mound of squirming towel laments.

"Sorry, Doc. So sorry," I say, though it doesn't sound super sincere when I can't help but laugh. I grab what I hope is Barbara's scruff as she growls her protests and Fionn releases a string of Irish-accented expletives. As soon as I've got her pulled off his face, he stumbles backward, his hair disheveled and his neck red with bloodied, crisscrossed scratches.

"What the *fuck.*"

"It worked," I reply with a shrug as Barbara continues to squirm in my grip. "You're welcome."

"I'm going to have to get rabies shots."

I turn Barbara toward me and she screeches and squirms, trying to take a swipe at my face. "I mean, she doesn't *look* rabid. But I don't know shit about raccoons."

"Well, I'm not going to take my chances and end up barking at my shadow, thanks," he says as he levels me with a stern look. When Barbara growls, Fionn's glare softens into worry. Even though he looks like he wants to hold on to his irritation, he can't seem to. "Let me take her for you."

"Nah, I've got a good grip on her. I don't have faith this hostage transfer would go well. She's spicy," I say as she punctuates my words with frustrated barks. "Just pass me a crutch and stuff one of those trail mix bags into my pocket." I nod toward a basket filled with very Fionn-esque healthy snacks. "I'll let her out the back while you get your battle wounds cleaned up."

Fionn's brows knit, a crease notched between them. "Are you sure?"

"It's the least I can do. Thanks for taking a raccoon to the face for me."

Fionn can't help but snicker as he slides his gloves off and drops them on the counter. He takes the package of trail mix and hooks a finger into my pocket. Fionn Kane does not flirt with me. Or at least, he tries his best not to. But his eyes don't leave mine as he slides the treat into my pocket and says, "It wasn't really by choice. But I'd take a raccoon to the face for you any day, Rose Evans."

Blush rises in my cheeks as I smile. And I know he likes it. I can tell by the way his gaze drops to my lips and lingers there. I consider calling him out on it, throwing a question or two out into the open to see what happens next as he bends to retrieve one of my crutches. But before I have the chance, there are three loud knocks at the front door of the clinic.

Fionn pats down his shorts, and that moment of unexpected playfulness vanishes from his eyes as they dart in the direction of the front of the building. "Shit. I left my phone at the front desk. I have no idea who that is."

"I've got Barbara, don't worry about it. Go ahead, I'll be totally fine."

He gives me a doubtful frown and three more knocks rap at the door. With an exchange of reluctant nods, we part ways, him toward the front of the clinic and me toward the rear with a single crutch and an irate trash panda. When I get to the back door, I wait until it's closed behind me before I lean the crutch against it, using my free hand to fish the trail mix from my pocket. I open it with my teeth and scatter the contents on the concrete walkway before setting Barbara down, using the towel as a flimsy barrier between us to keep her from backtracking and chomping on my legs. She looks like she considers it too, at least until I shoo her away in the direction of the food. With a final glare in my direction, she starts picking up peanuts and raisins with her dexterous little paws.

"So cute yet so murdery," I say, stuffing the gloves in my back pocket. "I think we're kindred spirits, Barbara."

She growls.

"Right. Enjoy your snack. I'm totally going to tell Dr. McSpicy you're getting in through the vent for giving me that ungrateful attitude." She looks up at me with her beady little eyes. "Okay, fine. I won't. But you need to check those manners next time."

I leave the crusty raccoon to her meal, grabbing my crutch

before I reenter the clinic. I'm halfway down the hallway before a single text from Fionn stops me short.

| Hide.

I dart into what must be Fionn's office as the light for the corridor flicks on and a familiar voice booms from the direction of the waiting room.

"Apologies, Dr. Kane. I know the clinic is closed and all, but I saw your truck out front and the lights on, so I thought I'd take my chances. It's just that my eye is a little sore, and I was wondering if you wouldn't mind just taking a quick look. Save me all the trouble of driving out to Weyburn."

"Of course, Mr. Cranwell," Fionn says, but his voice is pinched, his tone clipped. "We'll take Exam Room Two."

I linger in the shadows, staying out of sight in Fionn's office as he leads Matt to the exam room across the hall. My hand passes behind my back. I slowly pull my blade free of its sheath.

"So, tell me about what happened," Fionn says. Paper rustles as Matt gets up on the exam bed.

"Long story, Dr. Kane. Not an entirely interesting one either. Got some cocktail sticks lodged in there."

"You're sure that doesn't make for an interesting tale?"

Matt huffs a laugh, and the fine hairs at the back of my neck raise. "Maybe for another day."

Fionn hums a thoughtful note, and then there's silence, I imagine as he's pulling off the eye patch and examining the healing wound. "How long has it been since the injury?" he asks, despite knowing the answer.

"About three weeks."

"And you're still having pain?"

"Yes."

My hand tightens around my blade. That one simple word is delivered like a lie. I could give him real fucking pain. Take the other eye and make him beg for mercy. Realistically, would I probably puke everywhere if I did? Yes. But it would be worth it.

"How's the farm?" Fionn asks, pulling me out of thoughts of murder and chaos. "Wife and kids?"

"Same old, same old," Matt replies, and there's a hidden thread of darkness in the jovial tone of his words, as though he's telling himself a clever joke. "How about yourself, anything new and exciting in the world of Dr. Fionn Kane?"

Fionn's reply is delivered with clinical detachment when he says, "Nothing much to report."

Matt chuckles. My guts churn at the sound. I don't know whether to burst out of the shadows and slash Matt's fuck-ugly throat or chase after Barbara to hide out in her trash panda den. "That's not entirely true, is it? I understand you've got visitor staying with you. Someone not from around here. A woman with a broken leg."

"Word certainly does get around among small towns, doesn't it."

"How'd she run into such a spell of trouble to wind up at your house?"

"Mr. Cranwell," Fionn says on a sigh. "You know I'm not at liberty to discuss a patient with you."

"I'm not asking about her condition. I'm asking about how she got there."

"Considering she's not here to answer for herself, I'm not about to detail her circumstances to someone she's never met." There's a pause. I imagine Fionn giving him a stern look. I can picture with perfect clarity the way his eyes can turn as sharp as the cutting edge of a polished gem, so beautiful but still able to draw blood. "It wouldn't be very professional of me, would it?"

"You're right, you're right," Matt concedes, though his submission is not convincing. "I'm just looking out for you. Making sure you're all right."

"Why wouldn't I be?"

"You just never know who you might be dealing with, that's all. Outsiders can cause trouble."

"No more so than 'insiders.' Isn't that right?" I know Fionn well enough to know that I've never heard him sound like this. The words are simple, direct. They're delivered with coolness, an eerie sense of calm. But beneath them is an undercurrent. A lethality. A warning to stay away. *Or else.*

I might not be able to see their faces, but the tension between the two men feels ready to ignite. A curtain of unease descends, thick enough that I'm sure I could cut it with the blade clutched in my hand.

"Your postoperative recovery seems to be going well. There are no signs of infection or swelling," Fionn finally says. His voice is still cool, but it's lost the deadly bite in the tone. "I'll prescribe some tramadol for you."

"No need, Dr. Kane," Matt says. "I'd better stay alert. You know, busy time of year and all. I've got to stay vigilant. On my toes."

Fionn says nothing. I imagine the deferential nod he probably gives Matt, the way he watches and considers and gives only what he needs to in a tense situation. He'll be careful, calm. But he'll be roiling under that detached exterior. I know there's another side to him, buried beneath what he lets me see. And this time I can feel it, lingering in the air like musk.

I shift farther into the shadows when I hear footsteps, coming face-to-face with a photo of Fionn and two other men who have similar features. Dark hair. High cheekbones. Shining smiles. Blue eyes, each shade unique, the color of Fionn's the lightest of them all. They link arms over one another's shoulders. They're his brothers in Boston, Rowan and Lachlan, whom he's spoken of only briefly. I step closer to the photo as a set of curt goodbyes reaches me from the entrance. Even in a moment frozen in time, I can see the love and happiness that radiates from each of them. And Fionn has come all this way, chosen to separate himself from his brothers and his home, just for a chance to heal a broken heart. Maybe a chance to hide the side of himself he doesn't want anyone to see.

What if I'm tearing his sanctuary apart?

The front door of the clinic closes and a moment later, Fionn returns. I realize before I exit his office that I recognize him by the cadence of his steps alone. He stops in front of me, and I try to smile. But guilt is starting to chew a little hole in my heart.

"Are you okay?" he asks, his brow furrowed, his eyes pinned to mine.

"Yeah. Are you?"

I don't know what I expect him to say. But I know for sure that the last thing I expect is for him to wrap me in an embrace.

His arms are tense around me. Protective and sheltering. I'm so surprised that it takes a moment for me to return the gesture. As soon as I do, his heart jumps a beat beneath my ear. A little of the tension in Fionn subsides, as though he didn't realize how much he needed this too. Something about that aches in my chest. Maybe I tighten my grip around him just a little. Press my face to his chest a little harder. Close my eyes as I take in his scent, sage and citrus warmed by the sun. There's maybe a hint of raccoon too, but I let that slide with a faint smile.

We stay like that for a long while. When we separate, Fionn checks the front door of the clinic, making sure Matt is long gone before he beckons me to follow. He lifts me into the truck like he always does. He seems nervous to drop me off at home, where I'll be alone, but after at least five or six reassurances that I'll be okay, he leaves for the hospital to get his first rabies shot.

It isn't until later that evening, when I'm lying in bed and staring into the dark, that I realize something.

He never answered my question.

I don't know if he's really okay.

BEAST MODE

Fionn

The lights are low. Music pumps through the speakers. The smell of sweat and beer and bourbon permeates the air as I make my way through the crowd. My grip tightens on the handle of my bag, and I push past the people talking and laughing as they wait for the show to begin.

Maybe I shouldn't like this environment. I know what's about to come, after all. It's not really the kind of thing a man like me should condone. But the truth is, I love coming to these Blood Brothers fights. The split flesh to mend. A glimpse of bone. It's raw and visceral. This is humanity at its bloody core, fights hidden in the dark. My job might be on the sidelines, to fix the damage done during the bare-knuckled fights in a makeshift ring in a rundown barn, but I enjoy it, nonetheless. I'm close enough to feel the adrenaline of the battles and rivalries, and just far enough that I don't become a different man from the one I chose to be.

And maybe it will take my mind off Rose.

I can't deny how much I want her. Every day, little by little, it gets worse. Her infectious smile. Her uninhibited laugh. Her wild, unpredictable nature, as though she's not bound by the same rules as everyone else. She's so fucking beautiful it sometimes hurts just to look at her. The way she sits at the table to stare into her tarot cards with a braid looped over her shoulder and her fringe skimming her brows. The way her eyes sparkle when she teases me. No matter how hard I try not to let it, my desire for her chews at my resolve.

But I feel like I'm losing my grip on reality. Like I'm not the man I thought I could force myself to be. And that makes me infinitely more dangerous than she is. Because while Rose knows what she is and what she wants and how dark she's willing to be, I still have no idea what I'm truly capable of. Or what will happen if I let myself go.

I can't risk her. *I can't.*

I need some time to figure this all out. Time around something that gets me out of my own head and into the blood and guts of life.

When I make it to the side of the ring, my designated area, I set my bag down on the folding table and take out my white coat and stethoscope and put them on. I learned early on to do this first, or risk being punched in the face for taking up prime real estate next to the ropes. As soon as they're on, I wipe down the table and take out the things I know I'll need, placing them on a sterile disposable mat. Isopropyl alcohol. Cotton pads. A scalpel. Latex gloves. My suture kit.

"Dr. Kane," Tom says in his best announcer voice, sidling up to my table as I nudge my two metal stools into place next to the table. He gives me a flash of a chipped smile when I meet his eyes, his gaze traveling across the crowd before returning to me. This is his show. His lair. And he revels in every moment of the mayhem. "We've got quite a lineup tonight. I'm sure you're going to be busy."

"I'm always busy when I come here."

"Maybe extra busy this time," Tom says with a wink. "Fury and the Natural are up first. You ready?"

A spike of excitement snakes through my veins. I nod once. "Sure am, Tom."

"Great." He claps me on the shoulder. Then he turns to the ring, bringing a microphone to his lips. "Who in this shithole is ready for a fight?" he booms, his words chased by cheers and pounding feet and sloshing beer.

I've been here enough times over the last few years that I have this process memorized. Tom introduces the fighters. The packed audience yells their bets. They wave money in the air. Tom's grown kids and a handful of employees collect wagers. And as Tom booms the limited rules through the microphone, I ready myself. I'm coiled, even though I'm not the one about to fight. The match starts and I shift my feet on the sticky floor like I'm a mirror of the battle on the mats. When the Natural throws a hook, my fist tenses. When Fury ducks to avoid a punch, my head bobs too.

The fight goes the full three rounds. I patch the Natural up with a few butterfly bandages after the second, just enough to keep the blood from dripping into his eye, but by the end of the match, he's heading straight to me for stitches, the pain likely made a little duller by his narrow win in the ring. His buddy brings him two beers and he chugs the first one. I don't even bother mentioning that now is probably the worst time for alcohol given he needs at least six sutures. I just disinfect the wound and start my work, piercing his skin and drawing the thread through the tiny, bloody hole I create, tying each stitch with a precise knot.

I'm only three stitches in when a familiar voice grinds my progress to a sudden halt.

"Hey, Doc."

My heart surges into my throat and lodges there as I whip my head around and come eye-to-eye with Rose. She sinks a bite into a hot dog overflowing with mustard and relish and ketchup. Her eyes glimmer in the dim light as they take in the shock that must be spread across my face.

"Rose, what the fuck are you doing here?"

She shrugs, taking her time to chew and swallow before she wipes her mouth and gives me a mischievous grin. "Thought I might check out what y'all do for fun around these parts. The Suture Sisters are cool and all, but I figured crochet club and the gym weren't your only hobbies." She glances around us and returns her gaze to mine with a shrug. "Guess I was right."

"You're supposed to be at Sandra's," I protest, a wave of worry hitting me so hard I feel nauseated.

"I was at Sandra's, for a bit. But I got bored. One can only work on a sex swing for so long, I guess," she replies with a shrug.

"How . . . How did you get here?"

"Larry."

An irrational spike of anger hits my chest like a lightning strike. "Who the fuck is Larry?"

Her head tilts. "Chill, Doc. You're touchier than a Risley juggler with athlete's foot."

"I'm . . . *what?*"

Rose rolls her eyes at my inability to decipher her obscure circus lingo. "You're *irritable.*" I open my mouth to protest, but she's already shifted gears when she says, "You don't know Trucker Larry? He's your neighbor six houses down across the street." For a moment, I consider lying and claiming I know who the hell she means. But that won't fly with Rose. She merely grins around another bite of her hot dog and pierces me with her sharp, dark eyes. "Have you been living in Hartford, Doc? Or have you just been hidin' out in it?"

My gaze drops from hers as I turn her words over in my mind. I know she's right, of course, but it feels different to hear it from someone on the outside. I've had my head down, doing my work, keeping to myself. If a person hasn't come into the clinic, chances are I haven't gotten to know them. And even if they've been to my practice, can I say I've really made many friends in town? This Blood Brothers fight club is the closest thing I've had to socialization until I wound up with the Suture Sisters, and even this is realistically more of a job than it is a night off with friends.

A job.

I finally realize I'm here to suture somebody's face, and the gash across his brow is only half stitched up.

"Sorry," I grumble as I turn back to my patient.

"No need to apologize, Dr. Kane," the guy says as I slide my curved suture needle through his skin. "I'd rather look at her pretty face than mine too if I were in your position."

"Nah, you're the prettiest one here, Nate," Rose says, adding accelerant to the fire that's already burning through my veins. I turn my incredulous glare to Rose, who gives me a saccharine smile as she wipes her fingers clean then tosses the napkin into a nearby bin. She grips the handles of her crutches and points one in my patient's direction. "What, you're telling me you don't know Nate either? *Nate the Natural?* He makes those wicked-cool chain-saw wood sculptures all over town. The bear is badass, Nate."

"Thanks, Rose." Nate only grins when I narrow my eyes at him and pierce his brow a little more roughly than necessary for the next stitch. I try not to glance over at Rose as I concentrate on the work of my hands, and Nate can see it, my struggle to keep my attention where it belongs. So he takes every opportunity to ask Rose questions about her broken leg or her tarot cards, or worst of all, *How long before you're back on the road with the circus?*

"Last one," I interject before Rose has a chance to answer. I tie the final knot and clip the thread free, then rise from my stool. "See you around."

Nate gives me a slow smile that's equal parts teasing and pitying. "Thanks, man," he says, shaking my hand before he turns away. "Rose, stop by my shop next Sunday and I'll have something for you."

"No, you won't," I grumble, but no one can hear me over the drone of the crowd. I clean up my workstation, but really I hang on every word Rose says as she agrees to visit Nate's shop and compliments the new scar on his brow before giving him a brief hug. Even after Nate's moved out of my peripheral vision, I still don't look over at Rose. Instead, I busy myself with resetting my table, but I feel her dark eyes on me the entire time.

I finally set down the last item, a fresh, curved needle, when Rose says, "You okay there, Doc?"

No. "Yeah. All good."

"You sure?"

"You shouldn't be here," I blurt out. It feels like all the sound is sucked out of the room. Like I could pick Rose's voice out of the chaos, but her silence is just as loud. When I finally look up, she has her arms crossed despite leaning on her crutches, and it looks as fierce as it does awkward.

"Why not?"

"It's not safe."

Rose casts her gaze around us in an arc that sweeps across the ceiling and the crowd before returning to me. "Yeah, structurally this place is probably not great. One dodgy bolt and we'll all be crushed to death by rotten beams and broken dreams."

I give Rose a flat glare and mischief dances across her face. "You know what I mean. It's not safe for *you*. Your leg. This crowd. The person who could show up, if you know what I mean."

"You mean Matt? He's busy making hay. Lucy's younger sister's best friend's boyfriend told me at the car wash today."

"What were you doing at the car wash? You don't have a car."

"I was bored. Thought I'd take a little wander and got to talking," she says, unaware that two men have started a shoving match behind her, one pushing the other against the side of the empty ring before they're separated by their respective friends. "Anyway, this place seems just fine to me."

"You hurtle yourself though a metal cage on a death machine and you subsist on a diet of waffles and sugar. I can't say I trust your self-preservation instincts."

Rose lifts a shoulder and takes a lollipop from her pocket, holding my gaze as she slowly pulls the wrapper free and slides it past her lips. *Those fucking lips.* Strawberry red, glistening, sweet and plump. I can almost feel them, warm and yielding as they wrap around my—

"Next up is the Humphrey Hurricane," Tom booms into his microphone. Cheers and boos interrupt the ache that's already starting to build in my cock. I shake my head, trying to clear my thoughts and refocus on my purpose for being here. "And please welcome a brand-new challenger to the ring: Ballistic Bill."

The crowd descends into a frenzy of betting and shouting as the new guy ducks between the ropes and throws his hands in the air, turning a slow circle as he basks in the mayhem. He's fucking *enormous*. He shrugs off his black robe and he's like a square block of muscle and tattoos. Shaved head, wrapped hands, scarred face. This guy knows what he's doing. And I've seen the Hurricane fight. I've stitched him up. He's capable and fast, light on his feet. But I know the same thing the rest of the crowd does. The Hurricane is about to have his ass handed to him.

"Rose, seriously. You need to get out of here," I say over the cheers as Ballistic Bill roars like a feral beast. The crowd surges and a drunken onlooker bumps into Rose's crutch as though proving my point. He sloshes a few drops of beer on her arm, and it takes everything in me to swallow down a burst of rage as he apologizes to her before moving away. "It's not safe here. Fights break out on the sidelines all the time. You don't have anywhere to put your foot up."

"Chill, Doc." Rose brushes off the drops of alcohol and then hobbles toward me. She taps my hip with her crutch and I rise from the stool, internally berating myself for not giving her my seat earlier, though it's not like I want to encourage her to stay. As soon as I'm up, she plops herself down, then brings her injured leg onto the empty stool. "See? All good. Promise I'll move when you get your next patient. The Hurricane, by the looks of things. Yikes."

"Rose—"

"You should get us something from the grease joint." She nods toward the concession stand when I tilt my head and furrow my brow at what must be more of her circus lingo. "I wouldn't mind a beer. I'll hold down the fort and make sure nobody takes your doctory shit. If they do, I'll *stab them in the fucking eye*."

Rose whips my scalpel from the table and stabs an invisible assailant, twisting the blade, a look of maniacal glee plastered on her face. I cover her hand with mine and pry the knife from her grasp. "Please do not go stabbing anyone," I say as I take a sterile pad and disinfect the handle before setting it back in its place. "I'm only going to be the one to put them back together again if you do."

Rose shrugs as though that's not her problem.

"One beer."

"Might as well bring two, save you another trip."

"*One*. You're recovering. I'm your doctor. Doctor's orders."

Some fleeting wisp of emotion passes across Rose's face, the meaning of it too complex for me to discern from her furrowed brow before it smooths. "Fine. But I'll take a bag of Skittles too, please."

"I don't think they have Skittles."

"Trust me, they do."

Though I roll my eyes, we both know I won't deny her. It's hard enough not to bring an entire keg back for her just so she can have the two beers she wants while I keep her in sight. She grins at me as though she can read my thoughts. I shake my head at her, but when I turn my back and walk away, I smile.

The bartender sees me coming and I'm able to jump the line, grabbing the Skittles and a free beer and a bourbon for myself before I return to the table just in time for the start of the fight. Tom yells the rules into the mic. Closed fist only. No slapping, no elbows, no knees or kicking. Anyone knocked down has ten seconds to get back up. And then he steps back from between the two fighters, and with one simple word, the battle is on.

Fight.

The crowd roars as the Hurricane lunges forward with a hook that doesn't connect. Ballistic Bill leans away from a cross jab. And another. Another. A punch finally connects but only with Bill's arm as he blocks his face. He dodges more hits, allowing a few past his defenses, always leaning away just as a punch connects. The blows he lets through are nothing more than taps. The crowd cheers, and heckles, and shouts at both men. But Bill doesn't seem to notice. He's only focused on his opponent, his feet light and quick on the bloodstained mats despite his massive size. And he hasn't thrown a single punch.

"He's wearing him out," Rose says over the din of the audience, not looking away from the fight. She gestures toward the ring with a Skittle. "The Hurricane is so fucked."

Dread settles in my guts like a stone. Most fights here might be raw, but they're at least evenly matched. Not this time. And she's right—I can feel it in my marrow. The Hurricane is fucked.

I turn my attention back to the ring just as Bill delivers his first hit, a punch to the Hurricane's ribs. He stumbles backward. Bill clips his cheek with a jab. The Hurricane buries his head behind his forearms and blocks a few more punches. The crowd eats it up. But it's obvious. Bill barely follows through, hardly uses his shoulders. He doesn't put the momentum of his weight into the fight. These hits are only for show.

The buzzer rings, ending the first two-minute period. The fighters head back to their corners, where their buddies or amateur trainers pass them water and towels, leaning close to each man to deliver strategy or encouragement. Excitement skitters through the audience. I look down my shoulder at Rose and find she's already watching me, a grin etched into her face as she tilts her beer bottle in my direction.

"This is great, Doc. Thanks for bringing me here."

I frown. "I didn't. I've asked you to leave. Multiple times."

"I thought we were friends," she says with a sarcastic pout, but there's something about it that seems like genuine disappointment. The expression disappears in an instant and she turns her attention away from me to add her voice to the chorus of shouts around us as Tom calls for the fighters to return to the center of the ring. But I'm still looking at Rose, and it takes longer than it should to tear my gaze away.

The buzzer rings. The fight resumes. This time, Bill puts in a little more effort. He punches with more force. When the Hurricane loses stamina and backs away, Bill is on him, pushing him into the ropes. The newcomer is unrelenting. One blow after the next. The Hurricane takes successive hits to the ribs and when his arms inch lower and his frame hunches, Bill is there. A huge left hook slips right through his defenses and slams into the other man's jaw.

The Hurricane's back hits the mat and he doesn't get up.

Cheers and boos swell around us as the seconds are counted. The Hurricane barely stirs, his body splayed across the mat. When the match is finally called in his favor, Bill takes a victory lap around his opponent and then slips through the ropes to collect his winnings. I take his place to collect my patient.

"Hey, buddy. We're going to need to get you to the hospital," I say over the roar of the crowd as I kneel next to the Hurricane. He blinks his swollen eyes up at me, and I pull him into the recovery position. His friends pat his shoulder and keep him conscious as I turn my attention to Tom, the announcer hovering in the periphery. "What the fuck, man?"

Tom flashes a smile that might as well be made of dollar signs. "Great fight, wasn't it? The crowd is going *nuts*."

"You and I might have different definitions of *great*."

"Everyone who steps into this ring knows they might leave it on a stretcher."

"And everyone who steps into it should be matched so they won't fucking *die*."

The longer our eyes stay locked in a silent exchange, the more Tom's smile dissolves. We both know that if I accuse him of rigging this fight with a ringer, there will be more trouble in this barn than either of us can handle.

Tom knows I don't like it. But he also knows I won't risk lighting a fuse in a powder keg. His smile sneaks back onto his face when he says, "Don't pretend you don't enjoy a little mayhem, Dr. Kane. Why else would you keep coming back?"

"Because if you insist on running this club of yours, someone qualified needs to be here to put the fighters back together," I say as the Hurricane's friends get him up on his unsteady feet.

"Because they're going to wind up worse off if I don't. Or someone will end up dead. Because—"

Whatever half-truth I'm about to bark at Tom evaporates the moment I hear Rose scream.

I forget about my patient. The crowd. The lights and the noise. When I whip around, all my focus is on the place she should be. The place where she is *not*.

My table has shifted, my supplies scattered across its surface. One of Bill's friends tries to hold him back as he scraps with two other men, a third stumbling away from the altercation with his hand raised to catch the blood that trickles from a gash over his eye. *Where is she?* I call out her name, but she doesn't respond. The brawl shifts to one side just enough that I can see the floor. And then I spot Rose. She's been knocked off her stool, one hand clasped around her leg just above the edge of her cast. Pain twists her features into a grimace. She tries to push herself beneath the table and out of the way of the fight, brandishing one of her crutches as a weapon to keep the oblivious crowd away.

In an instant, I'm on my feet, gripping the ropes to duck between them. The sound of her scream still rings in my ears, setting my blood on fire. But I can't get to her fast enough. Not before Bill knocks into her cast and she lets out an agonized cry.

"*Get the fuck away from her,*" I snarl as I shove Bill with both hands. He stumbles into another man on the sidelines of the skirmish. By the time he rights himself and pivots in my direction, I've put myself between the fight and Rose.

Bill hardly takes notice of the men he was battling just a moment ago. His friends step in to shove them back into the heaving crowd. But Bill doesn't notice them. His eyes trail down the length of me as a sneer lifts one corner of his lips. "Stay out of it, bro. Wouldn't want to bust up that pretty face."

I could leave it there. Deescalate this situation. Chalk it up to bad luck. That's probably all it was, just a moment that went too far. A simple accident.

But then Bill's eyes land on Rose.

His menacing, predatory grin is stuck to her like tar. It clings on and I don't have to look over my shoulder to feel her recoil behind me, as though her pain and fear and anger are invading my cells. And then I forget all about the kind of man I'm facing. Just like I forget the kind of man I'm supposed to be.

My first hit slams into Bill's cheekbone. My second into his temple. I catch the moment of surprise in his eyes. In a blink, it transforms into rage. His fist arcs through the air, but I duck to deliver a hit to his ribs. He grunts in pain. It shouldn't be so satisfying when he lurches backward. My knuckles crunch into his brow. It shouldn't feel so fucking good when the skin splits open.

But it does.

Bill rallies back as blood pours over his eye. I take a punch to the cheek that makes the world around me vibrate and darken. But I stay on my feet and come back harder. My blood is lava. My muscles are stone. One fist after the other. One blow after the next. I don't even see the man I pummel into a bloody pulp. I just see Rose on the floor, her pretty face creased with pain, her broken leg clutched in a white-knuckled grip. I see the unshed tears in her eyes and I hear the agony in her voice. And all I want is to tear his fucking flesh off for hurting her. I want to punish him. I want to punish *myself*. Because I never should have turned my back on her. The moment she showed up, I should have insisted we leave.

It's my fucking fault.

Something cracks open inside me. A fucking *monster* tears free. I roar as I throw all my weight into a right hook that smashes into Bill's bruised jaw. His head snaps to the side and his muscles go slack and he falls to the floor.

For a moment, the barn seems completely silent. The people around me stare at Bill, bloodied and unconscious on the floor. Then they look at me. The man who's supposed to be the doctor for probably half these people and their families. With my stained white coat, covered in crimson splashes. My stethoscope discarded at my feet. And then, just as sudden as the stark silence, they erupt in cheers, raising their glasses, shouting and bouncing on their heels. They pat me on the shoulders and chant *Doctor, Doctor, Doctor* over and over and over. But even through the crowd, I still hear her. The only person who says my name.

"Fionn."

I spin around and push past a few people to get to the table where Rose struggles to keep her balance with the single crutch, the other lost somewhere among the crowd. Before I realize what I'm doing, I've framed her face with my hands, my knuckles raw and swollen next to her flawless skin. She's so fucking beautiful, her cheeks flushed, her plush lips open, her lashes still damp with tears of pain. My thumb coasts across her cheek and her eyes drift closed.

"I got knocked over. I'm okay," she whispers. I don't know how I can hear her over the noise that surrounds us. But I do. She grips my wrist with her free hand. "Are you?"

God, I want to kiss her. I want to feel the heat of her lips against mine. Would she want that? Would she melt against me if she did?

Or would the tension I feel between us snap and release something feral inside her? Inside *me*?

I lean a little closer. Her eyes search mine. Her grip tightens on my wrist.

A hand clamps onto my shoulder and Tom appears in the periphery. And just like that, the spell is broken. I turn my attention back to Rose. Her eyes are still on me.

What are you doing? She's your fucking patient.

And you're the most dangerous man here.

I let my hands fall back to my sides.

"Looks like there was a ringer in our midst the whole time," Tom says. With a clap on my back and a dark smile, he slips back into the crowd.

Though Rose keeps her thoughts shuttered from me, something lingers in the air between us. An electric charge. The scent of an oncoming storm.

And then she turns away.

REDUCTION

Fionn

"There's a beat-up chick here with a tall guy claiming to be your brother. He stole my fucking crutch," Rose snarls on the other end of the phone.

I rap my fingertips on my desk as a shit-eating grin spreads across my face. "Ask him to give you his childhood nickname."

"He's asking to confirm your childhood nickname," she says, but not to me. The defiant "no" I hear in the background is like a single-worded symphony in my ears.

"Great," Rose says, menace dripping from her voice. "Then I knife you in the balls."

There's a muffled protest from Rowan and an unfamiliar woman's voice interjects in the tone of a pained and tired plea. There are a few resigned words from my brother that I can't make out, a beat of silence—and then a burst of laughter.

"His nickname is Shitflicker," Rose finally says, and my triumphant cackle echoes through the empty clinic as I lean back in my office chair.

"That's my brother Rowan. Tell him I'll be there in about fifteen minutes." I hang up and the smile lingers as I push aside my paperwork and lock up to walk home. There's a car I don't recognize in the driveway when I arrive. I can almost feel Rowan's energy before I even reach the door. When I open it, he's at the table with Rose, and relief courses through my veins when she looks at me and smiles. It's a moment that only lasts as long as a blink.

The legs of the chair scrape across the floor as my brother rises and heads straight for me. "Where the fuck have you been, dickhead?"

"Work, dumbass. I had to get some paperwork out."

Rowan wraps me in a tight embrace. There's tension in his arms. I might not believe in auras, but I can sense his distressed energy like a halo that lights up the room. We separate just enough for him to press his forehead to mine the way we've done since we were kids, and then he lets me go to stare into my eyes. I've never seen him so wound up. So . . . agonized. His focus shifts to the living room and sticks there, and I follow his gaze.

"This is Sloane."

A woman with raven hair watches me from the couch, an angry boot print stamped on the center of her forehead, two crescent bruises beneath her lashes contrasting with her sharp hazel eyes. Her left shoulder hangs lower than the other and she cradles her forearm to stabilize it. She might be injured, but I've heard enough about her history from Rowan to know that she's probably the most dangerous person in my house right now. Which is saying something.

I go to the couch with Rowan on my heels, so close I can still feel his nervous energy humming at my back. When I stop in front of Sloane, he drops to a crouch at her legs. She lets go of her injured arm to take his hand. "I'm Fionn," I say, and she lifts her gaze from the silent exchange she seems to be having with my brother and turns her attention to me. "Can I have a look at that shoulder?"

Sloane swallows and nods, wincing as she tries to pry her injured arm from her body. I palpate the joint, feeling the head of her humerus and the edges of the glenoid fossa and the acromion of her scapula. "How did this happen?" I ask as I prod the swollen tissue.

"I fell off a roof."

"More like got tossed from a roof by that ugly motherfucker," Rowan snarls.

"He got what he deserved. And I consider it a win for me."

"Blackbird—"

"Murder games aside," I interject, "are there any other injuries I should know about?"

"Other than this?" Rowan says, pointing to her bruised face. The look Sloane gives me is unamused. "No."

I pull my hand away from her shoulder and gently press her nasal bones, but despite the dried blood that rims her nostrils, nothing feels noticeably broken or out of place. "Seems all right. Did you lose consciousness?"

"Yes, for maybe a minute."

"And she vomited."

Sloane winces, a hint of blush coloring her cheeks, but Rowan merely squeezes her hand. I hold my finger in front of her face and ask her to track it. Her dilated pupils lag slightly in following the motion. A concussion is likely, and she seems to already know it. "Yeah . . . You won't want to be driving for a little while. Try to take it easy."

"Figured."

"And the shoulder?" Rowan asks. He might try his best to hide it, but I've seen fear in Rowan more times than I can count. It's there in his eyes, in the tic of the muscle along his jaw. "Will she need surgery?"

"No," I say, and his breath of relief is audible. "Normally, I'd advise going to the hospital for an X-ray to be sure nothing is fractured, but I'm guessing you want to keep yourselves as off the radar as possible, given the circumstances." They both nod, and I glance toward Rose as she watches off to the side, her expression grim. "We need to get to my clinic so I can inject the joint with lido and manipulate the bone back into place. And it's going to hurt. But it will feel a lot better after that."

Rose's crutches tap on the hardwood as she hobbles closer to the couch. "I've got some button-up shirts that will fit you. I'll grab a few in case you'd rather cut that one off."

Sloane's expression softens and a tired smile spreads across her lips. "That's really kind. Thank you."

With a nod, Rose pats Sloane's good shoulder and swings her way to her room. Sloane watches until she disappears from view. When Sloane meets my eyes, there's so much I can read from them, so much she tries to tell me in a single, lingering glance. She likes Rose. She trusts her. But she doesn't trust me. Even though I've been through medical school. Even though I've saved lives. Fixed injuries. Delivered the occasional baby. Held the most vulnerable life in my palms. I can tell Sloane sees right through me.

You are living a lie, she seems to say as her eyes stay fixed to mine. *And if you hurt her, I'll kill you.*

I'm fucking paranoid. She's probably not thinking any of these things. She's a serial killer for Chrissakes, how else is she supposed to look at me other than unnervingly? I already know she likes to take the eyes of her victims and string them up in a web of fishing line, and according to my smitten brother, she does it while they're still alive. Of course she's unhinged, and I'm just a little freaked out about having her in my house. That's all this is.

Sloane's gaze finally disconnects from mine. It lands on my knuckles, where the scabs are still healing, their edges red. Then she turns her attention to Rowan, who doesn't seem capable of looking at anything but her. He doesn't miss the pointed glance she directs at my hands before I can hide them.

Okay, so she's definitely *ready to kill me.*

"What have you been up to, brother?" Rowan asks as he grabs my wrist. I close my fist and wrench free of his grasp, and he grins. "Getting into some fights, are we?"

"None of your business, Rowan."

"So that's a yes." I scowl at him and rise, heading to the kitchen for no other reason than to get away. Of course, being the annoying older brother he is, Rowan follows. "Got anything to do with the little banshee?"

"Her name is *Rose*, you fucking asshole," I hiss as I turn on him. Though I step right into his space, he doesn't budge. He just smiles at me like this is all a fucking game, one that he's winning.

"Another yes, then. What happened?"

"Do you remember that time about ten seconds ago when I told you it was none of your business? It's still *none of your fucking business.*"

Rowan falls into silence. I turn my back on him to fill a couple water bottles. His voice is softer than I expect when he says, "She was pretty clear there's nothing going on between you. Didn't get the impression she was happy about it though. So it begs the question, why not?"

I turn off the water and grip the edge of the sink. "Rowan—"

"And if you say 'Claire,' I'm going to punch you in your fucking throat—"

"It's not Claire." I wheel around to face him. Rowan's smirk might be teasing but worry still hides in his eyes. "It's *me*."

His eyes narrow, that smirk of his long gone. "What about you?"

"I'm her doctor, for one thing."

"Forbidden. I like it. Makes it ten times hotter."

I groan and swipe a hand down my face. "I'm not . . . I can't . . . I'm not ready for a relationship."

"Who said anything about a relationship, you *feckin' eejit*? You're putting too much pressure on yourself. You're allowed to have fun."

I roll my eyes. "I'm not going to *use* her for *fun*."

"Didn't say you would. But she is a grown-ass adult woman who might also want to have *fun*. Did you ever think about that?"

I'd like to say, *No, I have not*, but truth is, I think about it a lot. Probably every waking hour, in fact. How it would be nice to have something easy, something with no strings attached, no responsibility to hold myself to a standard that seems more and more impossible to maintain. It would be nice to be in the moment with someone, without worrying about the future and the kind of person I might not be despite the years I've spent molding myself to fit that box.

I open my mouth to try to rationalize my inertia, but the increasingly weak argument evaporates when I hear the guest room door close at the end of the hall and the *tap, tap, tap* of Rose's crutches as she enters the living space. Rowan gives me a pitying look and draws me into an embrace before she can join us. I sigh.

"Maybe you should give yourself a break," Rowan whispers in my ear. "You're a dumbass, but you're a good man. You deserve to have fun too. And I like the little banshee."

He claps me on my back and heads toward the living room, tossing a grin over his shoulder as he goes. But then it's Rose's magnetic pull that draws my attention away. She stops in front of me with a gentle smile, her eyes soft, three rumpled shirts hanging from the handle of her crutches.

"Let me know if I can help."

I'm more worried about her passing out when I start the closed reduction procedure, but I nod instead. "Maybe you can help distract her, if she wants."

"Yeah," she says as she watches Rowan help Sloane to her feet, his nervous energy peeling from him in waves. "Man-guy there is about as calm as a monkey on a gridiron."

"Man-guy . . . ?"

"Long story." With a final, fleeting smile, she leads the way out the door. We take two vehicles, Rowan and Sloane following Rose and me in their rental car.

When we get to the clinic, I inject Sloane's joint with lidocaine, and after fifteen minutes I start the procedure to manipulate her bone back into place. We take it slow, pausing to wait for her muscles to relax, for the pain to become a little more bearable. Rowan never lets go of her good hand. He reminds her to breathe. Tells her she's brave, and tough, and so strong. I don't know how much of it registers as she closes her eyes and grits her teeth against the agony. When the bone finally shifts into correct alignment, she takes a deep, unsteady breath. Rowan rests his head next to hers and I look to Rose, who's sitting in the corner of the room, her gaze not straying from the couple even though I'm sure she feels me watching.

After a few moments of rest and some pain meds, Rose gets Sloane into a fresh shirt and pair of leggings, and then I fit her with a sling before we leave.

Rose and I don't talk on the short drive home. We don't talk much over dinner either when I really think about it. We mostly converse with Sloane and Rowan, and not directly to each other, even when Sloane announces she's too exhausted to stay up any longer and Rowan briefly leaves to help her get situated in the other guest room they'll share. There's a tension that's settled between us, one I find difficult to pin down. I'd like to think it's instinct, that too many apex predators in one place has set us on edge. Or that it's the discomfort of being in the presence of two people who have so obviously just realized they're falling in love. But it's not that. And I know it. It's the tension that comes with wanting so much more than you're willing to take.

Now it's close to midnight. And I'm still wide-awake. Because there are muffled voices from the guest room across the hall where Rowan and Sloane are staying. Voices whose words are indecipherable, but the tone is unmistakable. Desire. Desperation. Demands. There's a low chuckle. I hear the creak of the mattress through the thin walls. A moment later, there's a loud moan from Sloane.

"Fuck. My. Life," I groan as I pull a pillow across my face.

It does not stop. For *hours*. I try falling asleep with my earbuds and a playlist of white noise, but all the white noise in the world can't cover up the occasional scream. I swear to Christ, I don't think I've ever wanted to murder my brother more than I have tonight. And I'm almost positive he's rubbing my self-imposed celibacy in my fucking face. *You're allowed to have fun*, he'd said just this afternoon.

Maybe he's right. Would it be so bad to want something easy if Rose wanted it too? If we made no promises about where it would go? She won't stay here forever. Once she's fully recovered, she'll be back on the road.

It's finally quiet when I sit up on the edge of my bed and put my earbuds away. I stand and leave my room as though summoned by a force I can barely resist, not stopping until I'm standing outside Rose's room.

I close my palm around the handle. Rest my head against the door. My other hand is poised to knock. I can almost feel the tap of my skin against the wood.

I let out a long, slow breath, and uncurl my fingers from the lever one by one.

I return to my room. Stare at the ceiling in the dark.

And for the first time, I ask myself:

What would happen if I stopped trying so hard to be a different man?

SCRATCH

Rose

I hobble to the door in Rowan and Sloane's wake as they head out onto the porch of Fionn's house and turn to say goodbye. The sun illuminates the speckled black marks beneath Sloane's eyes. The boot print in the center of her forehead is an angry stamp of purple. I wanna hunt down the motherfucker who hurt her and rekill him, whoever the hell he was. But despite her obviously painful injuries and her flighty vibes when she glances at the neighbors three doors down, I can tell. This woman is *happy*. At least, as happy as she'll let herself be. For now.

And her Shitflicker man-guy? He's over the fuckin' *moon*. Hopelessly in love. Ready to get the hell out of here and look after his woman. So it's no surprise that it's Rowan who kicks off the departure.

"See you around, Rose," he finally says. His wary gaze rakes over my face. I narrow my eyes at him, but I have to bite down on the inside of my cheek to stop from smiling.

"I'm sure you will. Drive safe, Shitflicker."

"Listen here, ya little banshee—"

"*Rowan,*" Sloane hisses as she wallops him in the stomach with her good arm. My grin begs to ignite.

"She *beat me* with her *crutch*, Blackbird."

"And then you ate three helpings of her waffles this morning and single-handedly drained her maple syrup supply. I think you'll survive, pretty boy."

Rowan shrugs, but there's a spark in his eyes as they slide to where Fionn stands just behind me. "I needed the calories. I had a busy night. Playing *sports.*" Rowan lets the innuendo linger like a barb before he cackles a laugh. A deep blush creeps across Sloane's swollen cheeks. Satisfied, he drapes an arm across Sloane's back before he presses a gentle kiss to her temple. "Come on, love. We've got a long drive ahead. Rose, it was good meeting you. Keep my little brother safe with that crutch, all right?"

"I'll do my best," I say, and with a nod, Rowan turns his gaze toward his brother, his expression softening.

Fionn steps around me, laying a hand on my arm to ensure I don't wobble on my crutches as he passes close to me. He probably doesn't notice the electric hum that travels beneath my skin in that momentary touch. I bet he doesn't register the way I glance down just as his hand lifts away. For him, it probably wasn't even a thought to touch me, just an action. A sleight of hand. A magic trick. So fast and so simple that I could have imagined it. But when I meet Sloane's eyes, I know she saw it. There's a spark in her blood-shot gaze. A little dimple peeks out at me next to her faint smile.

My gaze is still lingering on Sloane when Fionn says, "I'll miss you, brother. Maybe next time you should come for a simple visit. No drama. No . . . shenanigans."

"That doesn't sound like fun at all," Rowan replies as the two men clasp each other in a tight hug. When they separate, Rowan's hand folds over the back of his brother's neck, and they press their foreheads together. "Thank you for looking after my girl."

Fionn nods, and with a final round of goodbyes, they head to their rental car. We're alone once more. Just me and the doc. Standing side by side on his porch. The car slides away into the morning sun, as pretty as a sweet fairy-tale ending. The couple three doors down watches too, then turns and waves at us. We wave back.

For a flash, I can see it. My own fairy-tale ending. A quaint little house. A happy little life. My own little bit of magic.

But it's just that. A flash. A little trick. Because that's a life not meant for someone like me.

"They're gonna be just fine," I say, and when Fionn looks down his shoulder at me, I smile.

When we're back in the house, I flop down on the couch, putting my cast up on the coffee table with a *thunk* and a sigh. I press my hands over my eyes as though it might help push all my thoughts back into the depths of my skull. It might have been a rocky start with man-guy in particular, but I realize now that they're gone just how much their presence was a relief from tension that's been filling the walls of this home. Tension that maybe only I feel. As much as I loved having Rowan and Sloane here, their absence has already shown me that it's worse than I realized. I'm suffocating here, forced to sit with myself without all the chaos and distraction of a life on the road. And I don't think it's just a simple case of "itchy feet." It's not the familiar urge to get back on the road with the troupe when I've been off it for too long. It's

159

that I can't get away from all the things I convinced myself I never wanted. Not when I'm encased in them.

A deep breath fills to the bottom of my lungs and releases in a frustrated whoosh.

"You all right?" Fionn asks from the kitchen, his voice wary.

"Yeah."

"You sure . . . ?"

"Totally positive." I can feel him scrutinizing me from the other room. Fuck knows, the weight of his assessing stare on the back of my head does absolutely nothing but ratchet up the feeling of discomfort at least ten more notches. "It's just this damn cast," I mumble, which is a half-truth. My leg is itchy as fuck beneath the layers of fiberglass.

I just need a little relief. To let go of some of this pent-up tension. That's all it is. I mean, who wouldn't get cabin fever when they're used to being on the road and performing every weekend?

With a huff of a sigh, I reach for one of Fionn's metal crochet hooks and prop my leg back up on the coffee table. I shimmy the hooked end between my flesh and the cast, and then I *scratch*.

The relief is fucking *delicious*. Maybe one of the best things I've ever felt. And it's not quite enough. The more I scratch, the more my skin craves it. The sensation of need spreads and I chase the relief with the tiny hook.

I hit a particularly itchy spot, tilt my head back, and moan.

"Rose," Fionn barks from the kitchen.

I barely register when he repeats my name. "Occupied. Leave a message."

"*Rose*, Christ alive." I hear his quickened pace as he storms across the hardwood. I know what he's about to do. So of course I double my efforts with the crochet hook.

"Stay away, McSpicy," I say as I furiously shove the crochet hook beneath the cast and scratch my skin.

"It's going to snap and cut you."

"It's metal."

"You're going to injure yourself."

I bat Fionn's hand away when he reaches for my wrist. "You won't let me live off sugar alone. You keep trying to give me that green juice shit. Let me have *something*."

"You could get an infection," he snaps when he finally manages to catch my forearm. I whimper in protest as he pulls the crochet hook from my hand and tosses it out of reach onto the chair across from me.

"But I have pearls," I say with a saccharine smile. My grin turns wicked when Fionn's cheeks flush. He lets go of my wrist but still hovers behind the couch, his brows knit with a frown as he stares down at me. But there's more than just his doctory judgment in his expression. There's heat in his eyes, a flame that licks at my skin.

"They don't last forever."

"Some do."

"Not these ones."

"Shame."

Fionn rolls his eyes, irritation deepening their shade of sapphire blue. I sink into the couch and puff a sharp breath upward to ruffle my bangs. The shallow creases that fan from the corners of his eyes smooth as his expression softens, just a little. "You can't do that," he says with a nod to the crochet hook as he comes around the end of the couch. "Even a small scratch could become a problem beneath the cast."

"Yeah, Doc. I heard you the first fifty times."

"This is the second time, technically, but who's counting—"

"And logically speaking, I know that, but I'm willing to take the risk for a little relief," I say as he stops before me. The rest I leave unsaid. That this is just a fleeting moment, a single scratch that will hardly satisfy me when my whole being seems consumed by discomfort. My flesh. My thoughts. Inside and out, I feel like I'm trapped, bound by layers and layers of tissue I can't shed.

And maybe, for the first time, Fionn doesn't just see it in me and pretend it doesn't exist. "Okay," is all he says, more to himself than to me, I think. He kneels between the couch and the coffee table, meeting my eyes only briefly, just long enough to ignite a heavy beat in my heart. He turns his focus to my leg, gently wrapping one hand around the layers of fiberglass that encase my ankle, his other sliding beneath the back of my knee. "Hold still."

And then he leans in, his face so close to my thigh that his hair tickles my skin. He blows a long, thin thread of air beneath the edge of the cast. His breath is cool when it streams over my flesh. I swear I can feel it stir every individual hair that's grown in the dark. My heart pounds in my ears. Can he sense it against his warm palm? Does it riot against his hand? Does he think about the reasons why it seems to double in pace when he sucks in a breath and blows another burst of air beneath my cast?

"Does that help?" Fionn asks, and when I don't say anything, he glances up at me. I give a faint nod. But I think it's a lie. I don't think it helps at all. I think it makes everything worse. If he realizes that my gesture is untruthful, he doesn't say. He just watches, taking in the details of my face. His eyes have turned black, the pupils blown. As though he can't keep his gaze on me any longer, he turns away and blows again beneath my cast. "I know it's not as effective as my crochet hook," he says as he shoots me a chastising smile over his shoulder, "but it's the safest way."

I don't want to tell him that he's making it worse. Or that it's making *other things* worse.

My core clenches. I try not to squirm in my seat. But I can't help it, not when Fionn's thumb absentmindedly coasts over the tender flesh of my knee as he blows another steam of air beneath my cast. My thigh tenses, and I shift my hips, moving slowly in the hope that he won't notice, because I don't want him to stop. Even if it makes me nearly mindless with the need for more. Even though I'm just a patient or a friend in his eyes. Even if I know it's only going to hurt more when he lets go.

He blows into my cast. Again. And again. And again. I shift my hips and brace my hands on the seat of the couch, but don't even realize I'm doing it. My flesh is on fire. My center throbs, screaming at me in a demand for more than I'm able to give. I should put a stop to this. But I can't seem to form a single word, not when Fionn's hand is warm on my leg. Not when his breath stirs every sensation in my skin.

Fionn turns to face me, my ankle and knee still in his grasp. His eyes drop from mine, and I feel the caress of his gaze on the side of my neck, then on my chest. I realize only now that it's heaving with rapid breaths, as though I've just run a race. I swallow and his attention returns to my throat before lifting to my parted lips.

His voice is low. Quiet. There's maybe even an accusation in it when he asks, "Are you okay?"

Every time I want to bury myself deeper in that same cocoon that seems to smother me, he tears through it. When I want to lie, I find that I can't. The best I can seem to do is to leave out the truth. But this time, it feels like there is nowhere to run. Not with the way he watches every nuance of my body. I've already given away more than I could ever hide.

"No," I whisper as I shake my head. "Not really."

He doesn't look surprised by my answer. And if it's a reply he doesn't want to receive, he doesn't let on about that either. Nothing in his expression has changed. He still holds my leg as though he might simply turn back to his task and breathe this torture across my skin. "Is it not helping?" he asks.

"No. It's not."

He nods, as though this is the answer he expected. "What would?"

I could say the crochet hook. Or cutting the cast off. Or enough alcohol to knock me unconscious. I look down at his hand on my thigh, then back to his eyes. "Not that," is all I can muster.

Fionn's eyes are lightless. I feel as though I'm ensnared by them. Like there's no way I can free myself. And the way he looks at me? It's as though I'm exactly where he wants me—pinned by his unflinching stare. "What would help, Rose?" he finally asks.

We watch each other. The connection between us never breaks. Not as I lift my hand from where it's gripped to the edge of the couch. Not as I slide my fingertips down my short skirt, not as they trace my thigh. Not as I lay my hand on Fionn's. At first, I think nothing about him has changed. But then I see it, the quickening pulse in the artery that lines his neck, the subtle tightening of the corded muscles of his shoulders.

He could stop me. But he doesn't.

I wrap my fingers around the edge of his hand. I don't take my eyes from Fionn's as I slide his palm up my thigh, inch by agonizing inch. The world around us falls away. The only thing I see is him as I guide his touch across my flesh.

His attention doesn't stray from my face, not as my motion pushes up the hem of my skirt and our hands climb higher. Not when I slide his fingertips over the lace edge of my panties. Not even when I move at an excruciatingly slow pace to draw his hand down to my center, where the fabric is warm and damp. Only then do I stop, my hand pressed over Fionn's, my clit throbbing with need beneath his touch.

He still doesn't look down. I don't know what will happen when I lift my palm away. Maybe he'll stop. Tell me how this is a terrible idea. He's my doctor. He's invited me into his house out of the kindness of his heart. He's tried to help me, but this isn't what he had in mind. I fully expect that response.

But that's not what happens.

Fionn's gaze doesn't break from mine, his touch still on my pussy. With his right hand, he slowly lifts my ankle, pushing my leg into the air so he can duck beneath it. He lowers my leg to rest my cast over his shoulder.

"I . . . I can't offer you a relationship, Rose," he warns.

Something about his words stings deep in a hidden cavern of my heart. But why should it? It's not as though I could stay, even if I wanted to. Not with Matt lurking around. He's clearly a little too interested in my presence here. It's not safe for Fionn if I linger. And I definitely *do not* want to stay, no matter how much I romanticize moments in this small-town life. This is just a crush, that's all. On a *doctor*. All smart and kind and sexy. On a town. It's cute, with the welcoming people and the rowdy fight club and the knitting grannies who take no shit. But my home is on the road. In an RV. In a big top tent. Flying through a metal cage. A person like me doesn't pick a relationship over that kind of life. And a person like Fionn doesn't choose a relationship with someone like me.

I soothe the little sting with a shrug. "Never said I wanted one."

Fionn nods. He seems relieved. "Then we need to have rules."

"Maybe can we make some when your hand isn't on my pussy? Because right now is not the best time to form logical thoughts." Fionn lifts his hand away, and a crushing wave of unanswered need courses through my veins. "That's not exactly what I meant."

"Rules first. We don't want to fuck this up before we even start."

"Fine," I say as I roll my eyes. "No . . . cuddling."

Fionn nods. "Okay. That's a good one. No kissing on the mouth."

"No sleeping in each other's beds."

"No holding hands or PDA."

"No pet names. But Doc doesn't count. You're just . . . *Doc*."

Fionn breathes a laugh, the warmth summoning goose bumps as it fans across my skin. His molten eyes soften, just for a moment. "And we'll check in with each other, yeah?" he says, and I give him a faint smile. "We'll just keep talking."

"Right." I nod. My head keeps bobbing, my lips pressed into a tight line, every muscle in my body coiled tight until a hidden wire inside me snaps. "Except for right now. With all due respect, Dr. Kane," I say as I fold one hand behind his head, "shut the fuck up and eat my pussy."

He laughs. But it's dark and deep. His eyes are wolfish on mine as he lowers his head between my thighs. The first press of his mouth to the fabric covering my pussy ignites liquid heat in my chest. It sparks a craving, a need. But need is a venom. It burns. It claims. It conquers and defeats you. And I surrender to it. I forget everything about who I am, where I am, what this is. I just want *more*. More of his hands wrapped around my flesh, pushing my legs wider. More of the way he rumbles a throaty moan when I rake my nails across his scalp and grip his hair. I even beg for it when he bears his mouth down on my clit, still sheathed beneath the damp, silken fabric. *Please. Yes. More.*

When I drop my head to the back of the couch, he still watches me. Every time I look down at him, he's waiting, a magnet ready to snap me back into place. He wants me to watch, I can tell. It's in the crease that appears between his brows, the way he lavishes me with ravenous kisses through the thin material. He keeps my broken leg slung over one shoulder and then slides his hands up my thighs. One keeps going, slipping beneath my shirt to trail a path of tingling heat up my belly, to the center of my chest, to the hem of my bra. He pulls one of the cups down and runs his thumb over my nipple, coaxing it into a firm peak.

"Rose," he whispers. He pulls my panties to the side and lavishes my clit with his tongue until I close my eyes. I'm panting, sinking into a euphoric haze. "If you—"

"If I want you to stop, just tell you, yeah yeah, rules, blah blah—"

"If you *don't* want me to stop, Rose," he says with a dark smile and hooded eyes, "then you'll keep your eyes on me."

I swallow. "Okay . . ."

"Good girl," he says, and slowly descends, his gaze unblinking until the moment he presses his tongue to my clit and moans into my flesh. His expression is one of both satisfaction and need, as though this is something he wants, but it's still not enough. As though he'll always need more. I know how that feels. That sensation is already embedded into my chest like a splinter that will never be pulled free. In just a few brief moments, I realize I might have sacrificed more of myself than I bargained for with this arrangement. Because I don't know how I'll be able to walk away from this once it's over. And it's barely begun.

I want to close my eyes, for just a moment, but I don't. I can't bear the thought of Fionn stopping. Not as he tears my panties at one hip, not bothering to pull them all the way off. He plunges two fingers into my pussy and I know I'm soaking his hand. He pumps them in a slow rhythm, and I moan as he seals his mouth over my clit and swirls his tongue over the swollen bud of nerves. His fingers curl, stroking my G-spot, and I whimper, melting further into the plush cushions. When I rake my fingernails across his scalp he groans his approval, a vibration that pushes me closer to an edge I'm not ready to fall over. I want to draw this pleasure out. I want to live in every moment of Fionn's tongue lavishing my clit, of his fingers thrusting in my pussy. Of his eyes fixed to mine, dark and lethal.

And then he sucks on my clit, and I lose the battle to not fall from the cliff of desire.

My back bows. I cry out. One of my hands tightens around the edge of the cushion, the other around the back of Fionn's head as I press him to my center. He has mercy on me when I close my eyes and forget all about his rules and demands. Stars burst across the black canvas of my closed lids. My pulse drums in my head. I unravel in Fionn's grasp, and he chases every moment of my spiraling pleasure with his tongue. Only when he's sure I've had enough and can't take more does he lift his mouth away and slide his fingers free of my soaked pussy.

It's a long moment that passes with just the sound of my ragged breaths between us. I still haven't opened my eyes when he lowers my leg from his shoulder. But he doesn't release it. He scoops up the other one, and a heartbeat later, I'm being lifted from the couch. When my eyes flutter open, his gaze is trapped on my parted lips. For a moment, I think he's going to break his first rule and kiss me, but he wipes that thought away with a flicker of a smile.

"You didn't think we were already done, did you?"

"I was hoping not," I reply.

His grin turns rakish as he starts walking toward the hallway that leads to the bedrooms.

A single, unwanted thought passes through my mind, that maybe he's right. Scratching an itch can turn it into an open wound.

I grip tighter to his neck and let him carry me away.

RECKLESS

Fionn

As often happens when I'm around Rose, there's one question that wraps its tentacles around every other thought I have:

What the fuck am I doing?

It takes on a thousand meanings. What am I doing taking my patient to my bedroom? What am I doing fucking my friend? *What am I doing*—I swore I was going to stay away from relationships. A friendship is a relationship. There are rules in place, sure, but why the fuck am I not ending this before we start? I could have at least waited until the haze of lust had cleared so we could talk about this like two rational adults.

What the fuck am I doing?

I know what I'm *not* doing.

I'm not fucking stopping.

Not unless she tells me to. Not when Rose is lying in the center of my bed, her breath still unsteady from the way I made her come in the living room. And fuck, it was perfect. She tasted so sweet. I glide my tongue over my lips as I stare down at her now. Her tight pussy gripped my fingers as she came, as though her body was desperate for more of my touch. Her arousal coated my hand. I wanted her to watch as I sucked it off my fingers, but she seemed lost in another dimension of euphoria, and I couldn't bear to break her away.

And that doesn't seem like something a friend would do. A lover, on the other hand . . .

The doubts might still swirl, telling me this is an epically bad idea. I'm not a good person for her. No matter how badly I want to be someone else, I know now that there's another side of me beneath those curated desires, and I don't know how deep that darkness goes. But I don't think I have the willpower to resist her. She's so fucking beautiful as she sits up enough to pull her shirt over her head, leaving her black bra behind. Her panties are already torn, hanging from the thigh of her unbroken leg, and she slides them off and then kicks them to the edge of the bed, her eyes not leaving mine.

"I thought you said you weren't done," she whispers. A slow smile creeps across her face. Somehow, she even makes that cast look sexy. It's something about the way she's learned to adapt to it. There's a grace in her resilience that I find intoxicating.

"I'm not done," I say, though I don't move an inch closer, not even when her legs drop open like a dare. "I'm just . . ."

"Hesitating?"

"Taking my time."

"So . . . hesitating."

"I prefer 'making the most of it,'" I say.

I'm totally hesitating.

Her grin stretches as she watches me. It's hard to get anything past her. I feel like I might have managed to keep my deepest secrets close, despite what happened at the Blood Brothers fight. But it takes a lot of effort. Everything else seems to slip past my grasp, as though I'm split wide open and she's stepped inside to look around.

"Then I guess I should make it worth your while," Rose says. A spark ignites in her eyes. "Or mine."

With that, she slides her hand down her body, a caress that drops from the notch of her throat, between her breasts, past her navel. Her touch detours, from one hipbone to the next, teasing me. Her eyes haven't left mine. I still haven't moved. Not even when her fingers finally slip down to her pussy and she touches her clit. Rose's bottom lip slides between her teeth and she lets out a long, shuddering breath.

"I feel like I'm befriending myself in this friends-with-benefits situation," she says, her voice barely more than a whisper that dissolves into a moan. There's an earnest weight to her words, and maybe a little disappointment when she says, "You don't need to join me, Doc."

"Like fuck I'm not."

With a hand behind my head, I grasp my shirt between the shoulders and tug it off, letting it fall to the floor. Rose's eyes fall to my chest, to my abs. They latch onto the motion of my fingers as I release the buckle on my belt, my button next, my zipper after that. I take my time, riveted by her unwavering stare and the way she swirls her touch over her clit. I don't miss a moment of it, committing what she seems to like to memory. A pattern. A pause. I want to touch her the same way, or surprise her with something she loves even more. Something she can't do herself. I want to discover her, not just watch from the sidelines.

172

I pull my jeans and briefs past my hips. Rose makes no effort to hide the way she stares at my erection. Just like with everything else in her life, she's bold, brazen. Undeterred by what other people might think or the unspoken rules that bind us. Rose knows what she wants. And it's intoxicating to know that what she wants is *me*. Openly. She drags her eyes up my body like she's savoring every inch of my skin. It takes everything in me not to rush forward and bury my cock to the hilt in her pussy with a single stroke.

"Have you been tested?" she asks.

"Yes. I'm clear. It's been . . . a while. A *long* while."

Rose nods, no judgment or concern in her eyes, only lust. "I have an IUD," she says, not slowing the motion of her fingers over her clit. "I was tested last year. I haven't been with anyone since then. So if you're nervous about coming inside me, don't be." A little tremor wracks her shoulders as though the thought itself is pushing her closer to another orgasm. "I'd like that. A lot."

My head tilts and I grab my erection with a firm hand. "How much?"

"*A lot*," she repeats, her gaze fusing to mine, her expression ravenous. "In me. On me. Yeah . . . cum kink. It's kind of my thing."

My cock goes impossibly harder.

"If that's not your thing though—"

"That's my thing. Definitely," I say, and Rose's lips stretch in a bewitching smile.

"Then what are you waiting for?" she whispers.

Goddamn. She's so fucking perfect. And this is so fucking reckless. But there's no way I can stop it now. Even if this is all we have. Even if it becomes a hammer to my heart. I want her too much. I desire her too deeply. And she needs me as much as I need her.

I swallow, keeping my hand clasped around my cock as I step forward and prowl onto the bed. She lifts her hand from her center as I notch the tip of my erection to her entrance. "If there's anything you don't like," I say, not pushing into her inviting heat, "if there's anything that makes you uncomfortable. If you want me to stop, just tell me. I will stop."

"Okay. Same for you." Rose's eyes stay fixed to mine as she gives a slight nod. There's no teasing light in her eyes when she runs her hands up my arms where they're braced next to her shoulders. "I trust you, Fionn."

I search her face. There's no lie in her words.

It takes everything in me not to lean down and kiss her as I push into her tight heat to the sound of her gasp.

Even fitting just the crown of my cock into her pussy is euphoric. A revelation. It's been a few years since I've been with a woman, but I don't remember anyone feeling as good as Rose feels. I linger there, gripped by her warmth. Rose's lips are parted, her brow furrowed. Her fingers dig into my shoulders. "More," she breathes.

I take one hand and run it from her hip to her knee, lifting her injured leg from the bed. And then I push in deeper to the sound of her desperate moan. "*Fuck*, Rose," I hiss, sliding deeper still, not stopping until my hips are flush with her body. We're both breathing heavily and we've barely even started.

"You feel . . ." she starts, losing her words as I slowly slide out. I thrust in hard, and she lets out a desperate moan. "Fucking hell, Fionn. You feel amazing." I do it again, pulling out slowly and thrusting in hard. Rose tilts her head back and whimpers. "Goddamn," she breathes. "I love that."

I give her a few more hard thrusts before I pick up a pace of steadier strokes, and she moans again. "Tell me what else you love."

"This," she says. Her hands trace my back, mapping my muscles and bones. "I love this too." I grin, though she doesn't see it. Her eyes are pressed closed, a crease etched between her brows. I pull the lace cups of her bra down and seal my mouth over the peak of her breast, and lick my tongue over her nipple. She rakes her nails through my hair. "And that. *Yes*. God." I kiss my way to her other breast as I keep up the pace of long strokes in her pussy. "What about you . . . ? What do you love?"

"Every fucking thing about this," I say, the honest-to-God truth. "I fucking love your tight pussy. I love licking it. I love being inside it."

She moans with my words, her nails scraping at my skin as I unfasten her bra and toss it to the floor. "What else? What turns you on?"

"Chasing you down," I reply, struggling not to fuck her hard at the mere thought of it. I want to take my time and enjoy every second of what could be a one-time thing. "Finding you. Fucking you like a goddamn prize."

Rose shudders beneath me and I know instantly that she enjoys that fantasy as much as I do. I look down at her and she gives me a wicked smile. "God, yes. But what if you couldn't find me?"

My strokes slow. I hold her gaze. The urge to kiss her steals my breath. It takes every last thread of my restraint not to do it, and it leaves nothing else behind. Maybe she won't see that every barrier I try to keep up has crumbled, if only for a heartbeat, when I say, "I will *always* find you, Rose."

Rose's smile is so faint it could be imagined. The flicker in her brow so brief it could be a mirage. But if she thinks this is still a game or something more, she doesn't say. Because there are no more words after that.

I kiss her neck. She trails her touch across my skin. Our rhythm grows more urgent. Deep rocking strokes, desperate moans. My cock glides through her heat, her pussy tight around my erection. Her body grips mine as though it's a missing piece it can't bear to let go of. Her whimpers become more intense, and I know she's getting close. My palm glides down her body and press my fingers to her clit and within seconds, she's losing control. Her back bows off the bed. I quicken my pace. She calls out my name and I'm falling with her into ecstasy, keeping my touch steady on her bundle of nerves as I pull out quickly. "Look down," I grit out, gripping my erection with my other hand as a pulse of cum shoots across her left breast.

"Fuck, yes, Fionn."

I'm immediately pushing back into her. A pulse of cum spills into her pussy. I pull out again, and this time it lands on her belly. I thrust into her cunt, staying buried there, the rest of my orgasm spent inside her. I brace my arms next to her sides, both of us recovering our unsteady breath. The sight of her covered with my cum just makes me want to do it all over again until she's fucking covered with my spend. And the way she looks down at her body, I think she's thinking the same thing.

"That was hot as hell," Rose whispers. Her hands trace patterns over the tense muscles of my arms. Part of me worries that she might be uncomfortable or in pain with her broken leg. But as I take slow strokes inside her, my cock still erect and growing harder with every second that I recover, those worries fade away.

She looks down at the point where we're joined and bites one of her blushed lips. "Did I tell you that I really like being covered and filled with cum?" she asks, her eyes meeting mine with faux innocence. My cock twitches with building need.

"You know, I think you might have mentioned something about that." I thrust harder, starting to pick up a steadier pace. "But I'm a doctor. I'll need some empirical proof before I can be sure."

"Thank fuck," she says around a moan.

We fuck. We come. We fuck again. I come in her pussy. I come on her tits. On her belly. The sun is setting when we finally stop, both of us panting, both of us sated, though I can't say for how long. And as I pull out of her for the last time, I'm already wondering how I'll ever be able to stick to these rules.

I'm about to ask Rose if she's hungry or if I can bring her something to the bed. And if she says she wants to stay in my room and fall asleep together, there's no fucking way I'll say no. But before I can say anything, she's shimmying to the end of the mattress and then she's up, balancing on her good leg, the injured one bent to keep the cast off the floor.

"Wait," I say, untangling my feet from the sheets. "Let me help you."

"I'm good, Doc." She casts a smile to me over her shoulder before she hops toward the door. Her ass bounces with every jump and I have to clench my jaw to keep from begging her to come back so we can do it all over again. "Rules, remember?"

"Yeah," I say, my voice thin and quiet, as though my mind has been lost in a spell and I can barely make such a simple word. And as she stops at the door, I think that might be true.

Rose turns, fully facing me. Her skin glistens with my spend. It's smeared on her thighs, painted on her belly and breasts. With her other hand braced on the door handle, she trails a finger through the cum spread across her belly, drawing her touch upward, tracing the swell of her breast. Her eyes never leave mine as she raises that finger to her mouth and rests it on her tongue. Her lips close around it. She hums a satisfied note, and then she gives me a wink.

A thousand fantasies flood my mind, all of them of Rose. My cock grows harder.

"Night, Doc. Thanks for a fun time."

She closes the door behind her and leaves me sitting in the growing dark.

DESCENT

Rose

I can't remember the last time I was on a plane. And I know I've never been on one with a guy. At least, not a friends-with-benefits guy.

Especially not one who's got his hand up my skirt and his fingers in my cunt.

I stifle a whimper, but only barely.

"Shh," Fionn says, pumping his fingers in and out of my entrance with slow strokes. I try not to squirm, but it's nearly impossible to sit still. "Someone will hear you."

"As if anyone who's walked by hasn't already clocked what we're doing," I whisper back. "Your jacket is on my lap and your hand is obviously moving *right there*."

"Do you want me to stop?" he purrs.

"*Fuck* no."

And I mean that. I definitely do not want him to stop. In fact, I'm pretty fucking surprised that we're here in this situation. I thought after a couple weeks ago when we finally hooked up that

179

he'd never want to do it again. And sure, he spent a day or two mired in an unnecessary pit of self-loathing, but it only lasted as long as it took for the announcement to hit the local news that the search for Eric Donovan had been called off at Humboldt Lake. I'm not entirely sure if he thought it was a good thing or a bad thing, but it was enough of an excuse for us to fuck on the kitchen counter of his house.

And then Rowan called to ask if we'd come to the opening of his new restaurant. We said yes, and after I modeled a few cute potential dresses from the closet in poor ol' neglected Dorothy, we gave the creepy corn people of the Prairie Princess Campground a fun soundtrack as I blew him on my RV bed and he screamed my name. And now here we are. On a plane. Heading to Boston. With Fionn's fingers knuckles-deep in my pussy.

He adds his thumb to my clit and I nearly erupt from my seat.

"Safety first," Fionn says as he reaches across my hips with his free hand and pulls one end of the belt over his jacket, and then the other. He slides the metal clip into the release and then tightens it with a swift tug of the strap, trapping his other hand against my pussy. "Seat belts should stay on in case of turbulence."

"Jesus Christ," I hiss as his fingers stroke deeper. "Who *are* you?"

"I'm just reciprocating after the blowjob you gave me in the motor home the other day. That's what friends do. Besides, we're on a mini holiday from Hartford, technically. And we should celebrate being out of town."

"By breaking the rules?"

Fionn scoffs, sliding his fingers out to tease my clit with swirls and circles. "We're not breaking the rules."

"Doesn't this count as a 'public display of affection'?" I ask, breathless.

"Not technically. Besides, I filed an exception when we boarded. As long as I make you come, it doesn't count."

He plunges his fingers back inside me, and I turn away and bite down on my fist, pressing my forehead next to the window, where the night sky stretches toward a curved horizon of cloud. There's a ding of an upcoming announcement from the captain. "We have begun our initial descent into Boston. We'll be arriving at our destination at 11:17 p.m. The weather in Boston is heavy rain and forty-eight degrees. The flight attendants will be coming through the cabin to collect any remaining items. We wish you a pleasant stay in Boston and thank you for flying with us."

"Better hurry up, Rose," Fionn whispers against the shell of my ear as he presses harder to my clit with the edge of his thumb. I stifle a whimper in my fist. "They're coming through the cabin. You don't want to get caught with my fingers in your pussy, do you?"

The thrusts come faster. He strokes my inner walls. His thumb works against me, and I close my eyes, every muscle tightening as release unravels in my core. My free hand grips Fionn's wrist through his jacket, but he keeps going, not stopping until he's sure I've claimed every moment of pleasure from this moment. He withdraws his fingers slowly as though savoring the heat surrounding his touch and the mess that he's made of me. I can feel the slickness of my arousal between my thighs, the cool dampness of my panties as he shifts them back into place. When he's straightened my skirt, he takes his jacket back to lay it across his lap just as a flight attendant draws near.

"That was very naughty, especially for an upstanding medical professional such as yourself," I say with a wicked grin as Fionn lays one of his fingers on his tongue and sucks my arousal from his skin. He shrugs and repeats the motion with his second finger. "We could have gotten caught."

"That's what makes it fun."

"I said it before. Who *are* you?"

"And I told you before, I was returning the favor. That's what friends are for."

"I think there's a bad man in this good doctor," I tease. "And I like him."

Our gazes lock. The teasing glimmer in Fionn's eyes turns to something molten, burning brighter when it drops to my mouth. I could lean closer. So could he. Maybe he's thinking about it. Just like I'm wondering what it would be like to taste him, my arousal still lingering on his lips. And goddamn but does he look good with this hint of cockiness that lifts one corner of his lips. I think he's going to break away, but he doesn't, and my heart pounds against my chest like it's trying to push me closer with every beat.

The plane drops and lurches suddenly as we descend into the clouds and we both sit back, gripping our armrests, Fionn's hand clasped over mine. "Just like the Zipper ride, isn't it? It's my favorite at Silveria. I always like to give it a test run every time we set it up," I say with an untroubled smile as turbulence rocks the cabin. A few noises of surprise rise from other passengers. Fionn meets my eyes and blinks as though coming out of a fog. And then his hand lifts from mine.

"Yeah," he replies, but his smile is missing its earlier lightness. "Definitely feels like when you're on a ride and your stomach drops."

The plane jostles a few more times in the heavy cloud, but we both settle with our hands in our laps. Maybe I've been wrong in thinking I'm the only one wondering what happens when my cast comes off and life can go back to normal. Maybe we both needed this reminder—that our usual lives still exist, even if we're here outside our normal rhythm. And if the lines blur so much we can't see them, it's going to be that much harder when we slip back into ourselves.

For the rest of the flight, it's like we're both aware we're treading too close to boundaries that shouldn't be broken. Though he helps me every step of the way when we deplane and navigate the airport, we don't talk much, keeping everything light.

At least, I'm quiet until we reach the baggage claim and my suitcase doesn't appear. After that, I don't think I shut up for more than a minute. Not as we head to the service desk to get it tracked down, not as we fill out paperwork to get it delivered the next day to our hotel, not even as we finally get into a car and make our way into the city through the heavy downpour. I'm so annoyed that I barely even touch the bag of Cheetos that Fionn tries to appease me with.

"What in the absolute fuck," I say for the thirtieth time, waving a Cheeto around as our Uber slows on Franklin Street in downtown Boston. "Our bags were literally loaded at the same time. How does mine end up in Florida while yours is here?"

"Mysteries of aviation," Fionn replies.

"All of my clothes were in there. Literally *all of them*."

"We can get you something new tomorrow, it's no problem. And they said your luggage should arrive by the afternoon."

"My toothbrush."

"I have a toothbrush."

"Good for you. Rub it in, Doc."

"I mean, you can borrow mine. But I'm sure the hotel will have some at the reception desk." He watches me as I finally crunch down on the processed orange stick. "You're pretty upset."

"Damn straight, Dr. Observation." I sigh, realizing I'm way too snappy, though Fionn seems unruffled. "Sorry. It's just that my tarot deck is in that suitcase and I'm worried about it."

Fionn's brow furrows as his gaze travels across my face. "You didn't take it with you?" I shake my head. "How come?"

"I did a reading before we left and had a weirdly strong feeling to pack it in my suitcase. When Gransie tells me something, I've learned the hard way not to ignore her, even though sometimes I try," I say as I gesture down to my cast. "Doesn't usually work out so well to disregard her direct messages."

"You named your deck Gransie?"

"No. It was my grandmother's deck. Gran died on it. Literally. *Boom*." I clap my hands and Fionn startles. "Smack down on the deck, God rest her soul. Now she's like . . . attached to it."

"O . . . kay. I . . . I'm sorry for your grandmother's passing," he says, though it sounds a bit like a question.

"Don't be. She's living her best afterlife." I pop another Cheeto in my mouth. We slow to a stop across the street from the Langham Hotel, an impressive-looking granite building, the blood-red awnings giving it an air of sophistication in the ambient light of the city night. While Fionn gets the bags out of the car, I head to the corner of the street to wait for him. The rain has tapered off to a refreshing mist and I turn my face to the sky, closing my eyes.

That makes it *extra shocking* when I'm hit full force with a blast of cold water.

It's on my face. In my hair. Soaking my clothes. It trickles down my legs, into my cast and my boot. I look over in time to see the car drive away, probably totally unaware that it just splashed the fuck out of me when it sped through the giant puddle at the corner of the road.

"Oh, my Christ," Fionn says, his accent stronger with worry and surprise. "Are you okay?"

"Dandy," I say, wiping my eyes with the heels of my hands, which accomplishes nothing. "I get it now."

"Get what?"

I gesture to my open jacket. Even the interior pocket is drenched, hit with the full force of water. The pocket where I always keep my deck. "This is why Gran wanted a vacation to Florida."

Fionn gives me a sympathetic smile and slides his coat off, waiting as I peel mine from my body so he can settle it on my shoulders. When I glance up, he's annoyingly even more handsome than usual with the dusting of mist on his face and hair. "Let's get inside."

A few moments later, we're entering the austere lobby of the Langham Hotel. "We have a reservation for Fionn Kane," Fionn says when he places a credit card and his driver's license on the pristine white counter of the reception desk. The woman on the other side has a perfect manicure, a perfect smile, perfectly obedient hair that's swept back in an impeccably sleek bun. Me? I look like I've been dragged through the apocalypse, fought some zombies, and narrowly escaped with some horror stories and a bag of wet Cheetos. And I would rock the apocalypse, I really would. I'm a circus girl, we're built to survive the end of the world. But I'm not sure I'm cut out for the fanciness of the Langham with its brushed gold and cool gray and muted blue decor. It even *smells* expensive. Decidedly not like Cheetos.

Doc, on the other hand, looks completely at ease as he watches the woman type in his details and pass his license back. At least, he looks at ease until she opens her mouth.

"Welcome to the Langham, Mr. Kane. I have you checked in for four nights with a king bed."

Fionn blinks, his cheeks crimson. "I reserved a room with two queen beds, actually," he says as he leans closer to the counter, his eyes darting to me.

"Oh, I'm sorry, sir," she says. Her brows lower as she stares into her computer monitor and clicks the mouse repeatedly. "I apologize for this mishap, but it seems we only have that king premier room left from our standard rooms. There's a jazz festival going on in the city. It's quite booked."

I smile at her, though her focus is still on the screen. I'm about to open my mouth to tell Fionn and the receptionist that it's fine, when Fionn leans against the counter, a look of dismay in his eyes.

"Do you not have an executive suite? Something with a pullout sofa bed? I'll pay the difference," he says.

The receptionist subdues a subtle cringe of doubt as she taps her mouse. "If we have one available, I can offer you a fifty percent discount, which would bring it down to about eight hundred and ninety-six dollars per night."

"*Doc*—" I groan.

The woman behind the desk lets out a sigh. "I'm so sorry. There's really nothing else available, sir. Would you still like to proceed with the premier room?"

The disappointment in his voice is obvious when Fionn agrees. She processes his card and passes over the room keys and then we're heading through the lobby, me already a couple of steps ahead. "It's not a big deal, Fionn."

"You used my name," he says, and I dart a questioning glance over my shoulder. "You usually call me Doc. Or McSpicy. Are you pissed off?"

"Frankly? A little bit, because I know I look like a Cheetos apocalypse horror show—"

"What?"

"But the room is *fine*. I can just sleep on a cot." I toss an eye roll at him as we head to the elevators. "I'm, like, half your size."

Fionn scoffs. "If anyone is sleeping on a cot, trust me, it will not be you. That's the last thing I want."

"I've literally slept in the Berry Go Round. You know, the strawberries that spin round with the flat wheel thing in the middle? Yeah. I can sleep anywhere. I don't mind."

"I mind."

"I can see that," I say, a little flare of irritation licking at my restraint. "You'd rather pay nearly a thousand dollars a night to not sleep in the same bed as me."

"No," he says, stopping us both with a hand on my wrist. We block more of the corridor than we should, him with his suitcase and me with my unsteady crutches and black cast. But Fionn doesn't seem to care about anyone or anything else. He looks at me with a kind of ferocity that I sometimes feel in him, but rarely see. "No, that's not it, Rose. It was one of your rules. And I don't want to break it."

"I gathered that."

"I don't want to hurt you."

I level him with a flat glare. "Oh, *right*, I get it. Well, don't worry, I heard you the first time. You don't want a relationship. What makes you think that I do?" Fionn doesn't answer, just stares down at me as though he can't work me out, even though my words are perfectly clear. "I'm a big girl," I say as I pat him once on the chest before I grip my crutches and pull away from his loosening hold on my wrist. "I think I can handle sharing a bed."

I make it all the way to the elevator and press the button before I turn enough to look at him. Fionn is still standing where I left him, his brow creased, the ghost of a thoughtful frown lingering at the corners of his lips. The call button dings, and the doors slide open and he still hasn't moved.

"Just because you finger fucked me on a plane doesn't mean I want to get married, Dr. Kane," I say as two women exit the elevator arm in arm.

"You tell him, badass bitch," one of them says as the other gives me a high five when they pass by. Fionn looks like he's wishing the floor would open up and absorb him, and though the women give him a brutal side-eye, he doesn't tear his attention from me.

The elevator doors bang against the crutch I hold out to stop them, sliding open once more. I roll my eyes. "Are you coming or what?"

Finally, he moves, though it's like he's wading against a current. It takes him longer to get to me than it should.

I haven't even been in an elevator that many times, as weird as it might sound. But this ride to the fourth floor is one of the most memorable for sheer awkwardness. Only one of us has luggage. One of us is pissed off. And I think both of us are probably realizing this is harder than we thought it would be.

We get to the floor and trudge to the room, the wheels of Fionn's bag bumping along the carpet in a sad melody to accompany our tense silence. When we step inside, the room is much like the rest of the hotel—elegant, luxurious, but in a way that feels calming with its blues and grays and soft whites. I already feel like I've made it messy just by entering.

"I need a shower," I say as I take a few steps into the room and peel his jacket off, setting it on the back of a chair.

"That's not what I meant," Fionn says. I turn and look at him over my shoulder, that same perplexed expression from down by the elevators still fixed to his face.

"Huh?"

"When I said I don't want to hurt you."

I blink a few times, facing him fully as I replay the conversation, but I still come up confused. "What, do you have night terrors or something?"

"No—"

"Are you one of those people who kicks when they're falling asleep?"

"I don't think—"

"Do you have a sleep demon who's going to possess me?"

"What? *No.*" Fionn takes a step closer, shaking his head as though trying to get his bearings. I raise my brows, waiting for some life-changing confession. "No. I just . . . don't know if I'm safe for you to be around."

I tilt my head, trying to figure him out. "What do you mean?"

He runs a hand through his hair, grasping the back of his neck as he says, "The thing at the Blood Brothers barn. I snapped. I fucked that guy up."

"Yeah." I try not to smile, though I quickly fail. "You did. That was pretty hot."

"*Hot?*" he repeats, though despite the attempt to sound incredulous, he can't hide the spark in his eyes. "Beating a guy unconscious during a moment of blind rage is kind of the antithesis of my profession. It was pretty *bad*."

"Meh. You could have ripped his spine out through his throat," I say with a shrug. "*That* would have been pretty bad. Yet even hotter."

Fionn sighs and drops his head, running his fingers over his temples. "Rose, the point is, I do not want you to inadvertently get caught up in my shit if something like that happens again. I wasn't in control. I would never forgive myself if you were hurt because of me."

"What do you *really* mean? Like, you're worried about hurting me physically? On purpose?"

"No." He shakes his head, his eyes haunted. "Never on purpose. Never you." His gaze falls from mine as though he can't quite bear to look at me.

"Never me," I agree. "Because you've seen it and lived it too, haven't you? You've lived in the shadow of a monster."

My heart cracks a little for Fionn as he nods, though I see a sliver of relief in his eyes when he meets my gaze. "I might not be a monster like my father, Rose," he says. "But I've done things I shouldn't be proud of. And I'm not like you."

"What, you mean you're not total chaos and mayhem?"

Fionn gives me a faint smile, but it quickly fades. "I never embraced that part of me that feels no remorse for the sins I've committed. I never got to know that side of myself. I spent a lot of time and effort to forget it ever existed, and now that makes it unpredictable."

"Fionn," I say, coming closer until I'm standing right in front of him. I balance on my crutches and grasp both of his arms, waiting until he meets my eyes before I continue. "You think I haven't figured that you might have seen and done some things you aren't proud of? Or that you were more acquainted with darkness than you let on? Sorry, but even Rowan and Sloane were a bit of a giveaway. And I've seen the worst in people. I know what they can do to one another. But I trust you. Maybe you should trust yourself too." I reach up and place a kiss on Fionn's cheek, parting with a gentle smile. "It's okay to love your darkness and still love yourself. It doesn't make you a bad person. It makes you a whole one."

I leave Fionn standing in the center of the room and head to the shower. He doesn't join me like I thought he might. When I exit the bathroom in my robe a while later, he's sitting in contemplative silence. But when he looks up at me, it feels like the air is a little lighter in the room. And though his smile is faint, there's an ease to it, as though he can breathe for the first time.

He gives me a T-shirt and a pair of boxers, and I get changed, climbing into bed as he takes his turn in the washroom. I stick to one side of the mattress. But when Fionn comes back into the room and turns off the lights, sliding beneath the covers, he gently lays an arm over my stomach. I turn over and he gathers me to his side. I rest my head on his chest, his skin smooth and warm. His heart drums a melody into my ear. I've touched him before, of course. Run my hands over his muscle and bone. But this time feels different. It feels like home.

Fionn presses a kiss to my hair. "Goodnight, Mayhem."

"That's not a nickname, is it?"

"I filed an exception. Didn't you get it?"

I smile in the dark.

And then I fall asleep.

SURFACING

Rose

"I need all the details," Sloane says, her eyes fixed to Lark above the rim of her coffee cup. Lark tries to dart her crystalline blue gaze away to the patrons that pack the busy café, drumming her short fingernails on the glossy black table. "So? What happened with you and Lachlan?"

Lark shakes her head emphatically, her cascade of blond waves falling across her shoulder. She and I have both opted for something stronger than coffee, and Lark takes a long sip of her mimosa as though that will get her out of answering. I might not know Sloane that well, but I already get the vibe that she's not the type to just let a nonanswer slide. Lark finally balks and does her best to put on a convincing facade. "Nothing."

I try to hide my grin behind my Bloody Mary, but Lark can see the amusement in my eyes when she looks to me for backup. "You sure?" I say, and I can sense Sloane's delight next to me.

"Mmhmm."

"You were out with him on the balcony for a while," Sloane chips in.

Lark squares her shoulders and raises her chin. "A girl can get some fresh air without some interrogation."

"He's pretty hot though," I say. "Reminds me of someone, but I can't put my finger on it."

"He doesn't look like anyone. Except an asshat. A hot asshat, but still an asshat."

"He makes me think of someone too," Sloane says, tapping her lip thoughtfully as she turns her gaze to the ceiling. "Oh! I know. It's Kea—"

"Don't you dare, Sloane Sutherland. Don't. You. Dare. Keanu Reeves is a god among men and you will not ruin him for me by comparing him to *Lachlan Fucking Kane*." Lark shoots Sloane a menacing look before the server interjects to take her now-empty glass. She immediately asks for a fresh one. When he's gone, Lark turns her attention back to us. Or, more specifically, to *me*. "Besides, we shouldn't be dissecting my nonexistent love life. We should be asking about *you* and the good doctor Kane."

My cheeks flame and I take a long sip of my drink. The girls wait me out, of course. And I kind of love them for it. It's been so long since I've had female friends my age. In fact, I find it hard to remember a time when I did. So even though I'm a little embarrassed about this question, it's nice to be asked. I might have met Lark only a few days ago and I hardly know either of them, but they've welcomed me like I was always meant to be here. And I don't think I'll be ready to leave. Not Boston.

And *definitely* not Nebraska.

I glance down at my leg. The cast will be coming off when we get back to Hartford. And then it'll be time to hit the road. Rejoin Silveria. Travel from town to town. Go back to what I know. What's comfortable.

But maybe it's not so comfortable anymore. Maybe it feels a little tight. For all its benefits, especially for someone like me, the freedom of that nomadic life is sometimes just an illusion.

Maybe things would be different if I stayed in Nebraska for a little while . . .

I clear my throat, trying to dislodge that idea from making its way into my voice. "I don't know," I finally say with a shrug. "It's fun, whatever it is. And we're friends. But anything else is not really . . . *real*."

"Do you want it to be?" Lark asks, her clear blue eyes full of sympathy as she studies me, their teasing glimmer now gone. "Kind of seems like you might."

"I don't know if it's that easy. My cast is coming off in a couple of days. Staying at Fionn's was always meant to be temporary. I'm supposed to be getting back on the road. And even if I was in a good place to start a relationship, Doc doesn't seem like he is."

Sloane hums a long and thoughtful note. "I can't say I really *know* him, but he seems like a bit of a tricky one. I think maybe he is ready." She turns to me, giving me a faint smile. "But he might not realize it until you're gone."

A deep sigh fills and leaves my lungs. "Yeah. Maybe."

"Well, I for one hope it works out whatever way *you* want it to," Lark says, reaching across the table to squeeze my hand. When she pulls her palm away, she leaves a gold sticker behind. "And you're not getting away from us, no matter which way it goes."

"Yeah. You're definitely not. You've been stickered. You're part of the sticker-bitch crew now. Count yourself lucky she didn't put them on your tits."

I look down. "She'd have to find them first."

Lark snorts. "Shut up. You've got great tits. All perky and shit. Great nips. Advantage of an optional bra and they don't smack you around. Small is sexy."

"Lark is like a tit sommelier. Trust her judgment," Sloane says, then drains her cup and checks her watch. "I have to run to meet Rowan at the restaurant, but I'll see you girls tomorrow? I'd love to catch up one last time before you both take off."

"For sure." Sloane rises, placing cash on the table before she gives each of us a hug. We stick around for another drink, and then we both head our separate ways with plans to meet up the next morning before we each fly out. It's nearly six thirty when I get back to our room in the Langham, but Fionn isn't there. He's probably still visiting with Lachlan. I'm pulling my phone from my pocket when it buzzes in my hand with an incoming text. Lark's name flashes on the screen.

OMFG!!!!

??

Rowan motherfucking Kane just broke up with Sloane, that fucking piece of shit. I'm gonna kill him.

Man-guy?! Are you fucking for real?

I'm going to knife that fucker in the balls.

You take the balls, I'll go for the throat. Sloane will want the eyes.

Good. I hate the eyes.

I'm starting to type another reply, but Fionn calls before I have a chance to send it.

"Your brother broke up with that smokeshow Sloane—"

"Something is wrong, Rose," he says, and though he tries to keep his voice calm, I can still hear panic swimming through its depths. "I was on my way back to the hotel when Lachlan called me. Rowan is hurt."

"Did Sloane . . . ? Is he all right?"

"He'll be fine. *They'll* be fine. I'll explain later. But it's going to take me a while. I'll be late getting in."

"Are you okay?"

"Yeah. I'm good."

"Let me know if I can help. Good luck."

With a final worried goodbye, Fionn hangs up. I blow out a long breath through my bangs. I keep in touch with Lark for updates, though they're minimal. My suitcase was returned a few days ago, so I busy myself with my tarot deck now. I do a reading for Sloane and Rowan, whose pasts look troubled but whose future is bright with love. I shower and play with my hair, holding the length up to see what it would look like cut to a bob. I order room service. Watch some TV. Spend some time catching up on texts from José and Baz and Zofia, and all the others from the circus who've been checking in on me this whole time, but whom I've been a bit slower to respond to lately for reasons I don't feel ready to fully explore. Spend time with myself, something that I guess I rarely do. I let my mind wander. To imagine the different futures that might lie ahead. Maybe I'll rejoin Silveria and everything will go back to the way it was.

But what if I don't? What if I stayed in Nebraska? Would Fionn even want that? Or maybe I could come here to Boston, start over fresh. Try on another life. See if it fits.

I'm lying in bed, too worried about Fionn and the others, too caught up in these kaleidoscopic futures, when Fionn comes into the dim room.

"Hey," I say, sitting up a little to see him. He sits down on the edge of the bed and gives me a smile, but it's weary. Whatever he's had to do, it's spent his energy and left little behind. "Are you all right?"

A little crease flickers between his brows as Fionn's eyes fuse to mine. "Me?"

I blink at him, not sure how my words could have been misinterpreted. "Yeah. You."

"I'm okay. I'm fine, actually," he says, though the second confirmation sounds more like a mask than the truth. "Rowan's arm and hand were injured. Managed to get him patched up."

"His Tower fell," I say with a sage nod. Fionn gives me a confused look, and I gesture toward my tarot deck. "It was part of his reading. His little murder competition with Sloane was bound to catch up with them. But they'll be fine now."

"You knew about their game?"

I shrug, sitting up to rest my back against the padded headboard. "Gransie had some strong feelings that day they came to your house. And I guess I filled in the blanks. The boot print on Sloane's face was a bit of a clue. So was the whole 'blah blah we killed the fucker' and arguing about the winner stuff."

"Yeah," he says as he kicks off his shoes and climbs onto the bed to sit beside me. "Rowan's not the best at keeping that shit to himself."

"Maybe he should fly a little under the radar for a while."

Fionn fiddles with the edge of the bedding, tracing a finger across the white stitches. "Probably. I think he's always had it in the back of his head that he's got Lachlan to clean up after him when shit really hits the fan. But, tonight aside, it seems like he's a bit more under control since Sloane came on the scene."

"And he's got you," I say, and Fionn turns to look at me. "I guess it makes sense now."

"What does?"

"Why you never embraced the darkness inside you," I reply, giving him a faint smile. "They expected you to rise above it. To be the man they couldn't be."

The dim light. The city sounds. The way he watches me. The way I must be watching him back. Fionn's gaze drops to my lips and lingers there. My breath catches. I could lean in. Maybe I do.

His eyes don't leave my lips as he drifts just a little bit closer. Time seems to stretch around us.

I don't want this moment to shatter. I know its sharp edges will lodge in my heart if it does. So I don't lean any closer. And maybe he's scared of breaking, just like I am. Because neither does he.

But a current still charges the air between us. An ache deep in my core is desperate for his touch.

I slide my palm across the duvet and place my hand on Fionn's. He's still watching my lips as I curl my fingers around his hand. And then I pull it toward me. I let it slide over my bare thigh, moving slowly, then up my hip, skirting my waist, not stopping until we reach my breast. I know he'll be able to feel the hammering beat of my heart.

"You don't have to try so hard to be somebody else," I say, and Fionn meets my eyes. "I like the dark too."

I give him a slow smile that turns wicked, letting go of his hand to reach for his belt, undoing the buckle and zipper. I can feel him watching every motion as I pull his pants and briefs down to free his erection, taking his length in my tight fist. "I love a bit of something deliciously sinful," I whisper.

And then I spit on his cock. He hisses with desire as I stroke the saliva once down his length and then I lean down, enveloping the crown in my mouth. Fionn moans as I run my tongue around the head and then take him deeper, hollowing my cheeks as I suck. "*Fuck*, Rose. That mouth of yours is going to be the death of me."

I work the base of his erection with my hand as I lavish the head with attention, and then I'm sliding him deeper over the flat of my tongue, deeper and deeper until I swallow down the urge to gag. I start a rhythm. Slow at first. Long strokes. As far as I can take him. Sucking as hard as I can when I pull back. Fionn threads his hands into my hair and pulls it back from my face to get a better view. I look up, my eyes watering, saliva cool on my lips and smeared on my cheeks.

"So fucking beautiful," he says, and I hum around his cock. "Jesus fucking Christ, Rose. Do it again." I hum louder this time, and then I rake my fingernails over his balls. "God, *yes*. Yes, Rose. Don't stop."

There's no way I'm stopping. I quicken my pace, humming moans into his thick cock, cupping his balls. His muscles tense. He calls out my name and I know it's coming. I thrust my head down on his erection, taking him as deep as I can as his cum shoots to the back of my throat. I swallow him down. Every pulse. I work his cock until he's shuddering, breathless and hot, his skin slick when I run my fingers beneath his shirt to trace the lines of his abs. When I'm sure he's fully spent, I start to pull away. But I keep my eyes on his. I take my time. I open my mouth wider and glide my tongue along the underside of his length. He's riveted to the motion as I lick him clean in a long, languorous stroke.

I'm about to back away when Fionn prowls over me in a flash of motion. One moment I was sitting, watching him with a devious smile, and the next I'm flat on my back, looking into his ravenous eyes. "You think you're going somewhere?" he asks, caging me in. I fake innocence, raising my brows as I shrug. "You think you're going to swallow my cock and I'm going to let you get away unsatisfied?"

"I am satisfied," I say, running my tongue across my swollen bottom lip. His eyes track the motion. I see the hunter in him, looking out through blown pupils, one that's determined to devour its prey.

"Not satisfied enough," he says, shifting his weight onto one arm as he trails a finger between my breasts, slowly dragging his touch down the center of my body. "I'm going to bet that your perfect pussy is fucking soaked, begging to be fucked." Suddenly, his touch is moving in the other direction, back toward my chest. I let out an immediate whimper and he gives me a rakish grin in reply. "I thought so. Fucking desperate to be lavished with attention, isn't that right?"

I let out another whimper as his finger circles my nipple through my satin tank top. I nod.

"What was that?" Fionn asks, tilting his head as though trying to hear me better. "I didn't quite make that out, Rose."

"Yes," I breathe, and his finger resumes its path toward my center. "I need it."

I need you.

Though I don't say the words out loud, he can sense them. He grins, slowly making his way down my body, maintaining eye contact the entire time. When he gets to my hips, he pulls my sleep shorts off, tossing them to the floor before he lifts the thigh of my injured leg to lay it over his shoulder. He's so delicate with my broken parts, even when he's about to destroy the rest of me. It sets my blood aflame. I've never wanted anyone like I do Fionn Kane. And as he lowers his mouth to my pussy and presses my chest down with his wide palm as though he can capture every heaving breath, I know that will never change.

Fionn slides his tongue from my entrance to my clit, circling the bundle of nerves. He moans into my flesh, his eyes drifting closed. If he said my pussy was the best meal he ever had, I would believe him. He presses harder, rolls his tongue over me, hums his satisfaction right into me. And then he glides his tongue back down to my entrance to thrust it inside, pulsing it in my cunt. When he licks his way back to the top of my folds, he pushes a finger into my pussy, followed by a second, curling them with every stroke. The pressure doesn't let up on my clit.

"More," I beg, my head tilting back as he works me closer to a blinding orgasm. "Make me come on your beautiful fucking face. I want to see it smeared all over your skin."

When I look down the length of my body, it's pure predator staring back at me. Fionn's eyes darken. He growls against my pussy, a shock of pleasure. And then he catapults me into oblivion.

Fionn raises on his knees. He takes me with him, never breaking his mouth away. My legs are braced over his shoulders as he raises my ass off the bed. The sounds he makes are wild, animalistic. He fucking *devours* me.

I don't just moan. I don't just come. I scream his name and split apart.

My fists curl around damp sheets. Every breath I take is desperate, as though there's not enough oxygen in the room. The scent of sex and his citrus and sage cologne are heavy in the air. I'm sure I lose hearing, every sound dampened, even my own unraveling moans. Fionn doesn't let up, still chasing every last moment of my orgasm until I tap him to stop. The instant I do, he comes back to himself and lets go, as though he was in that other dimension with me. One where no other world existed beyond this moment together.

"Are you okay?" he asks, breathless. His lips and chin and cheeks glisten with my arousal. I feel the first burn from his stubble on my inner thighs, a delicious pain that I savor.

"I'm fucking fantastic." When I smile, relief and maybe a bit of pride find their way into his expression. I'm a sweaty, boneless mess when Fionn lowers my hips to the bed and backs off the mattress to retrieve my sleep shorts from the floor. He puts them on for me, gently sliding them up my legs, lifting my hips to center them. And when he's done, he brings me things I can't easily reach. Water. My robe. The crutches that I left just out of reach from this side of the bed. And when I'm eventually ready to go to the bathroom, he has the bed ready when I get back, the covers smoothed and turned down.

When we're finally both settled in bed, we don't stick to our sides. Just like we didn't last night. Same with the night before. We meet in the middle. I lay my head on Fionn's chest. He wraps an arm across my back.

"Part of me doesn't want to go home," I confess into the dark.

"Yeah," he whispers. "Me too."

But as a close my eyes, I realize, I'm not sure which home I mean anymore.

I'm not sure where I belong.

STROKE OF LUCK

Rose

I'm sitting in the chairs that line the corridor outside the orthopedic clinic within the hospital, waiting for Fionn. We haven't talked about this day. Not aside from my immediate appointment, at least. We haven't discussed me calling José, or going back to Dorothy, or how I should be getting ready to pull up stakes and leave for someplace new.

It's as though the aftermath won't exist if we don't talk about it. And I want to. I'm desperate to test those waters, but I'm unsure what will happen if I do. At first, I thought it was just me who was avoiding the topic of my departure. But Fionn doesn't bring it up either, and though my first instinct was that he didn't want to be impolite and kick me out, I'm not sure that's it.

Ever since we returned from Boston a few days ago, we've mutually gone back to our friends-with-benefits rules. Just like slipping into a familiar costume. But it feels like that suit doesn't fit like it should. When we had sex in the shower the other day, we both paused in the hallway when we left the bathroom as though trying to figure out how to go our separate ways. It's suddenly unnatural to sleep without Fionn's heart beating beneath my ear. And when we fucked on the kitchen table, it didn't feel like fucking. Not with the way Fionn trailed a path of lingering kisses up my neck and across my jaw. Onto my cheek. At the corner of my mouth. That was the kiss that lasted the longest. I fought myself to not turn into it. And I think he did too. It felt like he wanted to take *everything*.

It felt like making love.

Ever since that realization, anxiety has churned in my belly, winding ever tighter, threatening to unleash confessions that I'll never be able to put back. I think I won't be able to keep them locked down for much longer. And my tarot deck isn't much help either. I shuffle. I draw cards. I read their meaning and decide I don't like it. So I try again. But every time, the result is the same. Cards like the Moon. Or the Fool. The Ten of Wands. Every time I draw cards, the messages come back the same. Uncertainty. Fear. A decision that looms ahead, and one I feel ill-prepared to make.

"Christ, Gransie," I say as I slide the Moon back into the deck a second time. "I already know I don't know. Thanks for reminding me."

"Good things not in your future?"

My heart seizes beneath my bones.

I look up. Matt Cranwell stands in front of me, a small bouquet of flowers clutched in one hand, a slow grin creeping across his face.

"Maybe that's true. Good things probably aren't," he says as he leans closer, pinning me with his single eye. The other is hidden by a black patch, the strap biting into his skin. "Especially seeing as how Eric Donovan's truck was just pulled from the Platte River."

Ice crystallizes beneath my skin. I try not to look away, or let my skin flush, but how do you control your body when it begs to release your secrets to the world? I'm not a sociopath. I'm not cold and remote, emotionless about the world around me. I harbor anger. I want vengeance.

And I feel fear.

"I don't know what you're talking about."

"No? You haven't heard the news?" Cranwell takes a seat one down from mine, tapping his knee as he gives a thoughtful nod. "It seems poor Mr. Donovan's truck went ass-over-teakettle into the river," he says on the heels of a deep sigh. "They're still lookin' for his body. I'm sure something will turn up soon."

"Perhaps he's gone on a mission to spread the word of our Lord and Savior Jesus Christ to faraway lands," I say, crossing myself, though I have no idea if I'm even doing it right. "But if he found himself pissed drunk and died in a moment of stupidity, may he rest in peace. I bet he was a fine, upstanding citizen. Amen."

Matt chuckles. "Now, you wouldn't happen to know anything about the latter, would ya?"

"I'm not sure what you mean."

"The dyin' part. See, I had someone attack me not long ago. Just out of the blue." He smacks his fist against his palm, the flowers rustling in his fist. "*Bam.* Just like that. But I hit her back."

"I bet you have practice at that."

Matt's eyes darken. "And you know what that little bitch did?" he says, his voice filled with gravel and wrath. "She took my *eye.*"

He stares me down, his finger pointed to the patch over his missing globe.

"Why are you here?" I demand. Slowly, Matt lowers his hand, tilting his head. "Just to tell me about some guy's truck? Or maybe you want to spread the word about how you got your ass handed to you by a phantom woman?"

"I'm visitin' my wife," he says. "She'll be here a few days."

Rage narrows my vision to a pinprick, the world around us falling away. "Guess she didn't have good things in her future either." My gaze falls to the bouquet in his hand. "Chrysanthemums? Really . . . ?"

He glances down at the flowers. "What's wrong with them?" he asks, but it's obvious by his tone that he doesn't really care what answer I give.

"It's a funeral flower, you eggheaded dumbass. It represents death."

"Hmpf." He gives them a cursory glance, then throws the bouquet at the wall so it drops into the bin beneath. Some of the petals float free with the impact, drifting to the floor. He looks at me and smiles. "Guess I'll just have to go empty-handed."

"Why is she here?" I demand.

"Damndest thing," he replies, breaking his gaze away to look across the aisle at the flyers pinned to a bulletin board above the waiting room chairs. *Have trouble sleeping?* *Know the signs of stress!* *Physical activity and you.* Matt chuckles as though he's looking at his own set of tarot cards, divining their secret meaning and finding it fitting. "She just tripped and fell. A stroke of bad luck. Maybe the same as Eric Donovan."

"I still don't know who you mean."

Matt turns to face me. His gaze pins to mine, unblinking. "That's funny. Because—"

"Rose Evans?" Nurse Naomi leans over the threshold of the door to the orthopedic ward. I give her a nod. She looks so different from the last time I saw her. Her hair is shorter, darker. Her skin brighter, like she's glowing from inside. There's a confidence in the set of her shoulders that wasn't there before. Her eyes flick to Matt and back to me. "We're ready for you."

Naomi doesn't let me out of her sight as I stand. I try not to let my sweating hands tremble as they clutch the grips of my crutches. She gives me the barest hint of a smile. I give her a nod in reply.

"Say," Matt says behind me, "how did you break your leg, anyway?"

I turn just enough to give him one eye over my shoulder. "Tripped and fell, I guess. Just a stroke of bad luck."

I refocus on my destination, and I don't turn back.

I swing my way through the door that Naomi holds open for me. When I'm past the threshold, she lets it close, but gives Matt a final hard look through the thick glass before she returns to my side. "Hey," she says, laying a hand on my arm. "You okay?"

"Yeah, are you?"

I worry that she'll say no. That she'll break down with guilt. That the news Matt just relayed about Eric's truck will find its way to her eyes. But the only thing I see there is relief. "I'm doing really well. Thank you."

I give her an unsure smile as we start walking down the hall. "I didn't do anything."

"No," she says, as though she won't accept an argument. "You did *everything*." Naomi's steps slow. We stop in front of an exam room. When she turns to face me, there are tears in her eyes. "I really mean it. Thank you. What you did for me was life-changing." She shakes her head and runs a gentle hand down my arm. "And if some rando shithead gives you trouble . . ."

"I can handle him. But maybe you can look in on his wife? Lucy Cranwell. She's here, somewhere."

Naomi smiles and nods. Her eyes light with purpose. "Yeah. I can definitely do that." She nods to the open door. "This is you, Sparrow." With a brief hug, Naomi leaves me to enter the exam room. I watch as she walks away, her steps sure.

It's not until she's gone that a long breath leaves my lungs. The next inhalation is an unsteady one. My heart is beating too fast, as though I'm already running.

I'm standing in the center of the room with my eyes pressed shut when I hear it. His footsteps. I can tell it's him as he strides down the corridor. I recognize his presence before he even enters the room.

"Hey," Fionn says. When I open my eyes, he steps in front of me, his brows furrowing with worry when he takes in my expression. "Everything okay?"

"Yeah. I just—" A pair of nurses strike up a conversation at a station just beyond the open door, and I cut myself off. My smile is brittle around the edges. "I just . . . can't wait to see the fur situation."

Fionn laughs, gesturing toward the exam room bed. "Nothing I haven't seen before." I leave my crutches off to the side and hop onto the table, my heart still climbing up my throat. Fionn goes into full doctor mode, talking about the process, something about a saw and scissors and skin that I should probably pay more attention to. But in my head, I'm replaying the conversation with Matt Cranwell. The revelation. The unspoken threat. How much he already knows. What if there's more? What if he's just biding his time? What if he suspects Fionn was involved?

I have to get the fuck out of here. If he's intent on revenge, I have to lead him away from Fionn. It's me he's after, and I need to give Matt a new trail to follow.

An electric whine fills the room and I startle.

"What the hell," I hiss, pressing a hand to my chest.

"The . . . saw . . . ?" Fionn says, his brow furrowing. "The saw I just told you about . . . ? The one I just asked if you were ready for me to start up and you said yes . . . ?"

"I did?"

He turns it off and lays a hand on my cast. I can't feel the reassurance of his touch through the layers encasing my flesh. "Are you sure you're okay?"

No. I'm not.

I wish the nurses would walk away so we could talk properly. I wish we had some fucking privacy. I wish I could tell him right now that I feel like I've been hit with a wave that's swept me into the sea. Somewhere, deep down, I probably want to rage, or cry. But I'm too scared to do anything but lie. "Totally fine."

A flicker of worry passes across his face. "I'm going to start the saw."

I nod. The whine of the motor starts up again. Fionn presses the cutting edge to the cast in quick bursts in a straight line down the length of my leg. He stops on occasion to wipe the blade with a piece of square gauze soaked in alcohol to cool it down. He does one side of my leg and then the other. For all this time I've spent in the rigid embrace of my cast, it takes only a few moments to break.

"So . . ." Fionn says, keeping his eyes on the work of his hands as he uses a metal tool to separate the cut edges of the cast. "You should probably do some physio for a few weeks. You'll have some muscle atrophy. Physio will help to ensure you build yourself back up safely." He clears his throat and risks a quick glance at me. "I know someone good here. Her name is Judi. She's got time to take you. If you want . . ."

It feels like he's prying apart my bones and cracking open my heart.

"I really appreciate that," I say, my voice unsteady. Fionn looks at me and I catch the disappointment in his eyes, the realization he's about to be rejected. "I wish I could stay. Truly. But I have to get on the road as soon as possible."

"It's okay." His smile is almost a perfect replica of the gentle one he often gives me in times of uncertainty. *Almost.* "I understand. That was always the agreement."

I take his wrist and shake my head. The nurses keep chatting right outside our door. One of them stands in my line of sight and she glances my way. I can tell in that brief look that she's assessing our conversation, even while having her own. Of course Dr. Kane would be the subject of interest around here. I bet half the hospital staff already know I'm staying at his house. I'm sure they're just waiting for the smallest pieces of conversation to flutter their way.

Frustrated tears sting my nose. I refocus on Fionn. I'll be fucking damned if I'll let him think I'm leaving because of any other reason than the one I created. Not for one goddamn minute. "You *don't* understand, actually."

"It's okay—"

"I don't want to cause you any 'trouble whatsoever.'"

Fionn pauses his efforts to split the cast and really look at me. He takes in the subtle shake of my head. I squeeze his wrist. He blinks, clarity sinking in, his eyes widening only slightly before he clears his throat. "*Oh* . . . I see. It's no trouble, but I do understand." He lays a hand over mine. "We can chat about it later. I can get you some recommendations for exercises on the road."

I nod. My smile is weak, but it's there, and so is his. He took a risk. When it comes to me, he's taken many, in his own quiet way. Maybe it's my turn. "But maybe you can check in once in a while? Make sure I'm doing them right . . . ?"

Fionn's smile brightens.

"Yeah," he says. "I'd like that."

HURDLES

Fionn

The Uber pulls away, leaving me at the entrance of the fair-grounds. An unlit Silveria Circus sign hangs overhead. I make my way past rides and game booths and concession stands in various stages of construction. None of the workers look up, even though it's closed for the day. Maybe some of them knew I was coming, or maybe they just don't care. There's a buzz that seems to linger in the autumn air, a charge of excitement. The relief of being at home, the first off-season show about to begin in just a few days. Magic and money to make. And as I near the small tarot reader tent and duck my head inside, scanning the table with its red cloth and the velvet drapes lining the walls, I wonder if the excitement is not so much in the air. Maybe it's in me.

Of course it is, you bloody eejit. You're about to fuck Rose. It's a biological response, nothing more. Certainly nothing to be worried about.

I shake my head as though it might clear my thoughts, then leave the tarot booth. I head to the left of the big top, through the fairgrounds and the rides that are not yet ready for visitors, past

214

the fun house and the Tilt-A-Whirl and the swing carousel. My steps quicken the closer I get to the area where the trailers and RVs are parked at the far end of the grounds. I pull my phone from my pocket and check it for the tenth time since landing at Midland airport just outside Odessa, opening my last message to Rose.

> My flight was canceled but got the earlier option! I'll be there by seven instead.

She still hasn't responded.

I pocket my phone and hitch my backpack farther up my shoulder. I spot her RV at the far edge of the clearing, not far from a picket fence that skirts the grounds where other motor homes are parked. It seems like she's one of the only full-time circus staff who doesn't choose to spend the off-tour months living in the small, well-kept trailer park that's part of the permanent circus grounds. Her home stands out from the beige and white and aluminum options that are parked in the clearing. The sides are custom painted with an ombre of pink and orange, a flock of sparrows in flight across the sunset colors. The lights are on. The blinds are drawn. And there's a rhythmic sound coming from within.

I know that sound well.

It's an Echelon Stride-6 folding treadmill. One I bought her as a goodbye present to help with her recovery. And she's running. *Hard*.

She shouldn't be going that fast. It's only been a month since I took her cast off and she went on her way, meeting up with the troupe as they returned back to Texas. I frown as I approach the

RV. A sudden burst of anxiety floods my veins as I tighten my hand into a fist and rap three times on the door.

The rhythm of the running footsteps doesn't change.

I knock again.

I shift on my feet. Clear my throat. I wait, but there's no change.

"*Rose*," I yell on the third knock. "I knew you'd love that thing, but come open the door."

No answer. She must be wearing headphones, so I grasp the door handle and start to pull it open. I only make it an inch or two when Rose is there, her hand braced against the edge of the door to keep it from opening and a wild, panicked look in her eyes.

But the sound of running doesn't stop.

There's someone else here.

"Doc," she breathes, adjusting the belt of her robe, then pushing damp hair from her forehead. She's cut it into a bob, the damp waves and curls skimming across the smooth column of her neck. Her eyes dart to the direction of the sound and back again. "What are you doing here? I didn't expect you for another couple of hours."

Dying, that's what I'm doing. Clearly dying of total embarrassment.

"I, um. I'm sorry." I run my hand through my hair and back away a step. My skin is burning. My heart thrashes against my ribs. My vision has narrowed as though nothing exists outside the things I wish I could unsee. Like the damp blotches on the purple silk from her wet hair. The blush in her cheeks. The distress in her mahogany eyes. "I texted, but . . . I'm sorry. I didn't know you'd have someone else here. I'll leave."

Fionn, you fucking fool. This isn't a relationship. You said so yourself. What the hell did you expect? You have no right to be upset. Just go.

I flash a tight smile at Rose, but I can't bear to see the pity in her eyes. So I turn away. I'll get the fuck out of here and find the next flight home and lick my wounds with a bottle of bourbon and we'll forget this moment ever happened. We'll go back to being friends, *no benefits*. Or maybe just doctor and patient. *Jesus fucking Christ*—

"Doc, *stop*." Rose's delicate hand wraps around my forearm in a talon grip. Part of me wants to pull away and keep walking, but I don't. Not when she whispers a single word, filling it with a desperate note. "*Please*."

My brows tighten as I take in the way her gaze darts across our surroundings. She tugs on my arm, towing me toward her RV. I don't argue, though I don't exactly stride after her either. But she doesn't give up. And she doesn't let go. Not even when she opens the door, tossing me a wary glance over her shoulder.

I enter the RV. A shirtless man runs at a punishing pace on the treadmill that fills the narrow aisle between the sofa and the little dining table. His chest is covered with cheap tattoos. His skin glistens with sweat.

"I'm gonna beat your record," he declares with a crazed grin, his eyes latched to Rose.

"I should go—"

"No, *wait*." Though I try to pull away, Rose refuses to relinquish my arm. She gives the guy a grimace of a smile and a thumbs-up. "Keep going, Chad. Maybe you'll beat me, after all."

When Chad gives her a double thumbs-up in reply, Rose tows me closer to the front of the vehicle, not letting me go until she seems certain I won't try to push past her to leave. There's a chittering sound of an animal, and a raccoon's face suddenly appears from the driver's seat.

"Is that . . . is that *Barbara*?"

"Umm, yeah," Rose says through a pinched smile. She blushes when I raise my brows in a wordless question. "When I left Hartford, I drove past your clinic and saw her trying to break in. She fell from the vent by the roof. She hurt her paw. I couldn't just leave her to fend for herself."

"So you *took* her . . . ?"

"Pretty much."

"A wild, rabid raccoon."

Barbara hisses, but Rose doesn't seem to take that as proof of my point. "She's not rabid. She's pretty talented, actually. Cheryl's been training her with the poodles. She had her debut show last week."

I open my mouth to say something, but my brain can't seem to sort through the many questions I have fast enough to land on a single one. Chad, however, is ready to fill the void. "She has a pet *raccoon*," he declares from the treadmill. "Isn't that badass?"

I let out an audible *ugh* and refocus my attention on Rose. "You really don't have to explain, Rose. Well, more detail about the raccoon is probably warranted. But not about the guy. We never agreed to be exclusive."

"Thanks for the reminder, you fucking clown. But I do have some standards," she says as she rolls her eyes and crosses her arms over her chest, her brows knitting together for the briefest moment before her expression smooths to a veneer of barely restrained fury. "Dudes with tattoos made with a Bic pen in their garage don't fit the bill, ya know?"

"Then what the hell is going on?" A sinking feeling drops through my chest to simmer in my guts when Rose gnaws her lip. "Spit it out—"

"He should be *dead*," she hisses. "At least, that's what Sloane told me when I texted her. I gave him double what she suggested."

"What . . . ?"

"I laced his churros with enough speed to choke a gorilla. He puked all over me and then started pacing around in circles so I brought him here and stuck him on the treadmill while I got cleaned up. I think he might've taken some other shit before I got to him. It didn't take much convincing to get him to go for a little run, but then again I might have told a lie or two about letting him fuck me in the ass if he beat my nonexistent treadmill record."

I blink at Rose, trying to process everything that just spilled out of her mouth. Churros. Speed. Gorilla. Ass fucking . . . ? I shake my head and try to return to the medical part of her confession, though it's a struggle. I finally land on, "You gave him amphetamines?"

Rose snorts. "*A lot* of amphetamines."

". . . Why?"

"He deals 'study drugs' to local high school and college kids when he's not beating up his girlfriend, so it didn't seem like it'd be a stretch if he took a little too much and wound up dead. Fuck around and find out. I was just hoping the *finding out* part would come a little more easily."

"And your plan now is . . . what . . . exactly?"

"I dunno," she says with an irritated flick of her hand in my direction. "Maybe to make him run until his heart explodes in his chest and he bleeds from his eyeballs or some shit. I'm not a scientist."

We turn toward the man. His pace is relentless. When we face each other once more, Rose juts her chin out and tightens her arms across her chest, determined not to balk beneath my cold and clinical stare.

"I don't think he's just going to magically die on your treadmill, Rose."

"A girl can dream."

"Aren't you worried about what will happen if he does?"

"I had a great plan to ditch his body at the fishing hole off Loop Road. But I guess I'll just have to wing it. Gransie seemed pretty confident it would work out anyway. But it's a good thing you're here just in time for 'trouble whatsoever,' right, Doc?"

I give her a flat glare and then grasp her shoulders just long enough to keep her rooted in one spot so I can slip past her. When I stop at the treadmill, Chad gives me a beaming grin despite the effort it takes to keep running. I should probably take his pulse, which I'm sure is past two hundred beats per minute, or at least point him in the direction of a hospital. Hippocratic oath and all that shit. But then, who am I to crush Rose's dreams? It's not like Chad is asking for medical assistance. And if Rose has gone to this much effort, the guy is surely no saint. I'm probably doing humanity more good than harm by just letting him live or die by the rules of natural selection.

I drag a hand down my face. *Christ.*

With a fleeting, suspicious glance toward Rose, I turn my attention back to the man before me. "How are you feeling, Chad? Ready to take a break?"

"Nah, bro."

"In that case, how about we take this run to the great outdoors."

"Yeah, man," he says through panting breaths. "I'm ready to take on the fuckin' *world*."

I press the emergency stop button on the treadmill and Chad stumbles before jumping onto the foot rails. Disappointed that he didn't fall on his face, I turn and hold open the door of the RV. "Great. Do a few laps of the grounds or whatever. We'll catch up."

"You sure?"

"I'm a doctor, I never lie."

Rose barks a laugh behind me. I shoot her a glare over my shoulder and she throws her hands up in surrender.

Turning my attention back to Chad, I grab his wrist and tug him toward the open door. His pulse thrums like hummingbird wings beneath my fingertips. "We'll come find you. Promise."

Chad gives me a thumbs-up, his go-to move, I guess, then steps out into the clearing. With a deep breath of cool evening air, he raises his fists above his head. "Fuckin' eh, clown town."

"Fuckin' eh," Rose mutters beside me.

And then Chad takes off running at full speed.

"He's pretty quick," I say. We watch him sprint in a wide circle, then he shifts his trajectory toward the white picket fence that surrounds the fairgrounds.

"Give a man a shit ton of drugs and the promise of ass fucking, and he'll do anything. Even knit doilies." Rose pivots a slow turn on her heel to pin me with a sardonic grin, a devious gleam flickering in her eyes. "Oh wait, you started that hobby with neither of those two motivators."

"I already told you, I thought the Suture Sisters was a fight club. And it's called *crochet*, not knitting."

"My bad."

We turn our attention back to Chad as he picks up speed. His naked back glistens in the dim light. His legs and arms pump at an almost inhuman pace. His strides lengthen as he nears the fence.

"Not sure hurdles are a great idea," I say, scratching my stubble.

"He's committed now."

Chad lets out a whoop of determination as he barrels toward his target.

. . . And then one foot catches on a rock.

He pitches forward at the fence, his startled shout spooking a flock of starlings.

"That's—"

He comes down hard on the pointed ends of the pickets. A visceral cry of pain is sliced short. The setting sun illuminates a pulsing mist of blood. His body jerks and twitches.

"—not good . . ."

A garbled, liquid breath sputters from his lungs. Chad's body convulses, then goes limp, his head suspended from a picket and the rest of his body hanging against the bloodstained slats.

We stand unmoving in a long moment of shocked silence.

Rose reaches forward and starts to pull the door closed. "Well . . . maybe hurdles were a stretch."

"*Rose*," I hiss, pushing the door open. She doesn't let go of the handle and pulls back with equal determination. "I am a *doctor*. I have to go help him."

"Help him to what, exactly? Un-die? Good luck with that."

"He could still be alive. Call 911."

"Hard pass."

"You do realize that someone is going to find him and they could very well notice that his tracks lead straight back to your RV, right?"

Rose heaves a lengthy sigh and relinquishes her hold on the door handle. Before I can slip past her, she blocks my path with her hand braced against the frame. "Just don't try *too* hard, Doc. He's still a piece of shit."

"I'll take that under advisement," I say with a roll of my eyes. I pull her hand from the doorway and lead the way down the steps. None of the circus performers or crew are out in the clearing. We jog toward the fence where Chad's body is draped, slowing as we draw closer. And though I listen for any sounds of life, nothing comes. I guess it should come as no surprise when we finally take in the extent of the damage. The pointed end of the picket is lodged deep in his throat. I'm guessing he severed his spinal column. I check for a pulse anyway, even though I know I'm not going to find one next to the gaping wound and the wooden stake that obstructs his airway. Blood pours in a thick rivulet down the picket, shimmering in the dim light.

"Yeah. He's definitely dead," I say as I lift my hand from his neck.

"Is that your professional diagnosis?" Rose leans over the fence to take a closer look at his open, unseeing eyes and the crimson stream that drips from his slack mouth. She seems to quickly regret her efforts to overcome her squeamishness and clears her throat in a failed attempt to hide a gagging cough as she steps back. "I thought the blood-drool was a pretty good clue, personally."

"Call 911, smartass."

"You first."

I roll my eyes and withdraw my phone, but I don't dial 911. Not when Rose is watching me with her enormous eyes, a current of worry buzzing through their mahogany hues. I sigh and lower the device to my side.

"What's going on?" I ask, gesturing toward Chad's body. Rose doesn't look his way.

"I started it."

"I figured. Why?"

"You could probably take a guess. Or did you miss the part where I said he was a piece of shit?"

"That's not what I meant." I hold her gaze steady as Rose's head tilts, but the blush in her cheeks makes me think she knows exactly what I'm getting at. "I meant, *why are you doing this*? You clearly can't stomach the gore—"

"I can too—"

"—and you're hunting down these men you have seemingly no connection with. But you don't seem to have much experience doing it."

Rose crosses her arms.

"As far as I can tell, you're seizing opportunity as it comes and you're getting away with it by sheer luck. It's a fucking miracle that Eric Donovan didn't wash up somewhere with staples in his eyelids."

She snorts. "That was pretty cool."

"Rose," I say, taking a step closer. "Why are you doing this? Why are you risking getting caught? Why—"

"Because not everyone gets that chance, Fionn," she snaps. Sudden tears well in her eyes, but she blinks them away, hiding them beneath a simmering rage. "Not everyone is strong enough or lives long enough to fight back."

We stare at each other, Rose with her arms crossed, me with the phone still clutched in my hand, thoughts of calling 911 drifting further from my mind. "I've been in their shoes. My folks were such a fucking mess that I spent most of childhood with my Gran until she died. And then back I went to that fucking shithole. A piece of shit dad, in and out of jail. A mom so broken she couldn't look after me. I was about to repeat the same cycle as the hell I lived in. I was only fifteen when my first boyfriend hit me." Rose's gaze drops to the ground, and she shakes her head, her arms falling to her sides. When she looks up at me once more, it's not just the pain of inescapable memories that I see in her eyes. It's not just determination. It's a plea. "I got out. I took my chance and ran away. But it's not enough to just be one of the lucky ones. Not when men like Matt or Eric or Chad will just find a next victim. Someone new to belittle and torture and sometimes even kill. Women like Lucy, or Naomi, or Chad's girlfriend, Sienna? They need more than just an open door. They need a broken cage. How can I say no when they ask for my help?"

My shoulders fall. I press my eyes closed. Lower my head. *Help*, she says from memory, her voice untarnished by time. And she's asking for my help now.

"The Sparrow. That's what the women call you," I say, and she nods.

"Have you ever heard of Giulia Tofana?" she asks. I shake my head when I open my eyes and meet her unwavering stare. "She was an Italian woman in the seventeenth century. She made a poison from arsenic and belladonna. As the story goes, she disguised it as face cream, so all a woman would have to do is come to her asking for Aqua Tofana. Many of those women were just like Lucy. And I thought I could be just like Giulia. For a while, I guess I was. But sometimes . . ." she says, turning her gaze from mine, her eyes glassy as they fix to the horizon, "sometimes you fuck up. You make a mistake. And when I fucked up, it cost the wrong person their life."

She raises her left wrist to me. I've seen the small flower tattooed there before, the initials *V.R.* beside it. When she finally meets my eyes, they're filled with pain. With loss and guilt. I might not have all the pieces. But my imagination fills in the blanks with vivid detail. And suddenly the picture that once seemed so disjointed comes into view.

Her determination to overcome her squeamish nature. Her apparent lack of fear for the consequences she might face. Even her declaration every time I call her out. *I started it*, she always says. She's determined to never place the blame on the women who have asked for her help. She will not put the responsibility of the killing on them. And she's punishing herself, too. For fucking up. For losing someone she never meant to hurt.

I don't press Rose for more details. I just reel her in to an embrace. It doesn't matter how tightly I hold on to her, the ache in my chest doesn't subside. I know the kinds of pain she's felt. I've endured similar suffering, the kind that scars you in a way that never fully heals. But, somehow, it's worse being powerless to take those wounds from Rose than it is living them myself.

After a long moment, I take her shoulders and back her away just far enough that I can lower my head and look into her eyes. "I need you to go back to the RV," I say, already knowing I'll be met with her resistance.

"No, Fionn. I started it—"

"No, you didn't." Rose shakes her head, but I stay locked on her shining eyes. "You finished it. And I'm helping you. But I need you to go back to the RV and stay there. I'm going to call the ambulance. The police are going to come. And they're going to find exactly what this is—a stupid piece of shit who died in a dumbass accident."

Rose gives me a watery huff of a laugh and shakes her head again. "I don't want to leave you to clean up my mess."

"And I will not leave you to do this alone. You and me, Rose, we came from a similar hell. And I want to help you. But the only way I can do that is to make sure you're safe. Over there." I point to the RV. Rose looks toward it, but I can still feel her hesitation. "Lights off. Don't come out unless someone knocks. You were asleep and you didn't see a thing."

With a kiss to her temple, I turn Rose's shoulders and push her in the direction of the motor home.

She takes two steps toward the RV and stops to face me with a weary, worried smile. "Thank you for your help, Fionn."

I nod once. Her smile brightens. And then she turns away, walking back to the RV in the dusky evening light.

No one ever asked me for help the way she did that first time we met. And I realize now, as she steps into the motor home and turns off the lights, that no one has thanked me for it either.

Not until Rose.

CONFECTION

Rose

"Well?" Fionn asks as I enter the RV and plop myself down on the small couch across from the dining table. He sets a pile of black yarn aside and regards me with a worried sweep of his gaze. "What did José say?"

"The police are treating it as an accident, apparently. There's nothing really to say otherwise. Chad's kind of known for being a local piece of shit and has an arrest record as long as my leg, so something makes me think they're not going to look too hard once they find a shit ton of drugs in his system." I sigh and rap my fingers across the surface of the table. "We won't open this weekend. So, I guess I have a few more days off. Maybe not the worst timing."

Fionn simply nods in reply and watches as I blow out a long breath. It's been four days since the Chad incident, and though it seems like everything is going to be fine, it still feels as though a turbine has lodged itself in my chest, like the blades keep spinning in the wind but the energy has nowhere to go. Part of it might be nerves, sure. Anxiety for the unknown. The risk of getting caught. But another part of it is sheer excitement. The residual thrill. Getting away with something bad but so very, very good. And it unleashes all kinds of dark and dangerous magic in me.

"Everything all right with you?" he finally asks, and I realize I've been smiling to myself, probably a grin that seems diabolical. Though, judging by the way Fionn narrows his eyes and watches me, I don't think he minds.

"Yeah. I um . . . just . . ."

"Have an itch that needs to be scratched?"

I snort a laugh. He's still trying to bite down on a smirk, but he can't help but let it curl one corner of his lips. It's so fucking sexy that my core twists with immediate need. "That sounds so wrong, given the circumstances." Fionn's head tilts as he tries to decipher my meaning. I wave his confusion off with a flap of my hand. "Speaking of which, is that my sex swing you're working on?" I ask with a nod to the yarn sitting on the table.

"Maybe. Thought it should be a high-priority project."

"Yeah . . ." I say, letting the word linger as my imagination takes me to all sorts of scenarios, all of which involve Fionn and Tencel bamboo yarn.

"You sure you're okay?" Fionn asks. His eyes narrow in an assessing gaze, but I can see a hint of amusement in their depths.

I clear my throat and shrug. "Just pent-up energy."

"Maybe you should set up the treadmill."

"Actually," I say, uncrossing and recrossing my legs, a motion Fionn's eyes snap to, "I was thinking a run outside might be a good idea."

"Okay . . . Want me to join you?"

"Yes and no." I get up again, and I feel the confusion in his gaze linger on me as I pull off my long-sleeve top, leaving my tank top behind. My weight shifts from side to side, my muscles already tense with anticipation. "I, um . . . didn't get to say thank you after you helped with all that whole . . . impaling situation."

Fionn's brow furrows and he lifts a shoulder. He's trying to look nonchalant about it, as nonchalant as he can, I guess. "It's okay."

"I mean, I wanted to *thank you* thank you."

I can see the exact moment my words assemble themselves in his brain. Fionn's eyes darken and fix to mine. His muscles tense. His pulse pounds in his neck. He starts rising from his seat, but I hold up a hand to stop him.

"Hold up there, Doc. I didn't say I would make it easy on you. This is a circus, after all. I thought we should have a little fun. And trust me when I say it's something you'll enjoy. You've even said so before." A lazy grin creeps across my face. I take my time. Examine my chipped nail polish. Blow out a long, long, *long* breath. My gaze flows up the length of his body, from his socked feet to the jeans that hug the curve of dense muscle in his thighs, to his tapered waist, to his biceps that seem to challenge the hem of his shirt, to his neck that shifts with a swallow, and finally his eyes. Those eyes that are nearly black, locked to me as if soldered to my face.

I saunter one step closer.

"Close your eyes," I whisper.

Reluctantly, he does.

"No peeking."

He crisscrosses his heart. I snort a laugh, and he grins.

"You're not so innocent, but nice try."

"I swear. Doctors never lie."

"Sure. Well, use that big doctor brain of yours and count to thirty for me, and then open them." One of his eyes cracks open as he gives me a scrutinous look. "What did I literally just say?"

"Okay, okay," he concedes, raising his hands in defeat. "One . . . two . . . three—"

"Slower."

"Four . . ." The pause lengthens and I creep backward toward the door. "Five . . ." I sneak down the steps and silently slip outside the motor home. "Six," he says as I close the door.

And then I take off running.

I head past the motor homes and the closed game stands and silent amusement rides, darting toward the left, where I can pause behind a building and watch Dorothy. Sure enough, Fionn comes out far before the count of thirty must be up. His head swivels each way and then he looks down toward his feet. He must pick up enough of my tracks in the dust gathered on the worn path, because he starts walking in my direction. "Fucking cheater," I whisper through my wicked smile before I back away into the shadows.

There are a handful of workers out and about today, either tightening up rides or restocking games with fresh prizes in preparation for our postponed next show. They hardly pay me any attention as I sneak through the grounds and backtrack so I can align with Fionn as he progresses down one of the aisles between game stands. I follow him for a distance, and when he seems to stall and his attention is caught in the wrong direction, I sneak up from behind and grab his hand.

"What in the Jesus—you scared the shit out of me," he says, his accent heavier in his moment of surprise. "Does this mean I win?"

"*Fuck* no."

"Then what are you doing?"

"Toying with you."

"And what about *this*," he says as he raises our interlaced fingers. "You're breaking some rules here. We're technically in public. And this is holding hands."

"Oh is it?" I bat my lashes at him, and he gives me a flat glare in reply. "Are you going to punish me?"

Desire flares in his eyes, a pool of black ink that consumes the vibrant blue. "Yes."

My smile stretches so wide that my cheeks ache. I give him a pat on the chest. "You'll have to catch me first."

Before I've even finished my sentence, I've ripped my hand from his and pivoted in the direction of the concession stands. I know he's right on my heels. I can hear his rapid footfalls. I can feel the weight of the hunt on me. The way his gaze lies heavily on my back.

But he doesn't know this place like I do.

I know every twist and turn. Every hidden door. Every little cubbyhole and safe place to find refuge. So when I gain enough ground in the network of structures, I duck into the storage hatch at the back of the hot dog stand and try to quiet my rapid breathing, clamping a hand across my mouth to stop the laughter that begs to be set free. I hear Fionn run past my hiding place and then I lose all sense of sound except the heartbeat that roars in my ears. When it finally calms, I crawl out of my cramped little cage.

I creep along slowly, crouching low to the ground. Listening. Stopping. Starting again, just a few steps at a time. But no matter how many times I wait and listen, nothing comes. There's no sign of Fionn when I peer between the stands. No clues on the wind, no sounds in the air.

Doubt claws its way into my mind. He probably gave up. Or maybe he's irritated that yet another one of our rules has been broken. I bet he went back to Dorothy. I can almost see him setting up my treadmill to run a four-minute mile and then plop down on my couch with some trail mix and a disgusting vegetable smoothie while he crochets a runner for my folding table and watches some *Surviving Love* on his iPad. I don't know why I find all of that fucking adorable. Green juice should *not* be adorable, considering it tastes like licking the trampled grass of a fairground. Not that I've ever done that before when I've lost a bet to Baz or anything.

My head swimming with doubts, I take one last spin to assess my silent surroundings, and then I straighten, smoothing a hand over my jeans. I blow a long sigh toward my bangs and then with slow and careful steps, I start walking back in the direction of the games.

I don't make it more than a dozen strides before a weight barrels into me. A steel band clamps across my waist. A palm traps a startled cry in my mouth. I'm lifted from the ground and in a twist and turn of motion, I'm dragged into the dim light of a closed concession stand.

"Did you think I wouldn't find you?"

Every exhalation he breathes tickles the hairs at the back of my neck. My heart rate spikes. I whimper, but the sound is lost to the palm that covers my lips. He kicks the door closed behind him, throwing us into shadow.

"So," Fionn says, that one word hanging in the air with so much sharp and steady certainty that it could cut through it. He sets me down and walks us to the counter to press my hips against it, his erection hard against my ass. My belly clenches, a dull ache of need that demands his touch. "Why don't you show me what I've won?"

His palm is still clamped to my mouth, my unsteady exhalations spilling over the edge of his hand. His lips graze the shell of my ear and my eyes drift closed. His whisper is an intoxicating mix of sweetness and menace when he says, "You said you had a surprise for me if I caught you. I'm dying to know what it is."

God, I could live in this moment of anticipation forever. This moment when desire burns so bright that it could incinerate every rule and condition, if we just added a splash more gasoline to the fire. In this moment, there is no aftermath, no coming back to our senses. The only way out is to give in. Fuck the consequences.

Fionn takes his time to release each finger before he lifts his palm away. "Show. Me."

My heart climbs into my throat and lodges there. I toe off my shoes and, with one hand, undo the button of my jeans. I take my time with the zipper, willing myself not to rush. When it's finally at the last tooth, I slide the jeans and my panties over my hips, stepping out of them when they land at my feet. "Check your pockets," I whisper before he can figure it out.

Fionn keeps one hand braced on the counter to cage me in, and with the other he pats down his jeans. A low *hmm* resonates against my back as he brings a small bottle into view. A low chuckle escapes. "Bone yard snake oil cum lube," he says as he reads the label. "I have to admit, I like the doctor theme."

And then he goes still behind me. I bite down on a wicked grin as he sets the bottle on the counter and takes a step back. His hands grip my ass cheeks and separate them.

I twinkle my fingers in jazz hands. "Surprise."

"Jesus Fucking Christ, Rose," he says. I turn enough so I can see his face over my shoulder. His eyes don't shift away from what I know he's staring at—the multicolored handle of the Tutti Frutti vibrating butt plug lodged deep in my ass.

"I went with the circus theme too. Well, as close as I could get, anyway," I say. A hard swallow shifts in Fionn's throat before his gaze returns to mine. His eyes are nearly black, his pupils blown. "You seemed to be very interested in the ass-fucking idea when I said that I promised it to Chad. So, I took a bet that a little bit of anal might also be one of your things. If I'm wrong though—"

Fionn presses me into the counter, grinding his hips against me. His hard length pushes against the handle of the toy. "Trust me. It's my fucking thing."

With another roll of his hips, he steps back again, then grasps the handle. My pussy clenches. My clit throbs, begging for relief. My core burns with need and I want to beg him to turn on the vibration, but I stop myself. I want him to let himself out to play on his own terms.

And play he does.

He pulls the long, curved handle, sliding the toy out of my ass just a few inches before he pushes it back in again. Out and in. Out and in. With his free hand, he pushes my body down until it's flush with the counter and caresses my back. I brace my forehead on my folded arms and breathe through my increasing desperation to be fucked. The slow thrusts continue and I feel the heat of my arousal on my inner thighs. I moan as he pushes the toy in as deep it will go, and then, so slowly I nearly beg, he pulls it free.

"Stay there," he says. "Don't move."

I shift just enough to watch as he takes the toy over to the sink and washes it with soap and water, patting it dry with paper towels when it's thoroughly clean. He turns to face me when he's done.

"I'm going to need you to hold on to this because once I've filled your ass with cum, that's going back in. So open wide."

Though I fucking love the idea of everything he said until the *open wide* part, my nose scrunches. I'm not opposed, but I'm unsure. But then inspiration strikes. I know exactly what will make this appetizing. My eyes dart to farther down the counter and the motion doesn't go unnoticed by Fionn. He chuckles as he spots what I'm looking at: the cotton candy machine.

"Okay," he says. "How does it work?"

"Switch it on, and then turn the volt knob all the way to the right." He does. The motor starts up and whirs as the heater in the center of the machine spins. "Get the sugar from the tub under there," I say, nodding to the shelves next to him.

"What color?"

"Surprise me."

Fionn gives me a dark grin as he pulls out the tub of pink sugar. He follows my instructions to get a scoop ready and when a minute or two passes, I tell him to turn the machine off and pour the sugar into the heater at the center of the drum. "Now turn it back on and catch the cotton candy," I say. We laugh as he uses the toy to catch the floss as it flows from the heater. I teach him how to spin the plug to catch the spun sugar in a ball. He probably gets half of it wound around his hand. But he grins, his face lit with a wide, uninhibited smile while he swirls more and more sugar around the toy until it runs out and he turns off the machine. When he's done, the Tutti Frutti butt plug is covered with a mound of pink candy floss.

"How about now?" he asks.

I open my mouth and he smiles.

He slides the candy-covered plug into my mouth and the burst of sweetness floods my tongue. My eyes flutter closed, and when they open, he's watching me, his expression ravenous. I slide the toy from my mouth slowly and gesture toward him with it, the colorful silicon now covered in dissolving pink sugar. "I've never been fucked in the ass while eating cotton candy before. This is like every circus girl's dream."

Fionn passes me the extra mound of pink floss gathered in his hand and then steps behind me, loosening his belt. "Is it?"

"No. Probably just mine."

"I've never fucked a woman in the ass while she's eating cotton candy before either," he says as he pops the cap of the bottle of lube and drizzles the cool, viscous liquid down the crack of my ass. "So I guess we're even."

I wink at him over my shoulder and make a show of running the sugar-coated toy down the length of my tongue before I face forward. Anticipation in my veins is an electric hum. The sweetness in my mouth is the perfect accompaniment to his erection as he drags the tip through the lube, coating his cock. He's savoring every moment. He circles my pleated hole in a tease and then slides up the crack of my ass, then back down again, repeating the motion, taking his time. His hand caresses my arm in a wordless request to add more of the extra sugar to the toy, and I do. The tip of his cock presses to my hole in a slow pulse as I pull a section of cotton candy free and wind it around the body of the toy. And as I slide it back into my mouth, he pushes his way inside, slipping the tip of his erection past the tight ring of muscle.

"Jesus fucking Christ," he hisses, pausing with just the crown of his cock lodged in my ass. I'm already panting heavy breaths, desperate for more. "This tight little ass is fucking heaven, Rose." He pushes in an inch deeper and I moan. "Tell me what you want."

He slides back until he's free and I whimper. A dark chuckle escapes him and I swear that my blood is replaced with lava. He presses to my ass again and slides in deeper, my body shuddering. I pull the toy from my mouth. "For you to fuck me the way I know you want to without worrying about what will happen next."

Fionn pauses. I glance over my shoulder and meet his eyes. It's as though the shell of him has cracked. And what's behind those splinters and shards is ravenous. "If you want me to stop, tell me or tap on my arm," he grits out. My reply is silence. I tear another piece of cotton candy free and wind it around the toy before I stick out my tongue and lay it on the surface. And then I turn on the vibration and face forward.

A deep growl fills our shadows and Fionn thrusts all the way in.

This. This is what I want. Deep, rocking strokes. My hips gripped in his hands. Fingerprints on my skin. He thrusts into me. Again. And again. Sliding out to the tip. Pushing all the way in. Fucking me without worrying about the consequences. What tomorrow will be like. What rules we might break. He picks up a pace. Faster. Harder. I pull the toy out of my mouth and moan as he pistons into me with merciless, feral need. The plug is still vibrating. I shimmy my hand between my body and the counter, its stainless steel edge biting into my forearm as I position the toy over my clit. My entire being seems to wind tighter, from my muscles to my veins to my mind. The orgasm builds in my core and I cry out, not thinking about where we are or who might hear us. Fionn's hand folds around my mouth to trap the sound in his palm. And then he bites down on the juncture between my neck and shoulder and he drives into me, wild with need, mindless and desperate. Sparks invade my vision and I come hard, my lungs burning, every muscle tightening. My ass clenches around his length and Fionn roars my name. He pushes as deep as my body can take him, his length pulsing as he spills inside me, just like he promised.

His hands land on either side of my head while his thrusts slow. His arms tremble. And my body feels weightless, my bones liquid, my thoughts still and quiet in the haze that hums in my mind like static on a radio.

"Fucking hell, Rose," Fionn says as he leans back. I still hear the unevenness in his breath. His body is fighting to recover. He starts to pull out, but he takes his time, and when I look back across my shoulder he's watching the motion, taking in every inch as he slowly slides free. The moment the tip of his erection is free of my ass he's taking the toy from me. He turns off the vibration. And then he positions it against my ass as I rasp out his name. "I told you I was going to fill you and put this back in," he whispers as he slides it inside. I whimper, renewed need already building deep in my core. "You're going to keep that cum where it belongs and I'm going to fuck you again when we get back to your RV. But in the meantime"—Fionn flips me over, landing my back on the counter and spreading my legs wide—"I'm going to make this pussy extra sweet."

I watch, riveted, as Fionn tears off a piece of cotton candy and lays it on his tongue. He lowers himself to my clit. His eyes don't leave mine as he passes a slow lick to my swollen bud of nerves.

I lay my hand over his where it's splayed across my inner thigh. Our fingers lace and he squeezes my hand, not letting go. And it's in this moment, with his eyes never straying from mine, this new wave of need building in my veins, that I know that when it comes to Fionn Kane, I will break every rule.

And for the first time, I let myself wonder if he might one day feel the same.

CLAWS

Fionn

ONE YEAR LATER

Good luck tonight, Doc! Don't break your
face. It's pretty and I like to sit there ;)

> AHAHA thank you! I'll do my best.
> And even if it's broken, you'll still
> be on it. I promise you.

> Looking forward to tomorrow.

Me too! I've gotta work at 7PM so if your
flight is late, just let yourself in.

I slip my phone into my bag and pull my shirt over my head before I put both into a locker. I should be thinking about what I'm about to do as I walk into the crowd, headed for the ring. I should be listening to the introduction and the rules as I slip between the ropes. I should be focused on my opponent. But I'm not. I'm thinking about Rose.

I try to put space between us. But it never lasts. There's always a reason to pull us back together. Like Rowan and Sloane's wedding—I tried to tell myself to ease back and give us both some room to breathe. And what happened? We ended up fucking in the bathroom of Leytonstone Inn. We were just bringing shit to the venue the day before Rowan and Sloane's surprise elopement, and in less than ten minutes of arrival, I had my mouth around her nipple and my cock buried in her pussy. Not to mention the wedding itself. Rose was so fucking beautiful in her bridesmaid dress, her smile lit up with happiness for her friends. I ate her pussy in the staff room of the bar that night like it was my last goddamn meal. I would have found a way to do it in the courthouse too a few weeks later had we been there in person for Lachlan and Lark's unplanned nuptials. But it's not just the sex. That's only a bonus, if I'm being truly honest with myself. Every spare minute I want to spend with Rose. She's funny. She's whip-smart. She's unpredictable. She lives her life with a wide-open heart, like she loves every piece of herself and isn't afraid to show it. She embraces everything from her fucked-up chaos to her brilliant, bright light. I admire her in a way I've never admired anyone, because it used to seem impossible to imagine what it would feel like to live that way. But she makes me think I could embrace myself and life the way she does. These things about myself that I've hidden away, the secrets and dark urges, she seems to sense them. And she's not afraid.

And my own fears are eroding, replaced by need I couldn't shake even if I wanted to. A need to be with Rose. A need for more than what we have now. It's consuming me, one cell at a time, one moment to the next.

I don't see her nearly enough. When I'm not with her, it's fucking agonizing. I miss her presence in my house, how she made it a home. I miss it so goddamn much I've been keeping her plants alive and thriving for whenever she can visit, which is rarely, even though she's decided to spend the last couple months in Boston as the circus is getting closer to winding down for the season. She talks in noncommittal terms when it comes up. "Thought I'd stick around Boston for a bit, see what all the fuss is about. I felt bad not being at Lark and Lachlan's wedding in person and I could use some time off," she said with a shrug when she first brought it up over a FaceTime call. "Barbara's doing great with Cheryl and the poodles. The twins can borrow my bikes until I get my bearings. And Baz needs a bit of freedom. I'll lend him Dorothy now that he can drive. You know, just a favor to his mom, give her a bit of a break," she said the next week. "Besides, Lachlan said his place is empty. Might as well have someone to look after it, you know?"

"Yeah, of course," I'd replied, trying to sound equally nonplussed. "Makes sense."

"I've got a job in Saugus with an event company for now, just a temporary thing that José hooked me up with. But Rowan floated the idea of me working at 3 in Coach for him once I'm finished with the Saugus Frightfair gig. The restaurant's so busy. He said it would be a big help if I was interested in learning. If I can help keep a circus troupe in order, surely I can handle helping him manage the place, right? Might be kind of fun to try something new . . . ?"

I had responded with something encouraging yet bland, not wanting to come off as too excited. The last thing I wanted was to scare her off. But In reality? I was fucking *elated*. And I haven't stopped thinking about it since. Not when I'm at work. Not when I'm at home, lying in the dark, daring to imagine what a different future might be like.

Not even now.

My punch lands with a crack on Nate's cheek. His head snaps to the side. Spit flies from his mouth, but he stays upright. At least long enough for me to deliver another blow to his ribs.

The crowd roars around us. Fire burns through my veins, a current of flame beneath sweat-slicked skin.

I hit him with a right hook. Christ, it's so fucking satisfying. I keep thinking of that time I stitched him up as Rose watched. He was purposely pushing my buttons with his *come by the shop* bullshit. I punch him again. A jab. Another jab. When he threw his name in to battle it out with Killer Kane for a chance at dethroning me, I jumped to defend my undefeated streak.

He's getting tired. His hits are weakening. His footwork is slow. I fake him out with the threat of a left jab. And then I throw all my momentum into a huge right hook.

My fist lands on Nate's jaw. His heads snaps back. And then he falls to the mat, unconscious.

Satisfaction.

The crowd goes feral.

Tom counts down the seconds. Nate's head rolls from side to side. His legs slide across the stained and padded floor. But he doesn't get up.

Hands raised in victory, I take a turn around the mat, my mouth guard hanging from a smile that's probably a little bit wicked. Then I manage to wrangle the darkness that seems to be thriving more and more with each fight, and I attend to the man lying at my feet.

Though I tell him I'm sorry when he comes to, I don't think I really mean it.

"Another excellent show," Tom says, clapping me on the shoulder as Nate's friends help him out of the ring.

I unravel the tape around my knuckles, testing out the pain that's mounting in my joints now that the adrenaline is already wearing off. "Thanks."

"Same again next month?" When I nod, Tom grins, passing me a clean towel for a gash I didn't even notice on my brow. "Better get that looked at, Dr. Kane. Might need a few stitches. You can pick up your cash tomorrow at my dealership."

Towel held to my bleeding face, I duck between the ropes and leave the ring. I pick up my bag from the locker and head through the crowd, nodding the occasional thanks to the spectators who pat me on the back and chant my name. But I'm not here for the attention. Or the money.

I'm here to let my monster free. And there's only one thing that beast truly wants.

To claw its way closer to Rose.

My pulse spikes at the mere thought of seeing her soon. But I try to shake it off as I make my way into the bathroom, commandeering one of the two sinks in the small, run-down space that smells like piss and beer. The steps are mechanical to me. Wash hands. Gloves on. Sterilize the wound. I thread the needle then face the mirror. I start the first stitch, leaning close to my reflection as I pierce my own flesh with the curved needle.

"Great fight, Dr. Kane," a voice says behind me.

The monster inside me claws at my ribs.

"Mr. Cranwell." I lean back, pulling the thread taut. Our eyes meet in the mirror. Cranwell has a prosthetic eye now to lie over an ocular implant I already know he received in Omaha, the subtle differences nearly indistinguishable from his uninjured eye. Both track me in the reflection. "You're looking well. How are you feeling?"

"Better than you," he says as his gaze lands on the gash through my brow.

I let out a quiet *hmm* and refocus on my wound, inserting the needle for the next stitch. The bite of pain is a welcome delicacy for the darkness in me to consume. It keeps my attention where it should be—away from breaking Matthew Cranwell's neck.

Cranwell leans against the sink next to me, crossing his arms over his chest as he watches my progress. "So. I heard the buttoned-up town doctor was not just mending wounds but making them too. Had to come and see it for myself. It was a good show."

I nod my thanks.

"Do you think Eric Donovan put up a fight when your little girlfriend killed him?"

My eyes snap to his. Blood roars in my ears. The urge to rip his spine straight through his throat is overwhelming. The only thing that stops me is luck. Another man enters the bathroom, not noticing that we're staring each other down, me with my barely subdued rage, Cranwell with a smirk that I'm desperate to punch off his fucking ugly face.

"I have no fucking idea what you're talking about," I say when the man enters one of the stalls.

Cranwell's grin stretches. "Oh, right. She's not your girlfriend, is she? At least, that's what I heard. Probably a good thing for you. Don't want to have your perfect image marred by someone like Rose Evans."

An electric chill climbs through my flesh. "I meant I have no idea about the other thing. You know as much as anybody around town that he's never been found. Only his vehicle. You have no reason to be asking me anything about this."

"Of course, of course. Silly me." His head tilts. His eyes narrow. "Are you sure about that, though? She was in your home for a couple of months, after all. You sure you didn't see anything . . . untoward?"

"If this is your attempt at an interrogation, I must say"—I turn my attention back to the mirror, starting the next stitch, swallowing the rage that threatens to tremble my hand—"it's fucking amateur. And deeply unprofessional. But I guess that makes sense, considering the circumstances of your departure from the Sheriff's Office."

Cranwell chuckles, scratching at the graying stubble on his chin. "I ain't interrogating you, Dr. Kane. I'm just askin' a simple question. Because from where I sit, it seems strange that she would be in Shiretown just moments before Donovan was last seen. A little thing like Rose Evans? Buying a big ol' knife? But, hell . . . What do I know?"

I shoot a cold glare in his direction, then pierce my brow and pull another stitch tight. "Well, Mr. Cranwell, I can confirm *I* don't know what you're talking about. And I'm not sure you do either. Eric Donovan is *missing*. He could be anywhere. He could have fucked off to Mexico for all we know. The kinds of allegations you seem to be dancing around are extremely serious."

Cranwell's smile stretches, a predator ready to take down the competition in its domain. There's a threat behind every wrinkle of weathered flesh, every movement of muscle and bone. "Did you know someone about her size did this to me?" he asks as he gestures to his eye. "A woman. Hit me and stabbed me, right in the eye. For no reason. Came onto my property entirely unprovoked."

"Sounds to me like you don't know who did it. And I wonder why someone would want to attack you unprovoked. It's not like you've done that to anyone else . . . right?" I knot another stitch and wipe the blood from my brow before I start the next. "Oh, I heard Lucy moved to her parents' place in Minnesota and took the kids with her. I'm so very sorry for the dissolution of your marriage. I wonder what could have precipitated that."

A flash of rage passes across Cranwell's face. But he doesn't risk lashing out, not as a couple guys from the gym enter the bathroom and nod in my direction. "No fuckin' idea," he finally says.

"I'm sure. Now if you'll excuse me, I have something to attend to. Oh, and Mr. Cranwell," I say, letting my eyes drop down the length of him and back up again, "I'm afraid I can no longer be your doctor. I hope you'll understand." With a final, cutting glance, I focus on my reflection, harnessing every last thread of restraint to keep myself from killing the man next to me.

"That's probably for the best for both of us," he says, clapping me on the shoulder just as I pierce my skin with the needle. The point scrapes within my flesh. "Have a great night, Dr. Kane."

I don't look at him as he leaves the bathroom. I just finish my stitches, a line of ten that curves from my forehead to the swollen flesh of my upper eyelid. When I'm done, I pack my supplies, throw away my gloves and the gauze and the towel that's stained with slashes of crimson. I toss on a shirt and a hoodie. Splash some water on my face. And then I grip the edges of the sink. I lean closer to the old mirror, the surface marred by scratches and imperfections. I don't think I recognize the man looking back at me anymore. And maybe I like it.

I leave without another word to anyone, going home and straight into the shower. Despite the pain and the rage and the anxiety swirling in my guts, I still think of Rose.

When I shut my eyes, I can see her face, her lips parted, eyes hooded and locked on me. I can hear her moans. Her phantom touch is there on my back, caressing my shoulders. I grip my erection and imagine sinking into her tight pussy. Her desperate cries roll through my mind, swelling and falling in the same pace as I stroke my cock. Every detail is so clear. The feel of her flesh beneath my palms. The peak of her nipples. The blush in her skin. I can't help myself. In my fantasy, I lean closer. Closer, and closer, and closer, until I slant my mouth over hers and dissolve into a kiss I've imagined more times than I can count. It's this moment that throws me over the edge. This forbidden, broken rule that has my balls tightening and my cock pulsing and ropes of cum shooting across the tiles. It's the kiss that has me unraveling, barely able to stand beneath the scalding water, one hand braced against the shower wall. I don't just want part of her. I want *all* of her. I want to consume these boundaries between us until I finally feel whole.

I press my aching forehead to the cool tile and stand in the spray until the water runs cold.

It's a fitful sleep. I'm too riled up about Cranwell and excited about the trip to get any true rest. When I wake, nothing seems to happen fast enough. The plane seems to travel too slowly through the sky. The line at the rental car counter is too long. I can't navigate the city streets as deftly as I need to. I try an alternative route of back streets and alleys to avoid the traffic as I make my way to South End, where Lachlan's apartment is, the one he's letting Rose stay in now that he's at Lark's place. I get stuck in traffic anyway, of course, because Boston rush hour is like that. I'm so worried I'm going to miss her before she heads out to work that I park three blocks away. I only brought a backpack, thank fuck, so I toss it over my shoulders and run the rest of the distance to Rose.

By the time I reach the fifth floor, sweat mists my forehead, the wound in my brow pulsing with every beat of my heart.

"Rose," I say, knocking on the door. "Hey, Rose."

"*Coming*," she chimes from the other side. I can hear the excitement in her voice, the bounce of her steps across the hardwood as she approaches. The locks shift and click in the door. And then she throws it open.

"*Jesus fucking Christ*," we both say at the same time.

Her eyes are locked to my stitches and the bruise that colors my cheekbone and brow.

Mine are fused to her fucking terrifying face and ridiculously hot body, the strangest contrast I've ever witnessed on a single person.

She's wearing a black lace bra and matching panties, her figure a symphony of softness and strength. The lace follows the curves of her hips and the swell of her breasts, black satin straps shining with the rise and fall of her chest with every breath. There's no detail that goes unnoticed beneath my gaze, not a single inch of fabric or skin that isn't forever seared into memory.

And then I get to her face.

She grins at me, showing off a set of horrifying, pointed, yellowing teeth. Too many teeth, all jammed up together. Her lips and eyes and the very tip of her nose are painted black, the rest of her face in a stark white. Two curved black lines flow halfway up her forehead to make new eyebrows, her natural ones hidden under the thick makeup. She tilts her head side to side to jostle the three little bells sewn to each arm of her black-and-white jester hat.

"I'm channeling Art the Clown from *Terrifier*, but make it cute, with like, Dracula's grill from *Renfield*. You like?" she says, her speech a little garbled by the fake teeth. She does a slow spin to show off the thong, the little triangle of lace contouring around the globes of her ass to disappear between the crack. My cock strains against my zipper, at least until she faces me again.

"I'm so conflicted. I want to fuck you so badly but I also fear for my life. It's like wet dream nightmare fuel."

"Honestly, that's the most romantic thing I've ever heard. Though I'm probably not supposed to say that. Rules and shit, right?"

"Right," I say, trying to contain my disappointment at how casually she just reminded me of our current situation. Rose envelops me in a brief embrace and then stands back from the door for me to pass. "Rules and shit. Yeah."

"Come in. Tell me all about your match and that sexy new scar.

There's some rubbing alcohol and gauze pads in your guest room en suite by the way, in case you need to clean it up."

Fucking hell. A one-two punch. I feel like I'm back in the ring and this time, I'm getting pummeled by Rose instead of Nate. And honestly? I think she could take me. She's scrappy as fuck. "Thanks," I say as I let the backpack slide from my shoulders. I set it down next to the couch and trail behind Rose as she heads to the kitchen, taking the teeth out as she goes. A little shard of disappointment lands in my chest when she grabs a robe lying on the back of a chair and slides it on. "I appreciate it."

"No worries. So, the stitches?" she asks, pulling a beer from the fridge and offering it to me. When I nod, she slides it across the island where I take a seat, then cracks open a bottle of water for herself.

"The stitches, yeah. I fought Nate. Guess he got a couple of good punches in. I ended up knocking him out in the second round, though."

Rose pouts, the gesture exaggerated by her stark makeup. "Poor Nate."

"Nate's fine," I say, rolling my eyes. When they land on Rose, she grins as though she sees right into my jealous thoughts. "I did run into Matt Cranwell though."

Even with the thick layers of makeup, I can still see the flash of fear in her face. "Cranwell? What did he want?"

"To be a dick, mostly. I wouldn't worry. He's still got nothing to go on."

"Nothing more about Eric lately?"

I shake my head. "It comes up in conversation here and there, usually in reference to Humboldt Lake. People still seem stuck on it. They think the search was called off too soon."

Rose blows out a deep breath and nods. Her smile is weak, but it's still a relief to see it. "How about Naomi?"

"She's great, actually. Got herself a new boyfriend, one of the other nurses. She seems really happy." This time, Rose's smile is the real deal. She beams at me. Which, even with her natural teeth, is still disturbing as fuck. "I'm still not sure what to make of all this," I say as I gesture a circle toward her face.

"Well, I'll give you some time to think on it. I've gotta get going to the Frightfair. I'm going to be late." Rose comes around to my side of the island and slides a hand across my chest, giving me an embrace from behind. My hand circles her wrist. Her pulse drums a steady beat beneath my fingertips. I resist the urge to raise her skin to my lips, but only barely. "Thanks for fielding that ass-hole Cranwell. Must be shitty having him pop up every once in a while."

The truth is, I've been thinking more and more of moving back to Boston. It wouldn't be the worst thing either to get away from Cranwell. But my interest in coming home has very little to do with him, and everything to do with Rose. If she really is going to stay, it feels like the right time to consider it. If I'm being honest with myself, it's the real reason I'm here, one I'm more and more ready to tackle head-on. I need to see if she might also be ready to dissolve our rules. To see what it would be like for us to make a real go of this. And being here, with her hand resting so casually on my chest like it was always meant to be there? That only makes everything clearer.

"It's no worries," I finally say, still relishing her gentle embrace. "I can drive you there, if you want?"

"Nah, it's fine. You just got off the plane." She pats me on the chest, a final stamp before she slides her hand free and starts toward the hallway that leads to the bedrooms. I wonder if she could feel the way my heart drummed against her palm. I know it's not the right time, but I'm desperate to throw my questions into the empty space where her presence just lingered. The words were *right there*, ready on my tongue.

Rose changes into the rest of her costume, coming out a few moments later with black and white pants and a button-up shirt, both of which seem too big for her, which only adds to her unsettling appearance. She slides her tarot deck and selenite into one pocket, the creepy teeth into the other, then gives me a grin. "Uber is on the way," she says, holding up her phone. "I'll see you later?"

"Yeah, maybe I can pick you up? I'd like to chat about some stuff. Maybe we can talk on the drive home."

Rose's white painted brows flicker. "Sure . . . Everything okay?"

"Everything is fine, yeah." I take a step closer, leaning down to press a light kiss to her cheek. "Text me when you're about half an hour from being done. I'll come get you. And don't make too many people shit themselves tonight. Cleanup would be a bitch."

Rose winks. "I thought you wanted me to have fun."

"Mayhem in moderation."

"That's boring."

With a final smile, Rose heads out to catch her Uber, leaving me in silence. I stand in the center of the room, watching that door like I hope she might turn around and bounce through it.

I'm not sure how long I stand there. How long it takes for it to sink into my marrow. But I finally realize I don't care about the illusion of light anymore. My Rose blooms in the dark. And all I want is to grow there with her.

HAUNTED

Rose

This is my favorite time of year. And it might not be Silveria Circus, but in a way, this is even better.

A brand-new night fair. An epic haunted house. A creepy-ass tent for my tarot readings.

Saugus Frightfair.

It's a perfect October night.

My setup is legit pretty fucking cool. When unsuspecting fair-goers come in for a reading from a terrifying clown, I've got all kinds of jump scares at my disposal. I keep a remote hidden on my lap and buttons on the floor I can press with my feet. I can turn off the lights, set off a smoke machine, trigger doll heads to drop from the ceiling or screams from the hidden speakers or a ghost mannequin to pop out of a cabinet at the side of the room. Sometimes, other staff sneak in to scare the shit out of unsuspecting clients. People love it. Especially when they get so into the reading that they forget to anticipate the next scare. And my cards have been on fire tonight. Readings about exes and romance and secrets, about ambition and hope and love and loss.

Eventually, things finally start to taper off toward the end of the night. There are still loads of people milling around, but there are longer gaps between visitors to my tent. I wrap up a reading for a pair of teenage girls and when they leave, I take out the creepy teeth and decide it's time to turn off the neon open sign at the entrance of my tent. When it's switched off, I let the curtain drape across the door. With a quick call on my walkie-talkie to the fair manager, Wendy, to let her know I'm closing up, I pocket the device in exchange for my phone and send a text to Fionn.

> Hey :). I'm just finishing up for the night. You still want to pick me up? No worries if you're already in bed!

Yeah for sure. Thought I'd make my way there to have a look around. I hope that's okay! I'm just parking.

> That sounds perfect.

With a smile and a deep, contented sigh, I sit back down at my table, cleansing my deck before I shuffle it. I've been so busy lately that I haven't had much time to do a reading for myself. And maybe it's not just that. I've kind of enjoyed not trying so hard to interpret the chaos that lives around and within me.

But when my readings have seemed so spot-on tonight, resonating with almost everyone who's come in to sit across from me, it's impossible not to pick the cards up and think about the future. Especially when Fionn is in town, though I try not to read our relationship too often in case the cards tell me something I don't want to know. I'm happy with what we have, even though I want more. And if it's destined to go in the other direction from where I hope we're heading, I'd rather just enjoy what we have without being worried about how it will end. So instead of asking about my love life directly, I go to one of my favorite questions for a simple reading, shuffling as I say it out loud.

"How can I prepare myself for what's coming next in my life?"

I draw the first card.

Knight of Swords.

I sit up straighter. This is a card I rarely pull for myself, and when I do, it usually means I have to act quickly. But it can also mean someone or something destructive. Someone ruinous.

I draw the second card.

Death.

My blood runs cold, as though it's been drained from my limbs, leaving my skin chilled and my hair raised. Like any card, Death can mean many things. Transformation. Endings. Change needed for growth. But after the Knight of Swords . . . ?

I draw the final card.

Four of Swords.

Stillness. Pause. *Mourning.* Time spent recovering.

"From what?" I ask. But I don't think I want to know the answers to my questions anymore.

I stare at the three cards. Unease snakes across my spine. The longer I look at them, the more I wish they would change, or that I could see any other meaning than mayhem and destruction. But no matter how I try to spin the interpretation, there's only a sense of dread drifting around me.

I hastily shuffle the cards back into the deck, put them in my leather pouch with the selenite, then slide the pouch into my pocket. With a long sigh that does little to calm me, I sit back in my chair and press my eyes closed. I try to find comfort in the sounds of laughter and music outside my tent, in the scents of donuts and popcorn. I close my arms over my middle and think of Fionn's embrace, of the warmth of his presence and the calm that comes with knowing there's someone out here in this crazy world who sees the real me and doesn't turn away. And that's all I want now. Some comfort and calm.

"Time to go home," I whisper to myself.

"That's a shame. I was hoping you were going to tell me about all the good things that lie in my future."

My eyes snap open and land on a man looming at the entrance of my tent.

His face is painted in white, a contrast to the yellow of his teeth, his lips peeled back in a menacing grin. His eyes are fixed on me, framed by diamonds of black face paint. A red ball covers the tip of his nose, a wig of curly fuzz stuck to his bald head.

I go rigid in my seat.

"After all, I drove all night to get here just to *see* you. Get it?" Matthew Cranwell points to his face, where a glass eye covers the prosthetic that must now be in place behind it. His smile widens. "Do you like my new look? I think the nose really adds something."

"You're right. You look just as much like a clown as the first time I met you," I say, edging my foot closer to the buttons hidden by my tablecloth. "I heard your wife finally left your ugly ass. Took the kids with her too. Good for her."

A flash of fury passes across his face, but he banks his ire behind a menacing smile. "It's been good for me too. Lost a couple pounds. Quit the booze, just about. Got myself a new purpose, ya see. I've rekindled my love of hunting." He reaches behind his back, withdrawing a blade that's as long as the one I left in my apartment, sitting in its sheath on the nightstand. "And I've certainly fleshed out some very interesting details about you."

He takes a single step closer to my table.

"The Sparrow," he hisses.

A thousand thoughts swirl through my mind. How could he know? How *much* does he know? Did someone tell him? Who did he tell? His lips curl with the knowledge that his arrow has struck its mark. No matter how hard I try to keep the fear from my face, he sees it. And he *loves* it.

"That's right," he says as he takes a single step closer to my table. "Did you know I used to be a deputy for the Lincoln County Sheriff's Office? Ten years I worked there."

I say nothing.

"I might be a farmer now. But those skills? That training? It doesn't disappear. I started trackin' down all the places your little circus stopped. Does the name Vicki Robbins ring a bell?" When I don't answer, he tips the end of his blade in my direction. "It should. They never found out where she got the poison that didn't quite kill her husband. Shame he murdered her so quick. Maybe he would have gotten a confession from her if he hadn't choked her to death. But you and I both know it was the Sparrow who gave it to her."

"I wonder why someone would try to kill their husband?" I snipe as I tighten my grip on the seat of my chair until my fingers lose feeling. "Any ideas?"

Matt chuckles, a low and mirthless rumble that fills my tent with malice. "The more I started to look, the more I found a trail of untimely deaths in the small towns you passed through. At least one or two men every season. You must be responsible for, what, ten murders? Maybe twenty? Oh wait, make that twenty-one if you count Eric Donovan, isn't that right?"

"As far as I heard, Eric Donovan's never turned up. He might still be traveling the country, doing whatever dipshits do."

"You don't always need to find a body for there to be a murder," he says around a dark and triumphant smile. We both know he has enough knowledge of a potential connection between me and Eric that there's no protest worth making. But it's his next words that turn my skin cold. "Dr. Kane. He must know too, right? He's the one who did your surgery. Put you up at his house. Worked with Eric's girlfriend. He beat the shit out of a boxer at that fight club for knocking you over, as the story goes. And he covered for you that time I dropped in for a visit at the clinic. I know you were there, listening to every word."

"Leave Dr. Kane out of this—"

"I tried, actually. Spoke to him just last night. But he seems hell-bent on sticking with you. I know he was flying here today, I'm bettin' to see you, isn't that right?" Matt waggles his brows and squeaks his red nose. "So just how much does he know, exactly? Or is it even worse than that? Has he been helping you—"

"What the fuck do you want? You think you're here to arrest me? You were kicked off the force for being an incompetent douchebag, from what I heard. So if this is some kind of lame-ass attempt to get yourself back onto the roster, think again. It's never going to work."

He shakes his head. The white paint cracks and shifts and flakes on his face as his grin stretches. "Do I look like the kind of guy to pass you over to some idiot in a uniform when I can settle the score myself?"

His leather gloves creak. His fists tighten. The knife glints in the dim light. My own mask of makeup tightens on my skin as I mirror his smile. "Do I look like the kind of girl to go down without a fight?"

I hit the button for the lights and plunge us into darkness.

Matt crashes into my table. I pick up my chair and swing it in his direction. Pain spikes in my wrists and elbows with the impact. Our cries of shock and frustration are a harmony in the darkness.

I take a second swing, a return pass. The chair breaks against Matt and I hear what I hope is the knife as it flies from his hand to break the glass in the cabinet door. All I have left of the chair is the seat. And though he groans with pain and curses with rage, I know he's not done yet.

I use the only advantage I have now—my knowledge of this cramped space. I drop to the floor and crawl to the back edge of the tent as Matt thrashes around the darkness, destroying everything he touches in his search for me. I stay crouched and quiet, tearing at the canvas until the pins loosen from the grass. Wooden seat still clutched in my grip, I slide free of the tent and *run*.

An unhinged, dirt-streaked, grass-stained clown running through the fairgrounds attracts only yelps of surprise and delight from the patrons. No one notices the panic in my eyes. The way I stop and spin around and scan my surroundings for the man who wants to kill me. No one hears the heartbeats that roar in my ears.

No one knows the realization that blares through my mind, obliterating all other thoughts.

If I don't kill Matt Cranwell, he will kill me. And he will take Fionn down too.

I cannot let that happen.

I look left and right but there's no sign of Matt Cranwell.

"Why does this shit never go right?" I ask out loud as I pivot on my heel and scour the crowd. The scent of donuts and churros and burgers swirls around me on the cool breeze. Aside from the occasional staff costume I recognize, it's impossible to pinpoint a familiar face beneath masks and makeup. A little surge of panic ripples through my heart. Maybe Matt has taken off like any sane person would do. Maybe he'll bring in the cops after all. There's no reason to entirely bank on his narcissism and misogyny and fondness for physical violence to get the better of him. And Christ, what if he does think rationally and take this to the police? Fionn will definitely be dragged down into the thick of this mess with me. My imagination threatens to run wild with images of red and blue lights, courtrooms and lawyers and metal bars that slide closed and never open.

But I can't get caught up in all that now. I've got a job to do. "Get your shit together, Rose Evans."

I start another turn when a quick burst of movement catches my eye. I spot Matt next to the hot dog stand. He's peering around the corner of the glass display. Then Matt spots me, and unfortunately, he's picked up a second weapon, his knife clutched in one hand, and a hot dog skewer in the other. He straightens and comes out from behind the cart, creeping another step in my direction. "It's on, you fuckin' clown," he snarls through a feral grin.

I take off running.

Matt roars a threat of vengeance behind me as I weave through groups of teenagers with their popcorn and cotton candy, and staff dressed as zombies and witches and deranged clowns. I dart between stands and through narrow passageways. My heart riots in my chest. My stomach threatens a revolt. But I still keep Matt just close enough that he can find me. Just far enough that he can't catch me. And I keep my eye on the target I spot through the crowd.

The haunted house.

I run for the staff-only side door, tossing a glance over my shoulder as I scramble to pull the keys from my pocket and unlock it. Matt is in the distance but lasered onto me. He has a limp in his step that slows him down, but not by much. He snarls when I give him my best psycho clown grin. I push the door open and leave it ajar, and then I plunge into the darkness, ducking into the shadows.

A moment later, Matt bursts through the door.

"Fucking bitch." He starts limping down the corridor where performers can travel behind the walls to scare visitors from behind hidden panels and trapdoors. Screams and laughter and the dusty aroma of glycerin fog linger in the air. His head swings side to side as he looks for any sign of me, a weapon still clutched in each hand. I step from the shadows, pulling the door shut with a quiet *snick*.

I sneak behind Matt, the flat seat clutched between my hands.

"Where the fuck are you," he whispers.

I smile.

Ta-da, motherfucker.

I use all my force as I swing the wooden seat and hit Matt in the back of the head. He stumbles and screams. His weapons clatter into the shadows. He drops to his knees, his head clutched between his hands, a mess of rage and chaos. I set the chair down and slink past him as he writhes in the dark. I start feeling for the knife so I can fucking finish this, once and for all. And just as I think I've felt the sharp tip of something metal, a hand clamps around my ankle and yanks me back across the floor.

When I roll over to fight him off, his glass eye is gone, leaving his lid half closed. But that's not the one I'm focused on. My shocked gaze is caught on the other eye, bulging much too far beyond the confines of its socket.

"Holy fucking shit, it's true. I hit you so hard your eyeball popped out." I retch, barely managing to swallow down a swell of nausea. The lids are pulled back across the bloodshot globe, making him look both surprised and cartoonishly angry. I retch again. "Put it back in, for the love of God."

"I'm going to fucking *kill you*," he snarls. He pitches toward me, his hands tensed into claws that I'm sure he's desperate to clamp around my neck. With a sharp kick to his chest, I manage to keep him at bay long enough that I can scramble to my feet and take off running down the corridor. With a momentary glance over my shoulder, I see Matt staggering to his feet, the knife gripped in his hand. He stalks toward me, and I dart through a curtain at the end of the hall to enter the ground floor of the visitor's section of the haunted house.

I slip past a group of teens huddled together in a corner of the creepy kitchen display, giving them an extra scare as a worker dressed as a bloodied butcher frightens them with a plastic knife. I keep going past a couple who clutches each other when a staff member drops from a hidden platform near the ceiling. I head past the smoke machine and lasers that obscure a clown crouched beneath white tendrils of mist. Matt is still behind me, and I pick up the pace through the displays and jump scares and terrified visitors. Then I head up the stairs to the second level.

The labyrinthine second story is filled with narrow rooms and screams from the floor below. I back up into a shadowed space and crouch between a china cupboard filled with decapitated doll heads and a blood-spattered sheet, trying to slow my breathing and listen for Matt's work boots thudding across the floorboards. But he doesn't come. A couple passes. Then a group of four teens. But still no Matt.

I wait. Try to sense the presence of anyone in the dark beyond the manufactured screams and the haunting music that play through the hidden speakers. Maybe he's left. Come to his senses. Decided to seek treatment for his very fucked-up ocular situation. Or maybe he's off to call the police, the thing he should have done in the first place.

I need to find him before he does.

There's a quiet scuff of shoes against the wooden floorboards. This might be my best chance to face him. I stand and peer around the edge of the cupboard. But it's not Matt that I see.

It's Dr. Fionn Kane.

I'm not sure how he knows it's me, even in the dark, even with my horror clown costume when there are clowns all over this fucking fairground. But he does.

"Crap," I hiss as he strides toward me.

"Rose." Fionn's eyes dart from my face to the seat of the broken chair in my hand and back again. "What are you doing?"

"I'm, um . . . working . . . ?"

"And by working you mean running around yelling, 'Come get me, you ugly piece of shit,' and laughing maniacally?" His eyes narrow. "I thought I saw someone in a costume following you. I came to make sure you were okay."

"That's really . . . that's nice. I'm totally fine . . . just out here representing the spooky season atmosphere," I say with a shrug as he reaches forward and flicks one of the stuffed arms of my jester's hat, the bell on the end tinkling in reply. He frowns.

"You sure you're okay?"

"Yeah. Thanks." I try not to shift my weight on my feet, but I can't help the need to fidget under his unerring stare. "Why don't you go get us some hot dogs? I'm totally famished. I'll meet you there as soon as I'm done with my . . . thing."

"Your *thing*."

"My performance thing."

"I thought you said in your text that you were done for the night."

"Um . . . Yeah. Almost. Just one more thing."

I dig in the pockets of my baggy black-and-white pants, the fabric stained with a spray of blood that could be fake. Or not. When I withdraw a roll of food and drink tickets and hold them out for

Fionn to take, he watches my hand with suspicion. "So when are you *actually* done?" he asks.

"Maybe give me, like . . . twenty minutes?" It comes out as a squeaked question. My throat just seems to close around the words. Fionn's eyes snap to mine as though I've just confessed every one of my mounting sins. His chin dips toward his chest, and he pins me with a stare both wary and menacing.

"Rose—"

A floorboard creaks behind Fionn. A flash of orange light glints off a blade. I drop the tickets and grip Fionn's wrist to tug on it as hard as I can, enough to imbalance him and send him stumbling past me.

I deliver a solid kick to Matt's shin as I hear Fionn's shocked voice say Cranwell's name like a question behind me. "Thought you'd never catch up," I say. With a second kick, his knife flies from his hand and hits the wall. He snarls in frustration, searching the floor as I duck behind Fionn and shove him forward toward the next room. "Time to go, Doc."

We tumble into a mock bedroom with Matt on our heels, his irate string of swears punctuated by the screeches and screams and cackles that pour from the speakers overhead. There's fake blood everywhere. On the walls. The ceiling. The bed where a life-size possessed mannequin springs up from the mattress. An old TV that crackles static in the corner of the room. Fionn rushes forward, and his movement triggers the sensor for a strobe light. It pulses a disorienting rhythm of light and darkness.

Fionn reaches back for me and grabs my wrist as he stumbles toward a door on the opposite side of the room, hauling me forward. But Matt catches my shoulder. Spins me around. I'm knocked out of his grasp and a shocked cry fills the room. There's a blinding flash. It's the automatic camera, hidden to take pictures of frightened visitors. In the light, I see the horror on Matt's face, his features exaggerated by makeup and blood and shadows.

The strobe turns off, leaving only the dim green and blue lights mounted in the corners of the room. Fionn drills Matt with an unblinking, ruthless stare. Even when Matt looks down in horror at the knife Fionn presses into his abdomen, Fionn never breaks his gaze away. He keeps hold of the back of Matt's neck with his free hand, his fingertips digging into the painted flesh.

"You thought you were going to enjoy your revenge," Fionn says. With a swift tug, he draws the blade upward. Crimson floods from the wound, staining Matt's torn shirt. His mouth is open but only a strained noise of pain escapes, as though his body is too shocked to manufacture sound. "And how does this feel?" Another jerk of the knife. "Still pretty good?" A soft tear of flesh, followed by Matt's whispered plea for mercy. "Because I think it feels fucking *fantastic*."

Fionn whips the knife free of Matt's abdomen and tosses it behind him. He bunches Matt's shirt with both hands at the shoulders and pushes him to the wall where mannequins disguised as dead bodies hang from meat hooks. He slams Matt's back into the wall and keeps him pinned there with one hand as he tosses one of the dummies to the floor with the other.

"Please," Matt begs, his voice barely audible between the recorded screams and voices playing around us.

But Fionn ignores him.

Matt has no strength to fight back. No way to stop Fionn as he hoists him up and pushes his back against the wall, letting gravity drive the pointed hook into Matt's body. He gasps with a fresh wave of pain. Fionn takes a step back and surveys his work. Blood pours from the gash up the length of Matt's abdomen. It trickles from the corners of his mouth. Matt's limbs scrape across the wall, but they don't touch the floor. One of his hands raises above his head in a desperate search for relief from the metal hook, but he can only trace the rusted iron. He doesn't have enough strength to grab it. Everything is moving slower than it should, like he's a fly caught in amber, stuck in the sticky embrace of time.

Matt's lips move, but they can't seem to form words, just a slow series of motions that carry no sound.

But Fionn seems to decipher the plea, his focus still locked on Matt. He laughs, a callous and cold delight that quickly dies. "*Help?* You want someone to *help* you?" Fionn shakes his head. "Do you really think I would ever, *ever* let you threaten her and walk away? Do you seriously think you could hurt her, and I would just let you live? You don't deserve mercy. When have you ever given that to anyone else? So the only thing I'll give to you is *suffering.*"

With his final word, Fionn delivers a punch to Matt's face that renders him unconscious. His head drops forward. His breathing is shallow, a liquid rumble. And then it goes quiet.

We're both staring at the man on the wall when excited voices come from a few rooms away. Fionn turns to me and I'm sure my face is an identical mask of panic. "Get under the covers," I hiss, pointing to the bed before I rush to the mannequin lying on the floor. I whip the burlap sack from its head and pull it down over Matt's instead, cringing when I catch a glimpse of the bulging eye. With a few deep breaths to recenter myself, I turn to check on Fionn's progress. But he still hasn't moved.

"Come on, Doc. Under the covers. Make some creepy sounds." I take him by the hand and lead him there, forcing him to lie beneath the stained white sheet. His face is expressionless when I cover him over just in time to creep out a pair of couples who clutch each other and laugh. I keep them moving toward the exit, and as soon as they're gone, I take the walkie-talkie from my pocket and turn it on.

"Wendy, it's Rose, come in."

Static crackles on the line. And then, "I'm here, over."

"I'm on the second level of the haunted house. Someone puked all over the floor," I say, casting a glance to the dead man hanging from the wall as Fionn casts the blanket aside and rises from the bed. "I'll clean it up, but can you shut it down? Over."

"Yeah, the last group just went through for the night anyway. Do you need help? Over."

"No, I'm all good, thanks. It'll take a while, but I can finish here. I've got keys so I can do a final lockup. I'll see you tomorrow. Over and out."

I turn down my walkie-talkie, sliding it into my pocket as I let out a long stream of air through pursed lips. My arms tremble. My heart slams so hard against my sternum that it could break bone. Fionn is standing in the center of the room, unmoving, eerily still. He watches as I pull the jester hat from my head and let it fall to the floor. I must look fucking deranged with my hair in wonky pigtails and my black-and-white makeup probably smeared with sweat and my clown costume streaked and stained. Maybe I am as unhinged as I look. Maybe that's what he's thinking as he looks at me, his expression unreadable. The music and screams stop, plunging us into silence so abrupt and all-consuming it nearly hurts.

271

This has gone too far. This time, there's no coming back. I just don't know how to be anything but what I am. Mayhem.

"I started it," I whisper. But I think we both know that I'm not talking about Matt Cranwell. And for the first time, I feel remorse for what I've done. The choices I make might suit me, but maybe this life is only meant to be lived alone.

A tear breaches my lashes. Another quickly follows.

"I'm sorry," I say.

Fionn breaks his haunted, motionless vigil. He strides toward me.

And the moment his lips touch mine, I know I'll never be the same.

DARK CORNERS

Fionn

This isn't just a kiss.

This is what it feels like to break wide open.

I frame Rose's face with my bloody hands. I devour her with need. She grips the back of my neck and consumes me with equal desire. This kiss is all bite. It's teeth clashing. Moans and whimpers and sweeping tongues. It's urgency and demand. It's an unleashing of desire that we've pushed beneath unraveling rules and conditions for far too long.

I'm drowning in her, swept away in a current I couldn't escape if I wanted to. Her scent. Her taste. The more I take, the more I want. The more she gives, the more I need. I don't know how I ever lived without the feel of her mouth on mine or the vibration of her moan on my lips. Her electric touch hums in my flesh. It's the most alive I've ever felt.

I slide a hand down her face, her makeup smearing beneath my fingertips, deepening the kiss as I push her toward the bed. We both fumble with our clothes, me with the buttons of her costume and her with my belt. When we make it to the bed, I break the kiss just long enough to push the top sheet and mannequin off the edge and onto the floor.

"Anyone could walk in here," Rose says, her tone breathless as I guide her down to the mattress.

"I don't fucking care." I catch a glimpse of her smile before I dive back into the kiss, pulling her baggy pants down and then the leggings and thong beneath. I bite her neck just hard enough to make her gasp. I soothe the nip with a kiss as I run a finger over her pussy, trailing the liquid heat of her arousal over her clit. I swallow her moan, lavish her tongue with mine, consume every sound of pleasure she makes as I swirl my touch over her swollen bundle of nerves. She writhes beneath me. She hums at my touch. She breaks the kiss to frame my face with her hands, her eyes dancing between mine.

"I want you, Fionn." Her tongue sweeps across her lips as her gaze flicks to my mouth. "I *need* you."

The air stills around us. Time seems to slow. She's said words like that before. So have I. But it feels different this time. I raise my hand to her face as I hover over her, sweeping the fringe from her brow. She might have a crazy costume on, a face painted in smears of black and white, but all I see is Rose. Beautiful and bright. Shining through her mask like she was never meant to live behind one. I don't think she ever has. And for the first time, maybe I know what that freedom tastes like.

"I need you too," I say, my heart a molten core in my chest when her eyes flutter closed as my caress trails down her cheek. "I think I always have. I just didn't realize how much until you showed up and changed everything."

Rose's eyes open, inky pools in the dim light. They don't leave mine. She reaches between us and tugs my jeans and briefs down to grasp my length with a firm hand. When I shed my jacket and shirt, she lines me up to her entrance. I watch every subtle change in her expression as I push into her tight heat. Desperation and relief, pleasure and need, hope and secrets. All the things I think we both still want to say but are afraid to put out into the world in case they're too fragile to thrive in the dark. But they're still there, blooming in the night.

When I've slid all the way to the base of my erection, I pause, leaning closer, savoring the sweetness of her scent and the longing in her eyes. No one has ever looked at me the way she does. And I've never wanted anyone like I want Rose. Never admired anyone, never been as enchanted or enthralled by anyone. I've never been as awestruck by anyone, this woman who doesn't just live her life but blazes through it like a comet burning through space, setting fire to the sky. I've never wanted to open up the darkest corners of my soul and show them to anyone like I have to Rose.

I've never loved anyone like I love Rose.

I close the distance between us and seal my lips to hers. I pull out slowly. Push back in. We pick up a rhythm, slow at first, gentle amid the horror and violence that's melted into the backdrop like a distant memory. Rose's fingers trace patterns on my skin, following the ridges of my spine. She hooks a leg across my back and takes my cock deeper. Every gliding stroke is heaven, her heat an embrace that I never want to leave. I break the kiss to press my lips in a line down her neck. Across her collarbone. Down her chest. I pull the cups of her lace bra down and expose her breasts. She gasps when I take her nipple in my mouth and tease it with my tongue. I scrape it with my teeth just hard enough to make her clench tighter around me. Then I soothe the whisper of pain with my tongue.

"I'm not going to last," she breathes as I piston into her, the rhythm more urgent with every thrust. "I want to come with you."

I take her delicate wrist and guide it down between us. Her fingers trace the muscle of my chest and the ridges of my abs until I turn her hand down to her clit. "Then you'd better touch yourself. Because I'm about to fucking fill this perfect pussy."

I seal my mouth to hers and swallow the moan that tumbles free. Rose's touch circles between us. The current builds at the base of my spine. I feel her channel constrict around my erection. Her muscles tighten beneath my hands, one of them folded around her neck, her pulse a hammer against my palm. Her head tilts back but the kiss never breaks. Not as a desperate scream threatens to burst free between us. Not as my balls tighten and I spill into her, pushing as deep as our bodies will allow. Not as the orgasm rolls through me in waves until my heart threatens to break out of my chest, its furious beats deafening in my ears. Not even when Rose's muscles start to relax, her body boneless as my strokes gentle until they still. Even then, the kiss lingers. What was desperate becomes sweet. Soft. A tender, wordless conversation in the dark.

When it finally breaks, I stare into Rose's eyes. Reality starts to creep back in, one piece at a time. The quiet crackle of static on the TV. The scent of the fog machine. The green and blue lights.

The body on the wall.

The things I've done.

Rose. I need to get her out of here.

I pull out slowly, not ready to part, to embrace the dread of the unknown when I've just felt the first moments of clarity that I've been searching for all my life.

"You need to leave," I whisper.

Rose props herself up on her elbows, searching my face. Her skin glistens in the dim light with every breath, and I want nothing more than to feel her warmth again. "What do you mean?"

"I need to call someone to help with this," I say with a nod to the wall behind me as I pull my jeans and briefs up.

"We can do it—"

"We *can't*, Rose. But I know someone who can help."

"I can stay. I want to." A thread of panic weaves its way through her voice when she says, "I don't want to leave you alone here with this."

"Rose," I say, my shoulders falling when she shakes her head. "I can't. I'm the one who did this, and I'm not going to risk you getting caught up in the aftermath."

Tears shine in Rose's eyes as she sits up. "But—"

"*Please*," I say, kneeling in front of her. I take her face in my hands. Her lip wobbles with mounting worry and the effort to hold back tears. She tries to shake her head, but I pin her with a serious and steady stare, one that brooks no argument. "I cannot. Risk. You. *I will not.* Please, Rose. I'm begging you. Just go back to the apartment, and I'll be there as soon as I can."

The moment between us could be eternal. Every shift of her glassy eyes between mine, every breath she takes, every motion of my thumb as I caress her cheek. It all embeds itself into my memory. "Okay," she finally whispers, and I try my best to give her a reassuring smile. I lean closer. Press my lips to hers. And then I let go.

We pull our clothes back into place. Fix the bed. When we're done, Rose moves to the door but hesitates. "Are you okay?" I ask.

"Yeah," she replies. "Are you?"

I smile, though it's faint and probably not very convincing. "I will be."

Rose gives me a nod, her eyes tracking toward Cranwell's body and lingering there before returning to me. "Thank you, Fionn. I . . . I'll see you soon?"

"Yeah. It'll be okay. I promise."

With a final glance that carries the weight of fear and worry behind her eyes, Rose turns away and leaves.

It's not until I'm sure she's gone that I make a phone call I never thought I would make.

And then I wait, standing in the center of the room like I'm one of the mannequins, an unmoving statue among the mayhem and madness. It could be five minutes that passes. It could be an hour. I replay every moment of the night on a loop until the sound of approaching footsteps breaks me away.

"Well, well, well," a voice says from the darkness. I've only heard him a handful of times, but I'd recognize the devil any-where. "Out of everyone, yours is the call I least expected, but the one I most hoped for."

Leander Mayes steps into the light.

I stand straighter. "Thank you for coming."

"You Kane boys are so different, and yet, so much the same," Leander says as he saunters closer. He's completely at ease in the midst of chaos, much like he was the first time we met. I'd looked up to see him enter the room as I stitched Rowan's split lip. Lachlan still had his belt gripped tight around our father's neck, even though his final heartbeat had long since passed. And Leander grinned then, much in the way he grins now. "You've always looked out for one another. Always had each other's backs. I'm assuming that's why I'm standing here right now and not Lachlan or Rowan, isn't that right?"

"I thought you might be more . . . efficient," I say, though that's only a half-truth.

Leander's gaze pans around us and his smile stretches. When his eyes snag on the mannequins hung up on the wall, Matt Cranwell's closest to the corner of the room, he laughs. "Oh dear. You've been having some fun."

"Not exactly." My words feel like a lie.

He makes his way toward the body, slowing his steps as he passes by. He raises his hand, a photo pinched between his fingers. In the picture, Matt and I stare into each other's eyes. Me with a lethal glare. Matt with shock and fear painted across his face. At the bottom of the image is the knife in my hand, lodged deep into Cranwell's belly. "A souvenir," Leander says, and slides it into the interior pocket of his jacket as he gives me a wink.

I watch as Leander saunters toward Cranwell. He stops within reach and tilts his head as though he's contemplating a work of art. And suddenly, I feel like the beast I've been desperate to unleash has just found itself in a whole new cage.

"Very precise," Leander says, motioning toward Cranwell. "Surgical, even. Made a bit of a mess though." He leans closer to the body, inspecting the blood-soaked shirt and the torn flesh. He prods the wound with a gloved finger and Matt's bowels and intestines tumble out of the slit, pink ropes that glisten in the dim light and drop to Leander's feet, his shoes covered with waterproof booties. "Intestines make me hungry every time I see them, even despite the smell. Reminds me of sausages. Does this place have hot dogs?"

When I don't immediately answer, Leander turns just enough to look at me over his shoulder.

"Yes. But the food stalls are all closed."

"Shame. I'd really like a hot dog." Our gazes remain pinned to each other for a long moment, and then Leander turns his attention back to the body on the wall. When he removes the burlap sack from Matt's head, he barks a delighted laugh before leaning in close to examine the dead man's face. "Wow. Impressive. That must have been a hard blow," he says as he flicks the bulging eye. He pokes a finger into the other orbit where the glass eye once was. "I'm going to assume there was a prosthetic as well, yes? Where is it?"

My skin turns to fire. When Leander turns and raises his brows in a question, there's nothing I can give for an answer.

"Don't recall where you hit him so hard his eyes popped out?" Leander says. I shake my head, and the corners of his lips curl. "Pity. No matter. I can have a scent dog brought in. We'll find it."

He whistles and two unfamiliar men enter the room wearing hooded coveralls and carrying toolboxes and bags of supplies. "So, what did he do to deserve this fantastical and very fitting end, anyway?"

I think of Rose. Her face. Her *fear.* I think of the incandescent rage that consumed every cell in my body. The relief and

280

excitement when the blade pierced Cranwell's abdomen. The feeling of his flesh splitting open and the terror in his scream. "He started it."

Leander huffs, clearly pleased with my answer. "And you finished it." He pats Cranwell's pockets down until he finds his mobile phone. "I'll make sure this is all taken care of."

"I appreciate your help," I say, and he gives me a single nod in reply. "How much do I owe you?"

Leander pins me with an unblinking, unnerving stare that latches on and doesn't let go. His expression is blank, emotionless. And then, a burst of laughter. It's a sudden transformation that brightens his cheeks and crinkles the corners of his eyes. It would look normal if it wasn't for the predatory way he watches me.

"I don't want your money," he says. My heart falls to the floor, ready to be removed with the rest of the blood and gore spilled across the planks beneath my feet. And Leander Mayes sees it. He *loves* it. "I just want a little bit of your time. Your . . . expertise."

I glance over at one of the men as he fills a spray bottle with a solution in a silver container. He meets my eyes only briefly before his attention flicks to Leander and then shifts to the floor. "What do you mean?" I ask when I refocus on Leander, whose smile remains undimmed.

"What I mean is, I need your *skills*." Leander pulls a plastic bag from the interior pocket of his jacket and slips the phone into it. He walks toward where the two men have started working and picks up a spray bottle. He mists the liquid over the floor, and patches start to glow with an eerie blue luminescence. There are smears and streaks. Boot prints in blood. One set of prints is mine. One must be Cranwell's. But there's a much smaller set that glows with the damning light of luminol.

Rose.

Leander chuckles. "Looks like you had a little partner in crime." My hands fold into fists, a motion that catches Leander's attention immediately. He grins. Even despite the body hanging from the wall, and the knowledge that I've just brutally killed a man, Leander Mayes is not afraid of me. He turns his back to me and sets the spray bottle down next to the supplies. "Did you ever tell your brothers what you did?"

I don't want to answer, but when Leander faces me, it's impossible not to say something. "Do you mean tipping off your cousins about the money my father owed them?"

His smile stretches. "That too. But I was more referring to how you stabbed your father in the back and severed his spinal cord. Lachlan might have taken credit for that kill by strangling Callum Kane, but even he didn't know that you're the one who brought the bastard down, does he?" He studies me with that predatory glee still lingering in his eyes. "Quite a nifty little trick, isn't it? If you aim *just right*," Leander says with a sudden jabbing motion toward Cranwell's body, his fist closed around a phantom weapon, "there's hardly any blood at all. He must have felt nothing from the waist down. Just a quick *snap* and down he went so your brother could finish the job. Even I didn't realize at first. Not until I cleaned up that mess and stripped Callum of his clothes."

For as many times as Lachlan has called Leander the devil, I've not really understood why. But now I do. In just a few short minutes, he's got me trapped in a corner by my secrets and deeds and desires, unable to escape.

"What is it that you want, Leander?"

"I'm so happy you asked." He wanders back to the cooling body and leans toward it, inspecting Cranwell's slack expression. "I have a contract coming up. It's kind of a big deal, if I do say so myself. I've hired the best of the best. Cream of the crop, if you will. But even then," he says, his gaze drifting back to me over his shoulder, "I expect some casualties. Bodies that need repair on the battlefield, you know? And I need my people to be in tip-top shape for the duration of the contract."

I say nothing.

Leander turns back to Cranwell, but not before I catch a glimpse of his grin. "Some of my team might need a bit of . . . rejuvenation . . . when the work is done. Anonymity is paramount in certain circles, if you catch my drift."

I hold my palms up in a placating gesture, even though we both know they're smeared with crimson stains. "I'm not a cosmetic surgeon."

"You're a smart, motivated man," Leander says. "I'm confident you'll learn."

My gaze slices toward the two men cleaning up after my mess. They don't look up. They don't cast judgment my way. They just do their jobs, spraying and wiping and spraying again as though this is all perfectly normal. And as much as I'm still reluctant to admit it, I can't deny there's something comforting about this clandestine world where any transgression can be cleaned away. For a price.

"So you want me to play doctor. For how long?"

Leander shrugs. "Ideally? Forever."

"No."

Leander turns, his grin menacing. "The way I see it, 'no' is not really an option, Dr. Kane."

He's right, of course. I know it. And there's no sense in arguing with a man like Leander Mayes. I can only hope to negotiate. "How long is this contract?" I ask.

"Seven months. Approximately . . ."

"I'll do this contract for you," I say, every word clear and careful and confident despite the intimidating darkness that settles across Leander's face. "And after that, we'll discuss something that works for us both."

"Works for us both?" he repeats.

I shrug as though I'm unbothered, though my heart is pounding in my ears and my throat tries to close around my words. "You want to be sure you're completely satisfied with the service I provide . . . right?"

We both know I could kill his team, kill *him*, and they wouldn't even see it coming. And even though I just issued an unspoken threat, something about the gleam in Leander's eyes tells me he likes it.

"Excellent," he says with a startling clap of his hands. "We leave for Croatia tomorrow."

"*Croatia?* But—"

"Oh, did I not say this position required some travel?" Leander's lips peel back to reveal his shining veneers. "Oops, my bad. But don't worry, Dr. Kane. You'll be provided with all the equipment you could possibly need. And a nice bit of cash too. I'll double what you're making now."

I pause, reeling. "But my clinic . . . the hospital—"

"My team will take care of all that, don't worry."

"My house—"

"That too. It'll be well looked after until you're ready to sell."

"You expect me to just . . . leave? But I have a life there."

"Do you, though? Sure, some people in Hartford will have questions. And it's my job to make sure the answers are ready. But do you really think they'll wonder why the reclusive Dr. Kane suddenly decided to take to the road after years spent as little more than a ghost among them?"

My heart stutters like it's taken an arrow to its chambers. I open my mouth, but no words come out. Not even a breath of air.

"Oh, and one more thing." Leander straightens. He faces me. The silence is as heavy as the scent of blood and death in the room. "This isn't the kind of job where you want strays to follow you home. And you can't have anyone from home trying to find you either. It's for safety's sake, you understand? So you can't tell Rowan and you especially can't tell Lachlan. The last thing I need is for him to have another reason to be irritated with me. I've given him enough already lately."

I know my brothers, and so does he. If they felt that I was in danger, they would travel to the ends of the earth to find me. "Okay," is all I can manage.

Leander's smile is that of a man who knows he's won. He takes a slow step toward me. Another. And another. He claps me on the shoulder and lets his hand linger there as though his touch is reassuring. His gaze pans across the floor before meeting mine once more. His smile might be a touch pitying when he says, "And you can't tell Miss Evans. You wouldn't want to put Rose of all people in danger, would you? Especially not when I'll be trying to look after her best interests. The Sparrow is not the easiest person to keep out of trouble, after all."

With a final pat on my shoulder, Leander walks away, leaving me feeling as though my heart has just been torn from my chest and incinerated before my very eyes. I'm still staring at the floor, blinking away a sting that won't subside, when Leander knocks on the wooden frame of the door.

"I'm famished," Leander says from the threshold. "I'd really love a hot dog. How about you?"

I blink and blink, but that pain just won't leave. And neither will Leander. Not until I follow him down the stairs as he makes a call to bring in a search dog to find Matthew Cranwell's prosthetic eye. Not as we open the door to the cool October night. It clings on as we find one of the closed food stalls on the silent fairgrounds and Leander breaks in with a snap gun.

I make Leander Mayes a hot dog.

And when he's finally done, his point proven about how thoroughly he now controls my life, he arranges for a private car to drive me to Rose's apartment.

Familiar Boston streets pass by the window. And I feel like a ghost in this city. Because my life is in the hands of the devil.

And my heart has burned to ash.

UNTETHERED

Rose

I shower, scrubbing the makeup from my skin until it aches.

I throw on a robe and stare at myself in the mirror.

I wear a path across the floor of the apartment, to the end of the hallway and back again. The clock on the wall mocks me, time dragging on and on but never going anywhere.

It's one in the morning when Fionn finally walks through the door, and the moment I see him, my heart hits every bone on its way to the floor.

"Hi," I say.

The look he gives me is haunted.

I take a step closer, but he stiffens. The space between us is no more than ten feet, but it suddenly feels miles wide. "Are you okay?"

His voice is low and quiet when he says, "Everything is taken care of."

I've never seen him like this. Shut down. Consumed by something I already know can't be fixed. I can almost see the wall

287

around him. An impenetrable blockade. And it's meant for only one purpose—to keep me out.

I swallow. "Thank you. But that wasn't my question." My blood is surging so loudly I can hear it, a pulsating hum in my head. Dread is climbing though every cell in my body. "Are *you* okay?"

"I have to leave. Tomorrow."

"Why?"

"I can't tell you."

"Why not?"

Fionn doesn't answer this time. He just shakes his head, his eyes still pinned on me, all the light within them gone. My throat threatens to close around a painful knot. My nose stings. But I will the sudden tears away. Maybe he can see the struggle in my face, because Fionn's gaze finally shifts from mine and he heads toward the kitchen. I trail after him.

"What happened?" I ask, stopping on the other side of the island. Fionn takes a glass from one of the shelves and the bottle of Weller's Special Reserve bourbon I got specifically for his visit because I know it's his favorite. He cracks the lid and pours himself half a glass, knocking it back in a single hit. "Fionn? What happened?"

"I fixed it. Like I said I would."

"I would have helped you. I still can, if you'll let me."

"Help?" he says, holding me in a stare I wish I could break away from. It slices through flesh and bone, not stopping until it hits my heart. "'Help' is what got us here in the first place."

I shake my head. "I don't understand. What do you mean?"

Fionn sighs, pouring another glass of bourbon, draining it as fast as it fills. "I took it too far."

His gaze falls to my leg, where the scar cuts a jagged line down the side of my calf. A memory smacks me in the face. One of Fionn, a halo of light behind him. I was lying on the floor of his exam room. His beautiful eyes were full of concern. I recall the faint sound of his voice pulling me from darkness, imploring me to wake up. I remember now. *Help*, I'd said before I fell back into a dreamless sleep.

I started it. I started it all.

My hand raises to my heart as though it could ever stop it from incinerating. It aches beneath my bones. "What happened?" I whisper.

"I can't tell you, Rose. Please stop asking."

I refuse to balk at his sharp tone. Shoulders back. Spine straight. I deserve *some* answers. "Are the police involved?"

"No. They're not."

The relief I feel is fleeting, too brief to be captured for more than an unsteady heartbeat. "Then why do you have to go?"

"Because I have to. Because look at what we've done together." Fionn gestures toward the windows behind me and the city beyond the panes of glass. "I *killed* someone. And there are consequences for that. We can't avoid them this time. I can't. We have to stop this."

Everything he leaves unsaid hangs in the air.

The tears blur my vision. I try my hardest to blink them away. It's so difficult under his cold, remote stare. "Is this the conversation you wanted to have with me earlier?"

"No. But it's the one we should have had."

We stand unmoving, watching each other. If there's any pain or regret in Fionn, I don't see it. It's just a clinical detachment. A decision made, ready to be executed with the precision of a blade.

Don't you fucking cry, Rose Evans. Not this time.

I force a weak smile that disappears as fast as it comes. "Yeah. You're probably right. I, um . . ." My voice cracks and I clear my throat. Even the threat of an impending breakdown doesn't sway Fionn. He just watches, that hard and unforgiving expression still etched on his face. "I should probably skip town too. Take the mayhem back to the circus, you know? I'll catch up with Silveria. Time to get back on the road."

I take a step backward. Then another. "For what it's worth, Fionn," I say, and I think I see the tiniest of cracks in his facade before his brow smooths, "I'm very sorry. I'll miss you. So much. But I understand."

I don't wait to see what his reaction might be. I don't think there's anything I'd want to see in it anyway.

I stride away, my head lowered, the tears falling freely as soon as my back is turned. When I get to my bedroom, I lean against the door, sliding to the floor. My chest feels like it's splitting open. Like I'm crumbling apart. Blowing away like ash in the wind.

And I cry.

I don't stop until long after Fionn goes to his own room. His footfalls slow as they pass my door. But he doesn't stop. Doesn't knock or say anything through the wood that separates us. He just continues walking and with a quiet *tick*, he closes his door. It seals us in silence. An apartment that suddenly feels like a tomb.

"I have to get out of here," I whisper to myself, just to hear something other than the oppressive quiet that surrounds me.

When I rise, I pull my phone from the pocket of my robe and text José.

Hi José. Sorry to text so late. I
changed my mind about staying
in Boston. I'd like to come home.
Can I meet up with you tomorrow
and get Dorothy back?

I'm both surprised and relieved when the three dots immediately start flickering with his impending reply.

Of course. We'll be arriving at Fan Pier
about 1PM. See you tomorrow.

And then, a moment later,

Love you, pequeño gorrión.

A fresh wave of tears wells in my eyes. On one hand, I'm grateful for the love. I'm craving the comfort of familiar sights and sounds. I want to be wrapped in José's hug. I miss Baz's laugh. I need to fly through the cage with the twins. But on the other hand, I'm already mourning something I wanted but never had. I was just starting to take steps in a new direction. I don't want to go backward now. But there's no other choice.

I go through the motions of my nighttime routine and fall into an exhausted sleep that feels like a haze of static gray.

When I wake the next morning, it's just after seven. My first thoughts are of the pain of the night before. Memories of the hard edge in Fionn's eyes. I remember how high my heart had soared when he pressed his lips to mine, only to come crashing down a few short hours later.

Hand on my throbbing forehead, I trudge to the en suite and take a shower. I stand in the scalding spray, staring blankly at the white tiles. I'm not even sure how long I'm there before I tear myself away. I'm wrapped in my towel and still dripping wet when I check my phone on the bathroom counter. There's a text from Lark, a reminder about our plans to meet for coffee later this morning. I groan and press the edge of the phone to my forehead. I'm not really in the mood to meet up with anyone right now, but I can't just cut and run, not from one of the girls. I thought I'd have all this time to build the foundations of these new friendships into something solid. Something permanent with roots in the ground. I think Sloane and Lark expected it too. It wouldn't be right to just leave without telling at least one of them why I'm cutting out.

I reply with my confirmation, pack up my toiletries, and head to the dresser. I'm just pulling on my hunting blade and clothes when I hear Fionn speaking to someone on the phone in his room across the hall. I can't make out the words, only the low tones of his voice. My spine goes rigid. I didn't think about what it would be like to actually have to face him this morning. I don't think I can handle scratching at a wound that's still so raw.

I make out the clipped sound of Fionn's goodbye. And then, a moment later, I hear the shower turn on.

Five minutes. Ten tops.

I can make it out before he even realizes I'm gone.

I'm a tornado in the room, tossing open drawers to gather my clothes by the armful and shove them into my new backpack. My few framed photographs on the dresser are next. My washbag. Fuck the shampoo and conditioner and my worn-out razor. I'll get new ones. Fuck the beer in the fridge too, dammit. Dirty clothes from the laundry basket in the closet go on top. A little ass-backward, but I'm running against time. In less than five minutes, I'm creeping out of my room, shutting the door behind me just as Fionn's shower turns off. I throw on my jacket and boots and purse, set the apartment keys on the island, and, with a final glance around the place I've called home for the last month, I leave.

When I step outside, I tighten the straps on my backpack and start heading south, bringing up my map to guide the way to Lark's favorite coffee shop, Trident Café, which will take me a solid thirty minutes on foot. But I keep a good pace. I fend off the chill of the October air through my damp hair. I try to think about all the things I want to say to Lark, and all the things I don't.

I enter the shop not long before she's set to arrive. I order a coffee and claim a round table where Lark will be able to spot me as soon as she walks in. I'm taking the first sip of the blessed black liquid when my phone buzzes with a text. Fionn's contact photo appears on my screen.

Did you leave?

I press my eyes closed. A deep breath does nothing to calm the surge in my pulse. Normally, I'd make some quip about his credentials. I'd have a joke ready or a teasing jab. But today, my response is just a single word.

Yes.

293

The dots of Fionn's reply are immediate.

| Permanently?

I roll my eyes.

> Yes. I left my keys on the island.
> I'll make sure Lachlan knows he
> can grab them.

| You also left your tarot deck.

"What the *fuck*," I say out loud, the legs of my chair grating against the tile floor as I stand. I pat down my jacket pockets. I dig through my purse. I'm starting to tear through my backpack when I remember. It was in the leather pouch on my nightstand. I can picture it clearly. "Fuck. Fucking *fuck*."

I'm dragging a hand through my hair when my phone buzzes with another text.

| I can bring it to you.

> I'm having coffee with Lark. Then
> I'm going to meet up with Silveria
> at 1PM at Fan Pier.

| I have to be at the airport by then. But
| it's on the way. I can give you your deck
| back and drop you off at Fan Pier if

| you're okay to be there a little early.

I sigh, cursing myself. I'm not thrilled at the prospect of seeing Fionn after I made so much effort to get the fuck out of there. But I cannot and *will not* leave Gran's deck behind.

I'm deliberating, still weighing my options when a flash of blond hair catches my attention out the window. Lark strides toward the entrance of the café, her eyes meeting mine through the glass. Her smile ignites and she waves.

| Okay. Trident Café.

| I'll pick you up at 11:30.

Other than a thumbs-up to his message, I don't reply, setting my phone down on the table to embrace Lark when she sweeps in like a storm of sunshine and glitter, her wide smile a balm to my busted-up soul. Even surrounded by her warmth, a cold chasm seems to take up space in my chest. I know deep down that she would never walk away from our friendship on purpose. But I also know how much harder it will be to see each other after today. Lachlan is Fionn's *brother*. As much as I've come to love Lark and Sloane, I know it will be hard to stay close when doing so will only keep feeding the pain that's already consuming me. My heart makes its bruises known with every beat. It begs me not to take another blow.

"You look stunning, as always," I say as we part and take our seats across from each other.

"So do you," she says, though I see a flicker of worry as her brows knit together. A server interrupts her thoughts and Lark orders a latte, and I use that brief moment to try to put on a more convincing mask. It doesn't work, of course. Because Lark is like a fucking laser beam that cuts right through bullshit. "Everything okay? You don't seem like yourself."

I wave her off, but it only deepens the concern in her eyes. "I'm just . . ."

Lark's head tilts.

"I'm not . . . things aren't . . ."

Lark's hand darts out and encircles my wrist. The sudden kindness has tears threatening to well in my eyes. "Rose . . . ?"

"I'm going to join Silveria again." I force a smile, trying my best to infuse it with brightness. "I just need to hit the road again, I think."

Her head tilts in the opposite direction, just like her dog, Bentley, whenever I ask him if he wants bacon. "But I thought you were liking it here . . . ? Did Rowan not talk to you about working at 3 in Coach? I know he was going to. If it's work-related, I can just—"

"It's not work-related," I say. "I left the keys on the island in the apartment. Thank you so much for letting me use the place and I'm sorry for not clearing it out like I should've."

"Is this about Fionn?" she asks. I bite down on my lip to keep it from quivering. Lark squeezes my wrist and I shrug, shifting my gaze to the far end of the café. She sighs a long, sympathetic breath of frustration. "I'm so sorry. Do you want to talk about it?"

"No," I reply, shaking my head. "But thank you. Maybe another day." I lay my hand over hers and this time, when I meet her eyes, my smile is a little less forced. "I want to hear all about *you*. I want to hear about married life to that adorable asshat Lachlan."

For a long moment, Lark says nothing. I know what she's thinking. She wants so badly to offer support, but she doesn't want to force it on me. And I love her for that.

With a final squeeze of my wrist, Lark lets go and sits back to regard me as the server brings the latte to the table. When he leaves, she refocuses her attention on me.

"He's good. Really good. Things are . . ."

"Good?"

She grins. "They're *great*, actually. He's kind of amazing. It might be a while before my parents and sister warm up to him completely, but my auntie Ethel adores him. Even Bentley seems to like him."

"They do share a similar level of grump."

Lark lets out a breath of a laugh. "They do. Bonded by asshattery."

"You're all crafty and stuff," I say. "You should make an Etsy shop. Sell fancy handmade hats. Call it the Asshattery. 'Hats for asses.'"

"Oh my *God*. That's an amazing idea." Lark's eyes are so bright that sparks could tumble from them and I wouldn't be surprised. She's absolutely buzzing. "Lachlan might not love the idea," she says, a sudden frown flashing across her face to be swept away again just a blink later, "but you've totally got my creative juices flowing."

I snort. "I know about your juices." I toast her with my coffee cup, waggling my brows as I lower my voice to a whisper and say, "Your *murder* juices."

"*What?*" she hisses as she leans across the table, gripping its edge, her eyes darting around us before landing on me and narrowing. "How did you know about that? Did Lachlan tell you? I'm going to stab that Budget Batman in his neoprene balls."

"I . . . don't know about the neoprene balls part," I say, my face scrunching before I shake it off. "But it was a lucky guess. A stab in the dark, if you will."

Lark's mouth drops open, her cheeks flushed. "How? How the fuck did you know that?"

I hold up a hand and tick fingers off as I list my points. "Best friends with Sloane, who killed that jerkoff who kicked her in the face. You're buddies with Rowan, her equally murdery husband. Lachlan gives off hot tatted assassin vibes. You like crafts, I assume that probably has something to do with it. Simple deduction." Lark's mouth is still hanging ajar when I reach across the table and pat her arm. "Don't worry. In case you haven't noticed, I'm pretty cool with it. Which might be part of my . . . current problems."

My gaze drops to my half-full cup, but I still feel the weight of Lark's attention on my face. "Oh. *Ohhh.*" Lark sits back in her chair, her body relaxing in my peripheral vision. "And Fionn is *not* so cool with it."

"Yeah," I say, turning my spoon over on the saucer, watching my warped reflection on the silver surface. "Being on the road . . . being the way I am . . . It's hard to find someone. Even harder when you're not afraid of the dark. I thought maybe I did find someone, this time."

When I meet her eyes, the smile we share is bittersweet. "You did. You've got me, always. You've got Sloane. We're not afraid of the dark. And we're not going anywhere."

This moment is the first one where I've felt any real relief since everything spiraled out of control last night. I know with the way Lark looks not just at me, but right *into* me, that she means it.

Conversation gets a little easier after that. The weight in my chest eases. We talk about Sloane and Rowan and their mini honeymoon to Martha's Vineyard. We make plans to meet up at the circus while Silveria is in town for the next few days if we can get our schedules to line up. She texts Sloane to make sure she'll be able to come to my show. One last chance to say goodbye. We order another couple coffees, a croissant each. We talk about her married life, how their stars are finally aligning. We laugh and smile. And time ticks down to the last moment. I feel its hammer in every heartbeat.

"I'm going to miss you," Lark says, reaching across the table to take my hand.

"I'm going to miss you too," I reply. I smile, but it's fragile. Ready to break. "You know what they say about the circus."

"What, that the show must go on?"

"No. That the show can't begin until you jump."

Lark's expression seems to clear. She watches me, her eyes fixed to mine, a soft smile forming at the corners of her lips. My phone buzzes on the table and my heart skips over itself. A rush of nerves roils in my guts as I read the short message. Just two simple words. *Parked outside.*

"Doc's here." I pocket my phone. "Guess I'll see you around. Don't be a stranger." With a few final goodbyes and a crushing hug, I pull away and place a kiss on Lark's cheek and leave the coffee shop, swallowing down the tears that climb the back of my throat.

Fionn is parked at the curb, waiting in his rental vehicle. He pops the trunk as I draw close and I toss my backpack inside next to his. I remember the first time I rode anywhere with him. The way he slid his arm around my waist. The strength with which he lifted me inside his truck.

Anything I should know before we do this? he'd asked before we drove away.

Maybe if I'd just said something then, my chest wouldn't ache so much now. I wouldn't be hesitating as I shut the lid of the trunk, slowing my steps as I walk closer to the front of the car. Though I hate the thought of making life harder for Fionn, I think the pain I feel now was worth it. It hurts because it was real. It's how I know the truth. The only one that matters.

I'm in love with Fionn Kane.

And it's too late to ever tell him.

"Hey," I say as I slide onto the passenger seat.

I can feel Fionn watching me as I pull the seat belt across my body and clip it in. When we still haven't pulled away from the curb, I return his gaze.

"Hi," he finally says.

He turns away to check for traffic, but I still catch a glimpse of his face. There are shadows beneath his bloodshot eyes. A hollowness to his features, one that might not be noticeable to most people, but I've seen him from every angle, in every light, from far away and so close his features become hazy. I can see the evidence of a sleepless night.

I look out at the coffee shop, taking one final glance at Lark before we pull into traffic and drive away.

"Thanks for taking me back to Silveria," I say, checking my text messages. There's one from José confirming that they're nearing the city. It'll be one of the last shows of the season before we make our way home.

"Here." Fionn extends the leather pouch toward me and I blow out a long breath between pursed lips. I take the deck out just to feel the comforting finish of the worn cardstock between my fingertips.

"I appreciate it. Thank you." I imagine what he must have been thinking as he entered my room and realized I was already gone. Maybe it was a bit of relief, at first. He had the place to himself. Maybe dread sunk in as he spotted the deck on my nightstand. It's impossible to divine his thoughts from his stoic expression. He just gives me a single nod.

The traffic is backed up. We inch our way along. A playlist drones through the speakers at a quiet volume. I'm not sure if it's better to have music or silence between us. There's a fresh wave of tension in the air as Fionn looks at his watch and taps the steering wheel with impatient fingers.

"I can take an Uber to the pier," I say, looking out at the river of red brake lights in front of us. I don't think we've made it more than a few blocks in the last forty minutes since we pulled away from the coffee shop. "Maybe you can find an alternative route."

"It's fine," he says, glancing in his rearview mirror.

I open my mouth to argue when a call comes through on the car's dashboard screen. Lachlan's name appears and Fionn accepts the call.

"Hey, Lach—"

"Where's Rose?" Lachlan barks, panic infusing every note. "Is she with Lark?"

Fionn and I exchange a confused glance. "I'm here," I say. "Lark went back to your place a while ago."

"Shit. *Shit.*"

"What's going on?"

"She's missing. Something's wrong. I can't explain right now. I need to get home."

"We're not far," Fionn says.

"I'll meet you there."

"*Fuck*," Fionn hisses as Lachlan hangs up. His gaze darts around the wall of traffic that surrounds us. It feels like there's not enough air in the car. Like we're spinning through space, though we're not moving at all. Panic curls around us and squeezes. If we don't find her *now*, we won't find her alive. I don't know how I know it. But I do.

I lean closer to the passenger window. "There," I say, pointing to a side street ahead and to the right. The turn is blocked by the cars ahead, all of us stuck. "The sidewalk," I say, and Fionn is already moving, wrenching the steering wheel far to the right. He narrowly avoids the bumper of the car in front and jumps the curb to take the side road, cars around us honking.

"Was anything at all unusual? Did she say or do anything out of character?"

"No," I say, swiping a tear from my lash line before it can fall. "She was happy."

Fionn's expression is grim as we speed down the block so we can backtrack. "Did you notice anyone out of place in the coffee shop?"

"No. There was nothing unusual at all." Fionn glances in my direction as we near the next turn. "What if we can't find her, Fionn? What if—"

"We'll find her," he says as we take the corner far too fast, nearly colliding head-on with a car taking up too much space on a narrow residential street. Fionn brakes so hard we both lurch forward. The tarot cards tumble across my lap and into the footwell. We're going to collide. On instinct, Fionn's arm flies out in front of me, bracing across my chest.

We screech to a stop inches from the other car's bumper. A loud horn blares from the other vehicle, but it's as though Fionn can't hear it. All his attention is on me.

"Are you okay?" he asks, his arm still resting across my body.

I nod, the motion shaky.

"Are you sure?"

"Yes."

He tears his haunted eyes from mine, then brings his arm over my head to rest it on the back of my seat as he looks out the rear window and reverses, giving the other car enough room to pass. When he rights himself, he throws the rental into drive, stamps his foot onto the accelerator, and flies down the street. With one hand braced on the handle of the door, I take my phone from my pocket with the other, calling Sloane. She picks up on the second ring, her relaxed greeting destroyed by my tone as soon as I ask her where she is. It crushes me to tell her Lark is missing. She cries out on the other end of the phone. I hear the moment her heart splits in half. Rowan takes the phone from her.

"We're on our way home. We'll be there as soon as we can," he says, his voice grave. Then the line goes dead.

It takes less than ten minutes for us to arrive at Lark and Lachlan's building, a former textile factory in a quiet neighborhood. We're just getting out of the car as another vehicle growls down the empty street. It's Lachlan's vintage Charger, racing toward us, squealing to a stop just behind us. We jog toward the car and he opens his door as he tries his phone, panic written across his face. The call rings unanswered on the other end before connecting to Lark's voicemail.

"We called Rowan, but he and Sloane are in Martha's Vineyard for the weekend. They're on their way home but it's gonna take a while," I say as he pulls a gun from the glove box. "What's going on? Where the fuck is Lark?"

"I don't know," he says as he leads the way toward the entrance of their building. "She called me to say her aunt died. She was supposed to meet me at the nursing home, but she never showed. Conor just found information about the man who's been targeting her family. And now Lark won't respond to any of my calls."

Fionn and I exchange a weighted glance as we follow Lachlan into the building and up the metal staircase, Lachlan spitting venom about someone being in his shop as we take the stairs by twos. When we get to the door of their apartment above the textile floor, Lachlan hesitates, one hand paused around the handle, the gun clutched in the other. His eyes are every shade of desperation as he nods to us in a wordless request to stay back. And then he twists the handle and opens the door.

His knees buckle and Fionn catches his older brother. My hand is shaking when I cover my mouth.

The floor is coated in blood.

Lachlan stumbles into the room. He calls out for Lark, a heart-breaking, hopeless plea. But instead of her voice, there's a desolate whine. We rush after Lachlan to find Bentley lying on the floor, the dog panting heavily, blood staining the patches of white fur on his side. His dark eyes are pleading as he looks up at us.

"Save that fucking dog," Lachlan says to Fionn as he strides to the kitchen to gather tea towels from a drawer.

"I'm not a vet—"

"*I don't fucking care, save that goddamn dog.*"

Lachlan rushes in the direction of the hallway, calling out to Lark without receiving an answer. "I'll help you," I say, heading to the side table where I know Lark keeps some of her sewing supplies. I gather a needle and thread and scissors and bring them to Fionn. My hands tremble as I take over the job of holding towels to the deep puncture wound on Bentley's side so Fionn can prepare for sutures. "Good boy," I whisper, stroking his bearlike head as he gives me a mournful whine. For what feels like the countless time today, I swallow a swell of tears. "What did he mean, someone 'targeting her family'?" I ask as I lock eyes with Fionn.

"I don't know. It's the first I've heard of it," he replies. "She never said anything to you?"

"Nothing at all." I search his eyes, but Fionn's expression is grim. There's so much blood on the floor. A streak of it leads to the door, as though someone was dragged. I keep asking myself the same question, over and over. *What if we don't find her in time?*

Lachlan enters the room and we break our silent exchange. "I'll do what I can to stop the bleeding now and get him to the vet," Fionn says as Lachlan passes him a set of clippers. Fionn

305

doesn't delay, turning them on to shave Bentley's thick fur and reveal the extent of the damage. "Do you have any idea where Lark could be?"

"No," Lachlan says as his gaze pans around the room. It seems to snag on something lying next to a broken lamp on the floor. When he strides away, I follow, watching as he picks up a phone from the floor. He looks at the screen. And a heartbeat later, a bereft, soul-shattering scream fills the room. Lachlan breaks apart right before my eyes. He tosses the phone on the couch and buries his head in his hands as though he could crush the anguish right out of his skull.

We're losing time.

Bentley whines behind me as I wrap a hand around Lachlan's arm and squeeze. He looks down, tears shining at his lash line. "Think. There's got to be *something*. Something weird. Something out of place."

Lachlan takes a deep breath. Presses his eyes closed. The crease between his brows deepens before it suddenly smooths. His gaze snaps to mine. "Across the street. He was *across the fucking street*."

Lachlan pivots on his heel and strides toward the door. I don't even think about it. I'm not yet sure what conclusions Lachlan has drawn. Or who we're after. Or how dangerous they might be. But I know Lark is out there somewhere. And Lachlan is on to something, a trail that starts across the street. So I just follow. I make my declaration. I'm going to go too.

"Rose, don't," Fionn says. His voice breaks on those two words and it stops me as though I've hit a wall. "*Please.*"

Time grinds to a halt. I turn. The sight of him grips what's left of my heart. He's so beautiful. So broken, kneeling on the floor with his palm on Bentley's side, his hands covered in blood. My pulse surges. Any doubt that's left behind is washed away by the current humming in my veins. "Lark is my girl," I say. "I'm going to get her back."

"But—"

"I love you, Fionn Kane."

The panic on his face is wiped clean, replaced with shock. It's as though he can't make my words fit into any reality that lies before us. His lips part, but nothing comes out. And I realize, I don't need him to say anything at all. I know how I feel. And it's still enough magic to be real, even on its own.

I take a step backward, and I give him a smile that fades as quickly as it appears. "Save the dog or this asshat will kill you," I say.

And then I turn away.

I don't look at Lachlan as I pass him, reaching behind my back to pull the hunting blade from its sheath.

I don't know what trials I'm about to face. But I do know one thing as I feel the weight of this last secret lift from my soul.

The show can't start until you jump.

BATTLEGROUNDS

Fionn

My brother stares at me, his face a study in pain.

I feel like I'm struggling to break the surface and take a breath. I'm still drowning in Rose's declaration. *I love you, Fionn Kane,* her voice echoes in my mind. Her words didn't just slip into the world. They crashed into me. They swept clean the sediment of the other life that's been crumbling in my grip from the first moment we met. It was like a break between two realities. The man I've been trying to be. The one I am. The one who is hopelessly in love with Rose Evans. The one who would do anything for her, even tear out his heart.

Lachlan watches me like he's expecting something. Like despite how much pain he must be feeling, he still has room in his heart to feel pity. Maybe disappointment.

I swallow. "Keep her safe," I say, my voice threatening to close around the words.

"I will. I promise." With one decisive nod, Lachlan turns away and jogs after Rose.

I turn my attention back to Bentley, wiping my eyes with my blood-spattered sleeve. "Okay, my guy. Please don't bite my hand off," I say as I press my knee to his neck in case he tries to thrash. "You're not going to like this."

I find the source of the bleed and start a vascular ligation figure-eight suture. It's messy. With a sewing needle and a pair of scissors and a very unhappy, unsedated dog, I've got my work cut out for me. But I manage to get the nicked artery closed off in a few moments that feel hours long. As soon as the stitch is pulled tight, I toss the needle on the floor and heave the dog into my arms, heading through the open door.

"You need to stop eating so much bacon. You must weigh a hundred and fifty pounds." Bentley's responding grumble becomes a whine as I jostle him on our way down the stairs. It's a sound that catches in my chest like a barb every single time I hear it. "And *that's* the reason I never entertained vet school. I'm sorry, buddy."

We're nearing the bottom of the stairs when I hear Lachlan's voice outside, followed by Rose's clipped reply. I was so busy patching up the bleed in Bentley's side that I didn't consider the possibility that Rose would still be within reach. And now that's the only thing that matters. To reach her in time.

I hurry my steps. I need to see her face. She told me she loves me. And I was so shocked not just by her words, but by everything they unlocked, that I made the worst mistake of my life.

I didn't say it back.

"Rose," I call out, just as two car doors close in quick succession. "*Rose.*"

The engine of the Charger roars to life.

"*Wait*," I beg, even though I already know they'll never hear me. I crash through the door with the dog in my arms just as they peel away from the building in a speeding mass of black metal. I watch as the car roars to the end of the street and drifts around the corner, the tires squealing. In a flash of light on polished chrome, they're gone.

"Fuck," I hiss, and the dog whines again as though agreeing with me.

I manage to open the door of the rental and get the dog into the back seat, and then I run to the driver's side. I have no fucking idea where the nearest emergency vet is. I'm searching for one on my phone when a text comes in from Rose.

> Montague Muffins, INC, 2008 Woodland
> Road, Portsmouth.

> I'll be there as soon as I can.

She doesn't respond.

I find a vet a few blocks away and speed there. Bentley is still panting, whining every few minutes. After I get to the clinic and park at the curb, the dog mounts a grumbling protest at the indignity of being carried, but he doesn't have enough fight in him to argue. I burst through the doors, and by a sheer luck, it's his regular veterinary office. They whisk him from my grasp as I relay what little information I have in rapid fire. I give them my credit card and phone number, and then I'm back in my vehicle in under ten minutes.

As soon as I'm sitting in the driver's seat, I press my forehead to the steering wheel and close my eyes. *What the fuck am I doing?* Rose was *right there*, saying the words I've wanted to say to her, offering her heart to me like she couldn't bear to keep it when she should be protecting every broken shard. And after everything that happened yesterday and the sleepless night that followed, I hesitated, too shocked to process what was happening or how monumental it was. It's as though I've spent years looking at a broken puzzle, and with one final piece, everything suddenly fit together.

Everything makes sense because of Rose.

I open my eyes and look to my right. Her tarot cards are scattered across the passenger seat and footwell. I hastily gather them up. All but three are facedown. Of the face-up cards, one is a knight, riding into battle with a sword held high. The other is three longswords facing downward, with a fourth lying beneath the tomb of a knight, the Roman numeral IV in the top left corner. The last is a reaper, a scythe gripped in his skeletal hand. I flip them over as I place them back into the deck and rest them on the seat. I'm just about to look for the leather pouch when my phone buzzes in my free hand. It's not Rose, like I hoped it would be. It's Leander.

| You are not at the airport, Dr. Kane.

I don't reply, selecting Rose's message instead so I can copy the address into my map before I pull into traffic.

I know I can't get away from Leander Mayes. Not forever. But I need to get to Rose. So I race through traffic. I cut people off.

Swerve from one lane to the next. I jump the curb. Weave into the oncoming lane. Sweat mists my brow. The beat of my heart dampens the sound of horns as other drivers tell me off. But I don't fucking care who I piss off or smash up. I will plow through this whole fucking city if that's what it takes. I need to fix this. I need to tell her everything I should have in a moment that slipped through my fingers. Hell is going to have to wait.

In a chaos of squealing tires and adrenaline, I finally make it out of the city and onto I-95, heading north to Portsmouth. I've just passed Danvers when my phone rings.

Leander's name appears on the dashboard screen.

Fuck.

I ignore him. But ignoring Leander is pointless. As soon as it goes to voicemail, he's hanging up and calling again. And again. *And again.*

On his sixth attempt, I finally accept the call.

"I do not like being ignored," he says.

"I gathered," I grit out in reply.

"Where the fuck are you? The flight boards in fifteen minutes, and you'd better be on it."

"It's not going to happen."

"Dr. Kane—"

"It's Lark. She was attacked in her apartment and now she's missing. Lachlan has gone to find her, and I'm following."

There's a pause. For a moment, the line goes so quiet I wonder if I've lost him. "Where," he says, not a question, but a demand.

"Portsmouth. I've just passed Exit 78A."

"I'll call you back. And you *will* pick up."

The line goes dead.

Ten minutes later, my phone rings again, and I accept it right away. "I've rebooked your flight. You'll leave at nine tonight. You *will* keep me posted on your location and I'll have my driver pick you up and bring you to the airport. Unless you want Rose's extracurricular activities handed over to the FBI on a fucking silver platter, you *will not* be late, do you understand?"

"Yes."

"Good." There's another pause, and though I expect Leander to hang up, he doesn't. His voice is softer when he says, "As soon as you know the status of Lark, let me know."

"Leander," I say.

"What."

"Conor knows something about this. You'd better get to work."

Leander hangs up for the final time.

It's another twenty minutes before I'm finally pulling off the interstate and racing down Woodland Road in Portsmouth. I careen around the corner of a long drive next to a Montague Muffins sign and lurch to a stop in front of the industrial bakery facility, where Lachlan's car is parked off to the side of the empty lot. The only other vehicles are a fleet of several delivery vans lined up near a loading dock. I'm about to get out of the car when I glance down at the passenger seat.

The tarot cards have been jostled from the stack I made earlier. Three are now faceup, though I don't know how that could be possible. The first is the knight, riding into battle with his sword drawn. The last is the Four of Swords. I pick up the one in the middle. Death. His polished scythe sweeps above his skeletal head.

A chill races through the backs of my arms. It crawls up my spine. I try to reason this away. Coincidence. Physics. The fallacy of memory. But I *know* something is wrong.

I toss the card aside and run to the building.

The main door is unlocked, the foyer dark. I rush past unlit offices, glancing through their open doors for any sign of Rose, calling her name as I go. I get to the end of the corridor and push open the heavy steel door to the factory floor with enough force to send it crashing against the stopper, the sound echoing across the high ceiling and metal trusses.

"Rose," I call out as I scan the factory. I pass machinery, polished silver tables. The smell of baked muffins lingers in the air as though it's soaked into the concrete walls. "*Rose.*"

"She's here," Lark says from around a corner, her voice coming from the other side of the wide room, the far side lined with industrial batch ovens. Relief is a flood. They found Lark. She sounds okay. But as quickly as that relief comes, it's washed away. "Oh my God—"

"*Christ Jesus.* Fionn, help—"

I round the corner in time to see Lachlan crash to his knees at Rose's side, Lark following to crouch beside him, her blond hair matted with blood. My heart stops. Rose is lying on the cold concrete. Lachlan takes her head, lifting it from the floor. It lolls in his grasp, as though she doesn't have the strength to hold it steady on her own. Her eyes lock to mine for just a moment. The light in them seems to dim, and then it goes out.

I close the distance between us.

"What happened?" I ask as I drop to her side. I glance toward the body of a man lying a short distance away, his eyes lifeless, a gunshot wound leaking blood and brain from the center of his forehead. I refocus on Rose as I press my fingers to her carotid artery. Her pulse is racing. Her skin is cool, covered in a thin film of sweat. I've seen her like this before. "Where is she injured?"

Lachlan shakes his head. "I don't know—"

"Was she shot?"

"No, I don't—"

"You *promised* me," I snarl, methodically checking Rose for the source of her injury. There's no blood on her head or neck. "You fucking *promised* me you'd look after her."

"I'm sorry—"

"Rose, wake up. Come on."

"Fionn," Lark says, and when I turn in her direction, there are tears in her eyes. She holds up a tool, something long and silver with a sharp, straight edge. The metal is coated in fresh blood.

"*Fuck.*" I tear open the buttons of Rose's plaid shirt and then I see it, the hole in the right side of her tank top, the torn edges stained crimson. I pull her shirt up. There's not much external blood but the wound is deep, angled upward into her abdomen, skirting just below her last rib. He's hit her liver. And it's bleeding into her abdominal cavity. "Call the fucking ambulance."

Lark dials 911. I pull my shirt over my head and press it to the wound as hard as I can, scanning the room. "There," I say, pointing to a Uline first aid kit fixed to the wall. "First aid kit. Bring it."

Lachlan runs to grab the kit while Lark speaks to the dispatcher, taking the woman through the key details, the address and phone number and the nature of the emergency. She puts dispatch on speaker as I motion her over. "My name is Dr. Fionn Kane," I say as I get Lark to kneel down so we can elevate Rose's legs on her lap.

"The patient is female, age twenty-seven, unconscious, breathing is rapid and shallow, heart rate elevated. Stab wound to the upper right abdomen, possible liver damage. Internal bleeding."

"The person or persons who stabbed—"

"Dead," I say. "No other injured parties."

I run through more details about the scene and circumstances and Rose's condition as Lachlan returns with the first aid kit, opening it to withdraw the gauze pads for the wound and a rescue blanket. I pack the wound and apply pressure. It's all I can do, and I feel so fucking helpless.

Lachlan's eyes meet mine. Regret and distress stare back at me. *Call Leander*, I mouth as the dispatcher tells us the ambulance and police are on their way. He nods once, and though I know he doesn't want to leave my side, his gaze still tracks to Lark. I know he's worried about what will happen next. About keeping her safe when police show up to ask questions. A heartbeat later, he rises and strides a few feet away to speak to his boss in low and quiet tones.

"What can I do?" Lark asks.

Fucking pray. Pray to some deity I don't believe in. Rewind time. I would give anything to take Rose's place, if that's what it took to save her. "Take the phone and wait for the ambulance."

"Okay," she says, her voice a tight whisper as she rises.

"Lark?" I meet Lark's eyes, the crystalline blue surrounded by the shine of tears. Blood is caked in her hair and streaked across her face and neck. "Tell them to run. We don't have much time."

She swallows and nods, and then she runs, talking to dispatch as she disappears around the corner.

When she's gone, Lachlan returns to kneel by Rose's feet, raising her legs on his own. "I'm sorry, Fionn."

"I don't fucking care," I snap, kicking the first aid kit. The metal scrapes across the floor. We've already used all the gauze. The blanket. I was able to fix a fucking dog, but I don't have the means to help the woman I love. All I can do is hold on and hope. I stare down at her pale face, so beautiful and serene, her thick lashes unmoving as I increase the pressure on a wound that must have burned with pain until the moment she slipped into unconsciousness. Tears flood my vision. "I can't fix her with that," I whisper.

I can feel the weight of my brother's gaze on my face, but I don't look up when he braces a hand on my shoulder. My first tears fall on Rose's skin, settling on her chest where shallow breaths rise and fall in a rapid beat.

"Why didn't I tell her?" I ask. "I love her. Why didn't I say it?"

Lachlan squeezes my shoulder. I press my eyes shut and drop my head to my chest. "You're right that it's my fault, brother. For more than just what happened to Rose. It always has been. All the way back to that night with Dad. Maybe even before that."

"You're wrong." I swallow. Confessions that have waited for so long in the dark finally work their way to my lips, ready to spill into the world. "It was me. I'm the one who killed him."

I glance his way only long enough to catch his confusion out of the corner of my eye. "What do you mean?"

"I ratted him out to the Mayes family. That night he came back home, when the fight started, I couldn't let him win. You and Rowan were on the floor, both of you too much in shock to notice. You didn't see. But it was me. I stabbed him in the back."

I hang my head and stare at Rose. Maybe everything would have been different if I'd been honest all along. Honest with her about how I felt. Honest with my brothers for what I'd done. Honest with myself. "I'm the one who killed him."

"You didn't." Lachlan leans closer. His breath fans across my face. "Maybe you brought him down, but trust me, brother. I'm the one who killed him. I felt his last breaths in my hands. And I have no regrets about that. *None*." I can feel the weight of his attention on my face, but I still can't meet his eyes. "Why didn't you tell me before now?"

"You're my older brother. I couldn't bear to disappoint you."

When I finally look at Lachlan, there are tears in his eyes too. There's so much regret in the way he holds my gaze and looks into me. "I put so many expectations on you, and when that life you thought we wanted didn't fit the neat little boxes you'd made, you started pushing everyone away. You've been running. From me. Rowan. Now Rose. You've been running from any love for so long you didn't know when to stop. And that's my fault."

"What if I'm too late?"

Lachlan doesn't ask the thousand things that could mean. He just leans closer. "I know you better than anyone. You're going to get her into that ambulance. And you are going to save her, no matter what it takes." He wraps his hand around the back of his neck and presses his forehead to mine. "She's still fighting. So you keep fighting."

When he pulls away, I face Rose with renewed determination. He's right. I will do whatever it takes to save her.

The minutes that pass crawl through time. I talk to Rose. I tell her to hold on. *Keep fighting. Wake up, just look at me.* She's in a battle she's losing. Her abdomen is swollen. The last hints of color slowly drain from her face. The pink of her lips lightens. I press the gauze to her wound as hard as I can as I lean down to kiss her cheek, her skin cold and pale.

Lark bursts into the room with two paramedics and three police officers on her heels, the gurney wheels squeaking on the concrete floor. I give them the information I have. I lift Rose onto the stretcher, her limbs limp across my arms. The paramedics strap her down and lift the frame, locking it into place, and then we run. I hold her hand. I don't let go. Not as we lift the stretcher into the ambulance. Not as I climb into the back with her. I look back out the doors and my brother and Lark are there, flanked by officers.

Lachlan gives me a nod, his lips pressed into a tight line. I don't miss the way Lark squeezes his hand. "Fight, brother," he says. And then the doors close.

I turn my attention to the paramedic in the back as the other runs to the driver's side. Sirens roar to life. "I'm Dr. Kane," I say. The paramedic, a dark-haired young woman, looks back at me with determination. "What's your name?"

"Jessica," she says.

"This is Rose. And I fucking love her. I will not lose her. So here's what we're going to do." Oxygen. Heart rate. Blood pressure. I remove the gauze as Jessica sets up an IV with tranexamic acid. I repack the wound with fresh hemostatic dressing. The ambulance speeds through the countryside as we work together against time. And Rose is barely clinging on. Her body temperature drops. Jessica pulls blankets from the portable warmer and lays them over Rose as I take hold of her hand. "Come on, Rose. Fight it out."

And she does. Wherever she's gone within herself, she keeps fighting. For every breath. Every heartbeat. As we pull into the hospital and the ambulance slows to a halt, I know that making it this far was just one battle. The war is ahead. It's in the surgical room. But I don't know if she has enough strength left in her to endure.

The ambulance doors are thrown open. I run alongside the stretcher as Rose is wheeled through into the ER. I give the doctors on call every scrap of information I can. It's only moments before she's whisked away into surgery. Her hand is pulled from mine and all I can do is watch as she disappears behind the double doors and into the heart of the hospital.

I'm standing in the middle of the ER, still watching the doors as though she might get up and walk back through them. The sounds and smells of the ward start to creep into my senses. The beep of monitors. The scent of industrial cleaners. The voices of patients and nurses and doctors. But all I see is the absence of Rose.

My phone buzzes in my pocket. I finally break free of my stasis and look at the screen to see a text from Leander.

> Just a friendly reminder. Whether your girlfriend lives or dies, we have a non-negotiable deal. My driver will be at the main entrance of the hospital at 6PM sharp to take you back to Boston for your flight.

I blow out a deep breath and look toward the door for a long moment before I type out my reply.

320

> I'll be there.

I pocket my phone. I look one more time at those doors. And then I turn away.

I will do whatever it takes to save her.

OUT OF TIME

Fionn

"Hard to say goodbye, isn't it?" a voice says, and I inhale a sharp breath as I turn toward the door. I fumble to hide a tissue but there's no fooling the sharp, cutting gaze of Sloane Sutherland. Or, more accurately, Sloane Kane. Her eyes shift between me and the backpack next to my chair. "Heading out soon?"

"Yeah," I say. And then I turn back to Rose to watch the rhythmic rise and fall of her chest as she sleeps. "In a minute."

I don't watch as Sloane enters the room. I just want to absorb every moment with Rose that I can. There isn't a detail I've not tried to carve into my memory, from the swirling waves in her hair to the precise angle of her nose to the gentle curve of her dark lashes. I wonder how much she'll change when I'm gone. How much I'll miss. I'll think about her every day. The absence of her will be my first conscious thought in the mornings. My memories of her will be the last thing I think about when I fall asleep. I'll hear her voice in my dreams. Her teasing laugh. Her broken cry.

How do I know?

Because all those things are already true.

And the only thing that will keep me going through this torture is knowing that my absence will keep her safe.

I swallow as Sloane takes a seat across from me. "Where's Rowan?"

"Going back to our car with Conor to see if the guy who took Lark really did put explosives in our vehicle like he claimed when Lachlan found him. Didn't really want to leave it there, just in case."

"Lachlan and Lark?"

"They just finished up at the police station. They'll be on their way here soon. Leander's people managed to sweep through Abe's apartment to remove anything we wouldn't want the cops to know. So thank you, Fionn. I know you gave Leander a head start at cleaning up this whole mess," she says. I nod, blowing out a long breath. "Your brothers . . . do they know you're leaving?"

"No."

"Where are you going?"

I shake my head. "I can't tell you. I'm sorry."

"Why not?"

"Sloane, I can't," I say, brooking no argument. I pin her with eyes I know are bloodshot and framed with dark circles. "Please don't ask. I won't tell you."

Her expression gives nothing away as she nods once. I'm not sure what she's looking for when she searches my face. Maybe a hint of an answer. Maybe the secrets that live beneath my skin. I know she's good at carving them from souls, just like I'm good at keeping them.

With a quiet sigh, she shifts her gaze to Rose, lifting a delicate hand to sweep the fringe from her brow. Rose doesn't stir. "Is she okay?"

"I think so." I place a kiss on Rose's knuckles, her hand warmed between both of mine. "Infection is a risk. It's going to take a while for her to recover. But there doesn't seem to be any brain ischemia, thank God. She just needs time."

Sloane nods in my periphery. "I'm sorry you won't be here for it, Fionn," she whispers, and the burn in the back of my throat nearly chokes me.

"Me too," I manage.

"You got her past the hardest part."

"Did I?" We lock eyes across the gentle rise and fall of Rose's chest. Sloane is so stoic, or at least she is when Rowan or Lark aren't around. But I see the wisp of sadness in her eyes that she can't hide beneath her lethal mask.

"I don't know," she says, and we break the moment between us to look at Rose. "Maybe. Maybe not."

God, I fucking hope so. I just want her to be happy. To be safe. To thrive. To know she's so fucking loved, even from a distance.

"You saved Bentley," Sloane says, snapping me out of my thoughts of what the days and weeks and months ahead will be like. When I meet her eyes, she offers a faint smile. "Lark is so grateful."

I nod. "He didn't really appreciate it, the cheeky fucker."

"Yeah. He's a bit of a curmudgeon. Probably why he and my cat, Winston, seem to get along. Rose told me about Barbara. We could have made it a trio."

I try to force a smile, but it doesn't take. All I can think of is

Rose, with that fucking raccoon clutched in one hand, her grin diabolical. She laughed so freely when Barbara was gripped to my face under that towel. *Christ*, what I wouldn't give to relive that moment right now so I could hear her again. There are so many moments that filter through my mind. Rose's teasing smile at Sandra's, the black yarn balled in her lap. Her guileless eyes as she sat on the edge of the bathtub with her injured leg on mine. The love that I could feel in her touch when she traced the lines of my face in the shadows of the haunted house. What if I never see or feel or hear those things again?

Sloane rises, breaking me away from questions that consume me. "We'll make sure she's okay. One of us will be here when she wakes up. I'll give you some time to say goodbye. But I won't go far."

I trust Sloane to keep her word, not for my benefit, but for Rose's. That only makes me trust her that much more. "Thank you. I appreciate it."

She doesn't react as I turn my attention back to Rose. But she lingers. I can feel her sharp eyes watching, but for what, I'm not sure. "If you'd told me where you're going, I wouldn't be giving you this," Sloane says as she passes me a folded piece of paper. My brows draw tight as I take it with a tentative hand. I open it under her watchful gaze.

Sloane Kane, Data Science Department
Clinical Development Operations
Viamax
Radnička cesta 81/18, 10000,
Zagreb, Croatia

"If you want to send her anything, send it to that address in my name. It's the local office for my employer, Viamax. The internal post will make sure I get it. And I'll ensure it gets to Rose with the appropriate level of secrecy. I promise."

I swallow, my eyes darting between Sloane and the paper in my hands. "How did you know?"

"Lark. She called Leander. Managed to get it out of him." She shrugs when the unvoiced question still lingers in my eyes. "The promise of undrugged muffins sealed the deal. She had to swear on her life she wouldn't tell Lachlan or Rowan."

"But—"

Sloane waves my concern off. "She won't. She knows as much as Leander does that the boys would chase you down and fuck shit up and probably make everything ten times worse than it already will be. Like I said, she's grateful for what you did for Bentley."

A shard of hope seems to pierce right between my ribs, stealing my breath. Hope can be beautiful. But it can also be brutal. It can keep your head above water just long enough to drown you in the next wave. I'm scared of what will happen if I hold on to it. But I'm never going to let it go, no matter what tsunami I have to swim through.

I fold the paper and slip it into the interior pocket of my jacket before I take Rose's hand. "What if she doesn't want this anymore?"

"I don't know, Fionn. Some broken hearts can't be sewn back together." Sloane's gaze drops from mine, landing on Rose and lingering there. "But maybe that's why you have to leave yours here for her." She doesn't look my way when she turns and heads toward the corridor. I watch her walk away, Rose's hand still clutched in mine, the address like a pulse in my pocket, a beacon I can cling to. When Sloane reaches the door, she pauses, resting her hand on the frame.

"Rowan and Lachlan say you're the best of them. What that means to your brothers might be different than what it means to you," Sloane says as she looks at me over her shoulder, her hazel eyes bright with a challenge. "So prove it to the only person who counts."

I give her a resolute nod. Sloane gives me one in return. And then she disappears down the corridor.

My phone buzzes with a message in my pocket. Probably a reminder from Leander. Or the driver. I glance up at the clock on the wall. Five minutes is all we have left. I turn all my attention back to Rose. "Rose," I say, stroking her hair off her forehead. "Wake up."

Nothing changes in her. Not the pulse that flows in a slow, steady rhythm beneath the fingers I keep wrapped around her wrist.

The unanswered message buzzes a second time. How two minutes have passed already, I just don't know.

"Sparrow," I whisper, hoping the alias will jar something in her subconscious. But there's still no change in the cadence of her inhalations, no flutter in her eyes. I squeeze her hand. I hold it to my lips. But I know how much blood she's lost and the power of the medication coursing through her veins. And as much as I want her to wake up so I can have one last moment, I can't help but think that it might be a mercy for her that she's unconscious. What's the point in waking up just to say goodbye again?

My eyes drift to the clock, no matter how hard I will them not to. Two more minutes left. And just like when we wheeled her into this hospital, every second counts.

I press my free hand to her chest, right over her heart. The steady rhythm is imprinted in my flesh, carved all the way to the bone. "Our time is up, Rose," I say. A tear breaches my lashes and slides down my cheek. "This can't be some 'no strings attached, friends-with-benefits' situation anymore. That's over now."

My final hope is that she'll be so angered by my words that she will wake up, but that snuffs out when she doesn't even stir. The shots fired over the bow of my ship just land in still water. There's no volley. No fight to meet me in the fog. She might not be able to see it, but I give her a smile, because even in the dark and silent solitude of unconsciousness, she still sees right through me.

"It's over because I love you, Rose. I'm sorry I spent so much time and effort trying not to. It was only because I didn't think it was safe for you. I don't think I knew how to fit into your wide-open world. But from the very first glance, from the first word, I was caught in your gravity. I wanted to be near you. And I couldn't bear the thought of hurting you. But, lately, that's the only thing in our cards, it seems."

I shift my gaze to the tarot deck resting on her side table. The Lovers card is flipped over and waiting for her.

One minute left.

I know the driver will probably come to find me if I'm late. And I don't want Leander Mayes or any of his people anywhere near my Rose.

It's a slash across my heart when I rise from my chair. Another when I lay her hand across her waist. I fear the wound may never heal when I lean down to press a kiss to her lips. Her exhalation warms my skin. I breathe her in, the sweetness of her cinnamon scent marred by the clinical room that surrounds us. She was never meant for a place like this, and yet she keeps coming back to it.

I sweep the hair from her face and try to imprint the image of her into my mind. Then I take a card from the interior pocket of my jacket, glancing over my words, hoping I said enough and not too much.

Dear Rose,

The sparrow is such a simple bird. I always wondered why you chose it, or why it was chosen for you. Because you're the most exciting, outrageous, intimidating, incredible person I know.

Breaking your heart was undoubtedly the worst thing I've ever done. Leaving is the only right thing to do, even though it's the hardest. I can't tell you where I'm going or what I'm doing, or when I'll be back. And I know that's unfair to you. It might be enough damage done that you can never forgive me, and I understand if that's true.

So I will love you enough for the both of us. I don't expect anything in return. I'm so sorry I can't be with you right now. I promise I'll be back to tell you I love you in person. I should have told you so many times. Like when we walked home from Sandra's, and you asked me things no one has ever taken the time to know. Or when I came into the hotel room in Boston and you were standing by the window. I forgot how to even form the words to tell you how stunning you were. Or the time you fell asleep on my chest. I stayed awake so long just to feel your breath on my skin and imagine a life I know now that I could have had, if I had just let my fears go. I've loved you all that time, Rose Evans. And I won't be stopping. Not ever.

Look out for yourself. Don't cause too much mayhem, if you can help it.

Love,

Fionn

I look up to the clock. I'm out of time.

I leave the card on the side table. I trace the smooth skin of her cheek. And then I lift my hand away.

With one final look at Rose, I turn and leave.

SCRIPT

Rose

I'm sitting in my RV, visualizing every detail of the show to come. The exact turns I need to take. The pitch and whine of the engine. The smell of exhaust. It's my first performance since I got out of the hospital and came home to Texas. The first off-season show of the year. And it's the first time I haven't felt the swell of excitement for the metal cage that's been my home for the last decade.

Usually, I'm buzzing to perform. The first shows after a few weeks off are always my favorite, because they're the closest it will ever feel to that fateful day when I rode the Globe of Death for the very first time. I was only sixteen. I remember my hand trembling as I firmed my grip on the handle of my dirt bike and crept forward until I entered the metal cage. I'd been working for the circus for a year by that point, doing all the jobs I could possibly volunteer myself for, no matter how shitty they were or how long they took. I begged José for that chance in the cage. There wasn't anything to prove I could do it, no credentials other than I knew how to ride a motorcycle. I had nothing to go on but guts. I didn't

331

actually know if I'd be able to pull that throttle back with enough precision to spin through the globe until I was either upside down without losing control completely or chickening out and falling flat on my face. I just had *belief*. And as soon as I tried it and experienced the rush of adrenaline, there was no turning back. I chased that high every time I got on my bike and faced the globe. Being in the cage felt like freedom.

But now?

Now, it feels like I'm trying to squeeze myself into a life that doesn't fit me anymore. It's as though I've taken the two halves of my cast and put them back together and taped them on. Even though I could run and jump and swim and kick, I'm not doing any of those things. I'm just limping along, coping with a broken heart by encasing it in a familiar routine.

I take a deep breath. My hand presses over the scar on my side. Sometimes, I'm sure I can still feel the burn of pain beneath my skin. Maybe it's a phantom ache, one I imagine so I don't let myself forget that everything that happened was real.

Not that my girls would let me forget about them, at least.

> LARK: Good luck tonight, Boss Hostler!
> Thinking of you! You'll rock it.

> SLOANE: I'd say break a leg . . . but
> please don't.

> LARK: We don't want anything getting in
> the way of your mad dancing skills!

A photo comes in from Sloane next. The girls are standing on either side of a cardboard cutout of me, a photo they took at Sloane's wedding where I was pissed drunk at the little pub after the ceremony, dancing with an inflatable dinosaur as Rowan sang "The Rocky Road to Dublin." I'm not sure whose sunglasses I was wearing, but I liked them, so I kept them.

> That T-Rex was the real MVP.

> Miss you bally broads. See you in August!

I know that subtle reminder is not what they want to hear. August is still eight months away, and they were bummed that I didn't make it for Christmas. I just didn't think I could bear it, being around two other couples, especially not the brothers of the man I love who just . . . disappeared. Especially not when those brothers have questions that I simply can't answer, because I don't know why he left or where he went. Sloane and Lark told me what happened that day in Portsmouth at the bakery after I passed out, of course. The blood. The tears. The hospital. The things he said that I didn't hear when I was unconscious, clinging to life. How I was saved by his hands.

I slide my phone into the interior pocket of my jacket and then grab my helmet and get ready to leave.

When I pull my door open, Baz is standing there, his fist poised and ready to knock.

"Hello, young sir," I say with a theatrical bow. "What are you up to?"

Baz shrugs, then holds a white envelope up for me to take. "This came for you."

"A letter?" I ask. My gaze pans the circus grounds as though the mystery might unravel itself. I pin my attention back to Baz, my eyes narrowing as I take the envelope. "How?"

"Don't ask me, I don't know. I just work here." Baz winks and then he turns and starts jogging away. I don't know if he's being honest or spinning a lie—the older he gets, the harder it is to tell. I open my mouth to yell after him, but he disappears between two motor homes before I manage to get out anything more than "but."

I sigh and turn the letter over. My eyes immediately fill with tears.

I take it to the little folding table and sit down, reading and rereading the handwritten text.

To: Mayhem
Dorothy, Silveria Circus
Texas

In the upper left corner:

Secret Admirer
Nowhere without you

There's a stamp in the upper right-hand corner, one from Croatia, but there's no mark on it from a post office. It takes me a minute to just sit back down at the table and stare at the text. I run my finger over every line of script. I didn't see his handwriting much when I stayed at his place. But there is only one person it could belong to.

I tear back one slide of the flap and run a finger beneath the top edge of the envelope, careful not to damage the stamp or handwriting as I rip it open. Inside is a letter folded around something. When I take it out, a tarot card falls onto the table.

The Five of Cups.

I unfold the letter, carefully placing it next to the lone card.

Dear Mayhem,

You know more about tarot than I ever will. So bear with me. I might make some mistakes. Lord knows, I've made plenty already.

I want to start with the Five of Cups—not to look into the future, but to talk about the past and present, and the regret and sorrow the card symbolizes. I'm so sorry for the way I hurt you. You deserved more from me from day one, and I didn't think I was a good enough person to give it to you. And when I finally felt like I could be that man, I was forced to let you go. It was the last thing I wanted to do. But it was the only way to keep you safe.

The grief and loneliness represented by this card haunt me every day. There isn't a moment that goes by when I don't think of you. And maybe you've let us go, maybe you've moved on. Maybe this is the only letter you'll read. I have to accept that possibility might be true. Ultimately, all I want is for you to be happy, no matter what you need to do.

But I am not done fighting for you.

I love you. I'm not letting you go. I never will.

FK

I take a shaky breath, wiping away the tears that trail down my cheeks. Part of me holds on to the anger and loss I still feel at being ghosted, left behind with questions that might never be answered. But another part of me wants to be warmed by the first little bit of light that's seemed absent from the cold darkness of my heart these last few months.

I reread the letter, over and over until Jim knocks at my door to tell me I'm going to be late for the performance. I do my show and then come back to my trailer and read it again until I can recite it from memory. It's on my shelf next to my bed so it's the last thing I see when I fall asleep. When I wake up the next morning, it's the first thing I grab, touching it just to make sure it's real.

The next week, there's another letter. Another tarot card, the Moon. In his letter, Fionn talks about how it symbolizes secrets and deceptions and illusions. He tells me about the things he feared—his own darkness, the secrets that he kept from his brothers. He talks about the secrets he's keeping now too, but only in the loosest of terms. He worries about his brothers and the people he left behind. But it's the last lines of his letter I reread that night until I fall asleep.

The hardest secret I ever kept was the one I kept from you. It was not telling you how much I love you. How much that love has consumed me, even when I tried not to let it. You unraveled the life I'd convinced myself I wanted. I didn't think the man left behind was one I could trust. I thought I was keeping you safe from me by hiding those feelings away. But I was wrong. I'd give anything to go back and break every rule before the day we made them. Because I know now that I loved you even then.

Another week. Another letter. Two tarot cards this time. The next week, another letter, a single card. Week after week, they keep coming, each letter accompanied by at least one card, sometimes two or three. Every letter relates to the meaning of the cards sent with it. Every one ends the same way.

I love you. I'm not letting you go. I never will.

The closer we get to the first of April, the more the anxiety churns in my guts. Because that's when we hit the road and start touring for the season. Maybe my last season, for real this time. Or maybe not, I don't know. Maybe I'm clinging to this life I no longer want because it's safe. It's known. And the last time I dove headfirst into the unknown I ended up with an edge beveler in my belly and my heart torn out of my chest. All I know for sure is that Fionn's letters have been something I've come to depend

337

on, even on those days when I've tried to convince myself not to. I've even started replying, writing pages to fold and put into envelopes with nowhere to send them. I tell my own stories about anger and forgiveness and love and loss. And maybe hope too. It might be a one-sided conversation, but there's a relief in putting those feelings onto paper and sealing them up, even if they're never read.

I get a letter the day we pack up to head out on the road. It comes with the Knight of Wands. He talks about how I must be getting ready to leave soon. He knows the card can signify travel, and he wonders where I might be going. He wants to ask about my favorite places. Says he wishes he were here so we could talk. "If you've kept your fringe, you'd blow the hair from your brow as you think about it. And then your eyes would shimmer when you'd tell me about the best stops on the road." I write back and say I wouldn't need to think about it. My favorite stop is the one where I found myself laid up in Hartford, Nebraska. I wonder about the people I got to know there. Is Nate still fighting in the Blood Brothers barn? What about Sandra and the Suture Sisters, have they all started crocheting sex swings now? And why did we never make them form a cover band and play at a Blood Brothers fight with a name like that? Sandra and the Suture Sisters need crocheted merch. I would buy it. "I miss Hartford," I say in my letter. "I miss you most of all."

I seal that letter and cry myself to sleep that night. And the next morning, we set off for Archer City.

It's not a long drive. Our first trip rarely is, just so we can work out the kinks with new staff and old machines and performances that are getting off the ground after a winter season at home. It will take a few weekends before we truly get into the swing of things. We spend a few extra days setting up and practicing. We run an extra night of shows. The day of teardown, I'm about to peel off my dirty, sweaty clothes and hop into my tiny shower when there's a knock at my door.

"Mail delivery," Baz says when I open the door and he thrusts an envelope at me. My heart flips over. I reach out with a tentative hand, but he whips the letter out of reach before I can touch it. "Are these love letters from the guy who came to visit when that moron tripped on the fence and offed himself?"

"None of your business," I reply. I hang on to the edge of my door and reach for the paper that he flaps just beyond my grasp. I finally manage to yank it from him, but only because I think he lets me.

"I've never seen you get mail on the road before." Baz's teasing smile softens when I look up from the envelope. He's right. Some of the troupe get mail forwarded by third-party services, or they pick it up from friends and relatives scattered along the route. But I've never done that. Never had a reason to. "It's nice. Dude must really like you."

With a little salute, Baz shoves his hands in his pockets and then walks away whistling "La Vie en Rose." A stupid grin must be plastered across my face, but he doesn't look back to see it.

I didn't think another letter would come, but now that I have it in my hands, the relief and excitement almost overwhelm me as they compete for the space in my chest. I sit down at my table and slide the letter opener I bought in February beneath the edge of the flap.

Dear Mayhem,

If I've timed this right, you'll be at your first stop. I hope it went great. I never told you that I went to see you perform in Ely for the first time after your accident. I didn't want to seem like some kind of weirdo stalker. I guess telling you about it a year later in my fourteenth letter that was written in a secret location and sent by phantom postal service is already pretty stalkery. In retrospect, maybe I shouldn't have been so worried that you'd see me in the audience after all.

The Chariot card probably means a lot to you. I bet it comes up frequently in your deck with all the travel you do. It would have come up for me too that time. I got in my car and drove for thirteen hours just to see you ride in that insane metal death cage. I was so fucking worried about you. I know you know what you're doing, but I wanted to be there, just in case. But it went perfectly. You were amazing. You came out of the cage and took your helmet off and held it up to the crowd. You looked so fucking proud. And I was so fucking proud of you too.

Ride safe, Mayhem.

I love you. I'm not letting you go. I never will.

FK

I smile at the Chariot card before placing it with the others in the drawer of my nightstand.

Every week. No matter where I am. No matter how busy. No matter if the show is great or a near disaster, if it's raining or sweltering hot or, one time, even snowing. Every single week, Baz brings me a letter from Fionn.

And then, in the last week of July, it's José who brings it to my door.

"Hi," I say as he stands outside my RV in the evening sun, his hat in his hand. "Would you like to come in?"

"No, *pequeño gorrión*. I just . . . I came to give you this." He extends an envelope to me and I drop down from the last step to take it, watching as he shifts his weight on his feet. I hike my brows in a wordless question, and for a moment he seems to deliberate, torn in a war of emotion. "What are you doing here, Rose?"

"What do you mean?" I let out a puff of a laugh as I scan the fairgrounds, gesturing toward the motor homes and campers parked around me. "I live here."

"No. You don't. You *exist* here."

It's like a punch to the ribs, one that sucks out all my air. "This is my home."

"Yes. But you're not yourself here anymore. You don't seem excited to perform. You haven't even set up your tarot tent since we started the tour."

"If you need me to read tarot, I will," I say, folding my arms across my chest.

"I don't *need* you to. It's just that it used to bring you joy. And others too. You know there was this woman named Lucy at the last stop who found me to ask if you were still doing readings?"

My throat tightens. "Lucy . . . ?"

"Lucy Cranwell. Had three kids with her. She said she saw you in Hartford. That you gave her a reading that changed her life. Her whole *life, pequeño gorrión.* She wanted to say thank you."

"Why didn't you come find me?"

José shrugs, giving me a melancholy smile. "I didn't think you wanted to be found. At least, not by anyone but him," he says with a nod to the letter in my hand.

I drop my arms from my chest. He's right. I haven't opened my tent since we hit the road. I've been scared of how much my need for vigilante justice ended up costing the people I love. How much it cost me. But in my grief, I forgot how much it gave to people who need the kind of help that's not easily asked for. I look down at the envelope in my hand, knowing there will be another tarot card inside. And I can't help but wonder if it's time to become the Sparrow again.

"You're right," José says. "This will *always* be your home. But it doesn't have to be. I got a letter too." When I tilt my head and furrow my brow, José spins his cap in his hands. "Dr. Kane said he was sorry that he didn't take good care of you like I asked him to that day we met in the hospital. And he said he would spend every day for the rest of his life trying to make up for it. He told me not to tell you that part, he wanted to tell you himself."

I smile through a watery film. "You're such a gossip."

"That's part of the reason why I run such a good circus. I'm in everybody's business," José says with a wink. He grins, but his smile slowly turns melancholy. "He wants me to give you time off so he can see you. He loves you, Rose. We will always be here for you, of course we will. But this?" he says, gesturing to the white paper clutched too tightly in my grip, "This could also be your home, if you let it. Maybe it's time to go. I think you want to. Don't you?"

Do I? I don't know. Holding these letters in my hands and reading pretty words that I want so desperately to believe is one thing. Standing in front of the man who shattered my heart is another. It's been nine months since I last saw him. He's probably so different now. Maybe he's not the only one.

Indecision must be written in the tears that cling to my lashes. I catch the shine in José's eyes too before he draws me into an embrace. "Go, Rose. And if you don't come back, I wish you well." I nod. Press my eyes closed. Listen to his heart as we sway in the summer sun. "And take the raccoon with you. She keeps getting into the churro batter. Do you know how many batches I've thrown out?" I laugh, though it's half-hearted. When he pulls away, José frames my face and presses a kiss to my forehead. "I love you like a daughter, *pequeño gorrión*. That will never change."

"I love you too, José."

I give him a melancholy smile, and he gifts me with a flourish of a bow in return. And then he puts his hat on, shoves his hands into his pockets, and ambles away. When he disappears from view, I enter my motor home, my fingers trembling as I grab the letter opener and slide onto the seat.

I unfold the letter and the Star tarot lands on the table.

Dear Mayhem,

I can't be sure you're reading these messages. But this is my favorite card.

When I first bought this deck and thought of you as I shuffled the cards and turned over the first one, the Star is what appeared. I didn't know for sure what that meant at the time, but I felt like it represented hope. Like you were my North Star. And now, the part of the journey where I have to stay an ocean away is finally coming to an end.

If I'm right and all these stars align, you'll be reading this in Ellsworth, Maine.

And if you want to meet me, I'll be waiting every day at Lookout Rock. I'll stay at Covecrest Cottages but I'll wait from dawn to dusk at the lookout for you.

I hope you come, so I can prove to you that every word, every letter, is true.

I love you. I'm not letting you go. I never will.

FK

I set the letter down and pick up the Star card. He drew this card from a deck and thought about me. He hoped these letters would knit some kind of connection between us, but he had nothing to go on but a feeling. And that's the only thing he's had to hold on to all these months.

I look out the window toward the fairgrounds, watching the Ferris wheel spin against the sky.

And I just keep watching, even after the lights go out.

THREE OF SWORDS

Fionn

The sun is setting behind me, scattering orange and pink flashes of light on the ocean waves. The contract with Leander might be finished, at least for now, but the memories of it haunt me like a film over the world. I've been looking at the sea from morning to night for the past five days, and in some ways, I'm not sure how much I've really *seen* it. I've seen wounds I've sewn over the last several months. I've made unexpected friendships, and I've seen the faces of those same people twisted with pain and suffering. I've seen broken bones and gunshots and torn flesh. I've seen death. But I've also seen Rose. No matter how deep the darkness dragged me, memories of Rose have been there to warm the night. I've seen her face as I've watched the sea. I've heard her laugh. I've felt her kiss on my lips, the give of her flesh beneath my hands.

But they've only been memories. And the hope of seeing her again feels like it's drifting out to sea.

I look at my watch and my heart drops, scraping bone on its way to the cold stone beneath my boots. She should have gotten my letter three days ago. I came early, just in case. But Lookout Rock is thirty minutes away from Ellsworth, maybe forty-five if she's driving Dorothy. It's close enough that she could have taken her motorcycle and made it here even faster, if she wanted.

My head drops as I take a deep breath of ocean air and pick up the backpack lying at my feet. With one last look at the sea, I turn. The backpack drops from my hand as my eyes land on a person who could be an apparition.

Rose.

She's so beautiful that the breath flees from my lungs. Her dark hair shifts in the breeze. It's just like the last time I saw her—fringe that skims her brows, waves that caress her jaw. Her mahogany eyes drill right into me, tearing back layers as though she can see every sin I've stacked up around my soul. She's wearing her leather jacket and a low-cut tank top beneath it. Black jeans and motorcycle boots. She looks tough as hell. But it's not just her clothes or the way she stands with her hands buried in the pockets of her jacket. There's a hard edge to her expression. No teasing spark in her gaze, no laugh at the ready. No smile or warmth in her eyes.

I know I did what I had to do to keep her safe. But this is the first time I've really seen how badly I've broken her to do it.

"I'm so . . ." I nearly choke on my words. Take a deep breath. Start again. "I'm so happy you're here. It's good to see you."

I feel like I'm unraveling from the inside out. But Rose? She's unreadable. The woman who has always lived wide open with her emotions on display. "You look different," she says.

I glance down at my clothes, run a hand through my hair. It's still short, but a little longer than the last time we saw each other, a bit less refined. There's more stubble on my face, probably some dark circles beneath my eyes from the sleepless nights I've had worrying that she wouldn't come. I don't know about the rest of me, but she must see something.

"You look the same. Beautiful," I say. I take a single step closer. Rose doesn't move. "I wasn't sure you'd come."

"Me neither," she replies, shifting her gaze away from me toward the sea. For a long moment, she stays silent, her expression hard. "I needed some time to think."

Rose is not the type to sit and stew on things. She's the type to jump in and deal with the consequences later.

"I'm glad you came," I say, and she nods but keeps her eyes from mine. A swallow shifts in her throat. Though her expression doesn't change, I can see how much she's struggling beneath a mask of indifference. I feel like my heart is left behind on the stone, my chest hollow, scraped clean. "I have something for you."

When I reach down for my bag, I dart a glance her way. It's a little bit of a relief to catch her watching with more interest than she wants to admit, judging by the way she stiffens when our eyes connect. My lips twitch with a smile that she doesn't see as I rummage in my bag. When I straighten, I hold an envelope in my hand, but I don't offer it to her. I open it instead.

"The last card of the deck," I say as I withdraw only the card and hold it out for her to take, the envelope and a folded letter clutched in my other hand. There's a question in her furrowed brow, but she takes the card and looks at the image. She knows tarot. She knew this would be the last one left. "The Lovers."

She doesn't say anything, just looks down at the card, letting her hair obscure as much of her face as it can. I unfold the letter.

"Dear Rose," I say. *"It's so good to be able to finally use your name. Because that means I'm home now."*

Rose's nose twitches and she sniffs but still doesn't look up from the card.

"I'm sorry for everything I've put you through. I couldn't tell you where I was or what I was doing because it was just too dangerous. I couldn't bear the thought of someone finding their way to you. Even writing you these notes was a risk. I've never written letters to anyone before, but there were days when it felt like knowing you might be holding the same paper and reading the same words kept me alive."

When I glance up from the letter, she's watching me, a shine in her eyes. My fingers tremble as adrenaline floods my veins, my gaze lingering for a moment on the end of the line of a tattoo that runs the length of my left forearm, one of her heart's rhythms, traced with precision from a photo I took of her EKG as she slept in the hospital.

"The Lovers card represents choices in relationships. And the choices I made nine months ago were the hardest ones I've ever had to make. I had to break your heart to save you. I had to leave to love you. And I want to spend the rest of my life making up for the time we lost. I'm asking you to choose us, Rose Evans. I promise to spend every day doing everything I can to make you happy. There's no one else I'll ever love but you. So no matter what you choose, I'm not letting you go. I never will."

I lower my hand to my side. A tear breaches Rose's dark lashes and slides down her cheek. She's staring down at the card again as though it might tell her the future all on its own. Her lip trembles. I would give anything to touch her. To kiss her. But I'm just not sure if too much damage has been done and too much time has passed.

Rose wipes the tears away, but more follow. "I liked your letters," she whispers. "That one was my favorite."

Hope soars in my chest, so big it chokes me, yet so fragile I think a single breath could break it. "Mine too."

"I . . . I've been . . ." Rose's voice cracks. I take one small step closer, but she shakes her head and clears her throat. "You hurt me."

"I know. I'm so sorry."

"But I know it's my fault too. I was the one who antagonized Matt Cranwell in the first place. None of this would have happened if I hadn't done that."

"No, Rose. I'm glad you did." She meets my eyes, finally, and it feels like a relief when she does. "I never would have met you otherwise. I'd still be stuck trying to live in a box that I was never meant to be in. That's one thing that being away has confirmed— that the idea of the life I thought I wanted was just that. An idea. And despite testing it out for a long time, it never fit. The only time anything started to feel *right* was when you came along."

Though her expression is still troubled, Rose nods. She keeps nodding, as though it's hard to stop, until finally she tilts her head and shrugs. She shuffles on her feet. Ruffles her hair. It takes her a minute to even glance at me, her damp lashes shining in the dim light.

"So, like . . . what does choosing you . . . what does that entail, exactly?"

I can't help the stupid grin that erupts on my face, though I try my best to subdue it. "I think it's whatever you want it to be."

"Well . . . but . . ." She shakes her head and looks out to the sea, a crease notched between her brows. "I like cuddling. We'd have to permanently dissolve that rule."

I take another step closer. She's nearly within reach. My hand aches with the need to touch her, but I stop myself from moving closer. "I like cuddling."

"I like PDA. Holding hands and shit."

"I want to hold your hand."

"Dorothy only has one bed. I'm not unfolding the sleeper sofa. It's a pain in the ass."

"Perfect. I don't want separate beds."

"And you can't keep telling Barbara she has rabies. She doesn't like that."

"You have Barbara?" I ask, and she gives me a faint nod. "I thought she was performing with the poodles."

"There were some . . ." Rose pauses, her gaze lifting to the sky as she considers her words. ". . . *incidents*. With churros. And maybe one or two with the hot dog stand."

I sigh dramatically, but only to test out her reaction. Sure enough, her eyes slice to mine and narrow. "I won't tell her she's rabid," I say, laying a palm across my heart. "I promise."

Rose's arms fold tight across her middle, the card still clutched in one hand. She juts her chin out and blows a puff of air into her fringe. I've imagined that exact quirk so many times over the last few months that it feels like a punch to the chest to see it happen right in front of me. "Dani and Renegade totally deserved to win *Surviving Love*."

I bite down on a laugh. "I don't know if I can cosign that one—" Rose levels me with a sharp glare through a film of tears. "Okay, okay. Dani and Renegade deserved their win, even though his made-up name sucked and his actual name is Brian and I'm also ninety-nine percent sure they cheated on that last challenge with the fish."

"Fair," she says with an eye roll.

We fall into a long silence as she fiddles with the card and weighs her thoughts. Part of me wants to crash into her and wrap her in a crushing embrace. But I can almost hear the war going on behind her eyes. The fear of being hurt a second time can be paralytic. My circumstances might have been different, but I know the power of heartbreak's poison. I know that even if she does choose us, it's going to take time, and maybe a little space to heal. So I don't ask anything more from her. I don't press. I just wait as long as it takes.

"I liked that time we kissed," Rose finally says, and the first hint of doubt creeps into her expression as her gaze finally lands on me and sticks. "We'd have to dissolve that rule permanently too."

"Thank God, because I fucking hate that rule. I'd like to break that one first, if you'd let me."

Her mask comes undone as she nods, every emotion bursting through her broken facade. Tears blur my vision as I rush to close the distance between us. I've imagined this moment a thousand times over the last nine months, even when I tried to stop myself in case it never came true. The feeling of her damp cheeks beneath my palms. The taste of salt and sweetness on her lips. The warmth of her breath on my skin. Her scent, notes of spiced chocolate on the sea air. The reality of actually touching her is so far beyond what I'd truly let myself wish for. So I drown in her. I press my lips to hers and thank every god I can think of when her tongue caresses mine. Everything inside me that felt misplaced is realigned when she wraps her arms around my neck and her body molds to mine, like she was always meant to fit.

"I love you, Rose," I say when we pull apart and I press my forehead to hers. "I'm sorry."

She doesn't have words, only emotion, just a shake of her head. We wrap each other in an embrace. I hold on. And she holds me back. It's starting to get dark by the time we finally let go, with just enough light to see the path that leads back to the inn where fairy lights line a covered porch facing the sea. A storm of nerves circles my guts. All my medical training, and high-pressure situations, and now this time spent working with some seriously fucked-up people employed by Leander—all that cultivated calm seems to fly out the window when Rose looks at me with her dark, shining eyes. It's as though the thought of anything to do with her has me reduced to a pit of anxiety.

I swallow and try not to tense as I point toward the inn just down the cliffs from where we stand. "Did you want to stay with me?"

Rose doesn't answer. My heart folds in on itself.

"It's . . . it's got a nice view of the ocean . . ." She watches me, unmoving. "Umm . . . it has a pretty decent breakfast buffet. And waffles, you love waffles." I grip a hand to the back of my neck when her brows raise like she's expecting more. "It only has one bed though."

Finally, her smile breaks free, as though she'd trapped it just to watch me squirm. "That was the selling point I was waiting for, Doc."

We walk to the inn under the brightening stars, hand in hand. Every step we take makes me feel like I'm living someone else's life. Like I could blink and learn this is all a dream, some delirium that will wear off, and then I'll realize she was never here in the first place. And for a moment, I think it's going to be an even worse fate when we get to the parking lot of the inn, and she looks toward Dorothy to slip her hand free of mine.

"Hold on a minute," Rose says, taking a step back, and then another. "I'll be right back."

I nod. She gives me a flash of an unsure smile and then turns away, walking to the motor home with her hands shoved in her pockets. After a few brief moments inside, she returns with a backpack slung over one shoulder. "Just had to feed Barbara and get some stuff for the night."

"Of course." I hold out a hand and she takes it. Her touch is still hesitant, which seems unlike the Rose Evans I know, but I know it will take time to earn back the trust I tarnished. So I just stay steady, opening the door for her when we get to the inn, leading her to the room on the second floor that faces the sea. When we get inside, she goes to the windows and watches the ocean, sliding the backpack from her shoulder and onto one of the chairs.

"It's a nice view," she says, not turning away from the black waves that melt into the horizon.

"Yeah. It is," I say, watching her. "Do you want something to drink? I've got tea. Bourbon."

"Bourbon would be nice, thanks."

I nod, but she doesn't see, then turn to the small kitchenette to take the only two glasses from the shelf and fill them. I'm pouring the first drink when she speaks, her words turning my veins to crystals of ice.

"*Dear Fionn,*" she says, her voice barely more than a whisper.

I turn around, a slow pivot on my heel. She has a letter in her hands. The edges of it quiver in her grip.

"*I got your letters. I keep opening them. I finally decided I should write back. I've never gotten letters like yours before. And I've never written to anyone. It's almost ironic that they have nowhere to go.*"

Rose's eyes dart to mine, and I can't move. I'm rooted to the floor. "*I had a dream while I was in the hospital. That some broken hearts can't be sewn back together. And I wondered if mine would be like that too. I thought so for a long time. And then your first letter came. I was angry. I felt empty. But getting that letter was like receiving the first stitch. It hurt. But it helped too. Every one since then has closed a little bit of the wound, even on the days when I didn't want it to.*

"*The card you sent me today is the Three of Swords. You talked in your letter about how it represented heartbreak. There was pain and loss those last days we were together and in the ones since, you said. You worried about how I was feeling. But when I opened the letter and the card fell out, it was reversed. It means that the knives fall from the heart. Healing begins. That's what your letter meant to me. Another stitch in a wound.*

"*So I hope you keep writing to me. And I'll keep writing to you. I hope we heal ourselves and each other. I hope we'll stitch back together. Because I love you, Fionn. I'm not letting you go. I never will. Love, Rose.*"

She lifts her eyes to mine. And though I take a step in her direction, it's Rose who closes the distance. When I have her in my arms, everything else in the world seems to fall away. "I meant it, Rose," I whisper into her hair. "I'm not letting you go."

She nods against my chest. "Me neither."

For a long while, we stay that way, swaying to the music of heartbeats and breath. When we finally part, Rose takes off her jacket. I give her the bourbon and have my own. We sit on the bed, and she reads me her letters, one by one. We talk. We laugh. We fall asleep in each other's arms. We start the slow process of stitching back together.

For once, I'm awake the next morning before Rose. I write her a letter. This one is about happiness. Relief. Gratitude. I end it the way I always do, with a promise. That I will never let her go. Then I leave it on the pillow before I slip from the room to get her a coffee and waffles from downstairs. When I get back to the room, she's in the shower, her reply note already waiting on the little table next to the bed. Her letter isn't just about happiness, or relief. It's about want, and need. It's an invitation. I leave the coffee and breakfast in the kitchen and then I join her in the shower, and we make love beneath the spray, savoring every kiss, every touch, every whispered word that was left unwritten.

Every day we write each other letters. Every evening we read them out loud. We talk through the way we feel. Sometimes we make love. Sometimes we fuck. Sometimes we fight. Or we laugh. Or we cry. But every day we heal.

We leave the inn after a few days, and then we hit the road with Dorothy and no real plan of where to go. We just stop at different campgrounds. Some evenings, we meet random travelers. Sit around a fire, Rose glowing in the flickering light. Her laugh gets easier as time passes, and so does mine. Other nights, we keep to ourselves and talk about the life we both left behind in Nebraska and the future that lies ahead. She's ready to give Boston another try, she says, if I'm ready too. And I am. I know how much Leander would love to have me close as a physician on his payroll. He's texted me five times since the Croatian contract finished to offer me a permanent job in Boston, even offering to help me set up a legitimate clinic of my own in the city so I can be there if he needs me. He could force me into it with the mountain of evidence he still holds in his gasp, of course. But truthfully? I'm ready to say yes. And though I think she's trying not to let on, I know how much Rose wants to be closer to Lark and Sloane. I can hear it in her voice, see it in the way the idea lights up her eyes. "But maybe we could still take Dorothy out to stretch her legs in the summer," she said last night when she climbed into bed.

"Yeah," I'd said, pulling her against me. She laid her head against my chest and I pressed a kiss to her hair. "I really like that plan."

And now, three weeks after our reunion in Ellsworth, it feels like we're finally where we're meant to be. On the same path. We're walking side by side, our hands clasped, our shoes crunching on gravel as we draw closer to the cabin where Sloane's BMW and Lachlan's vintage Dodge Charger are parked. Barbara ambles along beside us on a leash and harness, sniffing the ground in her endless hunt for contraband snacks. The lights are on inside the cottage, illuminating the scrub grass that slopes toward a moonlit lake.

Rose squeezes my hand and I look down my shoulder at her. "You okay?" she asks.

"Yeah," I reply, giving her the most relaxed smile I can manage. She's not buying it, of course. Her eyes narrow on me as they sweep across every detail of my face. "It's just been so long since I've seen Rowan and Lachlan. I'm excited. Maybe a bit nervous."

My admission seems to appease her as she brings her other hand to circle my forearm. "They're going to be so excited to see you."

"Yeah, I just feel bad to have left it so long. I could have messaged them when I first got home."

Rose considers this, her head tilting side to side. "Yeah, but it was okay to take some time too. You needed it."

She's right. I did. Maybe I still need time. Not just to get over the last nine months of repairing traumatic injuries, or crash-coursing cosmetic surgery on the job, or living a life in secret apart from my loved ones. I also need to figure out what it is that I want from the future. Who I really want to be. Because the truth is, after so many years of trying to out-perform expectations, I think I need a minute to stand back and simply *exist.*

And if I'm lucky, no matter what we do next in life, that's the way it will be. Me and Rose.

We stop just behind the cars, watching the cottage, admiring its inviting glow. When Rose turns into me, I wrap my arms across her back.

"You ready?" she asks.

I lean down, pressing a kiss to her lips. She sighs against my mouth. How I ever lived so long without touching her, I don't know. And now it feels like I'll never get enough. When we pull away from each other, I sweep the hair back from her face, giving a final kiss to her forehead. "Probably not," I say.

"It's going to be great. A real *ta-da!* moment." Rose squeezes my waist in a tight hug and then lets go, taking a few steps back. She smacks a bug on her bare leg and I catch sight of her scar on her calf. One I helped to mend. But when I meet her eyes, I know that even from that first moment we met, it was Rose who healed me. "I'll go around to the deck and sneak in. You come in the main door," she says, her smile soft and reassuring. "It'll be great. I promise."

I nod once, because it's all I can manage. She picks up the squirming raccoon, then turns and jogs away to the front of the cabin. I'm left standing in the dark, watching her disappear into shadow.

When I'm sure she won't see, I pull a box from my pocket. I flip open the lid. The ring catches the dim light. If I were to look close enough, maybe I could see the night sky reflected in polished gold and precious gems. When we look up to the stars, we're looking back in time. But all I see is the future. And it's richer and brighter than I ever thought it would be.

I close the lid. Slide it back in my pocket. I hike my bag higher on my shoulder and take a deep breath. I walk to the steps of the cabin, determination in my stride, love and hope alive in my chest.

I'm going to make up for lost time.

MAPS

"What in the fuck is that?"

"An upgrade."

Sloane sighs and cocks a hip, trying to look as irritated as possible. She does an admirable job, but I can tell she's biting down on a grin. And she knows I know. She has to look away, probably in the hopes it will make it easier to keep up her disgruntled display. But it doesn't work.

"You told me once that no boys were allowed in the woods unless they had scales and a breeding kink," I say with a wicked grin.

"That was four years ago."

"So . . . ? I'm just making sure I've got clearance, you know? I don't see what the problem is. We're going to be in the woods."

"Not in West Virginia."

"It's still 'the woods,'" I say with air quotes. "And the last time I checked, you kind of enjoyed the Sol cosplay. I'm just taking it up a notch."

"Up a notch," she repeats with a snort. I shrug, and Sloane levels me with a flat glare. Her cheeks flush beneath her dusting of freckles. It's still my favorite shade of pink. "You think this is just a single notch?" She waves a hand toward my polyester dragon suit, this one enhanced by layers of scales glued to the fabric and even my skin, and a shit ton of green and blue makeup. "This is at least twelve."

My bottom lip juts out and she groans. "What, you don't think I'm pretty anymore? Are you embarrassed to sit next to me?"

"Yes," she deadpans. "*Hard* yes."

My prosthetic foam horns graze the roof of the car as I shake my head in feigned disappointment. I let out a deep, dejected sigh and Sloane curses, crossing her arms. I pat the passenger seat but she doesn't move, her feet still planted to the sidewalk. "Come on, Blackbird. Just get in the car. We've got places to be."

"If you're trying to fly under the radar—"

"Great pun, love—"

"—maybe showing up to the location of our annual game in a full dragon costume is *not the way*."

"It's a cabin. In the woods. In the middle of fucking nowhere. I'm sure we'll be just fine, love. Get in. We're going to be late and I want to chase you and fuck you on the forest floor before the others get there."

With another long-suffering moan, Sloane tosses her bag in the back and slides onto the passenger seat. "You're the worst."

"And you still love me. Now give us a kiss," I say as I lean over the center console with my lips pursed. She can't help but giggle this time as I wrap an arm around her shoulders and pull her closer, laying a kiss on her cheek as she squeals a protest that has no real fight to it. My painted lips leave a green smear behind on her skin. As soon as I let her go, she flips the visor down and rubs at the mark.

"You did use actual face paint, right?" Sloane's eyes slice to mine and narrow. "Please tell me this isn't poster paint or some shit."

"Of course," I say convincingly, though her glare doesn't soften. With a final grin at my wife, I key the engine, and we start making our way out of Boston. Do we get a few honks and hollers as we idle in the Friday afternoon traffic? Yes. Does Sloane groan and rub her forehead? Also yes. But every single time, it ignites her blush and summons her laugh. And I relish each flush of pink and every smile.

We stop once for gas and switch the driving responsibilities halfway through our six-hour trip, Sloane adamantly declaring that I'm either going to have to hold it or piss in a bush on the side of the road because she'll "rough gouge" my eyeballs and leave "crusty edges" if I even think about walking around in public. When we roll into Linsmore, it's nothing more than a gas station and a general store and a few dilapidated houses with weathered wood planks and cracked window panes and chipped paint. It's beautiful in the golden hour, the kind of light that makes you feel nostalgic for a time and a place where you've never lived, but it still gives you an ache in your chest. The town seems deserted, though it's clearly not with the mowed lawns and the stocked general store, but no one is around to prove it. A sign just past the town limits says BARN DANCE AND BARBECUE, EVERY FRIDAY FROM 7PM TO 11PM, 102 MAGNOLIA STREET, in retro lettering that appears to have been recently repainted.

"I guess that explains why the town is so empty," Sloane says as she glances down at her watch. "Seven thirty. Do you think the killer is there?"

I shrug.

Silence stretches between us. An uneasy dread creeps into my veins. I glance over just in time to catch the dimple appear next to her lip.

"*Oh no.* Blackbird—"

"Hey, BMW," Sloane chimes, and the car responds with a robotic "hello." "Show me the route to 102 Magnolia Street."

"I have found one route to 102 Magnolia Street," the car says, sounding like it's fully on board with Sloane's mission to get her revenge for my costume antics. An alternative route appears on the dashboard display. "Should I take it?"

"*Yes*," Sloane declares, at the same time as I say "no."

"Okay. I'll take you to 102 Magnolia Street," the car says.

"Blackbird . . . no . . ."

"Butcher, *yes.*" Sloane's wicked giggle is punctuated by the tick of the turning signal as she makes a U-turn to follow the car's directions. "You're the one who decided to spend six hours in a dragon costume."

"And you love cosplay."

"I also love winning."

"But we have to get to the cabin."

"And we will, after a brief detour."

"Then I should really come with you. For safety purposes and whatnot."

"Most definitely not," she says as she turns down a rural road. The Magnolia Street sign seems to mock me as we pass. We can already see the barn ahead, cars parked in the clearing next to it, light leaking between the planks of its walls. "I hate to point this out, pretty boy, but you're not really dressed for the occasion. This little getup of yours is not what I would call 'discreet.' So I guess you'd better just wait in the car."

"But the woods—".

"Sorry." She's definitely not sorry. Not with that fake little cringe and the exaggerated pout that follows. But there's nothing more murderously adorable than when she's determined to get under my skin and flay it clean from my bones with her competitive edge. I think it's my favorite version of Sloane Kane.

Even still . . . I fucking hate the idea of sitting behind in the car while she gets the jump on this year's Annual August Showdown. Though I refuse to admit it out loud, she's won more rounds of our murder competition than I have. And even though we've decided to extend our game indefinitely, it's not like I need to lose yet another year to my beautifully vicious wife.

Sloane parks the car at the entrance of a farm field gate on the opposite side of the road from the barn, where the vehicle will be out of view. I blow out a long breath and try to settle into my seat, though my prosthetic horns aren't making it easy to get comfortable.

"You look like you're regretting your life choices," Sloane says as she turns the engine off.

"Maybe one or two."

"Then I'll leave you with this lovely reminder that every time you try to take your teasing a little too far, karma comes along to bitch-slap you in the ball sack."

"That's . . . extreme. And also inaccurate."

"Is it? Remind me, how was that rump roast at Thorsten's? I could see if they have any ice cream at the barn dance, maybe?"

I cross my arms and glare through the windshield at the empty field of grass ahead. "Touché."

I don't have to look over to feel the radiant heat of Sloane's triumphant smile. But I do still glance her way. Her hazel eyes dance in the dim light. Her dimple winks at me with mischief. "I'll be back soon," Sloane says as she opens the car door. "Maybe with snacks."

Though I say her name in a final protest, she's already closing the door, her devious cackle following in her wake.

I twist as much as my costume will allow and watch as she jogs down the gravel road toward the barn, the urge to follow her nearly consuming me. But she's right. Though I'm sure this barn dance is a pretty close-knit affair where everyone knows everyone, Sloane at least has a chance of flying under the radar. I, on the other hand, do not.

"Rowan Kane, you *feckin' eejit*," I hiss as she disappears from view and I settle back into my seat. "You will *never* live this down if she wins."

And then I wait.

And wait.

And wait.

I'm debating whether I should get out and check on her when I look toward the barn and spot Sloane jogging back toward the car. It's only been forty-five minutes, just enough time for the sun to set and the colors of the sky to deepen, but it feels like *hours.* Relief fills my chest when she pulls open the door and slides into the driver's seat with a satisfied sigh.

"Productive?" I ask.

She shrugs, but her voice is just a hint too breezy when she says, "Not really."

"Did you find anything useful?"

"Only this," she says as she pulls a bottle of liquor from beneath her flannel shirt. She passes it to me with a grin so bright it blares her thoughts like a beacon—thoughts entirely centered on irritating the shit out of my broody older brother.

"What the hell is that?"

"Moonshine, probably. I overheard someone say it was whiskey but I have my doubts. So I hope dragons can sing, because I expect 'The Rocky Road to Dublin' at full volume tonight."

"Well," I reply as I read the homemade label before I place it on the floor behind me, "this dragon can't sing, but I'm certainly going to do it anyway."

"That's my Sol." Sloane leans over the center console and presses her lips to mine. Her scent of ginger and vanilla floods my senses as though it's permeating my skin, embedding itself where it belongs. I graze her cheek with my knuckles, tracing the constellation of freckles that dusts her skin, a pattern I know by heart. As my fingers thread into her hair, she sighs into my mouth, pressing her lips harder to mine, moving closer, and just as I deepen the kiss, she pulls away.

"Gross," she says, her nose crinkling.

"Gross? *Gross*, Blackbird? I am mortally wounded."

Sloane giggles as she opens the compartment in the center console to retrieve a tissue and wipe her lips off. "Your makeup. You can't taste that?"

"I was committed to the bit. I must be desensitized."

365

"That does *not* taste like lipstick, Rowan." She pulls the visor down and checks that she's rubbed any remnants of green from her mouth. With a sideways glance, she assesses my face, her eyes lingering on my lips before she returns her attention to the little mirror. "Are you one hundred percent sure you used face paint?"

"Umm . . . mostly . . . ?"

Sloane's head whips to the side and she pins me with a scrutinous glare. "What do you mean 'mostly'?"

"It wasn't staying on super well, so I . . . augmented it."

"Augmented it . . . with . . . ?" When I break my gaze away with a cringe, she whacks my arm. "Rowan Kane—"

"Poster paint."

The car sinks into an eerie silence. This might be how I die. My wife will probably murder me and dump my body into a field. I weigh my chances for survival. I can cook, that has to count for something, right? And she thinks I'm pretty—at least, she does when I'm not in a full dragon costume complete with foam horns and layers of silicone scales. But she's pretty fast. And stabby. And she goes for the eyes.

It takes a long moment before I look at her. When I do, I'm not sure she's actually breathing. She's so lethally still that I don't know if I should maybe just take my chances and run for it.

And then she bursts out laughing.

It's so loud and sudden that it startles me, and that seems to delight her even more. She laughs and laughs and fucking *laughs*.

"What's so funny . . . ? The bottle said it's water-soluble," I say, and she wheezes, tears leaking from the corners of her eyes as she parrots my words back to me through strained vocal cords.

"Did you test it?" she manages to get out, though only barely.

"No . . ." I flip my visor down and open the cover on the mirror. My face paint concoction has definitely stayed put. Which is maybe a bit concerning now that I think about it. It's been on there for *hours*. Maybe too many hours. I swipe my thumb across my tongue and rub at a spot on my cheek next to the scales. While the top layer smears, the skin underneath is definitely still green. "Ahh . . . *shite*. There's gotta be a way to get this off, right? Blackbird? You like makeup. And painting. So you know how to get this shit off, yeah? It'll come off . . . *right?*"

Sloane cackles through my questions, her eyes still watering as she keys the engine and reverses onto Magnolia Street. "Somehow, I don't think a homemade apricot-turpentine scrub is the best option. But don't worry," she says as she reaches over to pat my hand, "I still think you're pretty, even if you're permanently green."

"*Permanently . . . ?*"

By the time we reach the cabin, I'm sure Sloane regrets letting the word *permanent* tumble from her grinning lips. I pepper her with questions for the remaining thirty-minute drive, about skin and dye and *just how bad would it really be if I tested out this apricot-turpentine scrub idea?* That one earns me a much-deserved smack to the shoulder. I guess she's right. Testing out new things on my face has apparently not gone so well for me today, so ramping it up to another level is probably not the best idea either.

In fact, the whole costume was definitely not my best idea, though it seemed like a good one at the time. I guess I didn't anticipate a barn dance detour that would cost us a precious hour and a half of time. I was hoping to arrive early so I could chase my wife through the woods and make her laugh as I fucked her on the forest floor. At least I'm extremely successful in the laughter part. Too bad it's not just my wife who's delighted by my costume.

"You feckin' dumb bellend. What in the Christ Jesus are you wearing?" Lachlan says from the porch as we exit the vehicle. Sloane's grin is maniacal as she stands off to the side to watch our exchange with unrestrained glee.

"What the fuck does it look like I'm wearing, asshat?"

Lachlan makes a show of taking off his glasses and polishing the lenses with the bottom of his shirt before he slides them back on. "Looks like an idiot suit. Is that the right answer?"

Sloane bellows a laugh as Lark pushes open the screen door, drying her hands on a tea towel as she exits the rustic cottage. She lurches to a halt as soon as her eyes land on me. "Oh holy hell." Her giggle is devious, a bright contrast to Lachlan's derisive snort. "Is that suit clean?"

"Unfortunately," I grumble.

"Oh, *Rowan*—"

"Don't give him any sympathy, Lark. Pity makes him even more insufferable, the feckin' twat."

"But look at him. He's all sad and horny."

"Literally," Sloane interjects, whacking one of my yellow horns as she heads toward the porch to give Lark a hug. "Also permanently green."

"We need to talk more about 'permanent,' Sloane," I say as I grab our bags and the moonshine and then follow after her, my dragon tail swishing across the gravel behind me. When Lachlan groans and runs a hand down his face, I exaggerate the sway of my hips just to annoy him.

"We've talked about it plenty." Though Sloane doesn't turn my way, I can almost hear her eyes roll. "Talk about it with your brother."

"Eyeball Spider Lady," Lachlan says as he wraps Sloane in a hug, "how do you tolerate that pain in the arse?"

"He usually makes up for it in other ways." With a kiss on Lachlan's cheek, she lets him go and joins Lark's side. The two link arms to share a flurry of whispers, probably about whatever it was Sloane actually discovered at the barn. They head inside as I climb the porch steps to stop in front of my older brother.

"Give us a kiss, asshat." Before he can get away, I wrap Lachlan in a bear hug and plant a smear of a green kiss against his cheek, one of my scales falling off in the process.

"Gobshite."

"Bellend."

When I let him go, Lachlan still can't help himself. He lays his hand on either side of my head and presses his forehead to mine. "You're still a reckless little shit," Lachlan says, and though he tries to look serious, the glimmer in his eyes gives away his amusement. "But I still love you."

"Love you too."

With a clap to the side of my head, Lachlan grins and lets me go to pick up one of my bags and the bottle of moonshine, examining it with a furrowed brow. "What the fuck is this?"

"Homemade whiskey, apparently."

"Christ Jesus."

"Sloane found it at a barn dance in Linsmore. And judging by the way those two are conspiring, that's not the only thing she found." When I nod toward the two women whispering in the kitchen as they open a bottle of red wine, Lachlan follows my gaze and groans. "I think she's got a jump on us for the game."

"Well, I might have an idea or two myself."

"I thought Conor wasn't going to give you extra clues. Sloane will be so pissed if he is."

"You bellend," Lachlan says with an eye roll, keeping his distance from the two women as they head toward the living room with their glasses. When he seems to think they're safely out of earshot, we take their place in the kitchen, and he cracks open the moonshine. "I am capable of doing my own research. And I promised the eyeball spider lady I wouldn't mine Conor for information. I've seen what's involved in eyeball removal. I don't want her to make good on that threat," he says with a shudder before he pours a glass and slides it across the counter of the island. "Trust me."

Lachlan raises his glass in a silent toast and I do the same, and then we take a sip of the golden liquid. It burns my throat as it slides down to my stomach, where I'm pretty sure it'll eat through my guts. "Fuck, that is atrocious."

"Are you sure it's not battery acid?"

"No. I'm not sure at all. Though it's not going to stop me from drinking enough to serenade you."

"I think it might kill us both before that happens," Lachlan says as we both suffer through another sip.

"So you said you have information?" I say in a conspiratorial whisper as I lean closer across the island. "What kind of information?"

"Yeah, Man-guy," a chipper voice says from right behind me just as I take another drink of moonshine that shoots up my nose and spurts past my lips in a spray that hits Lachlan right on the shirt. "I want to know too, what kind of information?"

I spin around to the sound of Lachlan's "Christ Jesus" and the combined squeals of Sloane and Lark. The little banshee grins up at me, her dark eyes sparkling. She sets down a pissed-off-looking raccoon of all fucking things, though somehow, that tracks. "Rose, fucking hell. You scared the shit out of me." I move to give her a hug but she backs up a step, her hands raised.

"Whoa, now. That's a situation you've got there. You look like you're starring in the busted version of *Wicked*." She leans forward and pats my arm. "A for effort. Or . . . something."

Though I hear Sloane snort from the living room, it's my older brother's voice that seems to echo in my mind.

"Rose . . . ?"

Rose and I exchange a fleeting smile before I turn to look at Lachlan. I've never seen this expression on his face before, his brow furrowed, his eyes taking on a glassy sheen.

"Hi, Lachlan."

Lachlan takes a few slow steps around the end of the island, steps that quicken until he's rushing to embrace Rose, that shocked hope and guilt still etched into his face until he pulls his glasses off and wipes his eyes. They exchange whispers, things only the two of them are meant to hear, but words I catch anyway. Words about regret and choices. About time and promises. About how some vows are never meant to be made, because they are not in our hands to keep.

The screen door quietly closes, and Fionn steps inside the cabin. He lets his bag slide from his shoulder and drops it on the floor, never taking his eyes from Lachlan.

"I thought maybe you should have a doctor around. Just in case," he says, clutching the back of his neck.

I turn back to Lachlan, whose heart has been shattered for so long that its sharp edges have scored the pain right into his face. His eyes glisten with tears. His hand trembles when Rose lifts it from her shoulder.

"Fionn," is all Lachlan manages to get out, and then he's striding across the room. The two lock in an embrace that lasts long enough that it reminds me of others they've shared. Like the time Fionn graduated from medical school. Or the time we landed in Boston from Sligo and set foot in our own apartment, our first safe place. Or even that hazy memory of the hospital that first day we met our little brother. There was a heart-splitting sadness that I was too young to fully understand. So much grief for the loss of our mother, a pain that weighed heaviest on Lachlan's shoulders. But there was so much love too. It was there in the way Lachlan held our baby brother in his arms. Just like it's here in the way he holds on to him now.

"I'm sorry," he whispers. In all our years together, I've never seen Lachlan's shoulders shake like they do now. I've never seen him crack open and cry, not even when we were young. He grew up so fast. Spent his youth walking us through darkness, our beacon in a night that I once thought would never end. "I don't know how to fix it. I'm just so feckin' sorry, Fionn."

"It's not your fault," Fionn says, pulling back just enough to look into Lachlan's eyes. I notice for the first time how Fionn really *looks* different. Not like the man we thought he wanted to be, steeped in high expectations and buttoned-up formality. He looks . . . at ease. At *peace*. "I'm sorry, Lachlan. It was never your fault. And I would have gotten in touch or come home sooner, if I could have. I just . . . needed time. Time to reset myself, I guess. Time to figure things out without relying on you both to somehow do it for me. Well, maybe not him," he says with a nod to me. "He looks like a dumpster goblin."

Lachlan lets out a watery laugh and turns his glassy eyes to me over his shoulder. "I think we've just officially replaced your Shitflicker nickname. Dumpster Goblin suits you."

"Especially now that it's permanent," Lark pipes up. When I glance her way, she's wiping a track of tears from her cheeks with the heel of her hand.

"I really need to know if this is actually permanent," I say as I start peeling off a scale glued to my cheek. Fionn scratches his stubble as he watches me from beneath the arm Lachlan keeps slung over his shoulder. "Will it come off?"

"You didn't tattoo it on there, did you?"

"Of course not, dickhead."

"I'm sure you're probably fine."

"'Probably' does not inspire much confidence," I say, but Fionn only shrugs.

"You'll probably have to wait until the skin cells replenish."

"How long does that take?"

"A couple of weeks."

"*A couple of weeks?*" I parrot back to him as Sloane cackles in my periphery.

"Maybe. I mean, if you really scrub it twice a day. Otherwise, probably a month," Fionn says. I look over at Sloane but she just shakes her head. I do my best to look dejected, which really isn't so hard to do, and then I shuffle my way toward my brothers.

"I need a hug. Even dumpster goblins need love." With my arms outstretched, I grab hold of my brothers and though they protest, they still wrap their arms around me in return.

"You're an idiot," Fionn whispers to me as the three of us press our foreheads together.

"And you're a birdseed-eating twat," Lachlan counters on my behalf.

"And you're a broody asshat," I say, and he grins, the shine still bright in his eyes. I swallow, trying to force the sting in my throat from burning its way into tears. It feels like a displaced bone has finally been reset, like I couldn't take a breath without feeling a pain that dug between my ribs, and suddenly it's gone. And judging by the way my brothers both look back at me, they feel the same way. "Neither one of you would make as good of a dragon as me, by the way. But I still love you both."

"Yeah," Fionn says. "Me too."

Lachlan clasps a hand across the back of each of our heads. "Love you too, my boys. And I'm proud of you."

When we release each other, Fionn takes a step back, making a slow pivot on his heel. He looks at each one of us before his gaze finally lands on Rose and sticks there. "Now that we're all here," he says, "I have an announcement to make."

Rose's gaze flicks to Lark and Sloane, then to me and Lachlan, as though any one of us might know what Fionn is up to. "Announcement . . . ?"

"Well, really more of a question." Fionn takes a few slow steps toward Rose. She looks like she might want to run, but she seems fused to the floor. "I wanted to tell you that I love you, Rose Evans."

"I love you too," she whispers, tears gathering in her eyes as Fionn takes her hand, the other buried in his pocket.

"When you showed up in Hartford, it was the single greatest event of my life. You crashed in and tore my reality apart. I had taped up the broken parts of my life and you showed me that those pieces couldn't be sewn back together. They never fit in the first place. But you remade everything, Rose. I've admired you every single day I've known you. Your bravery. Your recklessness. Your huge, wild heart. Your willingness to embrace every part of yourself. You showed me how to care for the darkness, not to fear it or hide it away."

Fionn withdraws his hand from his pocket as he lowers to one knee. Rose's shoulders shake, the tears flowing down her skin.

"I love you, Rose Evans. I'm not letting you go. I never will." He flips open the lid of the box in his hand. A stack of three separate rings rests inside, made to look like a sunset of orange sunstone over a sea of sapphires and blue diamonds set in hand-etched gold. "Marry me, Rose. Let me love you forever."

Rose's joy can't be contained. It bursts from her in a cry and then she crashes into Fionn. He raises from his bent knee with Rose clutched in his embrace. There are tears and whispered words of love. They kiss. They laugh. And then Lark starts up a playlist as Lachlan breaks out a fresh bottle of whiskey. After a round of hugs and laughter and a toast with my family, I step away to finally get rid of my costume and scrub my skin beneath a hot shower.

When I return to the living area, the celebrations are still in full swing. I just stand back to watch for a minute. To marvel at the twists and turns that life takes. When I look a little more closely, I see the intricate pattern in the web. The map that brought us all together.

I'm watching my two brothers making up for lost time when I feel Sloane's hand around my wrist. I lift my arm and she nestles into my side.

"Hey, Butcher," she whispers.

"Hey, Blackbird." I press a kiss to the crown of her head. Fionn laughs at something Lachlan says, his touch never straying from Rose as the two sit cuddled up on the couch. Sloane sighs and I look down to see a contented smile lingering on her face. "I'm going to hazard a guess that you had something to do with that," I say as I nod in their direction.

Sloane shrugs beneath my arm. "Maybe."

"I'm sure your partner in crime was involved?"

"You're my partner in crime."

"The other one."

Sloane grins but doesn't tear her eyes from the scene before us. "What can I say, Man-guy? Lark is a hopeless romantic."

"Thought so." I turn toward her, Sloane's arms folding around my waist. I frame her face in my hands and press a kiss to her lips. "Thank you," I whisper into her skin. "I love you, Sloane Kane."

"I love you too, Rowan. And now that they're occupied," she says with a nod toward the living room, "wanna sneak away and go do karate in the garage?"

I smile down at my beautiful wife, those hazel eyes so full of love and joy, that dimple a flash of mischief next to her lip.

"I thought you'd never ask."

BLADE OF RAGE

I crouch behind the bushes and peer through the leaves, their shades of green vibrant in the morning sun that breaks through the canopy of oak and ash. The group huddles together at the edge of the rocky outcrop, taking turns with the binoculars. Lachlan and his wife, Lark. Fionn and Rose, now engaged. Rowan Kane. Sloane Sutherland, now a Kane too. I still hear her name the way Rowan called out for her the one and only time we met. *Sloane. Sloane!* His voice echoes in my mind in the desolate hours of night. One of the many nightmares that haunt the shadows of my room in corners where the light never seems to reach.

I glance down at the plaid shirt I'm wearing. Burnt orange. Navy blue. Buttercream squares crisscrossed with lines that have faded with time and wear. I run my fingers over the stitches I sewed into the torn fabric of the sleeve.

I'm going to give this to you but I need your help to get it off.

I lift my gaze to the group again. I've watched them before. Their easy interactions. Sometimes, their harder ones. A faint smile crosses my lips as I watch them whisper and laugh in hushed tones. Rowan's skin is tainted green from that ridiculous costume he was wearing last night. But when he wraps an arm across Sloane's shoulders and presses a kiss to her forehead before returning to his conversation with Lachlan, I can see the way she looks at him. Like he's the most beautiful thing she's ever seen.

I had love like that once too. I had Adam.

My eyes burn with unshed tears. Most days, I've learned how to swallow them. How to cut them up with the blade of rage. But today? Today is always the hardest day.

Three years ago, Adam was stolen from me in a storm of screams, in the roar of a chainsaw. He died to the final notes of the maniacal laughter of a deranged killer.

I would have died too.

Yes. He killed Adam. And I promise you, Adam will be the last person Harvey Mead ever kills.

I press my eyes closed. When I open them, the group is standing, brushing off their jeans, taking sips of water from bottles, shedding extra sweaters or checking knives or tightening straps on their backpacks as they get ready to leave the escarpment for the farm hidden in the valley. The one where a murderer lives. The next monster the apex predators have come to kill.

A spike of adrenaline drives through my heart, as sharp as the ones that Rowan drove through Harvey Mead's hands to nail him to the floor of his barn. An offering to the woman he loved. I watched, hidden in the tall grass as she came back to the barn with her injured arm held close to her side, a mummified body tucked beneath the other. She looked broken. But gleeful. Indomitable.

Fucking *indestructible*. Not just a survivor, but a reckoning. A woman with more power than I ever imagined possible.

I could be a woman like that too.

The group starts moving away, walking in single file down the narrow path. First Lark and Lachlan. Then Rose and Fionn. Rowan goes next. Sloane is the last to leave, casting a final glance toward the farm.

My heart catches in my throat as I move in slow motion, rising from my hiding place, a single step onto the same path that continues into the woods behind me.

Sloane's eyes snap to mine. They widen with surprise. Her hand tightens on the knife she holds against her thigh. And then I see it. Recognition.

Her eyes track down the length of the shirt I'm wearing. The one she gave to me when I was naked in the dark. When she meets my eyes once more, she smiles.

She nods. I nod in reply. And then she turns and walks away.

I watch until she disappears after the others. When the forest has gone still, I turn and head in the opposite direction.

Once upon a time, my name was Autumn Bower.

And I have my own story to tell.

SUSPEND

ROSE

I roll to a stop in the driveway and cut the engine to my Triumph, sliding my helmet off. I let it rest on the tank and brush the hair from my eyes so I can stare up at the house. *Our* house. Fionn's and mine. The first house without wheels that I've ever owned. It needs some work, don't get me wrong. The deck might as well be ripped right off. We'll start demolishing the kitchen this weekend. Fionn was so eager to get the renovations started that he and Lachlan painted our bedroom and replaced the carpet the day after we moved in. I can even hear the drill upstairs now, its whine floating down to me through the open guest bedroom window. There's music too. And Fionn's off-key singing. I smile and swing my leg over the bike. We've only been here a week, but it already feels like home.

When I enter the house, it smells like fresh paint and sounds like happiness. Barbara wakes up and stretches, half in and half out of the wooden box Fionn built for her next to the brick fireplace. I set my helmet down and then give her a scratch, lingering for a moment to look at the photos he must have unpacked today to set on the mantle. Some of my circus family. Some of Rowan and Lachlan. One from our first Annual August Showdown almost a year ago, Rowan's face a sickly shade of green from the poster paint that took a week to fade completely. And then there's one of my favorite photos, the biggest of the bunch. I pick it up, and smile down at our kiss, frozen in time. It's a photo from our wedding last month at Covecrest Cottages in Maine, the same place where we reunited. The place where it felt as though a last invisible thread pulled closed around a wound that took months to heal.

I run my finger over the glass that covers our faces. And then I set it back on the mantle. I don't linger, not when Fionn belts out the lyrics to "Don't Stop Me Now" by Queen as loud as he can upstairs.

I'm trying to sneak up the stairs, but I don't know yet which steps creak and which ones don't. Despite taking it slow, the fourth one is loud enough that somehow it alerts Fionn to my presence. I don't know how. It's as though his time with Leander has awoken a sixth sense that's been dormant for too long. The door to the guest room flies open, and a moment later, Fionn is standing at the top of the stairs with a drill in his hand and a grin on his face.

"Hey," he says, taking his phone from his pocket just long enough to turn off the music. "Were you trying to sneak up on me?"

"Maybe just a little," I reply, and his eyes brighten as though he's proud of himself for stopping me before I even got close. "How the hell did you hear me?"

Fionn shrugs and closes the distance between us, not stopping until he reaches the stair above mine. He leans down to press a kiss to my lips. That sense of home only weaves tighter around me. The scents of sage and paint and mint. His warmth, his touch. His taste. The way his fingers caress my cheek and tangle in my hair.

Our first kiss on the stairs. Fionn draws away but keeps me close, pressing a kiss to my forehead.

"I have something for you," he says, still close enough that I could count every shade of blue in his eyes.

"What is it?"

"A late wedding present." I tilt my head and he grins. "It's a show, not tell, kind of thing."

In a flash of motion, Fionn has picked me up and turned to deposit me on the step above him. In the next breath, his hands are covering my eyes.

"I thought you said *show.*"

"It's still a surprise. And not easily wrapped."

I grab the railing, and with Fionn's hands still over my eyes, we make it to the landing and turn in the direction of the guest room. "What if I don't like it?" I tease as we stop at the door.

"Well, it's not really the kind of thing I can return." Fionn lifts one hand away just long enough to turn the handle. The hinges creak as he pushes it open with a foot and then guides us over the threshold. "You ready?" I nod. "Three . . . two . . . *one.*"

He lifts his palms away and I blink as I take in the room.

There are no pictures or paintings. No dressers or desks. No bed. There's only one thing in the room. A single piece of furniture.

The sex swing.

I cackle a laugh and take in the finished project, a black crocheted piece suspended from a painted wood frame bolted into the ceiling. It looks suspiciously like an oversized plant hanger. "That is *amazing.*"

"All credit to the Suture Sisters. They helped to work out the kinks in the design."

I snort. "Yeah, I bet Maude led the charge on that one," I say as I walk closer to inspect the finer details of the stitching. "Did Bernard make the frame?"

"He sure did."

"It's epic." I stare up at the hooks as I tug on the swing. "Think it'll hold?"

"Only one way to find out."

Fionn's arm slides around my waist. His warm breath cascades across my neck between slow and luxurious kisses. "What do you think, Mrs. Kane?"

Goose bumps ripple across my skin. I close my eyes and smile as I raise an arm and run my fingers through the short hair at the nape of his neck. "I don't think I'll ever get tired of that."

"Tired of what? Kisses? I hope not," he says, pressing another lingering kiss to the juncture between my neck and shoulder.

"No. Of you calling me Mrs. Kane."

A rumbling *hmm* vibrates against my flesh. Fionn's fingers trace the sliver of skin at the edge of my shirt, then land on the button, slowly pulling it undone. "I'll never get tired of it either," he says against the shell of my ear. I shiver as he frees the next button. "*Mrs. Kane.*" He frees another button, letting his touch graze my navel in a slow caress. "You are so beautiful, Mrs. Kane. Your skin is so soft." His tongue traces a line up the length of my neck. "You taste so sweet. If only you knew the things I plan to do to you, Mrs. Kane. How I plan to devour you."

My breath shudders. Another button is pulled free. Then another. Another. In moments that seem to pass too quickly and yet not quickly enough, the shirt is sliding off my shoulders, falling to the hardwood floor. My bra is next. My jeans and panties. Then I'm standing naked, the weight of Fionn's ravenous gaze resting like a veil on my skin. I turn just enough to watch him reach behind his shoulders to pull his shirt off.

"Turn around, Mrs. Kane," he says, his voice husky with lust. I do as he asks, turning to face him. He doesn't come closer as his eyes trail the length of my body. They drag down my chest, past my navel, slowing over the narrow patch of hair at the apex of my thighs. I feel his need in every inch of skin his gaze consumes. Only once his attention has returned to my face does he step any closer. "I've been waiting to try this swing for so long."

"How long?" I ask as he lifts me with one arm, positioning the swing with his free hand.

Fionn chuckles as he sets me on the suspended yarn, and with just a little adjustment and a pause to ensure it's safe, he takes a step back. "Since you first brought it up."

A theatrical gasp passes from my lips, but Fionn hardly notices. Half of his focus is on my ankle as he slides it into a crocheted cuff, the other half on my pussy. "You were thinking about me in the sex swing at the Suture Sisters meeting? You scoundrel." Though we both smile, the amusement between us doesn't linger in the air, burning away in the heat of desire.

"From the moment you said it, I couldn't get it out of my head." Fionn slips my other ankle into the second cuff, and then I'm bared to him, my legs spread wide. His eyes stay locked to mine as his warm palm slides up my calf, skimming over the scar from the night we met before pausing there. He kneels between my thighs. My breaths come in pants. He blows a thin stream of air across my folds and I shiver, my fingers tightening around fistfuls of soft yarn. "I imagined you just like this." A slow lick passes over my center. "Spread open for me." Another caress of his tongue. "At my mercy." A lingering kiss. "Ready to be tasted."

I open my mouth, about to beg for more, when he seals his lips over my clit. My words dissolve into a moan. His tongue teases and circles. He kisses and sucks. He grips my thighs, imprinting his touch on my flesh. He feasts on me.

When I tilt my head back and close my eyes, Fionn growls against my pussy, nipping my clit with a gentle bite that's soothed with a kiss when my attention snaps back to him. As soon as it does, he smiles with approval, never breaking his gaze from mine. It's wicked. It's decadent. It's *perfection*. And when he slides two fingers into my pussy and pumps them in a building, quickening rhythm, it's an unraveling. My fingers tangle in the yarn. I whimper and beg. I come apart, suspended in a moment of ecstasy that seems like it will never end. He draws out my pleasure, savoring it. I feel like a delicacy in his hands, and he doesn't stop until I'm a mess of unsteady breaths and surging heartbeats.

"I like the swing," is all I can manage when I feel confident that I can make words a few moments later.

Fionn huffs a breath of a laugh, swiping his palm across the arousal glistening on his face. "I think we should still continue some testing. Best to be sure," he says as he stands, slipping the cuffs from my ankles. With his eyes fused to mine and a rakish grin lifting one corner of his lips, he unbuttons his jeans and tugs them over his hips with his briefs, freeing his erection.

"You're probably right. We should be sure to fully quality control the prototype before we make version two."

"Version two?" Fionn asks, and I give him a sage nod in reply as he lifts me from the swing just long enough to flip me over. My sweat-slicked belly and chest lie on the black yarn, my ass facing Fionn, my legs dangling off the edge.

"I figured we could try making a few," I reply as his palms caress the backs of my thighs and the globes of my ass. "Maybe start a collection."

"I love the way you think, Mrs. Kane." Fionn glides the crown of his cock over my folds before notching it at my entrance. I look up as he tangles his fingers into the crocheted yarn, gripping it in tight fists. With a swift tug, he brings the swing toward him, sheathing his cock with my pussy. I gasp. He rumbles a growl. For a breath, we don't move. "And I fucking love the way you feel," he grits out.

And then he fucks me.

His hips slap my ass with every deep thrust. I swing forward and back. Forward and back. Over and over. Pleasure is already coiling deep in my core with every stroke that glides over my inner walls, my body still sensitive from his touch yet ready for more. And he gives me everything. He slows when he knows I'm coming close to unraveling. He quickens his pace when the orgasm seems like it might slip from my grasp. He teases me with shallow motion and lavishes me with rocking thrusts. And when I'm nearly mindless with need, I slide a hand beneath the bottom of the swing and swirl my fingers over my clit.

"Please," I beg, desperation filling that single word.

His words are a strained and gravelly whisper when he says, "If you want me to fill your pussy, Mrs. Kane, you're going to have to come on my cock first."

As soon as those words leave his lips, I fall apart. Moaning. Begging. Clenching around him. Blinded by stars. Every muscle winding tighter and tighter until it feels like I dissolve.

With a roar, Fionn slams into me as deep as my body will take him. His strokes become unsteady as he empties into me, but he doesn't pull away, not until he's sure every last drop of cum is spent inside me. And we stay that way for a long moment. It's not until my skin starts to cool beneath a sheen of sweat that he steps back and slides free of my pussy.

"Goddamn, Rose," he says, lifting me from the swing to set me on my unsteady feet. "The swing was better than I imagined. What did you think?"

"I think . . ."

I trail off as we both look down at my body. My skin is imprinted with a beautiful pattern of stitches that we've both had a hand in making. It's a web of memory. A map of our history in my flesh.

When I look up and meet Fionn's eyes, I smile. And then I take a step back toward the swing, gripping onto the ropes of yarn to hop back onto the seat.

"I think we should keep testing it out," I say with feigned innocence as I spread my legs. "Just to be sure."

Fionn's grin grows wicked, his eyes dark. He rests his hands on my knees, spreading them wider. His palms slide up my thighs, painting them with the arousal that coats my skin. He steps closer, leaning down until his lips are only a thread's width from mine.

"Whatever you say, Mrs. Kane," he whispers.

He kisses me. He doesn't stop. The minutes and hours fall away. But each moment etches a map deep beneath my skin.

ACKNOWLEDGMENTS

First and foremost, thank you to YOU, dear reader, for spending some of your time with Fionn and Rose, and their friends and family, and Barbara, and of course the Suture Sisters, who I'm sure have started a thriving business selling sex swings on Etsy. It's hard to believe we're at the end of the Ruinous Love Trilogy, though it doesn't truly feel like the end in many ways. The most cherished thing this series has brought to me is gratitude. I am so deeply appreciative of the outpouring of love and enthusiasm from you, the readers. It's humbling that you even want to spend a few hours of your time with these stories, so to see you then fall in love with the characters is deeply moving. While writing *Butcher & Blackbird* was joyful, and *Leather & Lark* was challenging, *Scythe & Sparrow* felt *healing*. I had a blast. I threw in some truly bizarre shit. And it's difficult to describe, but I felt like Rose and Fionn loved me back in a way characters don't often do. I wasn't just watching their lives unfold. I felt like they were bringing me into their story, sitting me down with a massive cup of coffee, and saying, "Just hang out for a while and see what you find." I love them both, and I hope you do too.

Endless, enormous thanks to Kim Whalen from the Whalen Agency. You've been by my side at every step of this journey and I am so grateful for your unwavering support. You're hilarious as fuck and I adore working with you. Every time I drink from my matching tumbler, I'll think of you. HAHA. Thank you also to Mary Pender at WME and Orly Greenberg at UTA—thank you both for helping to bring these characters to a whole new world.

To Molly Stern, Sierra Stovall, Hayley Wagreich, Andrew Rein, and the entire team at Zando, thank you for bringing the Ruinous Love Trilogy far beyond what I ever expected it could be. That first thrill of seeing my book on the shelf in a bookstore is because of you, and I'm eternally grateful. Thank you also to copy editor Rachel Kowal who has (maybe) now come to terms with the fact that I'll never get lay versus lie right, HAHA.

In the UK, huge thanks to the team at Little, Brown UK, particularly Ellie Russell and Becky West, who have been so wonderful to work with and who were some of the very first folks in the publishing industry to rally behind the Ruinous Love series. Thank you also to Glenn Tavennec from Éditions du Seuil for being such a huge supporter of me and these characters. And I will always be so grateful to András Kepets in Hungary, who set in place the first domino that brought these partnerships to life.

Massive thanks to Najla and the team at Qamber Designs. You are so wonderful to work with. I had very little to go on when I first came to you with the request to make the series covers. I'd barely started writing B&B, and yet you absolutely nailed all three cover designs. Thank you so much!

To my wonderful PA and graphics wizard, Val Downs of Turning Pages Designs. Thank you for everything you do! You are so professional and supportive and talented, and an absolute delight to work with. I appreciate you so much.

I am enormously grateful to the amazing ARC readers and social media supporters of the Ruinous Love series. Thank you so much for taking the time to read, promote, and talk about these stories. Many of you have been on this journey with me since B&B. Some of you, even earlier than that. And I hope you know that it means the world to me that you'd take the time to offer your support and encouragement. I'm honored to be on this journey with you. I want to say a special thanks to Kristie, Chelsea, Lauren, and Abbie, who have been not only huge supporters of the Ruinous Love trilogy from the beginning, but who I'm truly honored to have become friends with.

Super special thanks to Jessica S. and Jessica M., who both so kindly vibe-checked things for me when I was in the "I want to BURN THIS" phase of writing. Jess S., you've been my friend on this wild and wonderful journey for so long, and I adore you. Jess M., the sister I never had, thank you for your support and guidance! Similarly, a huge thank-you to all my author friends. I'm lucky enough to say you're too many to name for fear of leaving anyone out, though I do need to shout out Santana Knox and H. D. Carlton in particular as you have really been there for me in some wild times. There's no one I'd rather be in a human centipede with (yeah, it's as weird as it sounds). I've learned so much from you. You've been a safe harbor in the turbulent sea that is publishing, and I'm incredibly thankful for your friendship.

Last but certainly not least, to my amazing boys. This book would not have been possible without my husband, Daniel, as much as he'd argue that point. He took the time to talk through story ideas with me, to read draft passages, to bring me food and water to keep me alive. When I would write late into the night, he would stay up to silently sit next to me no matter how tired he was, just so I wouldn't be alone. I love you so much, Daniel. You truly are an exceptionally supportive partner and the most amazing husband. And to my son, Hayden, thank you for your incredible hugs, your endless kindness, and your infectious laugh. I love you until the end of time and beyond. And if you've read anything before this page, you're grounded.

ABOUT THE AUTHOR

#1 *New York Times* and *USA TODAY* bestselling author and TikTok sensation with works sold worldwide in over eighteen languages to date, **Brynne Weaver** has traveled the world, taken in more stray animals than her husband would probably prefer, and nurtured her love for dark comedies, horror, and romance in both literature and film. During all her adventures, the constant thread in Brynne's life has been writing. With nine published works and counting, Brynne has made her mark in the literary world by blending irreverent dark comedy, swoon-worthy romance, and riveting suspense to create genre-breaking, addictive stories for readers to escape into.

Instagram: @brynne_weaver
TikTok: @brynneweaverbooks
Facebook: facebook.com/groups/1200796990512620
Goodreads: goodreads.com/author/show/21299126
.Brynne_Weaver